DM Me for Murder

DM Me
for *Murder*

A
Trending Topic
Mystery

Sarah E. Burr

First published by Level Best Books 2024

This novel is entirely a work of fiction. The names, characters and incidents portrayed in it are the work of the author's imagination. Any resemblance to actual persons, living or dead, events or localities is entirely coincidental.

Author Photo Credit: Doug Walters Photography

First edition

ISBN: 978-1-68512-557-8

Cover art by Level Best Designs

This book was professionally typeset on Reedsy.
Find out more at reedsy.com

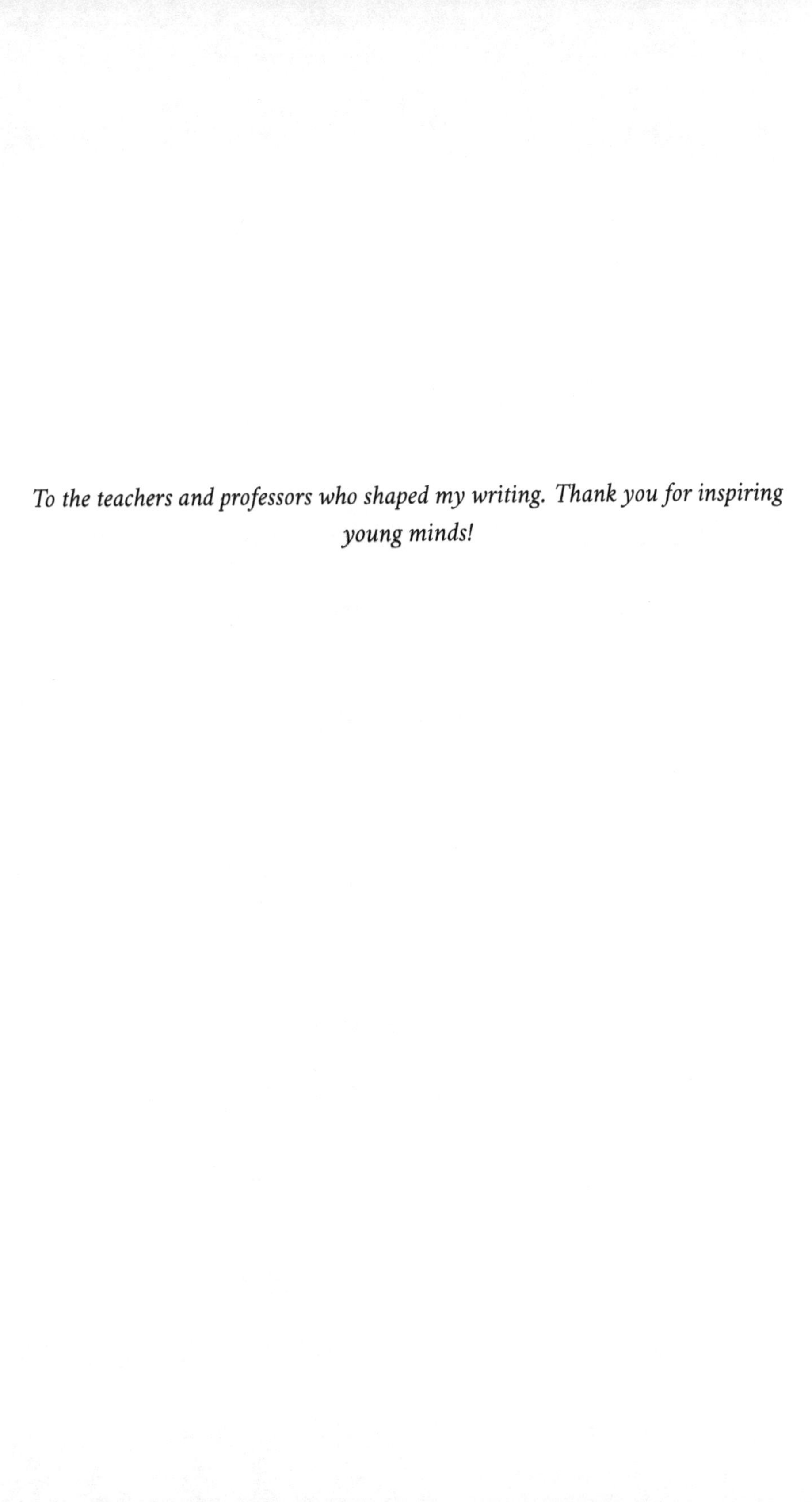

To the teachers and professors who shaped my writing. Thank you for inspiring young minds!

Praise for the Trending Topic Mysteries

"With #hashtags and @handles, a well-written mystery with some skilled twists and well-developed characters *#TagMe for Murder* is a hit!"—Dollycas, Escape with Dollycas into a Good Book

"If you are looking for a great mystery, you'll want this book to trend to the top of your to be read pile."—Carstairs Considers on *#TagMe for Murder*

"This book is the perfect mix of Nancy Drew and Instagram and a fun and enjoyable read."—*What Angela Reads* podcast

"I love Coco Cline…She is like a breath of fresh air in the cozy world."—Dollycas Great Escapes

"*#FollowMe for Murder*'s sleuth Coco Cline is confident, chic, and cool."—Lane Stone, author of the Buckingham Pet Palace Mysteries

"Ms. Burr has her finger right on the pulse"—J.C. Kenney, bestselling author of the Allie Cobb Mysteries and the Darcy Gaughan Mysteries

"Sarah Burr's *#FollowMe for Murder* is an accomplished, witty, and perfectly delightful mystery. The narrative unfolds with clear, precise details, and the heroine, Coco Cline, is indeed, someone we'd all want to follow."—Lori Robbins, award winning author of the On Pointe Mysteries

Chapter One

"Wow, nice digs." An impressed whistle zipped across my lips as I climbed out of the passenger's side of the sleek Mercedes sedan.

Amanda Highgrove adjusted her shades as she studied the stunning oceanfront property before us. "Crescent Hills is one of the more exclusive up-and-coming neighborhoods. Loads of new development projects going on."

She wasn't exaggerating. I'd counted at least thirty new houses in various stages of construction on our drive here. Central Shores was in for a big population boom.

I shook my head as we strolled toward the two-story modern home. "Looks like something out of *Selling Sunset*." Its massive windows, metal accents, and white walls screamed LA living, not small-town coastal Delaware.

Amanda giggled. "It makes sense why LaTàge booked the place. This is definitely her aesthetic."

A flutter of excitement jolted through me. "I still cannot believe we're about to speak with *the* LaTàge."

"Hey, this is no big deal, remember?" Amanda nudged me with her slender shoulder. "You are *the* Coco Cline, after all."

An unflattering snort escaped me before I could swallow it. "Omigod, stop. LaTàge is in a whole different stratosphere when it comes to influencers." I looped my arm through Amanda's. "But I love you for thinking I remotely have even a teeny bit of her star power."

My friend-turned-coworker patted the top of my hand. "Well, once CoA wraps this rebrand engagement for LaTàge, our services will be all anyone can talk about."

I grinned at the warmth with which Amanda said, "our services." I had brought her on this past June to serve as a temporary client engagement manager for my social media marketing business while I searched for someone to fill the role permanently. Turns out, it hadn't taken me long to find the perfect candidate. After only a few weeks, Amanda had asked to stay on full-time at Center of Attention, and I'd been more than happy to have her.

She glanced at her sparkly gold watch that probably cost more than my baby, my British racing green MINI Cooper, Jolly. "Eleven-o-clock on the dot. Shall we?" Amanda motioned toward the front door of the luxurious home.

Eager to be punctual, I raced toward the entryway and pressed the slate-gray doorbell. The porch had a very industrial look to it with a shiny, metal door framed by black iron. A steel railing with glass panels also ran the perimeter of the porch. Backless cement benches were positioned on either side of the door. Very chic, for sure.

Amanda dropped her tote bag onto the left bench and tapped her foot as we waited.

I glanced at my smartwatch, noting the seconds as they ticked by on my customized screen. "LaTàge confirmed our appointment, right?" I shuffled over to the closest window, trying to see inside, but some weird privacy tinting on the glass blocked my view.

"Yep." Amanda tucked a strand of silky blond hair behind her ear. "Ruby texted when they landed yesterday afternoon, so LaTàge should be all prepped to meet today."

I bobbed my head. Ruby Daniels needed no introduction. As LaTàge's personal assistant, content editor, and an official member of the "LaTàge Squad," Ruby was sort of an Internet icon, herself. You could always find her in the background of LaTàge's Instagram Stories, organizing LaTàge's life, editing a TikTok vid, or arranging her friend's next appearance or product sponsorship.

I pressed the doorbell again, taking another nervous glance at my watch. Eleven-o-two. Even though Amanda and I had been on time for our appointment, LaTàge was now making me feel like *I* was late. My desire to be punctual had grown into a flaw over the years, in that it caused me a great deal of anxiety.

Amanda's smooth forehead wrinkled slightly. She still maintained an enviable summer tan, even though it was a week past Labor Day. "Want me to text Ruby?"

I gnawed at my lower lip. "Let's wait a few more minutes. The last thing I want LaTàge thinking is that I'm uptight and cheugy."

Amanda snorted at the disdain in my voice. "Heaven forbid anyone think you were *cheugy*." She continued to chuckle at the term Gen Zers had coined when referencing us out-of-touch millennials.

"Hey, the struggle to stay relevant is real." I was only half-joking. As a social media influencer, I lived in constant fear that I would wake up one day and no one would care about my platform anymore. Not exactly great for one's psyche. "While this engagement with LaTàge could put Center of Attention on the map, it could also destroy us." A new source of worry joined the fray. If LaTàge gave the impression she wasn't completely satisfied with our services, it could spell an abrupt end to my beloved marketing business.

Amanda placed a palm on my forearm and squeezed. "You know that won't happen, Cokes. LaTàge already adores you and your work. She could have reached out to thousands of teams to help with her rebrand, yet she chose *you*."

"She chose *us*," I reminded her. I would have crashed and burned from juggling client engagements and running my lifestyle blog, *Trending Topic*, if it hadn't been for Amanda.

With a pleased grin sliding across her glossy lips, Amanda pressed the doorbell for a third time, and we waited.

And waited.

"Okay, it's been ten minutes." I finally turned to Amanda, my stomach in anxious knots. The breathing exercises recommended by my therapist,

Dr. Ashawari, were no longer doing the trick. My need to be on time had taken total control. "Text Ruby, will you please? I'm going to walk around the joint and see if LaTàge is out back. This place must have a deck or something." With the glorious mid-September weather we'd been having in Central Shores, Delaware, it wouldn't surprise me if LaTàge had fallen asleep outside while sunbathing.

Amanda dug her phone out of her designer tote and began tapping away at the screen. I took the porch steps two at a time and headed toward the south-facing corner of the house. Immaculate hedges lined the building and the initial curb appeal I'd felt slowly receded, replaced by a growing chill. While the house was architecturally gorgeous, looking at it now gave me goosebumps. Why did it suddenly seem so soulless and unnerving?

I rounded the corner, my gaze immediately drawn to the beautiful sandy beach less than two hundred feet in front of me. Aquamarine waves tumbled gently over the sand. "I would kill to wake up to this every morning." A pang of envy poked my chest. My two-story condo might be perched next to the Atlantic, but even my view wasn't this pristine.

Shaking my head free of covetous thoughts, I focused on the task at hand. With my sea-foam green gaze no longer distracted by the ocean, I quickly noticed a chunk of silky material billowing in the breeze. "Must be a curtain," I mumbled. The material looked like it was fluttering out from one of the large first-floor windows.

I scurried forward and found the curtain attached to a sliding glass door open by twelve or fifteen inches. I frowned. Had LaTàge left it ajar and gone to the beach?

I gathered the portion of the curtain that had blown outside and tried to tuck it into the house, but as soon as I let go, the breeze blew it back in my face. Based on the heavy, smooth feel of the fabric, the curtains had to be pricey. I didn't want them to get damaged and for LaTàge to be on the hook.

I reached out to close the glass door when something sparkly inside caught my eye. Momentarily startled by the sudden flash, I yanked my hand back before touching the handle. Sunlight shimmered through the opening, no longer blocked by the curtain or tinted glass.

Curious as to what I'd seen, I peered in through the doorway and quickly begged my eyes to adjust to the change in light.

"Omigod," I yelped as my brain finally processed the scene. The sparkly item that had caught my attention was a watch, even blingier than Amanda's, encircling the outstretched arm of a toned, dark-skinned woman sprawled across the tile floor. I didn't need to see her face to know who it was. Her iconic rainbow weave fanned out all around her head. "LaTàge!"

And from the looks of it, she was very, very dead.

Amanda's concerned, sing-song voice shook me from my dazed stupor. "Coco? Are you okay? I heard you—"

"Stop! Don't come in!" I didn't want my friend walking into a crime scene if I could help it. Not because I had fears about her contaminating it. I just didn't want her to be forever scarred by the sight of a dead body. But unfortunately, I held my palm up a second too late.

Amanda's blue eyes widened as she squeezed through the open threshold. "Oh, God. W-what happened? Coco, is she…?" She clearly couldn't bring herself to say the word out loud.

Panic and horror mingled in my stomach as I tried to calm myself down. After all, this wasn't the first dead body I'd come across. "Yes. I just checked her pulse." I'd darted inside to do so the moment I'd seen LaTàge in such a harrowing state. "We need to call the police."

Even though I did social media consultant work for the Central Shores Police Department and was good friends with many of its employees, I dialed 9-1-1 on my cell phone, careful not to use the fingers that had just checked the dead woman's wrist for any sign of life.

A perky, feminine voice answered. "Nine-one-one. What's your emergency?"

I sucked in a deep breath, my brain reeling. "Hi, my name is Coco Cline. I'm located at," I paused and shot Amanda a panicked look. *Where are we exactly?* I knew we were in a newly constructed neighborhood, but it was a large, expansive area, and I'd forgotten the house number.

Although she had tears streaming down her face, Amanda understood my wordless question. She opened her phone so I could see the Google Maps info on the screen.

"…located at seven-one-three Crescent Hills Drive. My coworker and I found the body of our client in her home." The phantom touch of LaTàge's cool skin against my fingertips made me sick to my stomach. "I think she's been dead a while."

"We've dispatched officers to your area, miss. Did you try any life-saving measures?"

I shot an unnerved glance at LaTàge. "I didn't. I didn't want to disturb the crime scene."

"Crime scene?" the dispatcher squeaked. "Has the victim been attacked? Miss, I need you to make sure you are in a safe space. Are you alone? You said your coworker was with you?"

Adrenaline flooded my veins. *Oh, snap.* Yes, I had immediately assumed that the unnatural way LaTàge was lying on the ground meant something bad had happened to her, but I hadn't even considered her attacker might still be on the premises.

Pinching the phone between my neck and shoulder, I reached for Amanda's trembling arm with my clean hand. "Yes, we're heading out to the street right now to wait for the police."

"Good." The dispatcher stayed quiet while I coaxed a whimpering Amanda outside. Only when I reported we were near our car did she continue with her questioning. "Did you notice anything or anyone unusual around you?"

Besides the corpse of an Internet sensation? "I'm sorry, no, but I don't live around this area, so I'm not super familiar with it." In my youth, Crescent Hills had just been a bunch of overgrown weeds and trees. The land had only been recently developed into residential homes, and this was the first time I'd visited the area since they'd broken ground. While there were plenty of new properties being built for middle-class families, the neighborhood we were in now was fancy enough to rival Canopy Cove, the upper-crust section of Central Shores where Amanda lived.

The echoes of emergency sirens rang in the distance just as the dispatcher said, "All right, miss, first responders have just turned onto your street. They should be arriving shortly."

I breathed a sigh of relief. In a small town like Central Shores, help was never far away. "I see their lights." I squinted, catching a glimpse of a police cruiser between the trees. "I'm going to disconnect now. Thank you for your help."

"You're welcome. Take care," the dispatcher replied before lowering her voice, "and I just have to say, I love your blog, Ms. Cline."

I'd already hit the End Call button before I fully computed her words. *What did I just hear?* I was never one to turn away praise from a fan, but had my 9-1-1 responder really just complimented *Trending Topic* during an emergency call?

I shook away my incredulity and pocketed my phone. I had other things to deal with. Like my most high-profile client ever being dead.

I rummaged through my bag with one hand, trying to find a bottle of hand sanitizer. I pushed away a hairbrush along with the cute but functional tie-dye pocketknife my boyfriend, Hudson Caruthers, had given me for a present. Knowing my penchant for pitting myself against cold-blooded killers, he'd had the all-purpose tool engraved with my name.

"Here." Amanda held out a Purell bottle she'd pulled from her own bag and squeezed it over my open palms.

I slathered my hands with the cool liquid, wishing I could wipe away the image of LaTàge splayed on the floor as easily as I could wash away the germs.

"C-Coco." Amanda's chin quivered as she wiped away her tears. "W-what did we just walk into?"

I draped an arm around her, lending her all the comfort my frazzled state of mind could muster.

"D-do you think someone," Amanda paused to take an exaggerated gulp, "*killed* her?"

"I don't know." Of course, my mind had jumped to foul play upon seeing LaTàge, but my previous experiences with murder might have clouded my jaded judgment. But what other explanation could there be? LaTàge wasn't known to use drugs, and healthy, twenty-five-year-old women didn't just drop dead.

I didn't get a chance to elaborate before a police cruiser pulled up behind Amanda's S-Class Benz. Officer Adrian Riley climbed out, his expression a tight mask of concern. "Hey, Coco. Dispatch says you've got a DB?" He closed the distance between us in three long strides.

I nodded solemnly. "In the kitchen, off the south-facing side door. Our client, LaTàge."

Adrian's dark eyes widened. "LaTàge? As in, 'dats how we dooz it?' LaTàge?"

If it had been any other day, I would have laughed my butt off at Adrian impersonating LaTàge's signature catchphrase. Instead, I grimaced. "Yes. She flew out here to work on a rebrand engagement with CoA."

"Wow. Lifestyles of the rich and famous, huh?" Adrian stroked the dark skin on his cheeks. "Well, okay. You two stay here. I'm going to secure the perimeter, since I'm first on the scene. Gavin and the team aren't far behind me." He unclipped his radio and began issuing commands as he headed toward the property.

"This is not good, this is not good," Amanda murmured repetitively as she watched Adrian's retreating figure.

I nudged her arm. "I know. People are going to be devastated by LaTàge—"

"I don't mean LaTàge," Amanda snapped rather forcefully.

When I raised my eyebrows at her harsh response, she softened. "Sorry. But that's not what I meant. Think about what you just said, Cokes. LaTàge flew out here to do a CoA engagement, and now she's *dead*." Amanda folded her arms across her chest. "This is not going to be a good look for *us*."

I stared at her, a bit stunned Amanda's thoughts had turned so selfish, but I then reminded myself that we all processed death and grief differently. She was probably trying to grapple with the terrible situation as best she could. And now that she had put the concern out there… "We don't even know what happened. Let's not get ahead of ourselves."

More sirens whined in the distance, and soon, another cruiser appeared, followed by a black SUV and a white van. I expected twenty-seven-year-old Lieutenant Gavin McInnis to leap from the driver's side of the police car—after all, the Central Shores PD only had two—but to my surprise, he stepped down from the tanky SUV. The station's newest recruits, Aubrey Milhouse and Jared Hubert, climbed out of the cruiser and joined him. Chief Lloyd McInnis, Gavin's uncle, had hired several officers in recent months, and he was looking to hire even more.

Gavin muttered some instructions to his subordinates, then headed our way, while Milhouse and Hubert hustled toward the white van.

My longtime friend tipped the brim of his hat in greeting. "Hi, Coco. Ms. Highgrove."

I resisted a snicker at the deferential way Gavin treated Amanda. Her father, Thurston Highgrove, was a generous police department donor and was currently working alongside Chief McInnis on a proposal to expand the PD's services, given Central Shores's expected boom in population. Thus, the Highgroves were treated like royalty.

"You both doing all right?" Gavin tilted his head to the side.

Amanda's eyes began to water again. "Oh, Gavin, it was terrible! I don't know how you deal with stuff like this day in and day out."

Gavin's pale cheeks grew red, and he reached for the back of his neck. "Adrian radioed that the deceased is a client of yours?"

My throat tightened. "Yes, she is. Was. Although, we'd yet to meet with her in person." I shifted my gaze toward Amanda.

"Yeah, everything had come through her assistant—Omigod, Ruby!" Amanda scrambled to dig out her phone. "I totally forgot I texted her."

"Did she respond?" I peered over her shoulder to see her screen.

Gavin's brow wrinkled. "Who's Ruby?"

"She's LaTàge's bestie and personal assistant," Amanda explained without looking up from her phone.

"Holy sh—LaTàge? *That's* who your client is?" Gavin's hazel eyes were dangerously close to popping out of his skull.

I nodded. I guessed Adrian hadn't shared that bit of news over the radio. Probably a smart move because once word got out, our sleepy little beach town would be anything but.

"Hey, boss!" Adrian waved as he approached our group. "Got a minute?"

Gavin gave us an apologetic glance before hurrying over to Adrian's side.

I watched them exchange a few words back and forth, Gavin's expression growing stormier by the minute.

Yikes, he's beginning to take after his uncle.

Amanda elbowed me in the side. "Um, take a look at this." She held her phone out to me. "Ruby responded."

I'd been so distracted by Adrian's reappearance that I'd forgotten Amanda had been scouring her texts. "What'd she say?" I asked, rather foolishly, because Amanda had the conversation open right in front of me.

"Nothing good." She pointed to the screen.

I read the clipped message, my heart vaulting into my throat.

Sorry. Don't know where LaTàge is. That mess is not my prob anymore.

Chapter Two

I shot Amanda a spooked look. "*'Not my prob anymore?'* What's that supposed to mean?" Ruby had been LaTàge's right-hand woman since LaTàge hit five hundred thousand TikTok followers.

Before Amanda and I could dissect the cryptic text further, Gavin and Adrian headed our way. Their steps were much heavier upon their return.

The sight made my heart plummet. "What's wrong, guys?"

Adrian pressed his lips together, clearly waiting for the young lieutenant to take the lead.

Gavin removed his hat and ran his fingers through his wispy, sandy-blond hair. "Coco," he said with a sigh, "when you checked LaTàge's pulse, did you check her neck or wrist?"

I straightened at the pointed question. "Her wrist. I couldn't see her neck through her hair, and I didn't want to disturb her body."

"Good call." Adrian gave me a slight smile.

Gavin sent him a silencing glare. "What else did you touch? The door?"

I shook my head. "Not really. It was open when I came around back. The only thing I touched was the curtain." I explained how we'd waited ten minutes for LaTàge to answer the doorbell, but after no answer, I went to check the back of the house. "I thought I'd find her sunning on the deck—" Emotion choked at my throat, preventing me from continuing.

"While you were inside, did you notice anything out of place?" Gavin prodded me further. "Anything that was obviously missing?"

"No, no way." Strands of my strawberry-champagne-dyed hair swished in front of my face as I shook my head. "I've never been here before. I literally saw LaTàge on the ground, checked her pulse, and then called nine-one-one."

Adrian had a notepad out and was scribbling away as I spoke.

"What do you mean 'obviously missing?'" I gasped. "Was LaTàge killed *and* robbed?"

Gavin narrowed his eyes. "I thought you didn't get close enough to the body to see anything?"

"I didn't." I held my hands up in defense. "I just assumed…lying there, she didn't look like she'd died naturally, Gav."

Amanda whimpered next to me. "I agree."

Gavin brooded a moment before he hunched forward with a defeated sigh. "It will be all over the news soon, anyway," he muttered, more to himself than to us. He lifted his hazel gaze. "Based on the ME's preliminary findings, we suspect foul play was involved."

Amanda's fingers clamped around my forearm. "LaTàge was *murdered*? Here, in Central Shores?"

Even though I had already assumed the worst, hearing confirmation was still a punch to the gut. How had this happened in my hometown? Again? "Do you know when? How?"

Gavin's nostrils flared. "Even if I knew, I wouldn't be sharing that information with civilians."

I rolled my eyes. "Oh, come on, Gav. We might be able to help. LaTàge was here to meet with us, after all." To say nothing of the department's two previous murder investigations that I'd had a hand in solving.

Gavin raised an eyebrow. "Do either of you know who would want one of the country's most popular influencers dead?"

I hadn't been expecting such a direct question. "Well, um, no, not right now."

Amanda simply shook her head.

Gavin's phone, clipped to his belt, began buzzing. "Then Adrian will take your statements, and you can be on your way." He already had the phone to his ear as he turned and stalked toward the house. "Deacon, where the heck is your team?"

Adrian winced as he watched the lieutenant retreat. "Don't mind him.

Gavin's just worried about this case turning into a three-ring circus."

"The media scrutiny will be awful." Amanda tugged nervously at her blond blowout. "I mean, this is LaTàge we're talking about." Her initial shock had clearly begun to fade into simmering curiosity.

"Speaking of LaTàge, do either of you know her real name?" Adrian asked, his pen poised at the ready.

"Uh, no." I nearly joked that LaTàge's real name was the Internet's best-kept secret, but thankfully, I realized this wasn't the time or place. "Did you check her belongings? Isn't it on her driver's license or something?"

Adrian tapped his notepad with the tip of his pen. "Do you know anyone who might be aware of her legal name?" He didn't make eye contact, intent on avoiding my question.

Well, two could play at that game. I thought back to Gavin's earlier remark when he'd asked if I thought anything had been obviously missing. "Was LaTàge's purse stolen?"

Adrian gnawed on his lower lip. "Her purse is still sitting on the countertop," he muttered out of the side of his mouth. "Phone, tablet, Kindle, all still inside. The only thing that seems to be missing is her wallet."

Amanda and I exchanged spooked expressions. "So, nothing with her full name on it?" I clarified.

Adrian shook his head. "So, if you know someone who might—"

"Ruby Daniels should." Amanda held up her phone. "Want me to call her and ask?"

"No, Ms. Highgrove," Adrian hurriedly answered. "If you can just give me her contact info, I'll reach out to Ms. Daniels myself."

I waited for Amanda to tell Adrian about the odd text Ruby had sent her, but Amanda merely shared Ruby's electronic contact card with the officer. After Adrian asked us several more questions and recorded us talking about our discovery, he thanked us and said the PD would be in touch.

Neither Amanda nor I spoke until we were buckled in her car. "This is bonkers." Amanda pressed her palms to her face, smoothing the creamy foundation on her tear-stained cheeks.

I leaned back against the headrest. "Bonkers doesn't even begin to cover it."

"Are you okay, Coco?"

The concern in Amanda's voice momentarily baffled me. How had the kind, considerate woman next to me once been the meanest girl this side of Drea from Netflix's teen hit, *Do Revenge*? We sure had come a long way since our cantankerous high school days.

"I'm fine," I hastily reassured her.

But she wasn't about to let me off the hook that easily. "Finding LaTàge? It must have been so triggering."

I took a deep breath, still trying to process *what* I was feeling. "Let's get out of here."

"Okay. That's probably a good idea." Amanda's smile seemed strained, and it was then I noticed her trembling hands.

My emotional compass may have been broken, but Amanda's clearly wasn't. "Hey, why don't I drive?"

"Thanks." Her chin quivered. "Sorry I'm not as tough as you."

"I'm not tough." If anything, I was boxing my emotions away, which was not a good coping mechanism.

We switched places, and soon, I pressed the gas and sped away from the eerie scene.

"Do you think we should call Ruby and let her know what happened?" Amanda broke the tense silence that had settled over us.

I shook my head. "Nah, Adrian's got her info. News like that should come from the police." As much as I wanted to speak with Ruby about the weird text she'd sent Amanda, I knew better than to get in Gavin's way right now. He had enough on his plate. He didn't need my interference.

"What do you think her message meant?" Amanda twirled a strand of her hair with a manicured finger.

I mulled over the sharp words. "It kinda sounds like Ruby might have quit working for LaTàge or something."

Amanda stared out the window. "I wonder where Katz and Miguel are."

Ah, the other two members of the LaTàge Squad. Katz, an edgy, up-and-coming designer, was LaTàge's stylist, whereas boyfriend Miguel was a fledgling influencer who was often seen on LaTàge's arm at red carpet events.

"They wouldn't have skipped out on this trip, that's for sure. Their little posse is glued at the hip. So, where could they be?" I shot a dubious glance at Amanda. "More importantly, where is Ruby? She never leaves LaTàge's side."

Amanda shrugged. "Well, if Ruby really quit working for LaTàge, why would she stick around? This was supposed to be a business meeting, after all."

I was still pretty flabbergasted that LaTàge wanted to meet with us on our home turf. Amanda and I could have just as easily arranged for a remote engagement, but LaTàge insisted on being hands-on during the process. She thought we'd "vibe together better" in person rather than through Zoom.

I pinched the bridge of my nose as anxiety began to mount. My swirling thoughts shifted to my consulting role with the Central Shores PD. Given my growing notoriety as an amateur sleuth, Chief McInnis had recently redefined my ongoing CoA engagement with the department. When I'd started working alongside the team earlier this year, I'd served as their social media liaison and spokesperson, but after two nationally televised takedowns, me being in front of a camera generally caused more of a stir than either Gavin or his uncle wanted. So, these days, I helped manage their online communities and their website. I could only imagine how the PD's Facebook page would explode after the news about LaTàge broke.

As I drove to Amanda's home on Millionaires' Row—the local term for Canopy Cove—I tried to reorganize my priorities. A young woman was dead, yes, but part of me couldn't help but fret over how LaTàge's demise would affect the PD and Central Shores. With three homicides in less than six months, our quiet, seaside haven was in danger of becoming a crime den. Chief McInnis's ambitious plans for expanding the department couldn't be approved by the town council soon enough.

I pulled into Amanda's circular driveway, parking behind my MINI Cooper. I'd driven here for a working breakfast before heading over to LaTàge's Crescent Hills abode.

"Thank you for driving. I'm feeling a bit better now." Amanda smiled weakly. "Although popping a Xanax definitely feels in order."

I wasn't sure whether she was joking as we climbed out of her Benz.

"Okay, so what next?" Amanda placed her hands on her hips, scanning me up and down.

"Why don't you take the rest of the day off?" I hitched my tote bag on my shoulder. "We cleared our calendar for LaTàge today, so you should give yourself a break. Decompress a bit." I paused. "And who knows? Gavin might need to speak with us later, once they're done with the scene."

Amanda shivered. "Good point. I guess it wouldn't hurt to stick close to home." She turned to head toward her grand, if gaudy, entryway.

"Give Arthur a ring, too," I called out. I knew from experience that having a loved one at your side to process traumatic events was a godsend.

Amanda shot a worried look my way. "What about you? Hudson's just started his press tour, hasn't he?"

I tried to ignore the longing pang in my chest at the mention of my boyfriend. "Yeah, he's due back next week. I'll be fine, though. I'll swing by Jasper's or Charlotte's place."

Relief fluttered across Amanda's elegant features. "Oh, good. Okay, talk to you tomorrow." She waved and went inside.

As soon as I sank into Jolly's warm embrace, I felt my poised exterior begin to crack. I'd been trying to stay strong for Amanda, but stumbling upon my third dead body was just as terrifying as finding my first. I may not have known LaTàge personally, but I'd followed her online for several years now. I discovered her fun, campy videos in my feed long before she made it big, so I felt like I'd been with her on her journey to influencer stardom. I loved her bubbly personality and the effortless way she handled herself. Even when she stumbled over her words during an Instagram LIVE session, she still remained composed and charming. My favorite LaTàge content of late was her posts about the random things she did with her beloved little dog, Hashtag.

I gripped the steering wheel in sudden panic. Where was Hashtag? I hadn't seen the adorable Miniature Pinscher anywhere in LaTàge's rental. He usually went with her everywhere, as long as dogs were allowed. Why, just last month, she'd posted pictures of Hashtag eating spaghetti on a balcony in Venice.

On instinct, my phone found its way into my hand, and I swiped through the lock screen. I dialed Adrian's number and waited while the phone rang.

"Hey, Coco, what's up?"

He sounded harried, so I pledged to keep this quick. "I just thought of something. Are there any signs of LaTàge's dog?"

"Dog?" Adrian's surprise was apparent. "No…why?"

I swallowed. LaTàge's wallet was missing, and now, possibly, her dog. "She doesn't go anywhere without him. He's a little Miniature Pinscher. Hashtag."

"That name rings a bell. I think Lana's showed me Reels about him before," Adrian murmured thoughtfully. His wife was an avid social media user and also a fan of mine. "I'll relay this to Gavin. Thanks for the tip."

I felt a little better at the sincerity in his voice. I was grateful Adrian took me seriously and didn't brush me off as some nosy busybody. "No probs. Good luck."

Hoping little Hashtag would be found safe and sound, I ended the call and navigated to another app. I opened Messages and selected my most-used group chat.

Hey, guys. Any chance you're free for lunch? Got some news.

Jasper Hastings, my best friend since second grade, responded with lightning speed. **Did Dad propose???**

I chuckled at the many running jokes in his simple text. Jasper often called me and Hudson Mom and Dad for childish, Jasper-ish reasons. My bestie also liked to tease us for not yet taking the plunge after four and a half years of dating.

Before I could come up with a witty retort, Charlotte Whittaker, my closest girlfriend, entered the convo. **H is still in NYC, J. Duh. M is working the café today so I'm free for food.**

H, J, and M? Are you channeling Prince Harry & Meghan or something? Please don't. Jasper tagged on a GIF of Moira Rose from *Schitt's*

Creek, rolling her eyes. **I'm in town until 3, so I can join.**

A wave of relief lightened the tension in my shoulders. If I couldn't hang with Hudson to decompress after the morning's trying events, my two ride-or-die friends were the next best thing. **Meet at Duneside in 20?**

Chapter Three

After receiving affirmative thumbs-up emojis from my besties, I put Jolly in gear and drove out of Mill Row. Sunlight streamed in through Jolly's moonroof, and I blasted the AC. While tourist season might be dwindling, what with back-to-school schedules, our September weather was very much still in summer mode. As the cold air brought a round of goosebumps, I winced at the unwanted flashback assaulting my memory. LaTàge's cool skin. Gosh, how long had she been lying there?

I tried to bury the image of her beautiful rainbow-colored hair fanned out across the sleek tile, but it remained at the forefront of my mind. In my hazy fog, I didn't recall noticing any blood at the scene. In fact, I really couldn't remember anything beyond LaTàge sprawled across the kitchen floor.

I turned on the radio to distract my morbid thoughts as I made the fifteen-minute drive from Canopy Cove toward the beach. I took the coastal route, and soon, the strip came into view. As our town hub, the strip offered residents and tourists a variety of small businesses and quaint eateries. Charlotte's café, Brewed to Perfection, perched at the south end.

My destination today, however, was a bit farther down the road. As its name suggested, Duneside was a seasonal lunch spot situated on the beach. Despite its perfect setting, my friends and I hardly ever ate there because it was nearly impossible to get a table during the summer months. With Labor Day in our rearview mirror, September was pretty much the only time we locals ventured inside.

I approached the diner, my gaze drawn to the big, black sign underneath Duneside's glowing red name. **SEPTEMBER 30TH – CLOSING FOR THE SEASON.** The countdown was on.

I parked in the crowded gravel lot. I climbed out of Jolly and locked his doors, taking a moment to scan the area for Jasper's sporty Porsche or Charlotte's new pickup truck. Seeing neither, I headed inside to grab a table.

The interior of Duneside was all jersey blue shiplap with white accents. Seashells, fishing nets, and buoys hung from the walls, embodying your typical oceanside haunt.

I approached the hostess, wary that there wouldn't be an open spot for us. I saw several familiar faces seated at various tables around the diner. Lacie Burbank, my childhood babysitter, chatted with her younger sister, Dionne. Fred and Natalia Beaufort, the owners of Central Shores's one and only French restaurant, ate quietly in the corner. Andre Nunez, the sommelier and proprietor of Central Shores's popular wine bar, dined with his new boyfriend, Garrett.

"Good afternoon, Ms. Cline. Can I help you?" the cheery hostess asked with a flip of her raven hair.

I hesitated a moment, wondering if it had been a wise idea to come to someplace so public. I couldn't risk people overhearing about my morning's exploits, but there was no way I could keep finding LaTàge a secret from Charlotte and Jasper. Luckily, from the looks of their demolished plates, everyone I knew seemed to be wrapping up their meals.

I relaxed and smiled at the young woman's warm greeting. While I didn't think I'd ever met her before, it was clear she recognized me. A perk—or con, depending on how you looked at it—of online fame. "A table for three, if you have it."

She bobbed her head as she studied the computer screen at her podium. "Ooo, do you mind waiting for a few minutes, Ms. Cline? We've got a table opening up soon."

"No problem." I sat on the bench in the cozy waiting area.

Two minutes later, the Beauforts shuffled their way past me. With heads down, Fred and his wife looked like they were trying to be invisible, but the popular restaurateur inadvertently made eye contact with me, and my mother raised me to be polite.

"Hi, Fred. Natalia." I waved at the middle-aged couple.

Fred managed a tired smile. "Hey, Coco. Nice to see you."

He sounded like he almost meant it. Fred's family had been going through a rough patch, and I'd had a hand in their drama making national news.

Natalia didn't meet my friendly gaze. Instead, she put a guiding hand on her husband's back and departed the diner.

I shuddered at the uncomfortable interaction, trying not to take things too personally.

The hostess reappeared a moment later to collect me. "This way, please." She escorted me to the corner table at which the Beauforts had dined.

I settled into my seat with a glance at my watch. Jasper and Charlotte should be here any moment.

I heard them before I saw them. Well, I heard Jasper.

"—don't make me do it, Mil. It takes away all the show's spontaneity." As he waltzed into the restaurant, Jasper tossed his left arm into the air, his right hand clutching a phone against his ear.

Charlotte, standing next to him, elbowed him in the stomach, likely signaling him to take his flamboyant behavior down a notch.

With a wave, I caught Charlotte's attention. A smile broke out across her gorgeous face, and she grabbed Jasper's muscular arm, pulling him in my direction.

Jasper continued to complain into the phone. "I don't care that she's a Grammy nominee. She didn't *win*." He nodded in acknowledgment as he plopped down on the chair across from me.

"Who's he speaking with?" I whispered to Charlotte.

She rolled her ethereal gray eyes as she claimed an open seat. "Who else? His *producer*."

I giggled at her snarky exaggeration. Charlotte may have been the nicest person I'd ever known, but after nearly four years of countless shenanigans, Jasper and I were beginning to rub off on her.

"I should have guessed." I flashed Charlotte a conspiratorial grin. Ever since Jasper had launched his talk show, *Divulge Direct*, he always seemed to be on a call with his producer, Millie Stabler, plotting his next move.

Charlotte reached for my forearm and squeezed. "Hey, you okay? You look a little down." She tilted her head with concern, the long waves of her amber hair rippling with the sudden movement.

I sighed. She knew me too well. "It's been a morning."

Jasper ended his call with the punch of a touchscreen button. "Why?" His icy blue eyes narrowed. "Has HRH finally snapped and reverted back to her old teenage self?"

I snorted at Jasper's nickname for Amanda. HRH—Her Royal Highness—alluded to the days when Amanda Highgrove had been the mean Queen B of our school. "No. I wish."

Both my besties noted the melancholy in my voice. Jasper set his snarky demeanor aside. "What's going on? Did something happen with Hudson?"

I appreciated his concern. "Hudson is fine. This…is a little bit more complicated."

Charlotte poked my arm. "Spill."

I leaned forward to share the latest drama with my friends when a server appeared at our table.

"Hey, Henry." Charlotte smiled at the older gentleman. As the owner of the most popular café for miles, Charlotte knew practically everyone in the area.

The elderly white man grinned back at her. "Hello, Sweet Charlotte. What can I get you and your friends?"

After relaying his order, Jasper folded his arms, a frown growing on his angular face.

"What's with the pout?" Charlotte gave his elbow a playful knock.

Jasper scoffed. "Out of the three of us at this table, *you're* the one he recognized?" He then rubbed his temples as if the thought pained him.

I giggled at his antics. "Relax. I don't think Henry is the key demographic for *Divulge Direct*."

"I'm on a quest to become a household name. *Everyone* is my intended demographic." Jasper slicked back his dark brown hair with a haughty sniff.

Charlotte groaned. "Ugh, if that happens, there'll be no living with you."

Jasper was in the process of transitioning his society and fashion magazine, *Divulge*, into a media conglomerate with the recent addition of *Divulge Direct* to his repertoire. Initially, *Divulge Direct* had been conceived as a local talk show produced by WMTG, the same network Hudson worked for. However, putting Jasper and Millie Stabler in a room together eventually generated a much more ambitious, grandiose concept. While *Divulge Direct* aired live on a local station, the show was also made available on podcast platforms worldwide. The two-for-one show format had exciting potential, and Jasper had been working hard all summer to make it a success.

"Who's Millie trying to bring on the show now?" I asked, curious what Jasper had been talking about when he'd sauntered into Duneside.

He waved the question away. "Later. You obviously have something to tell us."

I gulped. It had been comforting to occupy myself with my friends' lives and not dwell on finding LaTàge. "This stays between us, got it? No swooping in to give Millie the scoop," I said, shooting a pointed glare at Jasper, "and no telling Deacon I told you." My pleading gaze traveled to Charlotte. Deacon Lait worked for the Central Shores PD as a forensic tech. He was also Charlotte's boyfriend of five months.

Charlotte dragged her finger across her chest. "Cross my heart."

"Fine." Jasper blew out a forceful sigh.

I lowered my voice. "Amanda and I had our meeting with LaTàge this morning." In hushed tones, I hurriedly relayed just how horribly our consultation appointment had gone awry.

My pals were understandably floored. Even Jasper was at a loss for words, a rare thing indeed.

I sat back in my seat, an invisible weight lifting from my chest. "I had to hold myself together to get Amanda home, but guys, LaTàge is *dead*." I held my head in my hands. "And I feel like it's my fault."

"What?!" This admission snapped Jasper and Charlotte from their stunned stupors. "Of course, you're not to blame," Charlotte cooed.

Jasper folded his arms. "Yeah, don't be ridiculous, Cokes."

"LaTàge was here for a CoA engagement," I hurriedly countered. "If not for our meeting, she would be bouncing around LA with her crew."

Charlotte tucked a loose strand of my long, pin-straight hair behind my ear. "Coco, take a deep breath," she instructed in a nurturing manner. "You're not responsible for any of this."

My vision grew blurry as unwanted tears welled in my eyes. "I just—I can't believe it."

Jasper steepled his fingers together. "Do the police think she was…" he whispered, his head swiveling in an elaborate glance around the restaurant, "M-U-R-D…E-R-E-D?"

I almost laughed, as it was clear Jasper struggled with where to put the E's. But my response sobered me right up. "I don't know much, but Adrian mentioned LaTàge's wallet was missing from her purse."

"A robbery gone wrong?" Charlotte's brow furrowed with apprehension. "Where did you say she was staying?"

"Crescent Hills. In one of the new developments."

Jasper's gaze narrowed. "Where the heck is Crescent Hills?"

His question didn't surprise me that much. While Jasper had grown up in Central Shores, he'd only recently moved back to the area from Dover and spent very little time mingling with the commonfolk. "It's one of the new neighborhoods stacked with a bunch of boujee homes. Formerly known as the woodlands north of Canopy Cove."

"A few years ago, the woodlands were sold to several different property groups," Charlotte added. "Though, I think Ronny Durnst's company is the only one that's got McMansions up already. Crescent Hills is his site, right? Or is he managing Peach Blossom Grove?"

I shrugged. "You already seem to know more than me."

Jasper rapidly tapped his screen and studied his phone. "Peach Blossom Grove, Strawberry Lane, Colonial Drive, Liberty Circle," he murmured, reading the names of the new neighborhoods from some site. "…are these places gunning to be Mill Row 2.0?" He tilted his head.

My lip curled at his snark. "Yep."

He rolled his eyes. "I should have waited to snatch up a house in one of these spots. Instead, I'm stuck with you guys." When Jasper relocated to Central Shores, he'd purchased one of the free-standing condos in the same oceanside development in which both Charlotte and I lived. He liked to tease us about how we were suffocating him with our closeness, but always bashfully zipped his lips when I reminded him that *he'd* moved next to *us*.

Our server, Henry, returned with our drink orders and a basket of seasoned pita chips. Once he departed with our entrée selections, Charlotte took a thoughtful sip of her iced tea. "Gosh, having a dead starlet found in one of your houses is not going to be a good look for poor Ronny."

"Do you know him?" I asked, swirling my Diet Pepsi with a flimsy, eco-friendly straw.

She bobbed her head. "He comes by Brewed to Perfection regularly. Nice guy."

"Why was LaTàge staying at one of his new builds?" Jasper raised a dubious eyebrow.

"I don't know." My gaze drifted out the nearest window overlooking the churning Atlantic. "And what's weirder, the LaTàge Squad didn't seem to be anywhere in sight."

A girly squeak hummed across Charlotte's lips. "Omigosh, Katz is here? I just love their style. I can't wait for the new romper line they've been teasing to drop."

"It's been hyped for months. *Divulge* even got some exclusive pieces." Jasper stroked his chin. "But wasn't LaTàge going to be the face of the campaign? I wonder what will happen now."

His comment sparked a worrisome theory. Ruby's churlish text bubbled to the forefront of my mind. It was clear Ruby's relationship with LaTàge had recently soured. With all her friends seemingly MIA, I mulled over whether something had happened between LaTàge and the non-binary designer, as well.

Simultaneously, our smartphones all buzzed on the table. Jasper snatched his cell up first, swiping with the speed of Usain Bolt. His pale skin lost even more of its color. "Big yikes."

Intrigued by his reaction, I tapped the notification that had caused my phone to vibrate. It was the Apple News app, something the three of us all utilized, touting the headline, "**Internet icon and influencer LaTàge, dead at 25.**"

I sucked in a sharp breath. *"What?"* Gavin and the team had already released the news to the public? I guessed they must have tracked down LaTàge's next of kin. But seriously, what were they thinking, dropping this knowledge bomb so soon after LaTàge had been found? Had they even properly processed the crime scene? "Why would the PD share this?"

Charlotte, too, was devouring the news blast. "Uh, oh." She scrolled further on her screen. "This wasn't the PD's doing. Read on."

I did as I was told, tapping the alert, which linked me to a *PEOPLE* article.

Ruby Daniels, LaTàge's longtime friend and business associate, confirmed the news on her Instagram account, stating the following in a post, "I am completely shattered. My world, my light, my LaTàge, is gone. No cap, LaTàge was the best thing to ever happen to me. She saved me. RIP Queen. You will have justice."

Daniels' cryptic message suggests the popular TikTok star may have been a victim of foul play. LaTàge was rumored to be staying in Central Shores, Delaware, home to another well-known influencer, Coco Cline. What LaTàge was doing in the area remains to be seen.

PEOPLE has reached out to Ms. Cline, the Central Shores Police, and the Sussex County Crime Lab but has received no comment.

I blinked repetitively. Each time my eyes readjusted to the screen, more alerts and notifications blew up my phone.

"Holy Margot Robbie." Jasper's icy blue gaze was wide when he glanced up from his device. "Coco, this is…" He couldn't find the right words to describe the situation.

I continued to stare at the article, *my name* glaring back at me. Why had I been so publicly dragged into this mess?

Chapter Four

I couldn't ignore the other alerts on my phone any longer. I tapped the angry red badge on Twitter—I mean, X. The rebranded social media app had stopped counting how many notifications I had. My mentions were exploding.

@latageauxfolles: Our G.O.A.T is ded. Dies while with @CocoCline? Super sus. Wut is it with this sis and murder?

@longlivelatage: Justice for our gurl. Periodt. Get after this, @CocoCline. You owe her.

@lalalalatageluvr: Vibe check. Sending luv to the LaTàge Squad. Can't imagine how you are dealing @RubyDanielsOfficial @MigueltheMaster @KatzouttatheBag. Stay away @CocoCline. What did you do to our queen?

I tapped away from the growing list of mentions—some more like threats—calling me out for being the reason LaTàge was dead. I moved to the search section, and the list of top trending hashtags had my heart plummeting to my butt.

#JusticeforLaTàge

#LongLiveLaTàge

#RIPLaTàge

#CocoCline

#CrimeInfluencer

#CentralShoresisDeadly

I rubbed my temples as the dull ache of a migraine nipped back at me. I had reached the point in my life where seeing my name trend brought unbridled panic, not excitement. But having my beloved hometown up there with me brought even more alarm. "People are going to think Central Shores is the new *Murderville*."

"Without the funny guest stars." Jasper tried to make light of the situation, but I could tell even he was troubled.

Charlotte grabbed my hand and squeezed. "I'm sure this will blow over once the police release a formal statement."

I couldn't meet her gaze. Instead, I stared at the growing list of notifications on my phone. Buried among them, I discovered that I *had* received an email from some junior editor at *PEOPLE*, asking about my ties to LaTàge. No comment, indeed. They'd sent the email ten minutes before blasting their exclusive story across the web.

The buzzing notifications were suddenly drowned out by the staccato rhythm of my muted ringtone. Gavin's name filled the screen.

"I'm gonna take this outside." I showed Jasper and Charlotte the incoming call.

They nodded their understanding, and I hurried away from our table, trying not to draw too much attention to myself from the other diners.

Fresh ocean air washed over me as I scurried out into the parking lot, but it did little to soothe my nerves. "Hey, Gav—"

A slew of expletives greeted me on the other end. Not only from Gavin, but it sounded like Deacon, Adrian, and others were airing their grievances as well. "Oh, hey, Coco. I suppose I owe you an apology," Gavin said, finally uttering a coherent sentence. "For all those times you kept a murder investigation under wraps. I didn't realize how *impossible* a task it was."

I smiled uneasily at his evident sarcasm. "What happened?"

"We reached out to Ruby Daniels to try and track down more information about LaTàge." Frustration riddled Gavin's words. "She ended up coming by the house and saw all the activity. I guess someone from the county lab let slip it was a homicide, and now, the whole world knows about LaTàge before we even know who our vic actually is."

My eyebrows inched up my forehead. "You mean, Ruby wouldn't tell you LaTàge's real name?"

"She says she never knew LaTàge by any other name," Gavin explained. "Apparently, when they met, LaTàge introduced herself as LaTàge Luxe. It wasn't long before she was just going by LaTàge. Adrian did some preliminary records digging, and activity under the name 'LaTàge Luxe' popped up around eight years ago. Whoever she was before then, we have no idea. We can't find anything about her legally changing her name. California has a pretty transparent name-change process, and there's nothing."

"Wow." I whistled. I'd always assumed LaTàge was a stage name and that the influencer used her real moniker around her friends. "But Ruby wasn't just her best friend. She was LaTàge's assistant. Ruby must have booked travel or used a credit card or something."

"Ruby said she either used a business Amex or LaTàge made her use her own card for reimbursement. She never handled LaTàge's personal accounts, either. It was something LaTàge insisted she do herself 'to stay grounded.'" I could almost hear Gavin making sarcastic air quotes.

Odd. From their videos and online interactions, the two seemed so close. But Ruby didn't even know her bestie's given name? Moreover, why had LaTàge gone out of her way to keep Ruby at arm's length?

I heard muttering in the background, and I debated a moment before blurting out, "Well, is there anything I can do to help?" I already knew the answer. Gavin would snap and tell me to mind my own business, just like he had earlier this morning.

"Actually...yes."

"Huh?" I nearly dropped my phone on the gravel. "R-really?"

"Nothing like *that*, Coco," Gavin replied sternly. Somehow, he must have known my mind jumped right to helping him interrogate potential suspects. "We'd like to enlist your expertise to help us wade through LaTàge's online life. I know that's a bit out of your job description, but—" he lowered his voice "—we're up against a lot of hurdles, and it would be helpful to have someone who understands the influencer lifestyle explain her activity and her world to us."

The excited anticipation I'd felt a moment ago deflated. "You want me to give you the down low on her social media?" That hardly sounded thrilling.

"Her public-facing social media profiles might reveal whether she had credible threats against her. Even after we figure out LaTàge's identity, it's going to take a while to get the proper access to her phone and accounts—"

"Hold up." I stopped him, as what he said didn't ring quite true. "Why doesn't Ruby unlock LaTàge's phone for you? She should at least have access to that."

"We've already tried." Gavin sounded annoyed that I'd assumed incompetence on his part. "According to Ruby, LaTàge never gave her unsupervised access to her phone. Ruby only had control over LaTàge's inquiries email and calendar."

"Are you for real?" I couldn't comprehend Ruby not knowing her boss's passcode. While "personal assistant" was the professional term for someone in Ruby's role, she was really more like LaTàge's handler. Ruby organized and directed LaTàge's life, which meant she needed access to a *lot* of things, LaTàge's phone being one of them. Or at least, that's what I'd thought until now.

"Yeah," Gavin continued, unaware of my inner plight, "so we're stuck getting access to her phone records and activity the old-fashioned way." He didn't sound pleased.

I shuddered. Phone records were one thing, but smartphone manufacturers protected their clients' information almost to a fault. I'd listened to an *Anatomy of Murder* podcast episode where it had taken more than seven *months* for police to obtain the requested intel. "What about holding up LaTàge's face to her cell?" My stomach flipped at the mental image. "Even if she's dead, FaceID should still be able to recognize her."

"Come on, Cokes. Give us some credit." Gavin's exasperation was evident. "LaTàge didn't have FaceID enabled. Per Ruby, she didn't want Big Brother having her biodata or some conspiracy-theory excuse."

LaTàge's obvious mistrust regarding her privacy had me deeply concerned. It was a complete reversal from everything I knew about her, everything she portrayed online. I'd fallen for her open, transparent act, hook, line, and sinker. "Sorry." I hadn't meant to insult his skills as an investigator. "Ruby didn't give you any clues as to what LaTàge's passcode *might* be?"

"No. It was like pulling teeth to get her to share what she did. You'd think if your boss and gal pal was found dead, you'd be a little more cooperative. Or at least, show some concern." Gavin scoffed. "Guess she was saving all her tears for her TikTok Live."

Oh no. I'd only seen reference to Ruby's Instagram post, but it sounded like the girl had been busy making the rounds online.

"She and LaTàge's two other friends are coming down to the station tomorrow for formal interviews. Their lawyers are flying out this afternoon and advised them all not to speak with us alone." Gavin added, "Could we meet up beforehand? I'd like to get your input on some questions Detective Forester and I need clarified."

My ears perked up at the name. "Harriet's on the case?"

"Oh, yeah. Something this high profile? We'll be lucky if the state police or the feds don't try to swoop in and take over."

More murmurs floated over the line from Gavin's end. Their tone sounded urgent. "I need to get going. See you tomorrow? Ruby is scheduled to come in first. Can you swing by around eight?"

"Sure th—"

The call went dead.

"—ing." I frowned as I stared at my phone's lock screen. I wondered what had happened now.

More alerts cluttered my notification center, and my heart skipped with renewed panic. Tweet after tweet popped up. Some begged for me to avenge LaTàge, given my history of unmasking murderers. Others labeled me as a harbinger of death.

My anxiety spiked at the unkind words. I was used to being trolled on the Internet, but not about stuff like this. Strangers with nothing better to do often called me out for giving my "dumb" opinion or offering "stupid" advice. Others harassed me for my looks. My hair was too straight, my thighs were too big, my neck was too skinny, my elbows were too pointed...the list went on. All that, though, I could swallow. Being told *I* was the reason someone was dead? Not so great for my mental health.

One notification did lift my spirits. A text from Hudson.

Hey, babes. Hope you're doing okay. Saw the news. The whole LaTàge thing is all anyone can talk about here. Weren't you sched to meet today? Millie's already called 7 times about ideas for *CSH*. Reach out when you can, OK? Love you.

His message unleashed a flurry of emotions. Hudson had only been gone a day, but I missed him like crazy. I treasured his sweet "love you" note, but the other parts of his text had my stomach roiling. "Here" was New York City, where Hudson was working for the next week and a half. My super talented boyfriend had recently launched *Crime Sweet Home: A Look at Local Mysteries*, a *48-Hours*-meets-your-neighbors-type show produced by WMTG. Featuring active and solved cases throughout the Delaware region, it'd been on the air for about two months now and was already a major hit for the local network. So much so, Millie Stabler, who also happened to be the same executive producer for Jasper's *Divulge Direct*, had sent Hudson on a whirlwind publicity tour to hype the show on streaming platforms.

I typed back, **News is shocking but all is good. With Jasper and Char now. Lots to share off the record. When would be a good time to call?** I knew Hudson had his first major press interview today, this one scheduled with CNN. He was also hoping to track down some leads on a cold case he planned to feature on an upcoming *CSH* episode. A missing Cherry Springs woman, who was presumed dead, had some acquaintances who'd moved to NYC after her disappearance.

He responded almost immediately. **Why don't we FaceTime at 8? You can fill me in and I can tell you what Andy Coops looks like in real life.**

His teasing Anderson Cooper remark brought a smile to my face. I knew if I told Hudson right now that I'd been the one to find LaTàge, he'd probably be on the next flight home to comfort me. Thank goodness he wasn't really on social media anymore, or Hudson would panic at all the hate trending my way. I couldn't let my inability to steer clear of murder derail this amazing career opportunity for him. **It's a date. Break a leg <3**

With my message sent, I set my iPhone to Do Not Disturb. I couldn't handle the ongoing barrage of DMs, comments, and mentions. Instead,

I focused on something I actually had some modicum of control over: helping Gavin and the Central Shores PD navigate LaTàge's influencer world. Buoyed by the fact that Gavin had actually asked for my help with a case, I returned to Duneside to find that our food had been delivered.

I also discovered other customers must have checked their phones and seen the news, because Jasper and Charlotte were surrounded by three curious, familiar faces.

"Coco!" Lacie Burbank spotted me first. "Is it really true? LaTàge was here to see *you?*"

I flinched at her question. While Lacie hadn't sounded accusatory, the sudden influx of guilt that weighed on me felt suffocating.

Daniel Wu shushed her. "Come on, Lace. That's not fair." The attractive olive-skinned man smiled at me with sympathy. Daniel owned Mystic's Cards and Games, a steadfast establishment on the strip that he'd inherited from his dad. Mr. Wu had retired to Florida two years ago, leaving the game shop in his thirty-six-year-old son's care.

Lacie flashed an apologetic look. "Whoops. Sorry, that came out wrong. I just can't get over the fact that LaTàge is—*was* in Central Shores."

Daniel gave a wry chuckle as he moved his wheelchair back a few inches, allowing me to return to the comfort of my seat. "We should change the town slogan to Central Shores: it's to die for."

Lacie's younger sister, Dionne, smacked Daniel on the shoulder. "That ain't it, chief."

"Sometimes I feel like I need a translator to talk with your generation." Daniel rubbed his shoulder, giving Dionne a playful smirk.

Dionne ignored him and turned her brown-eyed focus on me. "You okay, Ms. Coco?"

Even though I'd told the recent college grad to drop the "Ms." numerous times, Dionne always showed me deferential respect that made me feel *much* older than twenty-eight. Yikes, soon to be twenty-nine at the end of next week.

"I'm fine. Thanks, Dionne. The entire Internet just seems to be mad at me." I balled my fist and propped my cheek against it, a wave of exhaustion barreling over me.

Lacie dusted off her hands. "Well, you'll set them straight, won't you? I mean, how could anyone from Central Shores possibly have anything to do with LaTàge's death, let alone the town's number one crime fighter?"

My cheeks glowed warm at Lacie's praise.

Jasper, who'd been suspiciously quiet up until now, bobbed his chin. "Yeah, you need to pin down which member of the LaTàge Squad did her in before the Internet decides to cancel you, Cokes."

"What are you getting at?" I raised a cautious eyebrow.

Jasper shrugged. "You dove right in when you thought *I* was on the hook for murder. I can't believe you're not already trying to track down a killer now that it's your neck on the line."

Reflexively, my hand brushed my collarbone. "Be real now. The police know I didn't have anything to do with this."

"Tell that to this guy." Charlotte slid her phone my way. A chilling meme stared back, featuring my face superimposed over the body of a little girl smirking as her home burned in the background. The creator had typed over the flames, **LaTàge's Career**.

I stared at the meme with growing dismay. Not only was it incredibly tacky and disrespectful to LaTàge, but it also hammered home the seriousness of the problem I faced. "That's awful."

"*That's* already been reposted forty-nine thousand times." Charlotte pointed to the tiny icons below the mean tweet.

I studied the faces of my two besties, very much aware Lacie, Dionne, and Daniel were hanging onto our every word. "Look, I'm sure once the real killer is caught, the Internet will forget all about me."

Jasper scoffed. "The Internet *never* forgets."

I stared him down, willing him to read my mind. *Come on. You know me. Twenty-plus years of friendship has got to count for something, right?*

Finally, Jasper's eyes widened as the metaphorical lightbulb popped on. "But on the other hand, you did promise Hudson you'd forfeit your sleuthing escapades. I'm sure the police will get to the bottom of this soon," he added sagely.

As I nodded in agreement, I noticed how our onlookers slumped with defeat. "Well, then, I hope it all works out, Coco. Good luck," Lacie offered as she and Dionne waved goodbye.

"See you around." Daniel gave a friendly salute before navigating his wheelchair toward the exit.

Charlotte's lips slouched in a pout. "Aw, I was kinda looking forward to playing super sleuth again. Especially when the suspects have the potential to be famous."

I stared at her. "Well, obviously, we're going to dig into this."

"Huh?" Charlotte did a double take. "But you just said—"

"Yeah, in front of those guys. I love Lacie, but we can't have other people knowing we're looking into LaTàge's death." My previous investigations had proven more than once the importance of flying under the radar. "At least, not until we've solved the case."

"Yeah, duh, Char." Jasper stuck out a teasing tongue at her. "Did you like my skillful misdirection?"

I placed a hand on Jasper's broad shoulder. "It was some of the worst acting I've ever seen."

"Hey!"

As Jasper and I tossed snarky yet loving insults back and forth, Charlotte swirled a fry in her ketchup. "So, what do we do?" she murmured. "How do we go about clearing your name?"

While I knew I wasn't officially on the hook for LaTàge's murder, I was definitely at risk of being tried in the court of public opinion. If I helped the police nab LaTàge's killer, like I had two times before, there would be no way the Internet could stay mad at me.

Right?

My whole career as a blogger and influencer was wrapped up in the Internet's approval. I had to make sure I protected my reputation, my livelihood. Not to mention, someone had decided to end the life of a bright young woman on my home turf. I may not have personally known LaTàge, but I felt like I owed it to her to unmask her assailant.

Before I answered Charlotte's weighted question, I took a bite of my

Grilled Chicken Greek wrap. I hadn't eaten anything since yesterday's send-off dinner with Hudson, and my hunger pains were catching up to me. "Well, first, let me fill you in on my call with Gavin."

In hushed tones, I told Jasper and Charlotte about Ruby's strange response to her friend's death, as well as Gavin's request that I educate the PD about LaTàge's life as an influencer.

"That's great!" Charlotte clapped softly with glee. "You'll have total insider access."

I grimaced. "I'm going to have to play it carefully, though. Gavin can't find out I'm doing a bit more digging than he bargained for." I held her gaze. "I hate to even ask this, Char, but are you gonna be able to keep our snooping from Deacon?" Her forensic tech boyfriend would be obligated to rat us out to Gavin or Chief McInnis if he discovered what we were up to.

Charlotte didn't miss a beat. "What Deacon doesn't know can't hurt him."

I smiled. I loved how much my friends had my back.

"Okay, and since I'm forever alone, that's settled." Jasper rubbed his hands together with anticipation.

"Nooooo, it's not." I glared in his direction. "*You* have to promise you won't utter anything about this to Millie *or* use intel we uncover as fodder for *Divulge Direct.*"

Jasper grumbled. "What's the point of helping you if I can't dish about LaTàge?" But before I could issue a sarcastic retort of my own, he held his hands up in surrender. "I kid, I kid. My lips are sealed." He mimed the action. "Until the case is closed, that is. Then, I'm spilling the tea."

"Fineeeee." I rolled my eyes in weary concession.

Chapter Five

"So, where do we start?" Charlotte repeated her earlier question, now that we had established the rules of our sleuthing engagement.

I tapped the Notes app on my phone. "Where we always do. Who would want LaTàge dead?"

"That's a pretty easy list, given that her entire life was out on the West Coast and not here." Jasper held up his fingers. "Ruby, Katz, and Miguel. One or more of the squad *have* to be involved. No one else even knew she was in town. LaTàge certainly didn't post about it."

"I'm not so sure about that." Charlotte pressed her lips together. "Check this out." She'd pulled up Instagram and selected LaTàge's profile picture.

A recent Story loaded. The video featured LaTàge clad in a flirty bathrobe, pouring a glass of champagne.

"My Lalollies," her melodic, upbeat voice declared, "always remember, no matter what cray is happening in your life, you deserve a good glass of bubbly." LaTàge raised the flute in the direction of the camera, her bright smile not quite reaching her big brown eyes. "Dats how we dooz it."

The short video was classic LaTàge. Showcasing her glam lifestyle while reminding her followers—her Lalollies—that they, too, deserved the best out of life. She was all about self-love and being proud of who you were. Watching LaTàge on Charlotte's phone brought forth another sudden wave of waterworks. The young woman had given the world so much joy with her wacky, wild ways. Whatever "cray" had been happening in her life, LaTàge didn't deserve to die.

I wiped away a stray tear and got back to business. "The location looks like the Crescent Hills kitchen." I pointed at the smooth, shiny countertop, a suppressed memory stirring. "I didn't get a super close look at the place, but it's def familiar. When was this posted?"

"Um, fifteen hours ago." Charlotte squinted at her screen as she did some mental math. "So, roughly around nine PM last night."

"Are there any more vids?" I hurriedly pressed. "We might be able to narrow in on LaTàge's time of death based on when she stopped posting." I wondered if Gavin and his team had thought to do this. Should I text and ask? Or would I risk offending him…again?

Charlotte tapped forward to advance to the next Story. "There's just one other from eleven hours ago." The clip featured LaTàge pouring another drink, this time out on a deck facing the water. Although, in the moonlit darkness, we could barely see anything beyond the sparkling bubbly and the shimmering waves.

"My advice, Lalollies?" Her wistful voice came from somewhere off-camera. "Take a moment every day to look up at the stars. Remind yourself that they are infinite, and so are life's possibilities."

LaTàge's heartfelt words were made all the more tragic by the fact her life must have been snuffed out soon after this recording.

Jasper checked his watch. "So, her final upload was around one AM."

"It doesn't narrow things down for us too much," I contemplated with a sigh, "but it's a jumping-off point."

Charlotte twirled a strand of her hair, a frown growing. "What are the chances that her killer uploaded these clips to make it appear like LaTàge was still alive? It's not like these were Instagram LIVE vids."

I mulled over the possibility. Had the killer tried to manipulate LaTàge's social media to give themselves an alibi? "Something like that would require access to LaTàge's phone. And from what Ruby has told the police so far, LaTàge kept her passcode close to her chest. Unless the killer forced the information out of her, I think we can assume LaTàge posted these herself."

"Besides, check how high in the sky the moon was in that last one," Jasper added. "It had to be at least midnight when it was recorded."

Charlotte stared at him. "Since when are you a lunar positioning expert?"

"The new astrologist we hired for *Divulge* does weekly moon readings at the office." Jasper sounded as though he were chatting about an employee bringing in donuts.

"And I thought the free coffees Maria gets were a perk." Charlotte snorted at the rather unconventional employee benefit.

I giggled. "Based on the camera work, it looks like LaTàge recorded these herself. Ruby, Miguel, or Katz weren't around to help."

"Maybe that's what they wanted people to believe," Jasper contended. "I still think they are suspects one, two, and three."

I turned my attention back to my Notes app and typed the names of the LaTàge Squad. "Okay, okay, but without getting tunnel vision, who *else* might have it out for LaTàge? We've got to cover all our bases. Was she feuding with anyone online?"

Jasper shrugged. "No one publicly that I can think of."

Charlotte studied her phone. "Didn't she recently post a reconciliation video with her medium?"

Jasper choked on a bite of his Cobb salad as he laughed. "I totally forgot about that. Although, truth be told, Madame Organa looked stoned out of her mind during the session. I doubt the little hack even remembers it."

"So, moon readings are totally normal, but mediums are scammers?" I knocked Jasper's arm for his hypocritical comment. I'd never admit it out loud, but I totally believed in psychic abilities. On a whim, I'd had my fortune read the week before I met Hudson. The clairvoyant told me the love of my life was just around the corner and would walk on peanut shells for me. At the time, I thought she was completely kooky and mixing up metaphors, but low and behold, the next weekend, Hudson sauntered up to me at a dive bar, stepping on peanut shells as he maneuvered through the crowd. "What were LaTàge and Madame Organa fighting about?"

Charlotte shrugged. "LaTàge got angry during a livestream reading Madame Organa did for her on YouTube. Something about the truth coming to light. LaTàge went on a rant that she's always been truthful with her followers and that Organa was trying to sabotage her."

The conversation I'd had with Gavin about LaTàge hiding her real name from her friends floated through my mind. Truthful, huh? "Sounds like Madame Organa hit a sore spot."

"Dang." Jasper whistled. "What a luxe life. Cokes, how come you never stream sessions with psychics?"

I took another bite of my chicken wrap. "Because my followers would revolt." LaTàge's whole persona was about being extra and bringing the drama, whereas I (hopefully) was a down-to-earth, how-to influencer, giving guidance and recommendations about products and lifestyle choices. "Was this confrontation between LaTàge and her psychic enough to make Madame Organa fly across the country and commit murder?" As I said it out loud, I pretty much had my answer.

No.

"I don't think so." Charlotte chewed on her lower lip. "But what if we're approaching this the wrong way? Didn't you say that LaTàge's wallet was missing? What if this is just some random, terrible robbery?"

I stewed on her concern for a moment. "Then why would Gavin ask me to dig into LaTàge's social life? What useful information would her online accounts contain if this was a crime of opportunity?"

"That's a good point." Jasper waved his salad-laden fork at me like a baton. "You're also forgetting that LaTàge was famous for never, *ever* carrying cash. She wouldn't be caught dead with it." He paused and cringed at his own faux pas. "She was like the unofficial poster child for Apple Pay. Why take her wallet and not all the electronics you said were found at the scene?"

"Yeah, that part doesn't make sense." Charlotte munched on a bite from her buffalo chicken burger. "You can at least jailbreak an iPad. You can't do that with someone's credit card without it being tracked."

I stared at her a moment. Jailbreak? While Jasper and I were incredibly tech-savvy, Charlotte…not so much.

She blushed. "Deacon has gotten me hooked on that new cyber forensics show on Discovery Plus."

"Well, it's paying off." I grinned. "So, if robbery wasn't the motive, why steal LaTàge's wallet if not for money or her credit cards?"

Jasper dabbed his lips with a napkin. "Souvenir, perhaps?"

A cold chill ran down my spine at the morbid thought. "Or maybe LaTàge kept something in her wallet the killer didn't want found. Like her driver's license with her legal name." But where did that leave us? Why would the killer care if people found out who LaTàge really was?

"I think we should focus our efforts on the people who knew her best," Jasper stressed. "Ruby, Miguel, and Katz." He counted their names off on his fingers.

Charlotte shimmied in her seat. "Ooo! Famous people! I'm so excited. How do we go about tracking them down?"

"This isn't a fangirling excursion," Jasper grumbled, giving her a narrowed look. "Any one of them could be a *murderer.*"

"Why would Katz kill the face of their new clothing line?" Charlotte challenged.

"Creative differences, for one," Jasper replied. "If LaTàge had invested in Katz's company, she might have felt entitled to have her opinions heard. Katz may not have enjoyed having their creativity micromanaged."

My pulse quickened at his theory. "Can you use your contacts to dig into their business relationship?"

"Sure." Jasper made a note on his phone.

Henry stopped by our table to ask us about our meal. We'd had a productive working lunch because all our plates were empty. "We'll take the check, please," I confirmed with a smile.

"Okay, so Jasper's going to poke into Katz. What about the others?" Charlotte asked once the coast was clear.

"Gavin told me Ruby is coming in for questioning after our consulting session tomorrow morning. Why don't we try to catch her before she goes in?" I suggested.

Charlotte shook her head. "No way. If Chief McInnis sees you chatting with her, that could raise his hackles. We gotta question her somewhere less conspicuous."

"Hmm, good point." I began mindlessly scrolling through my phone as I often did while thinking. My fingers had a will of their own, and soon, I was on Ruby Daniels's TikTok profile. She had uploaded a recent In Memoriam tribute to LaTàge, set to an acoustic, slow version of Beyoncé's song, "Diva."

"Tasteful," I muttered, only slightly joking.

I swiped through Ruby's timeline. She certainly had been busy pumping out videos left and right today. Each featured her in some state of distress, lamenting some factoid about her bestie, LaTàge.

"I just find it so weird Ruby doesn't know LaTàge's real name." I rapped my left-handed knuckles on the table. "I mean, you guys both know mine, and I haven't gone by Cordelia in over a decade." My given name tasted like sour milk on my tongue. Only my mom and dad called me "Delia" anymore.

Jasper brushed nonexistent wrinkles from his crisp, rainbow-colored polo. "I know, right? Like, how did her real name never come up? With all her travel and such, you'd think Ruby would have seen it on a license or a passport."

"Ruby told Gavin LaTàge wouldn't let her near that kind of stuff. Under the guise of 'staying grounded.'" I mused over this perplexing puzzle piece. "It makes you wonder why LaTàge wanted to keep her real name a secret. Was she running from something?" By now, my focus was back on my cell, still scrolling through Ruby's TikTok videos. "Hold the phone." I scooted forward in my seat as I snapped a screenshot of the video frame before it disappeared. "What does this logo look like to you guys? There, on the towels?" I handed the device to Jasper so he and Charlotte could take a closer look.

Charlotte squinted. "Umm, it's a bit blurry…"

Jasper, though, had no issue decrypting the pixeled image. "Looks like a Bonsai tree to me."

I grinned. Jasper's dedication to working from his phone paid off. He could decode a fuzzy photo in seconds. "Doesn't The Glades Hotel over in Crestview have a Bonsai tree as part of their logo?" Back in August, I'd collaborated with the hotel's marketing team to do a few sponsored posts on my Instagram account to hype up The Glades' new outdoor spa and serenity garden.

Jasper's eyes widened in recognition. "You think Ruby and the rest of the squad are holing up there?"

I gestured toward the timestamp. It was less than forty minutes ago. "I think it's highly probable. The Glades is one of the swankiest hotels for miles." I wondered why LaTàge had opted not to join them, but then remembered the stunning beach view from the modern manor in Crescent Hills.

Charlotte glanced at her watch. "Should we head up there now?"

"No." I shook my head. "We've got to be careful about this, remember? We can't let Ruby or anyone else figure out what we're up to." I paused as Henry approached our corner with our bill.

We each handed him a credit card, and he shuffled away, leaving us to our private conversation.

"My thought is," I began to map out my plan, "we ambush Ruby tomorrow after she's done at the station. I'll make up an excuse about her leaving something behind in the PD's waiting room and that I offered to bring it to her."

Jasper frowned. "What item are you going to use?"

I searched my brain. "Uh, a jacket?"

"In this weather?" He motioned out the window at the bright, hot sun.

Charlotte brightened. "What about a pair of sunglasses? You can make off that they looked really expensive, and you figured she'd want them back, not tossed in Lost and Found."

"If it were anyone but Coco," Jasper said with a scoff, "that might be believable, but Coco's supposed to *know* fashion for her blog."

"Hey, I *do* know fashion, thank you very much." I lifted my chin in mock defiance. "Why don't I use my trusty Tom Fords for the ruse?" My beloved shades had been a miraculous clearance find at T.J. Maxx. They originally retailed for over eight hundred dollars, so Ruby didn't need to know I'd gotten them on sale for a clutch sixty bucks. "Once Ruby tells me they're not hers, I can move the conversation in a different direction."

Jasper raised a well-groomed eyebrow. "You mean, *we* can move the conversation in a different direction."

"Yeah," Charlotte agreed, "we're not letting you near another suspect solo, Coco. Hudson would have our heads."

I grinned. "I would never turn you guys away."

"We're just like Nancy, Bess, and George." Charlotte giggled at her *Nancy Drew* reference.

Jasper rolled his eyes. "The only trio I will willingly associate myself with is Destiny's Child."

Chapter Six

We left Duneside by two, with plans to meet up tomorrow morning after my consulting gig at the PD wrapped. Jasper and Charlotte made me pinky swear not to do anything without a sleuthing buddy, and I intended to keep that promise. From past experiences, I knew how much trouble I could get into on my own. Besides, I had too much CoA work to catch up on this afternoon. Not to mention, I wanted to get a head start on the social media deep dive Gavin had asked me to do about LaTàge.

Charlotte took off toward the strip to check in on her café while Jasper and I drove back to our Sunny Shores neighborhood. Jasper lived up the road from my condo, so I beeped in farewell before his sports car zoomed out of sight.

I parked Jolly in the two-car garage, aware of the slight twinge in my heart at seeing Hudson's empty parking space. I looked forward to talking with him after his interview. With his journalistic instincts, he'd probably have great advice for how to approach my latest investigation.

Once I made it inside the safety of my house, I sagged against the kitchen threshold. What a whirlwind day. I closed my eyes for a moment, but the unwanted memory of LaTàge's rainbow-colored hair splayed out across the glossy tile haunted me.

"Time to get to work." I dusted off my hands, trying to shake the image from my head. I needed to focus on something else, or I risked my anxiety spiraling out of control.

The perfect task waited in my office. The Smiling Succulent, a CoA client, had commissioned a website update as part of their rebrand efforts. Now that I had Amanda to help run webinars and client meetings, I could focus more on brand design reinvigoration, which I loved. I enjoyed being digitally creative with colors and fonts and structuring information in an eye-catching, engaging way. To me, it was so much more stimulating than the work I did these days as an influencer. Don't get me wrong, I loved my followers and the life their support had given me, but after playing "the online fame game" for most of my twenties, posting about my carefully curated life sometimes felt stale and stifling. *I wonder if LaTàge ever felt that way.*

Thank goodness I had CoA to challenge me. I couldn't deny there were some days when I debated getting out of the influencer game altogether to give CoA one-hundred-and-ten percent of my attention. But I'd then think about my fans and the amazing community we'd built. Deep down, I wasn't ready to say goodbye to *Trending Topic* and everything positive that came with it. At least, not yet.

Eager to get lost in a bubble of creativity, I logged into Squarespace and navigated to The Smiling Succulent's domain. For the next two hours, I busied myself with configuring their landing page, making sure to showcase their impressive variety of succulents and their stellar customer testimonials. The shop, located in neighboring Ocean Hollow, embodied the same small-town charm I adored about Central Shores. The quaint, cozy storefront was a dream to design for.

By the time I finished, I realized my phone had remained blissfully silent for the entire design session. I woke it up, only to notice that I'd left it on Do Not Disturb. "Oops." Among the countless social media alerts, I had several concerned texts from Mom.

Delia, just heard the news. Wasn't that lady your client?

Do you know what happened?

Are you involved in something AGAIN?

I chuckled at her use of caps. Both Mom and Dad knew I had a tendency to insert myself into police matters. Mom had even helped me with my last case.

Hi, Ma. Yes, she was. Not sure what's going on. Gavin only asked for my help with some social media stuff. I didn't want to worry my parents, so I left out the part about Jasper, Charlotte, and I planning to track down Ruby Daniels for questioning.

Glad he asked you this time. He should know by now what an asset you are to the PD.

The obvious pride in her message made me smile. While my parents didn't really understand what I did as an "influencer" and the impact my work had online, Mom clearly believed I was a credit to the Central Shores community.

Can you come to dinner tomorrow and fill us in? Thea and the fam will be over.

My smile faltered slightly. I loved my younger sister; really, I did, but we weren't exactly the closest. We could usually make it through ten minutes of small talk, but anything longer typically devolved into sibling bickering. We were just two very different people. Thea, now twenty-six, was a mother of three. While she was nurturing and kind, she tended to be somewhat self-absorbed—and that's saying something, coming from me. I may enjoy the spotlight I garnered online, but I never demanded any perks from it. Thea, on the other hand, expected our entire family to revolve around her and her children's needs.

Mom must have telepathically sensed my hesitation, for she added, **With Hudson out of town, what else do you have to do?**

Irritation flared within me, but I tamped it down. I knew Mom hadn't meant anything sinister by it, but the little jab at my lifestyle choices stung, nevertheless. Long ago, Hudson and I had decided to live our lives together, kid-free. A decision my mother frequently lamented.

I gave in to her request. I *had* been planning to attend the new book club at the Central Shores Public Library, but family came first. **What time? Can I bring anything?**

Mom sent a slew of celebration emojis before asking me to pick up a nice chardonnay. I added the task to my Google calendar, reminding me to swing by Vine, our town's trendy wine bar. Sommelier Andre Nunez would have just what I needed.

With Mom's texts answered, I braced myself for my social media check-in. LaTàge was still trending, along with my name and Central Shores. A new hashtag had also joined the fray.

#CocoClineistheProblem

Super.

I practiced the deep, meditative breaths that I had been working on in therapy. Between my crime-solving exploits and the pressures of fame, talking through my feelings with a health professional had been the best thing I'd done for myself in a long time. I still had a ways to go in getting a handle on my anxiety and my underlying need to be in control, but as Dr. Ashawari always reminded me, "Life is a work in progress."

With a slightly calmer and more introspective frame of mind, I scanned my profile and tried reminding myself that these online strangers were hurting, lashing out at some faceless person connected to their beloved icon. It lessened the cutting sting just a little. LaTàge's fans continued to pummel me with mentions, demanding everything from my arrest to my assistance.

At least I could make the latter happy, or try to, anyway. Having completed the landing page for The Smiling Succulent, I could now turn my focus to Gavin's request for the Central Shores PD.

I reached for my tablet. The more screens I had at my disposal, the better.

The police wanted an understanding of LaTàge's social media presence and whether she had any threats coming from those channels. I snorted as I mulled over the somewhat naive request. Of course, someone as famous as LaTàge would have her share of stalkers and weirdos. I mean, I had less than one-sixth of her fanbase, and I received threats and creepy messages multiple times a week, if not daily. Unfortunately, being a punching bag for strangers came with the public figure territory. Interacting online seemed to give people a free pass to behave horribly toward one another. As much as I valued social media for giving me the comfortable life I led, I sometimes wished it would collapse on itself. Our collective mental health would be in a much better place.

The full scope of what Gavin had asked for was nearly impossible for one person to achieve, but I would do my best to review LaTàge's most active profiles and online social circles for potential leads. I'd start where LaTàge had gotten her big break: TikTok.

TikTok wasn't a member of my social media Holy Trinity, but that was partly because of my age. I was a millennial, and Instagram was my app of choice. TikTok was Gen-Z territory and had exploded onto the scene after my high school and college days. I did post there occasionally, but I mostly used TikTok to research marketing trends. Nerdy, fun business-related stuff.

LaTàge, however, was a different story. Her videos started gaining traction about three years ago, and ever since, her star power had only grown. While she had a large presence on Instagram, where I'd first encountered her, she really dedicated herself to growing her TikTok audience. It was a smart move, too. So many struggling influencers tried to be everywhere all at once, instead of picking a social media lane and committing to it.

On my tablet, I navigated to TikTok and searched for LaTàge's profile. As a public figure, LaTàge had millions and millions of followers, but she likely didn't follow many accounts herself. I'd start there. It would be interesting to see with whom she was connected.

I sucked in a breath at the number listed above the Following label.

Eighteen?

Such a small amount surprised me. "I wonder if she has a personal account for friends," I muttered as the following list loaded. Some celebrity figures had private, pseudonym profiles where they could fly under the radar. For LaTàge to do so, though, didn't seem in character. She'd always been so transparent about her life, living it all online for the world to see. After all, this was a woman who'd livestreamed her last visit with her gyno. But I supposed everyone had their limits. No doubt, there were parts of her life she'd want kept hidden. Her given name, being one of them.

I skimmed LaTàge's following list. "What am I *really* looking for?" I may be a social media marketing expert, but now, I had to think like a homicide investigator. A forensic social media crime analyst, if you will. Had LaTàge's online activity led to her murder? Who would have reason to want her dead?

I studied the eighteen profiles with growing impatience. There was something about this list that struck me as odd, but I couldn't put my finger on it. Most of the accounts belonged to other popular TikTok stars. People who had already uploaded their tributes about LaTàge's death from places notably nowhere near Central Shores. LaTàge may have been cool to the touch, but I doubted one of these folks somehow killed her and, by now, returned to their New York or LA apartments to post about their sorrow. It didn't seem plausible.

I pursed my lips as I switched to my phone and launched Instagram. LaTàge's profile info was nearly identical, except here, she only followed fourteen accounts. As I scrolled through her picture grid, a discouraged twinge began to unfurl at the base of my neck. How was I supposed to find answers here? How did Gavin expect me to put together a comprehensive look into LaTàge's online life in such a short amount of time? I was in over my head.

Wait a minute…No, Gavin couldn't be that diabolical, could he? Was this part of some sneaky master plan to get me to stay out of his investigation? To make me feel inferior and overwhelmed by an insurmountable task?

Cool it, Cokes, I told myself. Gavin and I might not see eye-to-eye on my value as an amateur investigator, but I doubted he would stoop so low *or* dedicate that many brain cells to thwart my meddling. He was my friend, after all.

I was about to toss my phone down when the odd thing about LaTàge's TikTok and Instagram following lists finally clicked. *Friends.* It wasn't about who was among the handles. It was about who *wasn't* there. And, for some unknown reason, on either app, Ruby's, Katz's, and Miguel's usernames were nowhere to be found.

Chapter Seven

My pulse raced with excitement at this intriguing realization. LaTàge wasn't following her loyal posse? When had *that* happened?

I thought back to Ruby's curt text she'd sent Amanda.

That mess is not my prob anymore.

A complete one-eighty from the teary-eyed videos she had been uploading all day at The Glades. During her heartfelt tributes, Ruby gave absolutely no impression that anything was amiss with their friendship. Was it all an act?

I absently scrolled through LaTàge's feed, my finger tapping on a vibrant image that caught my eye. It showed LaTàge, Ruby, Miguel, and Katz walking the red carpet at the Venice Film Festival. The four of them looked beyond fierce. Miguel and LaTàge were draped over each other, clinging on for dear life like always, while Katz and Ruby posed back-to-back. The group's expressions were stoic and aloof, yet excitement shone brightly in their eyes. I could guess why. Scoring an invite to an exclusive event like the Venice Film Festival was a big deal for LaTàge. It proved she was successfully transitioning from online influencer to all-out celeb. Something I used to dream about back when I was first starting out. These days, I was much more content in the comfort of my own home, stepping into the spotlight only when I wanted to.

I studied the timestamp on the photo. It had been uploaded less than two weeks ago, at the start of the month. *Hmm.*

I tapped back to the image grid on LaTàge's profile. Why had this photo caught my wandering eye? I noticed then that every image posted after the film festival was only of LaTàge or Hashtag, her pup. Her friends were nowhere to be found. A stark contrast from her usual MO.

I leaned back in my chair, my gaze drifting toward the ceiling. Two weeks ago, the LaTàge Squad appeared thick as thieves. But Ruby's text, the squad's Central Shores sleeping arrangements, and LaTàge's following list all suggested something was not right in influencer paradise.

But was it serious enough to warrant murder?

Another potential road bump entered the picture. The Instagram Stories LaTàge had posted from the Crescent Hills home would soon disappear forever twenty-four hours after their upload. I checked my watch. Had the Central Shores PD or county crime lab thought to archive the clips? It was a gamble to text Gavin and risk offending him, but not asking might cause the team to lose out on valuable evidence about LaTàge's movements.

I opted for a more neutral path. I logged onto the Zoom app from my phone and launched an Instant Meeting. The option to screenshare appeared seconds later. Excellent. I could record the meeting and capture the clips as I watched them. This way, I had receipts for reference and could easily share if our local law enforcement hadn't done the same.

It didn't take long to pull up LaTàge's Stories and screenshot them. I hoped a second viewing might bring to light some new information, but nothing caught my attention other than the champagne label. I recognized the brand because I had the very same bottle chilling in my fridge. Surprised LaTàge, who was used to the finer things in life, would dare drink $12.99 champagne, I ended the Zoom recording and made sure I saved the video file correctly.

Satisfied with my work, I was about to visit Katz's and Miguel's socials when a reminder flashed on my phone screen.

Babe Alert – CNN.

Oh, snap. The evening had flown by. Hudson's interview was set to air in thirty minutes. Just the perfect amount of time to whip myself up a light dinner.

One of the very cool things about running a highly visible lifestyle blog was that companies often sent me free product samples to try out in the hopes I'd feature them on *Trending Topic* or post about them on my social profiles. Tonight, I certainly benefited from this perk. WhipDish, a meal kit service, had shipped me a box of goodies to review. Much like more established brands like BlueApron and HelloFresh, WhipDish touted a wide variety of healthy, affordable meals that were easy to make. The best thing about WhipDish was that every meal could be prepared in under twenty-five minutes. As someone who had set off the fire alarm more times than I would ever admit, quick, easy meals were my calling. There was a reason why *Trending Topic* gravitated toward entertainment, self-care, and décor topics and away from recipes.

I listened to a true crime podcast while I sauteed cauliflower and broccoli in aromatics. I hoped the newest season of *Strangeland* might inspire my sleuthing, and I soon found myself enthralled by the story of a terrifying home invasion.

As I mixed the veggie blend with parmesan couscous, the host's soothing voice triggered an earlier memory from Duneside. Charlotte had floated the idea that LaTàge's murder was a robbery gone wrong. While we had initially dismissed it because LaTàge famously never carried cash, I had to wonder…what if the intruder hadn't known LaTàge was in residence? The houses—scratch that, *manors*—peppered throughout the Crescent Hills neighborhood screamed, "We've got money." What if some desperate or unsavory character had decided to test their luck on what they thought was an empty staged home?

I turned off the stove and took my dinner to the couch, my cell tucked in the crook of my elbow. I flipped on the TV and navigated to CNN before typing the Crescent Hills rental address into my phone's search bar. Lucky for me—*not*—reading the address out loud to the 9-1-1 operator had permanently seared it into my brain.

I took a bite of my grain bowl as the results loaded. Buttery, crispy goodness melted on my tongue. "Now, this is how to eat veggies." I beamed triumphantly at the yummy entree. WhipDish would definitely be getting a positive endorsement from me.

I expected to see LaTàge's rental pop up on Airbnb or Vrbo. Instead, all I got were related Crescent Hills listings posted on Zillow, Realtor.com, and Trulia. I scrolled down the list. Ronny Durnst's development company was nestled among the links.

I frowned. So, the house wasn't listed as a homestay. How had LaTàge booked the place, then? I clicked on Durnst Developers to learn more about the property as Arnie Gable's flawless features filled the big OLED screen.

I dropped my phone with a squeal at seeing who sat next to her.

"Good evening." The fashionable and fierce host nodded briskly at her audience. "Tonight, I'm joined by investigative journalist Hudson Caruthers as we discuss his new show *Crime Sweet Home* and how media platforms like TV and podcasting are breathing life into old cases."

The camera panned out, revealing Hudson in all his glory. His bronze skin gleamed under the bright lights, and his smile looked effortlessly composed. "Thanks for having me, Arnie." His smooth, velvety baritone made me shiver with delight.

I wasn't sure what to expect from the interview, but Hudson walked the tricky line between self-promotion and supporting a cause like a true pro. While he namedropped the show a handful of times, Hudson really focused on the good work the program was doing. *Crime Sweet Home* had not only helped unearth critical, new information in several cold cases, but it had also become a platform where families of victims could advocate for change.

"In one of our most recent episodes, we educated the public about Michelle Leu's case. Her killer was caught several months after her death, but there was so much more that could have been done to possibly prevent such a terrible outcome in the first place," Hudson explained, his tone serious but gentle. "Michelle's family is now pushing for better protocols regarding missing persons cases. They are speaking to Congress next week. Viewers can learn how to help at our website." Hudson rattled off the domain and urged people to support the Leus in their advocacy work.

My eyes welled with happy tears as the segment stretched on. He was doing so, so well. Gosh, I was proud of him.

Just as Arnie Gable was getting ready to sign off, her lips twitched into a smile. "Well, Hudson, it sounds like you might have your next featured case at the ready. Are you going to be exploring the murder of famed social media influencer LaTàge? In your own backyard, no less."

I straightened with a gasp, inadvertently knocking my grain bowl to the side. Luckily, I'd licked it empty. Arnie had just thrown Hudson a major curve ball. How would he respond?

Hudson cleared his throat, his face a mask of calm. "While the news is shocking and sad, I don't think the local police need *my* help bringing any more attention to this particular case."

"What about your long-time girlfriend, Coco Cline?" Arnie quickly countered. "She's been at the center of several recent murder investigations."

My jaw dropped. *What in the ever-living—*

Hudson simply chuckled, cool as a cucumber.

Arnie must have realized she wasn't getting a comment from him, as she smiled and sent the audience to commercial.

I, however, wasn't laughing. A mega-popular news anchor had just said I'd been at the center of *several* homicide cases. Two did not equal several, in my book. Arnie Gable made me sound like the Angel of Death.

I rubbed at the dull ache brewing in my temples. I also wasn't thrilled my name had come up during what was supposed to be Hudson's special moment. I hoped he wasn't annoyed.

I still had about forty minutes before our scheduled FaceTime, so I opted to take a hot shower in our en suite bathroom. The soothing smell of eucalyptus and lavender shower gel should help remove the knots from my neck.

By the time I toweled off, I surveyed the bathroom vanity, searching for my phone. A brief spike of panic at not finding it was quickly doused by the realization that I'd left it on the couch.

Once I was snug in my jammies, I curled up in the corner of the jersey blue sectional and unlocked the screen. It opened on the sleek Durnst Developers homepage, reminding me that I'd been searching for information on LaTàge's rental. *"Where coastal living begins,"* I read the business slogan aloud. The website's color scheme—an airy blend of teal, gold, and gray— lent itself to the luxury seaside vibe. Ronny's marketing team had done a great job.

My focus snapped back to the original reason I'd Googled the rental property in the first place. I wanted to explore the theory that someone had cased the joint online, knowing that it was fully furnished, but not yet a permanent home. Ideal for looting high-end electronics. LaTàge just happened to be at the right place at the wrong time.

I tapped around the site, finding the properties tab with ease. Every single listing featured a home or plot in Crescent Hills. Touting expensive fixtures and award-winning design, there wasn't a house available for purchase under three million dollars. *Three million dollars.* Yeesh, this was not the Central Shores of my youth.

One property, however, was notably missing. The house where LaTàge had been staying. Had someone from Durnst Developers already removed it from the site? I could understand why Ronny wouldn't want his property linked to the murder of a celebrity influencer, at least not immediately. Would LaTàge's death cast a pall over the area, or would it generate more buzz?

The more I scrolled around the website, it became clear that Durnst Developers specialized in residential homes, not rentals. There was nothing about leasing any of these places.

Still unsure how LaTàge had come to be staying at the Crescent Hills manor, I pocketed the question until tomorrow morning when I synced up with Gavin. Now, I wanted to focus my energy on Hudson.

I propped my phone up on a small tripod atop the coffee table. This way, I didn't have to worry about holding the device in my hand or risk exposing several chins while we talked.

As soon as the digital numbers swapped to eight, Hudson's contact info filled the screen.

"Hey, superstar!" I beamed as I accepted the call, and Hudson materialized before me. The live feed revealed him lounging on a big hotel bed.

My boyfriend's dark brown eyes crinkled with delight. "Hey, babes. Whatcha think?"

"You were amazing!" I gave him a play-by-play of my thoughts. "What did Millie say about the interview?" At the end of the day, his executive producer's opinion was the one that truly mattered.

"She seemed pleased." Hudson tilted his head to the side. "I think she's a bit distracted by the LaTàge stuff."

I chuckled. "Aren't we all?"

Hudson's gaze narrowed perceptively. "Are you doing okay? It must have been a shock to have your meeting called off by a national news blast."

I gulped. Now was the time to come clean. "Eh, I found out about it a bit more directly." I confessed how I'd been the one to find LaTàge's body.

Hudson was understandably dismayed. "Oh, God, Coco. That's awful. Why didn't you tell me sooner?"

I shrugged. "Because I knew you'd be concerned about me, and I didn't want to ruin your New York moment."

"I can be on a plane tonight." In a rush, Hudson propped his phone on a nearby pillow, so I could only see his profile as he swiftly typed on his work laptop. "I can conduct my other interviews through Zoom or Webex."

"No! Please, don't." I clasped my hands pleadingly, so he could see them on the video call. "I'm fine, really, I am. It was horrible and shocking, yes, but I'm okay. Really." I willed myself to be as reassuring as possible. "You don't need to fly home and rescue me."

Hudson studied me a moment, his expression unreadable.

"And honestly, I'd feel terrible if I ruined your PR tour," I admitted. "You've got so many cases that need the attention. I can't in good conscience get in the way of that."

A tender smile curled on Hudson's lips. "I hope you know how special you are."

My cheeks heated at the admiration in his voice. "Oh, believe me, I do," I joked.

He broke into full-bodied laughter. "Well, okay, but if you start feeling squirmy, call me, all right? Even if it's the middle of the night."

"I will. I promise." I bobbed my head in solemn vow. Feeling "squirmy" was the code word I used to describe the occasional panic attacks I suffered since being assaulted by an unhinged killer. Yet another thing Dr. Ashawari and I were working through in my weekly sessions. "So, did you really get to meet Anderson Cooper?"

Our conversation returned to Hudson's New York trip, and he filled me in on his time in the Big Apple thus far. "Tomorrow, I'm meeting Roberta Jones's former sister-in-law for breakfast. I'm hoping she's more talkative than she was with the police six years ago."

"Goodness, be careful." Roberta Jones was the victim from a missing persons case Hudson was currently investigating for *Crime Sweet Home*. The thirty-five-year-old woman was presumed dead—murdered—and based on his research, Hudson and his production team were sure that Roberta's estranged brother was somehow involved.

My boyfriend held up three fingers. "Scout's honor. We're meeting at a very public bakery, so there's no need to worry."

"I'll worry," I quickly countered. "I can't help it."

"Me either." An air of sadness settled over him. "I'm sorry I'm not there right now to help you deal with everything. It must be a complete circus."

I waved away his concerns. "It will blow over." Thank goodness Hudson had deactivated his Twitter/X account post-Elon Musk takeover, or he'd see my name and associated hashtags still among the trending news.

"The PD must be drowning in media requests," Hudson added. "Have you been roped into doing spokesperson work for them again?"

"I think me getting in front of a camera right now would be the worst thing I could do." I winced at the mental image.

"Eh, that's probably the right call." Hudson steepled his fingers together. "So, do you have any hunches about who killed LaTàge?" His question had a sly drawl to it.

I leaned closer to the camera, ready to get to the good stuff. "Well, Ruby Daniels sent Amanda a pretty strange text right around the time we found LaTàge's body. And some super sus stuff online has me thinking her friends might have had something to do with it. I don't think they were getting along."

A dramatic gasp whispered through Hudson's fingers. "Oh, no! You mean the LaTàge Squad got tired of being treated like props?"

I giggled at his silly delivery, but the snarky comment had also unmasked a fairly solid motive. Could it really be that simple? Were LaTàge's friends finally done living in her much-more-famous shadow?

I pushed the thought from my mind. I was getting ahead of myself. We hadn't even spoken to Ruby or the others. I needed to go into this investigation with an open mind.

To Hudson, I said, "Gavin asked me to come down to the station tomorrow to help him and the team understand 'LaTàge's World.'" I spoke cautiously, adding air quotes to keep my tone light. While Hudson wasn't a fan of my sleuthing escapades, he'd always been supportive of them. But that had been when he was here at my side. I didn't know how he'd react, being several states away. "You know, give them an insider's perspective of the industry, so they have an idea about what it all entails. Influencer Life 101."

"That's great, babes." Hudson matched my blasé tone, although his eyes sparkled with mischief.

Why did I get the feeling he was hiding something? Oh well, it takes one to know one, I supposed. I inhaled deeply, steeling myself to tell him I planned to track Ruby down tomorrow and question her about LaTàge. "And besides that—"

"You've decided to launch your own investigation to help get you back into the Internet's good graces?" Hudson propped his chin atop his interlocked fingers.

I stared at the innocent expression filling my phone screen. "How did you—"

"Your cohorts texted me earlier to let me know they planned to take good care of you while I was away." Hudson grinned.

I was both oddly touched and mildly peeved about Jasper and Charlotte going behind my back, but clearly, their promise seemed to have a calming effect on Hudson. "I don't need anyone taking care of me." I rolled my eyes. I hated the thought of being a burden to my friends.

"It's something we all want to do, Cokes. We just want you to be safe." Hudson must have read my mind. "And since there's clearly no stopping you when a mystery is involved, you're stuck with us as your sidekicks."

I melted at his words. "I'd hardly call you guys sidekicks. You're the greatest partners-in-crime a gal could ask for."

His smile turned serious. "I know I sound like a broken record, but please be careful. LaTàge's friends come from a completely different world than we're used to in Central Shores. If they feel threatened, who knows how they might lash out."

"You don't have to tell me twice." I shivered at the warning. My small-town influencer lifestyle was galaxies away from how LaTàge and her glamorous squad operated. I knew I had to be smart about questioning them, or they could tear me down with a single tweet. Or worse.

Hudson appeared satisfied with my answer. "All right, keep me posted. And you're sure you're okay hosting Willow and Reade until I get home?"

"Oh, totally. It will be great to hang with them." Willow was Hudson's older sister. She and her wife, Reade Michaels, were flying in from California for an awards banquet honoring Dr. Irene Caruthers, Hudson and Willow's mom. Irene, the first Black woman to head a department at my alma mater, Bayside University, was being recognized the following weekend by some anthropology organization. We were all attending the event, then going out as a family to celebrate her award, as well as my twenty-ninth birthday.

"I just wish you hadn't tacked my birthday onto your mom's big night." I winced at the gauche action.

Hudson shrugged off my concern. "Hey, Mom knew the banquet was on your birthday and made the suggestion herself."

I still felt guilty for making Irene share the spotlight. "Do the girls need me to pick them up at the airport this Saturday?" The Michaelses would be staying at our condo for a week and a half.

"Nah, they decided to rent a car. I told Willow to let you know when they're close, though."

Hudson and I chatted for a few more minutes about his sister's upcoming visit. I hadn't seen Willow and Reade since last Christmas, so I was looking forward to spending some quality time with them.

"Make sure you let Wills treat you to dinner a few nights, too." Hudson tried to stifle a yawn. "It will help relieve her guilt over imposing on your hospitality for so long."

I shook my head at Willow's unnecessary stress. "It's not an imposition when it's family." I made a mental note to give the upstairs guest room a thorough cleaning this week. Hudson and I rarely ventured upstairs, so it was bound to need some airing out.

"You're sweet for saying that, but I know how busy CoA has been lately," Hudson noted sagely. "It's gonna be tricky juggling work and their visit. Trust me, it will make Wills feel better."

I secretly loved that Hudson's sister had the same nickname as Prince William. It made me feel so posh when speaking about her. "Fineeee."

"Thank you." He attempted to suppress another yawn but failed.

I knew he was trying to keep the call going for my benefit, but he didn't need to worry. My nighttime anxiety had become much more manageable in recent months. "Okie dokie, time for me to get my beauty sleep. It's been a long day." I could see from the tiny reflective FaceTime thumbnail that my own eyelids were drooping. "Sweet dreams, babe."

"Love you, Cokes."

"Be careful," we both added in unison.

Laughing as I ended the call, I sank into the embrace of the couch cushions, treasuring the warm fuzzies inside my chest. I harnessed their power as I took in the nighttime shadows stretching across the condo. Shadows that would have scared me half to death a few months ago. But thanks to my therapy sessions, my anxiety was doing much better, and I no longer had dreams about my attacker choking me. No, tonight, my thoughts would be consumed by LaTàge, her tight circle of friends, and why one of them might have had reason to kill her.

Chapter Eight

I woke before my alarm went off Tuesday morning, surprised by the enthusiastic energy coursing through my veins. Usually, I didn't feel this peppy before seven 'o clock, but I suppose I was a little excited to track down and meet Ruby Daniels in the flesh.

As I brushed my teeth, I carelessly checked my phone to see what notifications had come in overnight, like I did every morning. Regret rained down on me as soon as I was greeted by a barrage of angry tweets. How could I have forgotten this online nightmare? I still had countless mentions and DMs from people about LaTàge's death. At this rate, it would be impossible for me to wade through them all. It also meant anyone reaching out to my account about something other than LaTàge would likely get lost in the shuffle.

My brow furrowed, and I stuck out a sudsy, toothpaste-covered lip in a pout. I hated feeling like I was ignoring my followers. Since I'd hired Amanda to help with CoA clients, I'd been building better habits when it came to engaging with folks on my socials. This week, though, it would be slow going, responding to their comments. I prayed they'd understand this little blip.

I studied my besieged X profile while I rinsed with mouthwash. A wary idea floated to the top of my to-do list. Should I make a statement? Would that stoke the fires or calm the frenzy? What would I even say?

I tabled the notion for now. Once I spoke with Gavin and the team, I'd figure something out.

Next, I conscientiously selected my wardrobe. I usually kept things casual during my consulting sessions at the PD, but they weren't my main focus today. I needed something that would both impress *and* put Ruby at ease. I had to dress as Coco Cline, influencer and lifestyle blogger extraordinaire, not Coco Cline, nosy Central Shores busybody.

I opted for a form-fitting navy dress paired with a metallic belt. With ankle booties and shimmering silver earrings, I looked a wee bit vampy for work, but hopefully, no one at the station would ask why. They'd chalk it up as one of my flighty Coco-isms.

I debated sending my friends a text to inform them about our sleuthing dress code; however, it seemed pointless. Charlotte could wear a paper bag and still look like a million bucks. And Jasper would need no reminding. He dressed to impress his dry cleaner. He'd know that we needed to dazzle Ruby with our style.

With my sleuthing armor donned, I collected my work bag, phone, and keys before locking the front door. Twelve minutes later, Jolly and I arrived at the municipal center of town, although Central Shores looked like nothing I'd ever seen before.

News vans lined the normally picturesque street with reporters and their crews situated throughout the Commons. Beyond the small park stood a crowd in front of the old brick building housing the police station.

I gulped. *This looks fun.*

I navigated Jolly through the chaos, struggling for the first time in my life to find a place to park in my hometown. I kept my head down, so as not to catch the attention of reporters, and decided it was best to park a few streets over. I didn't need anyone snapping a picture of Jolly's license plate and blasting it online.

I ended up nabbing a spot three blocks away in a quiet residential neighborhood near the high school. A quick time check told me I had less than five minutes before my meeting was scheduled to start. Cue a rush of unwanted anxiety. If I was on time for a meeting, I was late. If I was late for a meeting, I was basically worthless. At least, that was what the old me had believed. The "new-and-improving" me took a few deep breaths and told myself it wasn't the end of the world. From the looks of the mob in the Commons, Gavin and his team had bigger problems than my minor tardiness. Yet, as I hurried toward the police station with an eye on the time, the knots in my intestines refused to lessen. I said I was a work-in-progress, right?

I pulled my phone out of my bag and began to compose a quick message to Gavin, letting him know I'd be a few minutes late. But he beat me to the punch, as a message in our ongoing conversation popped up.

Hi—running behind. Reporters are swarming the Commons. Park near the elementary or high school. AR will pick you up.

I stopped in my tracks, sagging with relief. **Am @ HS now.**

AR is on his way.

I waited in the shade of a poplar tree, flagging down Adrian a few minutes later once I saw a police cruiser turn onto the street.

"Morning, Coco. Sorry for all the hoops." Adrian smiled as the passenger window rolled down. "Hop in."

I greeted him as I climbed inside the vehicle. "I saw all the reporters. Talk about wild. You guys doing okay?"

"We're keeping our heads above water." Adrian drummed on the steering wheel as he pulled back onto the road. "That's all we can ask for at this point."

"All those news vans…is Chief McInnis going to make a statement?" I twiddled nervously with the worn leather handles of my bag. We needed to do something to get this situation under control. But what could I do that wouldn't add fuel to an already raging fire?

"Nope. We've been told it's a media blackout on our end. All communications will come from SCCL."

I grimaced at this update. I doubted Chief McInnis liked his authority being usurped by the Sussex County Crime Lab.

Adrian must have noticed my reaction. "It's actually good news for us. Means we can focus more on the investigation than dealing with the media circus. Something the chief was eager to give up in order to partner with county on the case."

"I'm glad to hear that." I stared out the window.

Adrian adjusted his aviator sunglasses. "Yeah, me too. Jurisdiction battles are often a pain to navigate, but McInnis has been more than happy to let SCCL take the helm this time, what with the call from the governor he received last night."

"The governor?" I raised my eyebrows. I shouldn't have been shocked. This was an incredibly high-profile case for Delaware.

"Yup." Adrian lowered his deep voice, despite us being alone in the car. "This is between you and me, but I don't think the chief wants Central Shores on the hook for this investigation. Harriet and Director Morrison will take the heat if this doesn't get solved ASAP."

I considered this nugget of intel. I certainly didn't blame Chief McInnis for wanting to pass the buck, but I worried how this might affect my sleuthing operation. I could probably sweet talk my way out of trouble if Chief McInnis and Gavin—who'd been my date to junior prom—found out I was interfering with their case. It would be much harder getting myself out of hot water if the higher-ups at SCCL got wind of my involvement.

Note to self: don't get caught.

"If County is in charge, do you guys really need little ol' me to go over LaTàge's socials?" I asked out of genuine curiosity.

Adrian cleared his throat. "Well…just because SCCL has taken the reins doesn't mean we aren't doing everything we can to help them. At least, that's how Gavin sees it. He believes that if we can prove ourselves, it will help sell the community services expansion project the chief is trying to get funding for."

"What do you mean, that's how Gavin sees it?" I stared at him suspiciously, sensing he was omitting some juicy office drama based on his tone.

Adrian sighed. "He and the chief aren't exactly seeing eye-to-eye about LaTàge's case at the moment. Gavin thinks it's a chance to prove our value, while Lloyd believes we should let Director Morrison run with it."

"I find it hard to believe the chief would be willing to hand over jurisdiction just like that." I wasn't accustomed to McInnis playing nice with the county team.

"He's been a bit preoccupied about preparing for Central Shores's future,"

Adrian admitted. "With the hundred-something new homes going up in Crescent Hills, Liberty Circle, and the surrounding developments, we're bracing for a big population boom. Chief McInnis wants to be ready to support everyone. More cruisers, more officers, more part-time staff. He wants it all."

"Can't blame him." The manors posted on the Durnst Developers website last night were just the tip of the iceberg when it came to new growth in Central Shores. "Isn't that all up in the air now? Won't LaTàge's death scare away potential buyers? I mean, it's no secret our crime rate is on the rise."

Adrian shrugged. "Crime is on the up and up everywhere. The last two murders we've had in Central Shores were closed within a week." He shot me a smirking sidelong glance. "Stats like *that* impress people looking for a home. Besides, I wouldn't worry about Crescent Hills or any of the other new neighborhoods becoming ghost towns. Durnst told us he's had several offers on the house where LaTàge was staying come in since yesterday."

"What?" I squawked as Adrian drove around the back of the police station, heading for the garage they shared with the fire department.

The seasoned officer chuckled. "Granted, the wannabe buyers didn't even know which house they were putting an offer on. They just wanted a piece of LaTàge history."

"Yeesh." I rolled my eyes. "People are weird."

"Ain't that the truth." Adrian put the cruiser in park, and we climbed out. He ushered me in through the garage entrance, and soon, I found myself standing in the narrow station corridor.

Adrian checked his watch. "Gavin and Harriet are finishing up an interview now. Should be done in five or ten minutes. Hang tight. Want a coffee or anything?"

I shook my head. I planned to grab a drink at Brewed to Perfection when I rendezvoused with Charlotte and Jasper. "I'm good. Harriet's here?" I would have thought the county detective would be working hard alongside her team at their state-of-the-art lab.

"Believe it or not, it was her idea to have you debrief them about LaTàge's online activity."

I felt my eyes grow large. "Seriously?" Harriet was interested in my help? A proud, goofy grin spread across my lips.

"Datz right," Adrian mimicked LaTàge's sweet, throaty voice. He then thumbed over his shoulder. "I'll be out front with Maude if you need anything."

I waved my thanks and leaned against the wall opposite the conference room. Poor Adrian didn't even have his own desk at the precinct. It sure would be nice if the chief's request for a new Community Safety Center was approved. His team worked hard and deserved a larger, more modern space conducive to their efforts. What with the four new hires Chief McInnis had recently brought on and his plans to expand the team even more, a station makeover was definitely warranted.

"Coco?" a low voice grumbled. "What are you doing back here?"

Ah, speak of the devil. I hurriedly straightened from my slouched position and tossed a bubbly smile at Chief Lloyd McInnis, who stared at me from his office doorway. Well, more like glared.

"Hi, Chief." I pointed to the closed conference room. "I was summoned by Gavin and Harriet."

His salt-and-pepper eyebrows drew together. "Why?" His tone dripped with suspicion.

Under his intense scrutiny, I shifted on the balls of my feet. Even though Gavin and Harriet had really asked for my help, I still felt edgy in the chief's imposing presence. "They have questions for me about LaTàge."

"I see." He disappeared momentarily from view, returning with a bulging folder and a briefcase tucked under his arm. "Nasty business up in Crescent Hills. Although I must admit, it certainly helps the case I'm trying to make for more department funding." Chief McInnis closed his office door. "You know, raising more awareness about the Community Safety Center proposal would be nice. Could we do something online to garner more support? Without it, I fear Roger Sullivan and his cronies will continue to drag their feet."

I bobbed my head sympathetically. Our mayor normally operated in the town's best interests, but the Central Shores CSC would be an expensive project, meaning a rise in local taxes. And a tax increase during an election year was never a good look for politicians. "Of course. I'd be happy to create a campaign and run it by you. Maybe a feature in the PD's newsletter, too?"

"Sounds good." He glanced at his watch. "Is the mob still out there?" Chief McInnis peered down the hallway toward the front of the building, his blue eyes growing stormy.

"Yeah. Adrian brought me in through the back."

The chief growled. "Director Morrison sure is taking his sweet time scheduling his fancy press conference. It would be nice to get these gnats outta my hair." With a gruff nod goodbye, he slipped out the station's back entrance.

Chapter Nine

I sank against the wall with relief, having made it through our conversation unscathed. While the chief's bark was generally worse than his bite, I didn't enjoy being in McInnis's line of fire. Luckily, he seemed too preoccupied with his CSC proposal to really question my presence here.

I was about to dig out my phone to help pass the time when the conference room door swung open. "Of course, Detective. Let us know if we can be of any further assistance. Derrick, you'll sign those docs?"

I recognized the owner of the suave, smooth voice as soon as I saw him. Ronny Durnst looked exactly like his website photograph, which surprised me. I would have assumed his tanned skin, white smile, and perfectly coifed chestnut-colored hair were all Photoshopped, but you know what they say when you assume.

The property developer noticed me standing in the hall and flashed a megawatt smile. "Coco Cline, right?" He held out a manicured hand in introduction as the door snapped shut behind him. "Ronny Durnst."

His friendly charm put me at immediate ease. "Nice to meet you, Ronny. Despite the terrible circumstances."

"Tragic. I can't believe it, to be honest. LaTàge seemed like a nice, down-to-earth girl. To have something like this happen to her…" His pinched gaze trailed down the sterile corridor.

I studied him dubiously. "Down-to-earth" was *not* an adjective I would have used to describe LaTàge. "Did you know her?"

"Not well, mind you," Ronny clarified. "I only met her and her friend yesterday afternoon upon their arrival. Derrick—my business partner—and I gave them a quick tour and the keys to the house."

Hmm. A friend, huh? So, someone else had been with LaTàge at the Crescent Hills manor at one point. Who? Ruby?

"LaTàge mentioned more than once," Ronny continued, "how grateful she was that she and her squad were able to stay on the beach. Very sweet and gracious. Nothing like I imagined her to be."

His comment about the LaTàge Squad staying at the house piqued my interest. If that had been the plan, how had Ruby ended up at The Glades? "You mentioned a friend. Who was it, do you know?"

Ronny stroked his chin. "I'm usually good with names…Roxie? Rita? No, Ruby!" He snapped his fingers. "Her name was Ruby."

"How'd she seem?"

Ronny shrugged his broad shoulders. "She was the one with the diva attitude if you ask me." His lips curled downward. "She wasn't very nice. Very distracted, too. I had to tell her about the security system like four times."

"Security system?" My heart leaped into my throat. "That's gotta be good news for the police." Cameras and access points would most certainly paint a picture of the crime.

Ronny winced. "Not so much. After we left, LaTàge reached out and asked Derrick to disable the cameras. Something about respecting her privacy. I wish he had pushed back on that request, but what's done is done."

While I understood LaTàge's need for discretion, the terrible irony was almost too much to bear. I concealed my clenched fists behind my back. *You've got to be kidding me.* The scenario was just like every true crime podcast trope I'd listened to where the security cameras mysteriously weren't working. At least I hadn't thought LaTàge's body was a mannequin when I found her.

Noting Ronny's disheartened change in attitude, I switched the topic. "I was checking out your website last night. You've got some amazing properties on the market—"

"You're over in Sunny Shores, aren't you? Interested in upgrading?" In what had to be a record-breaking rebound, Ronny's crystalline blue eyes now had a salesman's gleam to them.

I inwardly squirmed. How did this guy know the neighborhood I lived in? Outwardly, I plastered on a timid smile. "No, thank you. Not yet. I was just wondering how LaTàge came to be renting one of your homes."

"Oh." Ronny's enthusiasm tapered off as the conference room door opened behind him. "Honestly, it was all Derrick's doing."

"What are you blaming me for now?" A tall figure appeared behind Ronny. This man was pale and gangly, with tousled dark brown hair and brooding gray eyes. Next to the charming, suave Ronny, this guy's vibe was the definition of "meh."

"I was just telling Ms. Cline here how LaTàge came to be renting Seven-one-three from us." Ronny waved a hand in an introductory fashion. "Ms. Cline, this is Derrick Payne, my business partner."

"How do you do, Ms. Cline?" Derrick gave me a smile as tight as his handshake.

I acknowledged him kindly. I hadn't seen Derrick's picture anywhere on the Durnst Development website, so I wondered what kind of business partner he was. "You were the one who set up the rental?"

"Well, I convinced Ronny it was a good idea." Derrick shuffled his feet. "LaTàge reached out to us about leasing a place, and I suggested we comp her the visit. I thought it would add some mystique to the property if our brokers could say a famous influencer stayed there."

I honestly expected Derrick's remark to drip with condescension—many people didn't take us influencers seriously—but to my pleasant surprise, his expression brightened at his words, going from "meh" to "nice guy."

It was Ronny who rolled his eyes at Derrick's mention of "a famous influencer."

I was about to ask how Durnst Developers had even gotten on LaTàge's radar when the conference door opened again, and Gavin appeared.

"Hey, Coco. Come on in." He nodded at the two businessmen. "Mr. Durnst, Mr. Payne, we'll let you know when we're able to turn the property back over to you."

Ronny held up his hands. "Please, I'm in no hurry. I just want this maniac caught." He gave me a small smile. "Nice to meet you in person, Ms. Cline. If you ever would like a home with more space…" He slipped a business card into my hand before strutting down the hall and out of view.

"Sorry about him." Derrick grimaced. "Sales guy, through and through." He then trailed after Ronny with a wave goodbye.

I mulled over their odd partnership. *Opposites attract, I guess.*

"Looking to relocate?" Once we were alone in the hall, Gavin folded his arms and assessed me with a smirk.

I dropped Ronny's card into my bag. "No. But that doesn't seem to be a word in Ronny's vocabulary."

"You got that right. He tried to place both me and Harriet into new homes." Gavin ushered me inside the conference room with a chuckle.

"As if I'd want to live in this crime-ridden town." Harriet Forester glanced up from a stack of paperwork with a wry smile. "Good thing Mr. Payne was here to keep his buddy in check. Clearly, he's the brains of the operation. Hi, Coco. Thanks for coming."

I greeted her with a friendly smile. While the county detective and I weren't exactly close, we had developed a good rapport with one another. "Of course. Happy to assist however I can." I studied Harriet for a moment, noting she wasn't dressed in her normal sharp power suit. Today, she wore camel slacks with a navy-striped blouse. Her mousy brunette hair was braided, and there was a light dusting of rouge on her pale skin. She looked completely different but somehow familiar—

"All right, Coco, we won't keep you long," Gavin interrupted my inner musings and rubbed his hands together. "Before we begin interviewing LaTàge's friends, Harriet and I hoped you could give us a deep dive into their social circle dynamics. How they all knew each other, why they traveled together, lived together, etc." He pointed to the whiteboard. LaTàge's name and picture were scrawled across the top, along with photos of Ruby, Katz, and Miguel.

"Are those *mug* shots?" Stunned, I pointed at the grainy, unflattering images of Ruby and Miguel.

Harriet folded her arms as she stared at the board. "Yup. Daniels had a few shoplifting charges six years ago, and Torres was busted stealing his stepdad's car when he was nineteen."

"Wow." I had no idea. But then again, if I had one, I wouldn't go airing my criminal history across the Internet.

"So, can you tell us how LaTàge ended up surrounding herself with these people? We've got Ruby Daniels, twenty-seven, Miguel Torres, twenty-four, and Katz Keaton, twenty-eight." Gavin perched on the edge of the conference room table. "What's their deal?"

I shared with them what I already knew and what I'd learned while researching LaTàge last night. "Okay, so, three years ago, Ruby Daniels was working for a boutique pet photography studio out in Los Angeles."

"Hold up." Harriet raised her hand. "A *pet* photo studio?"

I nodded. "People bring their animals in to be photographed in fun costumes and scenes. Ruby did the set design and the lighting. LaTàge came in with her pup, Hashtag, and witnessed Ruby's talent in action. By the end of the session, LaTàge approached her, asking if Ruby wanted to work for her. By this time, LaTàge was already doing makeup tutorials and gimmicky videos on TikTok and Instagram, but her following was still rather small. She needed someone with design talent to help her edit content if she was ever going to gain more traction. Ruby accepted the job offer, and within six months, she was able to quit her day job and work alongside LaTàge full-time."

Harriet released a low whistle. "So, LaTàge became an overnight sensation. Sounds like Ruby was responsible for a lot of that?"

I shrugged. "Ruby did a lot behind the scenes, but LaTàge *was* the talent. Her charisma and eccentric behavior were the main reasons why people loved her so much. Not to mention, people went nuts for her content that featured Hashtag." My concern for the little animal resurfaced. "Did you find him at the house?"

Harriet shook her head. "One of the things Ruby actually told officers yesterday was that LaTàge boarded her dog for this trip. He's staying at an 'exclusive' pet hotel back in California. Her words, not mine."

I sagged with brief relief.

"So, LaTàge plucked Ruby from obscurity." Gavin stroked his chin as he examined the whiteboard. "What about the others? Katz and Miguel?"

"Miguel and LaTàge met at an influencer gala hosted by Meta last year," I explained. "They partied the night away and have basically been inseparable ever since."

Harriet wrinkled her nose. "Influencer gala?"

"Facebook and Instagram celebrated their most prominent users, as well as some up-and-coming personalities."

"So, Miguel is also an influencer?" Gavin's brow furrowed.

I nodded. "He mostly focuses on promoting fad diets and workouts. I'm not a fan because almost nothing he does is backed by science or doctors, but he keeps people returning by posting thirst traps."

"When you got it, flaunt it."

I grinned at Harriet's deadpan reaction. I liked this more casual, fun side of her. "Miguel also has nowhere near LaTàge's massive following."

"So, what, are he and LaTàge 'true love goals?'" Gavin rose from the table and stalked over to the whiteboard.

I chewed on my lower lip as I debated my answer. "Honestly, I sometimes got the sense that their relationship was more transactional than anything. LaTàge had a handsome piece of arm candy at her side wherever she went, and Miguel got a boost to his public profile."

"What makes you think that?" Gavin stared at me astutely.

I ran a hand through my hair. "I don't know how to describe it. Here." I held out my phone and pulled up a video that had appeared on my newsfeed last night. "Does this look like a couple who is head-over-heels in love?" I showed Gavin and Harriet some behind-the-scenes footage of a red-carpet photo call LaTàge and Miguel had attended. While they were all smiles and laughter for the cameras, once the photos were done, they couldn't put enough distance between each other.

"Hmm." Gavin's frown grew as he studied the footage. "I wonder if he'll play the role of grieving boyfriend when we interview him." He glanced at Harriet.

"He sure was playing that role last night." I showed them one of the many tribute posts Miguel had uploaded. This one praised LaTàge as his queen, his everything.

Harriet scoffed. "What a poet. Okay, what about Katz Keaton?"

"Ruby brought Katz on to be LaTàge's stylist two years ago. LaTàge wanted unique, one-of-a-kind pieces, so Katz designed LaTàge's wardrobe themselves. Their designs became a part of LaTàge's identity. Then, six months ago, Katz announced the launch of their own clothing line. LaTàge threw a big party to celebrate, announcing she would be the face of Katz's designs, as well as a business partner."

"Interesting." Harriet tapped on Ruby's, Miguel's, and Katz's pictures. "So, we have three people who were all financially linked to LaTàge in one way or another." Her shrewd gaze met Gavin's. "They all benefited so much from her life. We need to figure out what could be gained by LaTàge's death."

Gavin nodded. "Did anything else stick out on her accounts, Coco? Any weirdos posting threats?"

"I mean, sure, there were a bunch of unsavory comments, but that's par for the course when you're as well-known as LaTàge." I smiled apologetically, knowing this wasn't what Gavin wanted to hear. "I think we'd find more incriminating information in her DMs. That's where the real hair-raising stuff tends to live."

Harriet sighed. "We're working on it. But getting access takes time."

"If only Ruby knew her passcode…" I murmured. I still couldn't get over that LaTàge's friend and personal assistant didn't have access to her phone. It flipped everything I knew about the lifestyles of the rich and famous on its head.

A knock on the door interrupted our discussion. Gavin glanced at his watch. "Ms. Daniels isn't supposed to be here for another fifteen minutes," he muttered with a frown. But before he could open the door, Adrian stuck his head in.

"Um, Boss? You're gonna want to take the call on line one." Adrian pointed to the massive landline phone sitting in the center of the conference table.

Gavin gave him a cryptic look before reaching for the receiver. He then pressed the button next to a red flashing light. "Lieutenant McInnis speaking." He listened intently for a moment before his face grew slack. "I see. Mm-hmm. Yes. I'm terribly sorry, sir. You're staying where? Grandview? Okay, we'll be over to speak with you shortly. Yes. Thank you for calling, Omar. Goodbye." Gavin set the phone down on its cradle, his complexion drained of color.

"Care to share what that was about?" Harriet studied her colleague with growing curiosity.

Gavin stroked his chin, his expression still dazed. "That was Omar Jackson."

"Mr. J?" The man's more familiar name slipped across my lips. Omar Jackson owned Central Sports, a local chain of fitness clubs. He worked out of the Central Shores location on the northwest side of town. He'd also coached girls' junior varsity volleyball when I'd been on the high school team. His niece, Deja, had been in my grade. "Why'd he call?"

Gavin's shoulders straightened as he took a deep breath. "To give us the info we've been looking for. LaTàge's real name. It's Laila Jackson, his daughter."

Chapter Ten

"What?" I choked on the question. LaTàge was Omar's *daughter*, Laila Jackson? "That's impossible."

Harriet folded her arms as she studied both Gavin and me. "Why?"

"Well, for one thing, LaTàge touted to her followers that she was twenty-five years old," I pointed out. *Although, she wouldn't be the first celebrity starlet to fudge their age.*

"Hey, you're right." Gavin stroked his chin. "Heck, Laila was a senior at CSH when I was a first year."

I nodded. I'd been a sophomore at Central Shores High when Laila Jackson graduated.

"So, unless she's some child prodigy, that puts her age around thirty-one." Harriet headed over to the whiteboard to assess LaTàge's photo. "What exactly did Mr. Jackson tell you, Gav?"

"He said he saw the news this morning about LaTàge's death," Gavin recounted. "Since we hadn't reached out to notify him, he wondered whether we knew Laila and LaTàge were the same person."

I stared at him, dumbfounded.

"Omar underwent heart surgery yesterday morning, which is why he's only hearing about LaTàge's death now," Gavin continued. "He's recovering at Grandview Hospital, over in Rockaway."

Harriet wrote the name Laila Jackson on the whiteboard with a question mark. "We should speak to him as soon as possible. See if his claim is credible."

I ambled toward the whiteboard, staring intently at LaTàge's iconic face. I tried summoning memories of Laila Jackson from high school but couldn't bring any to light. I had little idea what happened to her after she graduated, but if Mr. J was telling the truth, Laila had somehow reinvented herself, shaved six years off her age, and become "LaTàge."

"Reality is stranger than fiction, so they say," I mumbled in disbelief.

Gavin folded his arms. "If LaTàge really is Laila, this turns the case completely upside down."

"Why?" I tilted my head.

"Well, we're no longer dealing with a victim with no connections to the area. Laila Jackson grew up here. Her dad is a successful businessman and a deeply respected member of the community." Gavin counted his reasons on his fingers. "It makes the suspect pool that much wider."

The metaphorical lightbulb dawned above my head. "So, you're thinking Laila—not LaTàge—was who the killer was after?"

Gavin shrugged. "Anything is possible at this moment. And it makes sense why only her wallet was missing."

My mind conjured images of credit cards and a driver's license. "They wanted to hide her real name."

The intercom on the phone crackled to life. "Hey, Boss." The speaker distorted Adrian's smooth voice. "Ruby Daniels is here."

Gavin ran a hand through his sandy blond hair. "Great," he grumbled. Clearly, this new development about Laila had left him a bit shaken.

Harriet reached for a white blazer slung over the back of a nearby chair. "I'll head to Grandview to speak with Mr. Jackson. One of my county guys will meet me there." She tugged on her cropped jacket when it hit me. Why she looked so familiar. I'd featured the very same outfit on *Trending Topic* not three weeks ago.

I swallowed a little squeal of delight. Detective Harriet Forester was reading *my* blog for fashion advice. My, how far the two of us had come.

She cocked her head in my direction, obviously noticing my twitching reaction. "Ms. Cline, I think we've gained a better understanding of LaTàge's influencer world. Thanks for taking the time to come down and speak with us."

Ugh. I could tell by her light, clipped tone that I was being dismissed. "There's one more thing I think you guys should take a look at," I hurriedly added. "LaTàge's last Instagram posts. She uploaded a few Stories from the Crescent Hills house. I thought they might be helpful in determining her time of death." I reached toward my bag to grab my phone.

Gavin cleared his throat. "Thanks, Coco, but Harriet's tech guy already archived all her active posts. Any content that was public facing, we have access to."

My cheeks grew warm as embarrassment unfurled within me. Of course, they'd thought to do this. "O-oh. Awesome." At least Gavin didn't seem too miffed that I'd assumed otherwise.

Harriet headed for the conference room door. "I'll call you on my way back to SCCL and fill you in on my chat with Mr. Jackson," she said to Gavin. "Once we have an affirmative ID, Director Morrison will want to have a joint press conference with the department."

I pursed my lips together. It sounded like Chief McInnis would have to take the heat from the media mob outside the station a little while longer.

Gavin bobbed his head. "I'll let the chief know." He cleared his throat before turning to me. "Thanks again for coming down, Coco. If we have any more questions about LaTàge, I'll let you know."

I deflated at getting sidelined so quickly, but then remembered it was in my best interest not to draw too much attention to myself for the time being.

As much as I wanted to meet Ruby and hear Gavin interview her, I knew that wasn't in the cards. I may have been on the PD's consulting payroll, but I was not an investigative member of their team. I was their social media guru.

I was about to wish Gavin good luck and scoot down the hall after Harriet when he gripped my elbow to hold me back. "Got a sec?"

Curious about what else he needed, I nodded. "Of course."

"Look." Gavin fidgeted a bit before releasing a big sigh. "I know county is lead on this investigation, but I think it would be a big win for our department if we're able to contribute information that triggers an arrest. Help us move the needle with the Community Safety Center proposal."

Adrian had mentioned as much when he'd given me a lift here.

"Given your tendency to stick your nose where it doesn't belong…" He paused and held my gaze. "If you do come across something, could you share it with me sooner rather than when you're in the middle of confronting a killer?"

I blushed as he referred to my previous exploits. "Are you asking for my help, Lieutenant?"

"No!" His response came in a rush. "Not as an officer, mind you. But as a friend, *if* you uncover info through your unconventional channels, I promise I won't read you the riot act."

I couldn't believe my good fortune. "Is this some kind of trick?"

Gavin chuckled. "Between that response and your comment about saving LaTàge's Stories, I take it you're already looking into her death?"

"Well, uh…" I debated what to say. I wasn't sure if he was setting me up or if this olive branch was actually real.

"Hey, I'm serious. I come in peace." Gavin held his hands up in surrender. "I know I should tell you not to interfere, but I also know you won't listen. I've seen the awful stuff people are posting about you online. You've got a lot at stake, Cokes. I get it." His expression softened. "Just know I'm willing to listen if you've got information to share. You *are* a member of this team, after all."

A confident smile spread across my face. "It's a deal."

"Great. Although," Gavin said with a stifled cough, "let's keep this between the two of us. What with the chief being so busy."

I held my hand out to shake on our under-the-table arrangement. "My lips are sealed." While Gavin, who'd been a good friend of mine since childhood, had grown to trust my investigative skills, his uncle viewed me as more of a hindrance than a help.

"And whatever you get up to, be careful," he stressed.

Buoyed by Gavin's willingness to give me some leeway to poke into things on my own, I bid him goodbye and floated down the hallway toward the front of the station.

I practically skipped into the waiting room before realizing I probably should've gone around the back of the building, much like I'd entered. Through the window blinds, I spied photogs loitering outside, and I had no desire to cross paths with them.

However, the sudden sight of bright *Little Mermaid* red-colored hair left me momentarily starstruck. Sitting in one of the cheap waiting room chairs with her arms crossed was Ruby Daniels in the flesh. She could've been Lupita Nyong'o's double with her heart-shaped face, dark eyes, and full lips. She wore a shimmering obsidian-and-gold jumpsuit, which I guessed was her haute couture take on "mourning black." She stared straight ahead, looking bored and intoxicatingly mysterious all at once.

I opened my mouth to say something to her when the sound of throat clearing pulled my attention toward the reception desk, where Adrian and Maude Langford both sat.

"You'll probably want to leave through the back, Coco." Adrian pointed a thumb over his shoulder. "It's even crazier out there now that Ms. Daniels has shown up."

"Sure, sure." I turned my attention back to Ruby, trying to figure out what to say to her.

"Don't bother." Maude scowled, seemingly having read my mind. "She's got those ear pods in. Hasn't heard a thing we've said to her."

Adrian chuckled. "They're AirPods, Maude."

Behind her thick glasses, Maude rolled her eyes. She'd been the daytime receptionist for Central Shores since I was a kid and had no patience for any technology newer than 1980.

The door behind me opened, and Gavin stepped into the waiting room. "Ms. Daniels? Right this way, please."

Ruby continued to stare straight ahead.

I tapped the sides of my ears, indicating to Gavin that he had noise-canceling earbuds to contend with. He sighed and marched forward, positioning himself right in front of Ruby. "Ms. Daniels?"

Ruby finally blinked. She held up a finger, silently asking him to wait, while she swiped through her phone with her other hand. "Sorry. I was listening to my daily meditation." The twenty-seven-year-old's smokey voice had a hint of California lilt to it.

Gavin nodded, doing his best to bury his annoyance. "Right this way, please," he repeated.

Ruby rose from the creaking chair with leonine grace. The lifts on her black biker boots put her at eye level with the lieutenant. "Great." She made the word sound like it had five syllables. "My lawyer also texted. He'll be here soon." Then, completely ignoring me, Maude, and Adrian, Ruby slung her black tasseled bag over her shoulder and followed Gavin into the inner sanctum of the station.

"Sweet gal." Maude snorted once the door slammed shut behind them.

I frowned at our non-interaction. Had Ruby not noticed me? It wasn't like I was a complete stranger to her. Maybe she was just too consumed by LaTàge's passing to be aware of her surroundings.

Whatever the case, I hoped Ruby would be a little more forthcoming when Jasper, Charlotte, and I spoke with her later at her hotel.

Since Ruby had just gone in for her interview, I needed to kill some time before the next phase of our plan kicked off. Luckily, I had just the thing to keep me busy. With the new bombshell intel that LaTàge might be Laila Jackson, I wanted to do some recon on my former schoolmate.

I wished Adrian and Maude good luck with their day and bid them farewell before Maude buzzed me back through the metal door separating the waiting room from the department offices. As tempted as I was to listen in to Ruby's interview from outside the conference room, I couldn't risk getting busted. I might be on Gavin's good side right now, but if Chief McInnis stormed in and caught me interfering, I doubted things would end well for me.

Instead, I hightailed it for the backdoor and skirted through the garage. I didn't plan on returning to Jolly just yet, however. No, my destination was the Central Shores Public Library for some good old-fashioned research.

Chapter Eleven

I kept my head down as I walked along the outskirts of the Commons, making note of the intricate cracks in the brick sidewalk that circled the charming park. Luckily, the frenzied news crews were still too preoccupied with Ruby Daniels' earlier arrival to notice me scurrying away toward my intended destination.

The Central Shores Public Library was the largest of the four buildings surrounding the Commons. The colonial-style architecture was beautifully constructed, albeit a bit rundown, but I could spot some recent repairs to help spruce up the exterior façade. The new director, Noelle Paige, had done an admirable job engaging the community and enticing more people to use the library's resources. For a time, I'd worried the institution wouldn't survive the year, but with a monthly book club and a new children's reading center, it seemed like fresh life had reinvigorated the place.

I neared the entrance and noticed a flyer taped to the front door, advertising the reading group I'd been planning to attend before Mom usurped my evening. As I studied the bright graphics, I considered pulling Noelle aside and offering her CoA's services. Getting the word out online about the local book club would generate more buzz for the library, and it would be a nice boost of publicity for CoA to be seen volunteering within the community. A win-win for everyone.

I pushed the ornate wooden door inward, inhaling the musty scent of old books that permeated the air. Rows of tall shelves lined the main aisle leading toward the circulation desk. Warm overhead lighting created an earthy glow, further enhanced by numerous house plants scattered around the main floor. It exuded a cozy vibe, perfect for curling up with a book in the leather recliners and on couches positioned throughout the spacious room.

I hastened toward the circulation desk where the library director stood with her hands on her hips as she stared at a pile of books.

"Hi, Noelle." I waved at her, careful to keep my voice at a respectful volume. "How's it going?"

Her broad shoulders straightened once she realized she had company. "Oh, hello, Coco. Nice to see you." A smile broke out across her pretty face. Her rich brown skin was smooth, refusing to give away her age. If I hadn't known she'd been a librarian for twenty years, I would have thought she was thirty. "I was glad to see your name on the book club roster."

"Unfortunately, I won't be able to make it to tonight's meeting. A family thing popped up." I winced in apology. "But I'll definitely be at next month's," I quickly added.

Noelle's smile turned to a look of alarm. "Oh dear. I hope it's not something serious?"

"No, nothing like that." I waved away her concern. "Just my mom getting her way."

Noelle chuckled. "Now, that tracks. Moira Cline doesn't take no for an answer. For which I am glad." As town council chair, Mom had made it her mission to get more funding for the library and, thus, had become a government advocate on Noelle's behalf. "You didn't need to come all the way down here to tell me you couldn't make it, though."

"I'm actually stopping by to do some research." I leaned against her pristinely organized desk. "I was wondering if you have any CSH yearbooks in your collection."

Noelle's brown eyes twinkled with pride. "We have every year since the school opened."

Score! "I'm trying to remember what clubs I was a part of when I was a sophomore," I fibbed and rattled off the year Laila Jackson had graduated Central Shores High.

Noelle extricated herself from the circulation desk and beckoned me to follow her. "All local materials are housed in this section." She led me over to an imposing shelf in the corner of the library. "Maps, copies of the *Central Shores Gazette*, annual reports, you name it."

I scanned the familiar purple and gold spines, traditional of the CSH yearbook. "Here we go." I stood on my tiptoes to grab the thick volume in question.

"Want to try one of our new reading rooms?" Noelle offered, motioning to a distorted glass door nearby. "We just unveiled them last week." Clearly proud of this development, Noelle beckoned me toward the doorway.

I peered inside, delighted by what I found. A desk with a collection of pens and pencils was pressed up against one wall, while a compact, cozy armchair was perched in the opposite corner. On top of the end table next to it was a small beverage station, complete with a mini Keurig machine and a pod tree with multiple offerings.

"Wow, Noelle. This is so awesome." It certainly did look like the ideal place to read.

"Thank you." She beamed. "All due to that funding your mom got us." Her smile suddenly turned to a frown. "Too bad Moira hasn't had the same luck with securing the votes for the Community Safety Center initiative. She and Lloyd presented a great proposal at the last town meeting. Even Thurston Highgrove showed up to lend his support."

I struggled to keep surprise from my expression. While I knew Amanda's father was in Chief McInnis's corner, this was the first I was hearing about my mother's involvement in the CSC project. Some daughter I was. No wonder Mom wanted me to come for a visit. We had much to catch up on. "I imagine constructing a whole new building and beefing up staff is a bit pricier than renovating a few reading rooms," I finally replied.

Noelle chuckled. "And therein lies the problem. But if Mayor Sullivan and the rest of the council don't realize the value in being prepared for all those new woodland homes to sell, well, then, it's their necks on the voting chopping block come November."

She made an astute point, but I hoped our local officials would see reason sooner rather than later. Gavin and the team were stretched thin enough as it was.

"Make yourself at home." Switching back to the matter at hand, Noelle ushered me inside the reading room. "But don't spill anything," she added in a firm librarian tone before sliding the door shut.

I placed the Central Shores High yearbook on the desk before assessing my beverage options. I selected a lemon ginger tea K-pod from the tree and fired up the Keurig. Underneath, in the end table cabinet, I found some compostable cups.

A minute later, I settled into my temporary workspace, inhaling the invigorating scent of ginger as I flipped open the yearbook. Black-and-white images from my adolescent past greeted me as I thumbed through the pages. Central Shores may have been a small town, but it was also home to a community school district. With so many kids from all over the coastal area, CSH had the funding to support numerous extracurricular activities, clubs, and sports. I'd dabbled in many of them throughout my high school career. But as much as I would have enjoyed gushing over photos of Jasper and me from *Beauty and the Beast* (we made phenomenal townspeople), I skipped over the yearbook's highlights from the school's musical and focused on the senior class tributes. It didn't take long for me to find Laila.

Unlike many of her classmates who had wide, eager grins in their senior photos, Laila's smile was tight and strained, not making its way to her big, dark eyes. As I stared at her, I tried to find a resemblance between her and LaTàge. She certainly was beautiful, but softer than LaTàge's thin face and sharp angles. I dug my phone out of my bag and tapped until I found an image of the late influencer from head-on. I placed the device on the yearbook page, studying the women side-by-side like I was doing a *Highlights* hidden picture puzzle. The only vague similarity I could determine was the shape of their eyes and chin. Everything else was different. LaTàge's nose was more defined, her cheekbones more prominent, her lips fuller. Heck, even her eyebrows had a different arch to them. The differences were extensive, but if plastic surgery were involved...

"Why would you do this to yourself, Laila?" I mumbled under my breath.

My gaze moved to the text beneath Laila's senior photo. Here, graduates shared their future plans and reflected on their time at CSH. Laila's was brief.

Laila Jackson is graduating with high honors and a scholarship to UCLA. She plans to study fashion journalism. During her time at CSH, Laila was a member of the photography club, a Buddy-to-Buddy mentor, and an editor for the school's newspaper, The Shoreline. She is grateful for her family's support and dedicates this yearbook to her parents, Omar and Trisha.

I swallowed as a sad memory hit me. Little more than a decade ago, Trisha Jackson, Mr. J's wife, had been diagnosed with stomach cancer. After a short yet hard-fought battle, she passed away the summer following my first year at Bayside University. I vaguely remembered the community coming together to support Mr. J, but I couldn't recall Laila being in the picture. Was my memory failing me, or had something happened to prevent Laila from being beside her dad at Trisha's memorial?

Other than Laila's graduation feature, I couldn't find much about her in the yearbook. On a whim, I dialed Jasper's number. While I tried to block out most of my high school social experience due to Amanda's bullying, Jasper had embraced it, using it as fuel to power his tycoon ambitions.

"Have you been kidnapped?"

I chuckled softly at his stern greeting. Like many millennials, I was mildly allergic to the phone, always preferring to text rather than call. However, for a case, I was willing to grit my teeth and bear it. "No. I have a few questions about our high school days." I kept my voice low. Even though I was in a private reading room, I wasn't sure how soundproof they were.

"Ew," came Jasper's deadpan response. "Why? And where are you?"

"I'm at the library. Are you alone?" Jasper often oversaw his growing *Divulge* empire from his home office, and sometimes, he invited team members over to brainstorm layout and content ideas for future issues.

"I am. I blocked off my calendar since we're on Ruby Watch." I heard him moving around his condo. "I also needed some quiet time to storyboard my next *Direct* episode. What are you at the library for? You've heard of the Internet, right?"

I lowered my voice even more. "What I'm about to tell you stays between us for now, got it?"

Jasper sighed, the force crackling against my phone speaker. "Yeah, yeah, yeah. If I break my promise, I get your firstborn child."

I snorted at his remark. Jasper was not a fan of children, so it seemed ample punishment for breaking a promise. However, since I had no plans to procreate, it was also something he wouldn't suffer repercussions from. "While I was at the PD this morning, Omar Jackson called."

"Mr. J?" Jasper sounded intrigued. "What for?"

"He told Gavin LaTàge was really his daughter, Laila."

Jasper gasped. "*What?* Shut the front door. LaTàge was actually someone with ties to Central Shores?"

I nodded, then remembered he couldn't see me. "Do you remember Laila at all? She was two years above us."

"I'm trying to think." Jasper went silent for several seconds. "Man, the only thing that comes to mind is her shushing Deja once when Deja said something particularly nasty to me. I was at my locker, and Deja made some snarky comment about my fluid sexuality. Laila happened to be walking by and told her cousin off. It was like the one time I ever saw them interact."

I frowned at the memory. No doubt, Deja had come after Jasper to impress Amanda. During our freshman year, it took Deja several months to prove herself worthy of being a member of Amanda's mean girl posse.

"Other than that, no," Jasper continued on the other end of the line. "It's like once she graduated, Laila completely fell off the face of the earth. Not that she ever stood out much in school, to begin with. She was pretty quiet."

"What about when Trisha Jackson passed away?" I pressed. "Do you remember Laila coming back for her mom's memorial or anything?"

"You know what, I don't. I think I stayed at NYU that summer." Jasper paused. "But I *do* recall Mama Hastings making a comment about the whole affair. She mentioned how sad it was that Laila refused to put aside her differences with Mr. J and stand with him at the memorial. Luckily, Deja and Terrance were there to support him."

I mulled over this tidbit. It seemed Laila *had* attended her mom's funeral, but she'd stayed away from her dad and her cousins. "So, Laila and Mr. J had some bad blood between them around the time Trisha died?"

"I guess. Although over what, I have no clue."

I tapped my finger on the yearbook picture of Laila. "I wonder if Amanda would know. She and Deja were tight back in high school."

"Think Amanda 2.0 remembers that?" Jasper asked dryly. "She certainly has a selective memory regarding our teenage years."

I giggled at the sarcasm in his comment. While the Amanda Highgrove we were friends with today was a complete one-eighty from her high school self, she never had outwardly apologized for treating us like scum. "I'll touch base with her and see. Maybe Deja dished to her about some family drama. But if Laila *is* LaTàge, this puts a whole new spin on our investigation."

"You bet it does," Jasper agreed. "Does that mean our Ruby Daniels plan is off the table?"

"No way," I replied. "I still want to talk with her. See if she knew anything about LaTàge's ties to Central Shores."

"Sounds good. Let me know when you're ready to roll out. We're meeting at Charlotte's, right?"

"Yup. I'll text you when I'm heading down to the strip." As the owner of a hulking, four-door truck, Charlotte was the only one in our sleuthing squad with a comfortable car for more than two people.

We ended our call, and I went back to staring at Laila's yearbook photo. While Jasper hadn't been able to add much, his mom's comment rang in my ears. Laila had once clearly loved her parents, made evident by her yearbook dedication. So why had she opted to cause turmoil for Mr. J at Trisha's memorial three years later?

I dug my tablet from my bag. A library book couldn't answer my lingering questions. I needed the Internet.

Pulling up Google, I typed in **Laila Jackson, Central Shores,** and waited for my results. As the first page loaded, my excitement at seeing the number of search hits dimmed once I began to skim the text. I had a slew of info on Central Shores and people named Laila Jackson, but nothing mentioning both. Knowing Laila had gone to UCLA, I removed Central Shores from my keywords and added her alma mater.

A few promising results came up. Laila had been named to the Dean's list for the first six semesters of her college career. She had joined the university's campus paper, and a collection of her bylines popped up. However, an unsettling awareness dawned on me as I continued to scan the results. There was no mention of Laila after her junior year. Her articles with the paper stopped. Her appearance on the Dean's List ceased. Had something happened during her senior year to make her drop her extracurriculars and cause her grades to slip?

"Duh, Coco," I chided myself for my overt foolishness. "Her mom died the previous summer."

I continued to skim the results but found no further mention of Laila. I then switched to my favorite place to gather intel: Facebook. I typed Laila's name into Search and studied the faces staring back at me. I quickly opted to filter out alternative spellings of her name. I didn't need to see the profiles of Layla's and Leila's. When the list of accounts showed only Laila Jackson profiles, I went to work comparing their photos to the headshot in my old yearbook.

"She's not here." I frowned at my tablet. Facebook had been all the rage when I was in high school. Everyone wanted to be on it, especially once Zuckerberg opened the platform to anyone over the age of thirteen. Originally, you had to have a college email to use the social media platform, but that was done away with when I was in middle school.

I continued to check the accounts, this time clicking on them one by one. Did Laila not have a Facebook profile?

I cleared my results and typed in LaTàge's name. Her verified page popped right up, displaying her millions of followers underneath the title. Could Laila Jackson *really* be LaTàge? Had Trisha's death triggered something within Laila that made her want to change her name, her age, her entire personality, and be reborn as LaTàge? The thought left me mystified.

My phone buzzed next to my now cool cup of tea. A text from Gavin.

Got a minute?

I texted back, **Ofc. Call?**

The device buzzed to life a half-second later. "Hey," I answered with casual nonchalance. "What's going on?"

"I wanted to update you. I just spoke with Harriet after wrapping with Ruby. Omar's story checks out. LaTàge is—*was* Laila Jackson."

I sat back in the cushy desk chair, my jaw dropping open. "Omigosh." I don't know why the news left me stunned. I guessed the questions I'd been asking myself moments before Gavin's confirmation seemed too fantastical to be real. But with this news that Laila was indeed LaTàge, another question added itself to my list: how had Laila managed to pull off such an elaborate act of deception? Charlotte's earlier mention of Madame Organa, LaTàge's medium, prophesying that the truth would soon come to light floated through my memory. No wonder LaTàge had been so freaked out by the reading. For years, she had fooled millions of people into believing she was a twenty-five-year-old trendsetter from LA. Had her lies come back to haunt her?

Chapter Twelve

"Now," Gavin continued speaking, oblivious to my internal debate, "the reason why I'm calling you with this information is twofold. One, you were at the station when Omar's bombshell dropped, so I knew you'd probably spiral until you found out for certain. As for two…" He paused, and I heard him take a steeling breath, "Omar is recovering from extensive heart surgery. He was under the knife for most of Monday, so that's why he couldn't phone until this morning. He certainly doesn't need the media scrutiny about LaTàge being his daughter right now. Not with everything else he's dealing with. Both Terrance and Deja were adamant about that when Harriet left."

My mind raced. Terrance and Deja must have been visiting their uncle in the hospital. Did Deja know her cousin was *the* LaTàge? How had the Jacksons kept such a juicy secret for so long?

"So," Gavin explained with a sigh, "the crime lab is not going to release LaTàge's real identity until he's had more time to heal. You know what this means?" His tone became a low growl. "You're going to have to keep this news under wraps, Coco."

I gulped. "Um, sure. You can trust me." *Telling Jasper doesn't count, right?*

"Yeah, don't make me regret it."

"How was Omar able to prove Laila was LaTàge?" I burst out. The question had been gnawing away at me ever since Harriet had departed for the hospital. "I mean, anyone could say LaTàge was their daughter." I also found it hard to believe that someone as conscious of their social status as Deja wouldn't be letting the world know she was related to a famous influencer.

"He was able to provide photos of Laila with the same birthmarks found on LaTàge's body. We also cross-referenced Laila's information with the California DMV. Her address on file matches the residence leased to LaTàge's LLC."

I ran my fingers through my matted hair. Wow, now that they had a name, so much additional info made itself available for police to access. "This is so wild. I mean, we all *knew* Laila. How did we not know she was LaTàge? How did the Jacksons keep such a big secret?"

"Omar claims no one in his family, beyond him, had any idea Laila reinvented herself." Gavin sounded somewhat skeptical over this. "He hadn't heard from her in years, and it was only a few weeks ago that he began making an effort to rebuild their fractured relationship."

I continued to scratch at my head. "Do you know why Laila had become estranged from her dad in the first place?"

"Not yet, but believe me, Coco, we'll be looking into the Jackson clan as we conduct our investigation," Gavin replied. There was a sudden, brief shuffling sound on his end before he continued in a much louder voice. "Did you hear that clearly? *Our* investigation. You've done your part, for which we are grateful. But now, as a contracted department employee, you need to keep this quiet and not draw any attention to yourself."

Something about his stern, stilted delivery seemed off. Given our earlier tête-à-tête about me funneling intel his way, I wondered if Chief McInnis was now within earshot of the conversation.

Gavin then whispered into the line, "Deja is some hotshot politico now, and she made all kinds of remarks to Harriet about not dragging their family through the mud. She won't be happy if she feels like she's being targeted. Got it, Coco?"

Got it. Translation: Be careful about questioning Deja. She could cause trouble if she thinks I'm snooping into her cousin's case.

"Message received. Thanks for the heads up, Gav." Regardless of who LaTàge really was, there was still an angry online mob out there that faulted me for her death. If I could clear my name by helping the police uncover the truth through my own unconventional methods, I would. Gavin had to follow protocol and get warrants for things. I didn't have to play by those stingy rules, which could ultimately work to Gavin's benefit. "I will keep this stuff about the Jacksons to myself." And I was being truthful…sorta. Once I filled in Charlotte and my friends and I were on the same page, *then* I would be the picture of discretion.

"Okay. Good." Gavin's voice softened. "Once County does release Laila's name to the public, it would be great to have you help manage the department's socials. See if anything useful comes in. And, of course, all the information from our earlier discussion still stands."

His coded message reaffirmed my belief that Gavin wasn't intentionally shutting me out. He was only pretending to for appearances' sake. "Sure thing."

"All right. See ya, Coco."

"Bye." I ended the call, pursing my lips as I stared at Laila's yearbook photo. While this new development surely put a twist in the case, I still wasn't about to give up our pursuit of the LaTàge Squad. If Omar was being truthful and no one beyond him knew who Laila had become, the LaTàge Squad still seemed like the most viable suspects in her murder. Yet, I found it hard to believe that Laila had kept this secret from her cousins all these years. Terrance, maybe, but Deja was all over the 'gram. How could she *not* know who LaTàge really was? Yes, granted *I* hadn't made the connection, but Laila wasn't a relative. She'd been an upperclassman and one I'd hardly interacted with.

My call with Gavin also indicated another important point. He was no longer questioning Ruby Daniels, which meant it was time to mobilize the troops.

Omw to B2P. Ruby is done @ PD. I sent the group message to Jasper and Charlotte before tidying up my makeshift workspace. Discarding my cup in the compost bin, I then headed toward the circulation desk to return the yearbook.

Noelle glanced up from her computer as I approached. "All done?" she asked with a cheerful smile.

"Yes. Thank you. I love the new reading room." I motioned over my shoulder. "What would you say to CoA doing a little social media campaign to spotlight them and the monthly book club? Totally pro bono. More folks should know about all this great renovation work you've done."

Noelle tilted her head. "You don't have to do that, Coco. The library can pay for your services."

"I know, but I'd really love to donate the time."

"Well, then, I won't say no to that." Noelle clapped her palms softly together, ever mindful of her surroundings. "It would be wonderful if students learned about the reading rooms. A nice place to do their homework and such."

I nodded. "For sure. I can create some flyers to put up at the high school, along with some social media stuff."

"Let me give you what I've already drafted for our newsletter." Noelle rolled her desk chair to a nearby filing cabinet. As she rummaged through a drawer, I noticed a beautiful bouquet perched near her computer monitor.

"Those peonies are gorgeous." I pointed to the stunning assortment.

Noelle's cheeks darkened as she scooted back into place and handed me a leaflet. "A gift from my boyfriend."

"Boyfriend?" My eyebrows rose in surprise. "I didn't know you were dating someone."

Noelle twiddled with her book-themed lanyard. "It's only been a couple of months. But he's wonderful."

"May I ask who the lucky guy is?"

Noelle looked like she was about to tell me when her desk phone rang. She instinctively answered, "Central Shores Public Library. How may I help you?"

She listened a moment before she met my gaze with a grimace. "Sorry," she mouthed. "This might be a few minutes."

I made a hand sign that I would message her about a volunteer CoA engagement and waved goodbye. I needed to get to Brewed to Perfection. While I assumed Gavin had told Ruby to remain in the area, I couldn't be certain that she wasn't preparing to depart Delaware at this very moment.

Noting the gathered crowd of reporters outside the station, I did my best to steer clear as I hightailed the few blocks to my car. Fifteen minutes later, I parked in the residential lot behind the strip, spying Jasper's car nestled a few rows away. I couldn't suppress a reflexive cringe. No doubt, my friends would lightly poke fun at my neurosis over being the last to arrive.

I grabbed my bag containing all the necessary items for our sleuthing adventure, making sure I had my Tom Ford shades tucked away to play their part in the ruse. The ones I was wearing, a label ironically called Petty Trash, did their job well enough, but I missed the familiar feel of my regular sunglasses.

With hurried steps, I wove through the parking lot and down the alley between Jewel's Ice Cream and Harper's Pub. Jewel's had a sign outside stating they would be closing at the end of the month. A twinge of sadness echoed through me. As much as I loved my hometown, Central Shores in the off-season always seemed a little less joyful. Several shops closed or had restricted hours during the winter months, giving ghost town vibes until spring weather rolled around.

Brewed to Perfection occupied the southernmost building on the strip. Since I'd last visited, Charlotte had used window chalk to draw cute fall images, announcing the return of her yummy Pumpkin Patch Lattes and Autumn Harvest Chai. The smell of cinnamon and sweet spices buoyed my spirits as I glided through the doorway. While I wasn't a big fan of what the autumn season did to Central Shores's vibe, I was totally here for Charlotte's new menu.

"She hath arrived." Jasper spread his arms in dramatic fashion as he swooped toward me, acting like we hadn't crossed paths in ages rather than speaking on the phone not thirty minutes ago.

Charlotte waved from behind the counter, closing a thin, colorful binder with her other hand. "Need a caffeine pick-me-up before we jet?" She slid the binder out of eyesight with fluid grace.

"Yes, please." I bobbed my chin enthusiastically. I'd skipped out on my morning coffee in preparation for this very moment. "What were you guys working on?"

"Nothing special. Jasper was just helping me select a font for the menu." In lieu of my usual caramel macchiato, Charlotte busied herself making me a pumpkin latte.

I propped my elbows on the counter, surveying the empty shop. I doubted it would be that way for long. Charlotte's café was one of the few businesses that didn't suffer too greatly from the change of season. "Would you like my opinion?"

"Excuse me, *my* advice is good enough," Jasper cut in.

I was about to jokingly beg to differ when the storeroom door whipped open.

"Hey, Ms. Coco." Maria Ortiz, Charlotte's full-time barista and a recent college grad, smiled in greeting as she appeared. "Loved your latest post. I need to get myself a capsule wardrobe, stat." She rubbed her hands on her navy apron. "It would make getting dressed for work so much easier."

"A total timesaver," I agreed, touched she had read last Saturday's *Trending Topic* article. Capsule wardrobes were very popular, especially among young professionals. With interchangeable pieces that all complemented each other, a capsule collection provided an outfit suitable for any occasion, all while keeping the size of your closet under control. Perfect for apartment living.

Jasper shuddered with mock horror. "Ugh, I can't imagine limiting my wardrobe to thirty pieces. I'd rather turn my second bedroom into a walk-in."

"You *did* turn your second bedroom into a walk-in," I responded dryly.

"Oh, right."

Maria giggled at Jasper's coy reply. "Well, when you have access to all the amazing clothes that you do, why say no?"

"Right? You get it, Maria. Why say no?" Jasper snapped his fingers. "That's got a good ring to it. Maybe I'll do something on *Divulge Direct* to combat the rise of the capsule wardrobe."

I rolled my eyes at his theatrics. "Is that a war you want to start?"

"When you have a platform like *I* do, Coco," Jasper said with a sniff, "you want to shine a light on the injustices of the world."

"Ooookay." While I wanted to tease him that his podcast hadn't yet hit one hundred thousand downloads, I could see Jasper was enjoying the attention from Maria, so I let him have his moment.

She continued to pepper him with questions while Charlotte made my latte. "Do you have any super famous people scheduled to appear on the show yet?"

"We're getting there," Jasper hedged evasively. "Right now, we're booking a lot of *new* voices to help them carve out their space. You know, artists dropping their first single, up-and-coming designers, debut actors, the like."

I giggled to myself at Jasper's clever spin on his guest list. Since *Divulge Direct* was a new concept backed by a Delaware-based news station, "big names" weren't exactly clamoring to be featured on his program. Yet. I did have faith that Jasper would rise to the top. It would just take some time.

A rush of ocean air brushed past me as the front door swung open. I turned around to see a familiar figure in business casual attire saunter into the café. "Hey, Rand. Long time, no see."

Rand Windham removed his white visor and winked as he strolled toward the counter. "Heya, Coco. And Jasper! Man, it's nice to see you, bud. Heard you moved back to town." In a total bro-move, Rand playfully smacked Jasper on the shoulder.

Jasper's nose wrinkled slightly at the invasion of personal space, but he summoned a friendly smile. "Hi, Rand. Yeah, it's great to be back."

"Cool, cool." Rand's congenial grin turned to the others. "Hey, Charlotte. Maria. How you ladies doing? Could I get an iced chai?"

"Coming right up, Mr. Rand." Maria leaped into action.

He flinched once Maria's back was turned. "She makes me feel ancient," he muttered. "I'm not *that* much older than you guys." Rand had been a few years ahead of us at CSH. He'd been your stereotypical football star, although a knee injury he received his junior year at the University of Delaware had robbed him of the chance to go further.

"Don't worry, she still calls me Ms. Coco," I murmured softly, so as not to embarrass Maria.

"How's life been treating you, Hastings?" Rand absently fiddled with his long-sleeved polo, plucking at the embroidered Ocean Hollow Marine emblem. He worked there as a "yacht broker," helping clients find and buy high-end boats. "You're doing some fashion-related stuff, right? I think I see it on my feed."

Jasper's brow arched with surprise. "You do?"

Rand chuckled. "Ha, my buds razz me for following a lot of girly stuff, but it totally helps me shop for my wife. Gotta know what to get her when the waters need smoothing over, right?" He nudged Jasper conspiratorially.

"Really breaking down gender barriers there, pal." Jasper shook his head with bemusement at Rand's mildly problematic remark.

I searched my mental contacts list, scrambling to remember whom Rand had married. Whenever I saw him around town, Rand didn't usually comment on his home life. He tended to talk about—

"Man, I hope the weather's as great in Rhode Island as it is here. I'm heading to Newport for their annual boat show next week."

I bobbed my head conversationally while inwardly, I withered. *Anchors away.*

"*Another* boat show?" Charlotte chimed in with a bright smile. "You don't say."

While she may have sounded serious, I could tell from the sparkle in her gray eyes that she was teasing the poor guy.

Rand, bless him, didn't notice. "Heck, yeah. September's full of them." He brimmed with unabashed enthusiasm for his vocation. "I'm hoping I can swing going to Tampa at the end of the month, too. Racking up those frequent flyer miles, am I right?"

"Sounds like it." I laughed politely. Rand was a super nice guy, if a bit one-track-minded. It was probably why wealthy people trusted him when it came to buying a boat.

"All right, Cokes. Here you go." Charlotte slid a steaming Pumpkin Patch Latte toward me while simultaneously waving away my credit card. "Maria, you good to tackle the rest of the day?"

Her barista motioned to the empty café, apart from Rand. "I think I'll manage."

"I promise I won't cause *Ms.* Maria too much trouble." Rand slid his visor back over his sandy brown hair. He gave me and Jasper a wink that said, *Two can play at this game.*

Charlotte, however, didn't take managing her coffee shop lightly. "If things get busy, just give me a call, and I'll pop on back." For the longest time, she had been afraid to leave her brainchild in the hands of anyone else, but dependable Maria had earned her trust. Now, Charlotte regularly left the café in her care.

"Yes, ma'am. I hear ya." Maria shooed us out of Brewed to Perfection.

We said goodbye to Rand and headed for the exit. As the door closed behind our little trio, I feigned a gag. "Ack, Maria calls you ma'am?" We weren't *that* old.

"Yeah, it's a habit I can't get her to break." Charlotte released her long, amber hair from the usual ponytail she wore while on the clock.

Jasper patted her on the shoulder. "First-world problems, huh?"

We all laughed.

"My truck is parked around back." Charlotte motioned with her thumb. "Should we grab an early lunch here or someplace in Crestview?"

"I hear the restaurant at The Glades is super swanky." Jasper adjusted his bright paisley tie.

I scanned his crisp chinos and button-down shirt. He certainly hadn't needed any reminding that we had to dress to impress Ruby and her crew. Charlotte, too, looked gorgeous in a long-sleeved violet dress that would make even Ana de Armas envious. "Sounds like the perfect place to debrief after we chat with Ruby."

"Have you told her?" Jasper nudged my arm as the three of us walked toward Charlotte's truck behind her café.

Charlotte whipped her head in my direction. "Told me what?"

"Not yet," I muttered. "Once we're on the road, I'll bring you both up to speed."

With that, we climbed into the truck cab and buckled. Charlotte plugged The Glades Hotel into Google Maps and set off. During the twenty-three-minute ride up the coast to Crestview, I filled Charlotte and Jasper in on the wild revelation that the internationally revered LaTàge had once been a Central Shores native. After, of course, making them swear up and down to keep Laila's identity a secret.

"I didn't realize Omar even had a daughter." Charlotte, who'd moved to Central Shores less than five years ago, was flabbergasted by this development. "He only ever mentions Deja and Terrance when he comes by the café. Granted, Omar treats those two like they're his own."

I leaned forward from my spot in the backseat as I'd generously conceded the front to Jasper's six-foot-three frame. "He's a regular?"

"Sure," she answered as she drove along the coastal road. "The whole family is. They all come by at some point during the week. Deja's usually too busy to make small talk, but both Omar and Terrance are sweethearts." A frown grew on her lips. "I knew about Omar's heart surgery. Gosh, to have to deal with the death of a child, too. Poor guy."

An idea sparked in my mind. "How weird would it be if you visited him at the hospital?"

From the rearview mirror, I saw her eyebrows knit together. "Interrogating a grieving man while he's in poor health isn't a good idea, Cokes."

"We wouldn't be *interrogating* him," I quickly rebuffed the notion. "Just checking to see how he is."

She shot a dubious glance over her shoulder as if she didn't quite believe me. "Mm-hmm."

"Charlotte has a point. Not a good look to be badgering an old man. Especially if Deja found out." Jasper added his two cents. "Something like that could get back to Chief McInnis, and the short leash Gavin put you on would snap in an instant."

"Fine. Fine. You're right." I slumped back in the seat. "I just want to know what happened between Laila and her family to cause such a gaping rift."

"Do you think it has something to do with her murder?" Jasper cocked an eyebrow.

I shrugged. "I really can't even guess. I mean, from the sounds of it, Mr. J had to be at the hospital for pre-op when Laila was killed."

"Omar didn't do this, Cokes." Charlotte's certainty rang clear in her voice.

"He's a good man."

And I thought Stacy Lockner's killer was a nice person. I decided to keep my humble opinion to myself. The idea that the well-respected Omar Jackson could kill his own daughter *did* seem a bit outlandish. But then again, this whole case was blowing my mind left and right.

"Let's focus on Operation Ruby." Jasper clapped, redirecting our nervous energy. "Regardless of Laila's ties to Central Shores, it's beyond weird how Ruby has been acting. Her online tributes seem way too over the top, even for a member of the LaTàge Squad."

I dug my phone out and loaded Instagram to see her latest content. Ruby had posted five separate videos lamenting LaTàge since this morning. "Yeesh. No kidding."

"Seems a bit much, right?" Jasper turned around in his seat. "Almost like she's overcompensating."

I watched the most recent video. Ruby's head rested against a black leather car seat, the camera capturing her svelte figure as the vehicle pulled away from the curb. I could make out the Central Shores Police Station through the car's window.

"Guys," Ruby whimpered through a heavy sob, *"I just got done speaking with law enforcement about my sweetie, LaTàge. They seem totally clueless, but I am demanding justice for my girl. I will not rest until her killer has been apprehended, even if it means staying around this dinky town to keep tabs on them. Much love, fam."* The video ended with her wiping her tear-stained cheeks and blowing kisses at the camera.

"Holy Billie Eilish." Charlotte shuddered.

Jasper let loose a low whistle. "Dang," he said, adding several syllables. "I hadn't seen that one. Gurl be slinging mud all over the place."

I replayed the video, wincing at her remarks. I wondered if the police had seen this yet. No one from the Central Shores PD or the Sussex County Crime Lab would be pleased by her unflattering words.

"If he didn't already know," Jasper commented, "Gavin is now surely realizing just how good he's had it with you." He glanced down at my phone. "You never went off and put the popo on blast like that."

A small smile twitched on my lips. "I think he already has. Otherwise, he wouldn't have been so forgiving about my interest in the case."

"It's good that he's open to receiving intel from you," Charlotte chimed in.

"We just have to stay out of trouble," I cautioned. "How are things on the Deacon front?" I felt guilty about asking her to keep our investigation from her boyfriend. "Since Gavin suspects what I'm up to, it's totally fine to clue Deacon in."

Charlotte's expression turned wistful. "If only there was time. We've hardly spoken two words to each other since yesterday. It's all hands on deck, and he's been super busy coordinating the forensic techs." As the team's lead, Deacon had a lot of responsibility on his shoulders.

While I knew how hard busy schedules could be on a relationship, it was a bit of a relief to hear I hadn't put Charlotte in a completely impossible position with my selfish request.

"He *did* mention how it would be much easier for us to stay connected if we lived together."

I was glad neither Jasper nor I were the ones driving. "What?!?!" Our combined shock had Charlotte reaching for her right ear.

"Ow, guys. Come on, it's not *that* big of a deal."

Jasper knocked her arm. "Um, yeah, it kinda is. Have you ever talked about moving in with one of your boyfriends before?"

Charlotte's brow furrowed. "I guess not."

When I befriended her nearly four years ago, Charlotte had been experiencing a terrible dating streak. One that had continued until she met Deacon this past spring. "Char, this is awesome. I'm so happy for you. Deacon is a great guy."

A hopeful grin spread across her face. "You don't think I'm being rash? I mean, we've barely been together six months."

"That's five months and three weeks longer than any relationship you've had since *I've* known you," Jasper cheekily replied. "I think he's a keeper."

"Really?"

"Honey, if Deacon batted for my team, I'd have a go at him."

Charlotte and I burst into laughter at Jasper's deadpan delivery. "Okay, good. I'm glad to hear you both are on board." Charlotte beamed. "I wanted your opinions before I said yes."

"In all seriousness, what we say shouldn't matter at the end of the day," I sagely reminded her. "What do *you* want?"

"To wake up next to that beautiful, brainy man every morning." Charlotte's face reddened at her steamy admission.

Jasper held his hand in the air for a high-five. "Gurl, get it."

Chapter Thirteen

We spent the remainder of our drive peppering Charlotte with questions about her boyfriend. Since Deacon rented an apartment in nearby Cherry Springs, Charlotte had floated the idea of him moving in with her since she owned her home in our Sunny Shores development. He seemed to be on board with the situation as long as she let him pay for utilities and groceries, further cementing his awesomeness in my mind.

By the time we parked in front of The Glades Hotel, I'd almost forgotten the purpose of our drive. It'd been nice to chat about my friends' lives and all the good things happening to them. It also kept my wandering thoughts from revisiting the terrible crime scene Amanda and I had stumbled into yesterday.

While Jasper and I waited on the sidewalk for Charlotte to register her truck with the valet, I clutched my phone and navigated to my text messages. I selected my convo with Amanda, wanting to check in and see how she was doing. I may have become slightly accustomed to finding dead bodies, but this had been her first time.

Hey. You doing OK? Yesterday was tough.

Once I'd sent the message, I opened our shared CoA calendar. Amanda had several client calls this morning, and she'd CC'd me on a few outbound communications. I nervously nibbled on my lower lip, feeling like an awful boss. I should have instructed her to take another day to recover. Given the terrible circumstances, our clients surely would've understood.

Charlotte joined Jasper and me under the sleek, steel-blue hotel awning.

"All set. So, what's the plan to track down Ruby?"

"We get the front desk to call up to her room with our lost-and-found request." I dropped my phone back into my bag and grabbed the Tom Ford shades, the bait for our grand caper.

Jasper snorted. "This place has a rep, Cokes. The Glades isn't going to ring a VIP client for some randos at the front desk."

"You and I aren't exactly randos." I pointed back and forth between the two of us. With his *Divulge* acclaim and my own local celebrity, Jasper and I were known public figures up and down the Delaware coast.

Charlotte crossed her arms. "Rude." She turned her nose up with a teasing sniff.

I smiled apologetically.

"We need to catch Ruby off guard," Jasper quipped. "If the front desk calls ahead for us, she'll have time to prep."

"That's a good point." I pictured us sneaking down long, gold-painted hallways like Daniel Craig's James Bond in *Casino Royale*. "But how do we know which room she's staying in?"

Jasper held up his iPhone. "Lucky for us, she's not in a room. Have a look." He handed me the device before continuing, "She just posted to her Instagram Stories two minutes ago. She's being 'consoled' by a bartender out by the pool." His use of air quotes only added to his dripping snark.

Charlotte and I watched the short clip. Ruby was sipping on a massive gin & tonic while tossing her long, fire-engine red hair in the direction of the studly bartender. "Wow. She looks torn up." Her demeanor was completely different from the last video I'd seen. I glanced at the timestamp. "It's five o'clock somewhere, right?"

"How do we get access to the pool?" Charlotte motioned to our chic attire. "We didn't come geared up for swimming."

"Let's grab a table at the restaurant," I suggested, a plan hatching. "I'm pretty sure there's an outdoor dining area overlooking the grounds. Once we're seated, I'll sneak off and chat with Ruby."

Jasper growled. "No way. No confronting potential killers alone, remember?" He raised a sharp eyebrow. "Char can watch the table while you and I corner Ruby."

"Hey, no fair! I want to meet her, too." Charlotte stomped her foot in a pout.

"Fine, fine, fine. We'll all take a strategic bathroom break or something." I smoothed my dress and confidently strutted toward the revolving entrance door. I had a role to play. Outside of Central Shores, I was Coco Cline, celebrity blogger and influencer.

Jasper and Charlotte flanked me on either side as I surveyed the glistening, posh lobby. It hadn't changed much in the three weeks since I'd last been here, having a celebratory drink with the marketing team to conclude our CoA engagement. A large, somewhat gaudy fountain created a soft, calming ambiance with its trickling waters. A gold-plated reception desk adorned one side of the cavernous room, while the glitzy restaurant entrance was on our right.

A stately doorman dipped his chin in greeting. "Hello, welcome to The Glades. Checking in?" He eyed the area around me for any luggage.

"No, we're here for lunch." I smiled sweetly. This older white guy didn't strike me as the demographic to subscribe to *Trending Topic* or my socials, so I doubted he knew who I was. "We're hoping to dine outside." I pointed to the far side of the room, where floor-to-ceiling windows exposed a corner view of the Olympic-sized pool.

"Of course." The doorman smiled conciliatorily before his gaze fell on Jasper. "Oh! Mr. Hastings. So nice to see you again. Are you dining with these ladies? Would you like your usual table?"

Keeping my lips firmly pressed together, I turned an expectant glare toward Jasper.

He winked. "Thanks, Giles. My usual outdoor spot would be great," he said to the doorman.

When Giles turned around to escort us toward the restaurant, I smacked Jasper on the shoulder. "You had an in all along?" I whispered through gritted teeth.

"Watching you do mental gymnastics is fun." Jasper snickered. "I've been taking a lot of business lunches here lately. The boss betch vibe is strong."

Charlotte giggled. "Okay, then, *Mr.* Hastings."

The doorman stopped in front of the maître d', a tall, familiar-looking woman dressed in an impeccable cream suit. The silky fabric was gorgeous against her dark skin.

"Mr. Hastings would like his outdoor table," Giles instructed.

"Hello, Mr. Hastings," the maître d' greeted Jasper warmly. "How nice to see you."

"Hi, Simone."

Her astute gaze slid to me. "And Ms. Cline. Lovely to have you join us again."

I remembered how I knew her. Simone had been the person who'd brought a bottle of champagne into the marketing team's office during my last visit. "Thank you." Her recognition filled me with bubbly pride. Why couldn't all our sleuthing adventures roll out the red carpet for us like this?

Simone led the way to a grand portico where lush green plants shielded us from the noontime sun. From our spot on the deck, I could just make out a sliver of the pool on the other side of the grounds. The G&T in Ruby's Story had been pretty big. I hoped she'd be nursing it for a while.

"Can I get you all started with something to drink?" Simone asked with clasped hands.

We ordered unsweetened iced teas. As inviting as the signature cocktail menu looked, my besties and I wordlessly agreed to keep clear heads for questioning Ruby and anything that came after.

"Simone, darling, could you point us in the direction of the washrooms?" Jasper inquired with debonair flair. "I think we'd all like to take some time to freshen up."

"Of course. Inside, down the right hallway, past the guest lounge."

We thanked her, and she left to alert a server of our beverage order.

"The *guest lounge,*" Charlotte said with an airy drawl.

I giggled at her feigned hoity-toity accent. "Come on. Let's find Ruby."

Our covert trio did its best to keep to the shadows, being careful not to make eye contact with anyone else dining or working in the restaurant.

Once we found the hallway Simone mentioned, Jasper, Charlotte, and I hurried in the opposite direction as she'd instructed, following the signs for the pool area.

"Got our cover story in check?" Jasper slid his Gucci shades onto the bridge of his nose as we emerged into the sunlight.

I clutched my decoy sunglasses in my hand. "You bet. I even saw her in the police station waiting room, so she shouldn't have any problem believing me." Ruby *had* to have seen me, right? Even though she'd ignored Maude, Adrian, and me, she still must have known we were there.

"All right. Sell it, betch."

Jasper whistled as we arrived at the sprawling pool deck. The Glades had spared no expense with the serene, glam environment. Plush white lounge chairs were peppered around the massive pool, along with several cabanas stationed at the deep end.

I scanned the people sunbathing outside. Given that it was post-Labor Day, September temperatures were still warm, but tourist season had drawn to a close, so there weren't many visitors to scope out.

"No sign of Ruby," I muttered out of the side of my mouth.

Charlotte bobbed her head in agreement. "She must be in one of the cabanas."

"Incoming." Jasper placed his hand on Charlotte's back and nudged her forward. "Hottie bartender at two o'clock," he spoke in silly code. "Deploy our resident glamazon as a distraction."

I chuckled at his antics while Charlotte stuck her tongue out at him. "No fair."

"Yes, it's tragic being beautiful." Jasper rolled his eyes before coaxing her on.

Charlotte sniffed. "How do you know he's even into women? Awfully presumptuous, I'd say."

"Because as soon as he spotted your legs, he started making a beeline toward you. Now, go!" Jasper hissed, nudging Charlotte toward her prey.

Taking one for the team, she shimmied over to the approaching staff member. With a toss of her long amber waves, she had him under her spell, giving Jasper and me the perfect cover to scurry toward the cabanas.

Our search for Ruby didn't last long. Her throaty laughter drifted on the breeze, fluttering from behind one of the drawn white linen curtains.

"Yeah, I think we should keep things quiet for now. It won't be a good look so soon after…well, you know."

Jasper's eyebrows shot toward his slicked-back hairline as he glanced my way.

I, too, felt my eyes bulging. Was Ruby talking on the phone, or was she not alone?

We leaned closer to the curtain, trying to hear a response, but all that answered was what sounded like Ruby swirling the ice in her drink.

"Yeah. No, no," Ruby hurriedly added. "You do you, bae. I'm keeping my lips sealed. Especially now that I have the police up my butt."

Jasper and I both stifled snorting giggles at her language, but it was good to hear Ruby was taking Gavin more seriously than she'd let on in her Stories. The question we now had was, what was she trying to hide? Murdering her bestie boss?

"Mm'kay. Talk soon. Kisses." She appeared to be signing off her call.

Seizing the moment, I tapped on the cabana's wooden frame. "Excuse me, Ruby Daniels?"

"Yeah?" Ruby's tone was wary and annoyed.

I drew back the curtain, summoning a bored look. I didn't want her knowing how starstruck she made me feel. I had to appear aloof and unfazed if I was going to pull this off. "Hey, Ruby. Coco Cline."

Ruby, clad in a barely-there black leather bikini, sat a little straighter in her lounger, but she didn't get up. "Omigod, girl! Hey. Uh, what are you doing here?" She pulled a robe on to cover herself as Jasper loomed behind me.

Pleased with her quick recognition, I gave her a small smile. My influencer status might actually help loosen her lips. "I wanted to check in on you, what with everything going on. I saw you at the police station earlier and noticed you left your shades behind." I held out my peace offering, even though Ruby had big, blingy sunglasses on her face.

"Oh, wow. Thanks, babe. That's sweet of you." To my surprise, she took my beloved Tom Fords without a second glance and tossed them onto the teak side table next to her near-empty drink.

I cringed as the plastic clattered against the wood. *Um, what?* Had dear Tom just become a casualty of this plan? "No problem," I summoned a feeble reply.

"So, you were there at the station? Wow. Sorry I didn't see you." Right before our eyes, Ruby transformed into a grieving friend. Gone was the laughing, secrets-keeping woman we'd overheard mere seconds ago. "I must've been in a shocked stupor. I think I still am."

I swallowed back a burgeoning objection as I stared hopelessly at my favorite shades. How was I going to get them back? *Focus, Coco. We gotta get Ruby to trust us.* "Uh, yeah. You looked really torn up." I tried to sound sincere. "This is my friend, Jasper Hastings." I motioned him forward.

Ruby studied him cautiously. "Why does your name sound so familiar?"

Jasper waved his hand with a bowing flourish. "I'm the Editor-in-Chief of *Divulge* magazine and the host of the new show, *Divulge Direct.*"

"Huh? Oh, right. That's a fashion mag, yeah?" Ruby bobbed her head, her tone bored once more. "I think Katz mentioned wanting to appear on your platform. What with their upcoming launch and all."

Beside me, I could feel Jasper struggling to contain a squeal of glee. "Ruby," I interjected before he could hijack our interrogation and turn it into a business meeting, "I'm so sorry about La—LaTàge. What a nightmare." Yikes, I'd almost said Laila.

Ruby pushed her sunglasses back into her red hair, revealing her teary, dark eyes. "It's hard to believe she's gone." However, she still didn't sound too upset. More like annoyed.

"I feel awful," I continued, trying to get her to share more. "I mean, you guys flew all the way out here for a CoA engagement, only to have it end up like this?"

Ruby scoffed. "I bet you do. The Internet is all over you right now." She swooped a finger through the air, and her expression became almost a bit envious. "LaTàge would be thrilled with the attention she's getting."

I risked a spooked glance toward Jasper. *That was a bit cold.*

"You were the one who found her, weren't you?" Ruby arched a perfectly threaded eyebrow my way.

Her question brought forth the unsettling memory. I flinched. "Yeah. When LaTàge didn't answer the door for our meeting, I went around back to see if I could find her."

"That show home is luxe, isn't it?" Ruby interrupted, changing the subject. "If I'd had known how fancy it was, I never would have said no to staying there."

Had she switched topics because the thought of LaTàge lying dead saddened her or made her feel guilty? Either way, Ruby's comment intrigued me, and I remembered my earlier conversation with Ronny about LaTàge renting the house for her friends to share. "Oh, so, she didn't rent it for herself?" I opted to play dumb.

"No way." Ruby shook her head. "LaTàge *hated* being alone. She practically begged us to crash with her. It turned into a whole 'thing' that we weren't." She rolled her eyes at the mention of drama. "And now I'm left to wonder if she'd still be alive if we did."

Jasper folded his arms casually across his muscular chest. "Why didn't you stay?"

Ruby motioned around her cabana. "LaTàge got the house totally last minute, so Katz, Miguel, and I were already booked here."

"The Glades wouldn't let you cancel?" I tilted my head.

Ruby grabbed her G&T from the side table and took a hearty sip. "Not without a hefty cancellation fee."

Odd. I was about to ask her why LaTàge just wouldn't pay it when Ruby's phone chirped.

She grabbed it and read the notification, a scowl spreading across her features. "Ew. Gross."

Jasper and I waited for her to elaborate.

Ruby flopped back against her lounger. "Ugh, so stupid. My lawyer says I have to stay in the area until my alibi is cleared up."

Jackpot.

"What? Why?" I sputtered, seizing this perfect opportunity. "The police don't think *you* had something to do with LaTàge's death, do they?"

Ruby threw her phone onto the neighboring lounge chair. "The rent-a-cop I spoke to is totally blowing some very innocent remarks way out of proportion."

"Like what?" While I wanted to defend Gavin's honor, I knew it wouldn't score me any points with Ruby to take his side.

"Like—" She cut herself off, her almond-shaped eyes narrowing on me. "Wait a minute. You're all over the 'gram about solving murder mysteries. Are *you* trying to find LaTàge's killer?"

Before I could begin to protest, Ruby leaped from her chair. "Omigod. You totally are." She reached for my forearm, her grip surprisingly strong. "Gurl, you've gotta help me. I had nothing to do with this mess. I just wanna get out of here without getting canceled and live my life."

I searched her pleading gaze, a myriad of panicky thoughts running through my mind. The last thing I needed was Ruby Daniels posting on the interwebs that I was playing detective again. Such a high-profile shoutout would not go over well with Chief McInnis, Detective Forester, or anyone.

Then there was, of course, my suspicion that Ruby very much *did* have something to do with her bestie's demise. While her plea for help seemed genuine, I couldn't unhear the nasty comments Ruby had made on the phone moments before we waltzed into her cabana. Not to mention, it sounded a bit cruel that she was ready to put her friend's death behind her and "live her life." LaTàge had barely been dead forty-eight hours.

"Okay, calm down." I pried Ruby's fingers loose and invited her to sit. "Why do the police think you killed LaTàge?"

Ruby fiddled with her overly processed hair. "Well…" She paused, sizing Jasper and me up. "This stays between us, right?"

"Only if it stays between us that I have an interest in LaTàge's case," I countered, my tone dancing along the intimidation lines.

"On my grandmama's life." Ruby tugged at a gold chain hanging from her neck and showed us an icon of Jesus on the cross.

I bowed my head solemnly, striking a shady deal I hoped I wouldn't regret.

Ruby hadn't exactly proven to be the epitome of discretion.

"All right. So, when we dropped LaTàge off at the beach house after dinner on Sunday, she tried getting us to stay with her one more time. I mean, don't get me wrong, the place was a dream, but we couldn't waste the money by bailing from here. Things kinda escalated and, when we finally left, I told LaTàge I was done working for her."

Jasper stifled a theatric gasp. "Done, done?" he repeated.

"Done." Ruby shrugged. "I love—*loved* her as a friend, a sister, but I just couldn't afford to keep up appearances anymore. None of us could."

I wrinkled my nose in confusion. "Afford to keep up appearances? What do you mean?"

"Look, this is bound to come out sooner or later," Ruby murmured, swiveling her head to make sure there were no shadows lurking outside the cabana to overhear our conversation, "but LaTàge hadn't paid me, Katz, or Miguel, in weeks. She was totally broke."

Chapter Fourteen

I didn't think I could be surprised further by this case, but such spicy tea knocked the wind from my sails. LaTàge, *broke*? She was one of the most famous influencers in the country. She'd just attended the Venice Film Festival. She was supposed to be the face of Katz's new clothing line. Where in the name of Zendaya had all her money gone?

"What happened?" Jasper appeared as shocked as I was. "LaTàge had more endorsement deals than Kylie Jenner. How'd she burn through all that cash?"

"Gurl just wasn't good with money. She was paying us ridiculous salaries. Spending a fortune on clothes, booze, and food." Ruby rattled off LaTàge's offenses. "Don't get me started on her gacha game addiction."

My stomach coiled. "How long had she been having money troubles?"

"Things got real this past spring when Katz wanted LaTàge to formally invest in their label. LaTàge counteroffered to be the face of the campaign. I should have known then something was janky." Ruby took another sip of her cocktail. "But I didn't figure out *what* until July when LaTàge was asked to donate to several charities. Instead of donating the money herself, she launched a few GoFundMe campaigns for the organizations and publicized them on her platform."

"I remember those posts," Jasper spoke up. "She raised quite a bit for each cause."

Ruby nodded. "She did. However, when one of the organizations tagged LaTàge's Insta handle, thanking her for the endowment, I noticed the amount LaTàge donated was smaller than the amount she'd raised." Her brow wrinkled slightly. "When I asked LaTàge about it, she shrugged it off and told me I was mistaken. She even suggested I was too overworked and not keeping tabs on everything she needed managed. As if. All she ever let me touch were her calendar and bookings email. Girl was weird about her accounts. You'd think most people would love dumping their stuff onto someone else's plate, but not LaTàge."

Jasper and I shared another knowing look. Ruby's story aligned with what Gavin had told me earlier about her not having access to LaTàge's personal data. "You think LaTàge skimmed money off the top of her fundraising campaign to keep her influencer business afloat?" I asked.

Ruby shrugged. "While I don't have the receipts to prove it, I'm almost certain she raised more than she donated."

"Yikes." Jasper *tsked* his disapproval.

"It only got worse from there. LaTàge soon started asking me to use my credit card for expenses rather than her business Amex. She said it was for tax purposes and that she'd reimburse me. She did at first, but then the excuses started pouring in." Ruby rolled her eyes. "It wasn't until two weeks ago that we noticed our direct deposits hadn't dropped. When Miguel confronted LaTàge about what was going on, she assured us it was a bank error and that things would soon be resolved. After this trip, in fact."

"Really?" My mind spun with potential theories. Did LaTàge think our rebrand campaign was going to bring in a ton of new followers and sponsors? I swallowed a nervous gulp. What would've happened if CoA hadn't delivered the results LaTàge had been expecting? Had Amanda and I dodged a professional bullet now that the engagement was off? "Why did LaTàge decide to come here for our collaboration? If she was so strapped for money, why make the trek?"

Ruby pursed her lips together, the gloss nearly blinding me. "Don't ask me. LaTàge was dead set on hitting up Central Shores for some reason. She had this idea to do some major brand rehab to help drum up buzz for Katz's clothing line launch and came to me with *your* name." Ruby narrowed her gaze. "I suggested we do a remote engagement, or have you fly out to us, but she was really intent on meeting you on your home turf."

Her words sparked an idea. Up to that point, during our chat with Ruby, I had been focused on LaTàge the Influencer, keeping Laila Jackson at the back of my mind. But what if Laila Jackson had been looking for a reason to return to *her* hometown, and a Center of Attention consultation had been the perfect cover?

"Did LaTàge know anyone in the area?" Jasper stroked his chin.

Ruby shook her mane of long red hair. "Other than Coco? No." She stared at us like we were a few eggs short of a dozen. "Why would she?"

Outside of the cabana, I heard a familiar flirty giggle. Charlotte was still hard at work keeping the hotel staffer away from our poolside interrogation, but we had to wrap things up, or someone from the restaurant might come looking for us if we didn't soon return from "the bathroom."

"Do you know anything about LaTàge before she was 'LaTàge.'" I used air quotes to emphasize I was talking about her public persona.

"Odd." Ruby cocked her head. "The police asked me that, too. I've only ever known her as LaTàge Luxe. Born and raised in LA. Had no living family. Didn't talk much about her past. She worked odd jobs and made makeup tutorials online until we began collaborating together. The rest is history."

I considered the fake bio Laila had adopted. Born in LA? No living family? I shuddered. What had happened between the Jacksons after Trisha's death to make Laila metaphorically kill off her dad and cousins? "So, you don't have any idea who she was before she was LaTàge Luxe?"

"What do you mean?" A glimmer of apprehension flickered in Ruby's eyes. "LaTàge *was* LaTàge." She fidgeted in her lounger, growing visibly agitated.

I remembered my promise to Gavin about keeping the name Laila Jackson to myself and quickly changed my line of questioning. "Can you give us a rundown of what happened Sunday night?"

Ruby slumped against her lounger. "It's such a blur. LaTàge and I flew into BWI and rented a car to make the drive here. Miguel and Katz came out on a later flight than we did. They didn't arrive until four in the afternoon. By then, I'd gotten LaTàge settled into the house, and we all went out for hibachi. It was fun…until it wasn't."

"What do you mean?" Jasper asked.

"LaTàge was acting super sus. She kept swiveling her head around the restaurant, almost as if she was worried she'd be spotted." Ruby's expression grew perplexed. "But like, that's what we *live* for. I totally didn't get it. Miguel finally got tired of it and told her to relax, then they started bickering, and the night dissolved from there. They didn't speak at all during the drive back to the house."

I frowned. "Did Miguel and LaTàge fight often?"

Ruby shook her head. "Rarely. Miguel is such an easy-going and great guy." She wiped a dreamy smile from her face. "Usually, he didn't let LaTàge's antics get to him." Her gaze dropped to the floor.

I studied her pinched expression, curious about this sudden change in dynamics between LaTàge and her friends. Like Miguel, for instance. Was it harder for him to play nice with his girlfriend now that the money was no longer coming in? "What happened after dinner?"

"We dropped LaTàge off at the Crescent Hills place." Ruby took another generous sip of her G&T. "Once we got there, she tried to get Katz and me to stay with her, which led to another argument about money, and I finally blurted out I couldn't work for her anymore."

"How did LaTàge take the news that you were quitting?"

"Not well." Ruby scoffed at my follow-up question as she set her now-empty glass down. "I told her I obviously still wanted to be her friend, but I needed to find a way to make my own money since I wasn't getting paid by her. I needed to be free from her ridiculous non-compete."

Jasper raised a sharp eyebrow.

"LaTàge made us all sign them," Ruby continued without additional prodding. "As long as I was 'employed' by her, I couldn't take on sponsorships of my own. Miguel couldn't be seen with other women. And Katz couldn't style anyone but her."

"Yeesh. Dictator, much?" Jasper's tone may have been joking, but his expression was uneasy.

"I wanted out. Miguel and Katz did, too, although Katz refused to speak up. They were our DD for the night and thought we were all overreacting." Ruby hugged herself. "Maybe we were, but I don't know why LaTàge just wouldn't release us from our non-competes. It would have solved everything. We could generate our own revenue streams and all still be friends. Besides, if we didn't receive a paycheck from LaTàge within a month, our contracts would have been nullified anyway." Ruby stared down at her lean, long legs. "Still, after our blowout, LaTàge begged us to stay. She promised things would go back to normal soon enough, but I was done. Don't get me wrong, I loved LaTàge like a sister, but I…just *couldn't* with her anymore." Her comment was heavy with genuine sadness. It was the first time I truly believed Ruby missed her best friend.

My pulse quickened. "So, what happened when you told her things would never go back to normal?"

"LaTàge revealed a side of herself I'd never seen." Ruby's expression darkened. "We'd been through so much together, but she took angry to a whole other level. She told us we'd be sorry we ever crossed her."

The clear threat sent a chill down my spine.

Ruby noted my reaction. "I won't lie. I was freaked out. Katz, too. They have so much riding on their label launch. Miguel…he just stomped out of the house. Said there was no use reasoning with LaTàge."

"Did you tell the police about all this?" Jasper asked.

Ruby's chin quivered. "Not in so much detail. I just confirmed that while I'd ended a working relationship with LaTàge, I was still very much her friend."

Great. While the truth didn't paint Ruby and her friends in a flattering light, neither did her hiding the severity of their final argument. "When did you drop LaTàge off at her rental?"

Ruby reflexively glanced at her watchless wrist only to find it was bare. "We probably left her around seven-thirty. The three of us were back at the hotel by eight."

Seven-thirty? While I was totally shooting from the hip, LaTàge hadn't looked like she'd been dead for more than twelve hours when I'd found her at eleven o'clock the following day. "Did you guys leave the hotel afterward?"

"I didn't. I-I don't know about Katz and Miguel." Ruby's gaze darted to the side in slight hesitation. "We all went our separate ways after we returned. I needed some time to decompress. I went to the gym for a bit and was back in my room before ten."

From out of the corner of my eye, I saw Jasper's nostrils flare. He'd caught her reaction, too. Ruby wasn't being entirely truthful with us.

"Um, yeah, for sure." Charlotte's voice chirped right outside the cabana. "Hey, guys," she hissed a moment later. "Are you still there?"

I pulled back the curtain and invited her inside. As Charlotte breezed into the tent, Ruby's shoulders straightened, and she quickly adjusted her legs to accentuate their shape. Charlotte's natural beauty had a habit of making others around her feel slightly inferior in Central Shores, and it seemed LA trendsetters weren't immune to her charms, either.

"We need to go," Charlotte muttered out of the corner of her mouth before turning her attention to Ruby. "Hi, Ms. Daniels. Big fan."

Charlotte's fangirling immediately relaxed Ruby's on-guard stature. "Thank you. I appreciate that." She sounded sincere. "Are you a friend of Coco's, too?"

"Yes, Charlotte Whittaker. I'm also her personal drink artist." Charlotte reached out her hand for an introduction with a completely serious look.

Jasper nearly choked as he suppressed a snorting cough. I, too, tried to keep my expression straight. *Where had that come from, Char?* Even people like LaTàge didn't have *drink artists*.

Ruby, however, seemed to take my bestie at her word. "Drink artist, huh? Guess LaTàge will be wanting one of those next—" She halted mid-sentence, the horrific shock of her friend's death seeming to hit her for the very first time. "Oh God, I can't believe she's really never going to text me again."

Jasper, Charlotte, and I shared sympathetic murmurs with the grieving woman. "We'll let you go, Ruby." We'd unearthed a good bit of intel, but needed to return to our table before Simone hunted us down.

"Wait. You're going to help me, aren't you?" Ruby sounded like a scared child. "I didn't do anything to LaTàge, Coco. I swear. You gotta believe me."

Despite some of her questionable responses, I honestly believed her, and that made what I had to ask next even harder. "What about Miguel and Katz? Could either of them have killed LaTàge?"

Ruby gulped, her eyes wide and frightened. "No. No way."
She didn't sound very confident.

Chapter Fifteen

With a promise to do our best to help her, my friends and I bid Ruby farewell.

"Do you really think she'll keep her mouth shut about us asking questions?" Jasper raised a skeptical eyebrow as we skirted back inside The Glades restaurant.

I sighed. "I hope to Florence Pugh that she does. Ruby seems to have faith that we can track down the truth."

Charlotte threaded her arm through mine. "Well, you've proven yourself more than once. Ruby's lucky to have you in her corner."

"Are we sure she didn't do it, though?" Jasper countered. "LaTàge sounded like a total nightmare to work for."

We arrived at the restaurant and sat down at our table, finding that our drinks had been delivered. Judging by the melted ice, they'd been there for some time.

As soon as we settled in, Simone materialized at our table like a hospitable ghost. "I do hope everyone is all right?" Her wide-eyed expression oozed with both concern and curiosity.

"Apologies for the disappearing act, Simone." Jasper nonchalantly waved away the topic. "I roped the girls into helping me with a minor PR emergency. You know how it is. There's always some fire to put out."

Simone nodded, although, from the looks of her arched brow, I couldn't quite tell if she believed him. "I'll send your server over."

Once we'd selected our meals and our waiter disappeared with our order, Jasper and I gave Charlotte a recap of everything she'd missed inside the cabana.

"Yeesh." Charlotte grimaced at the end of our tale. "The fight the squad got into Sunday night sounds nasty."

Jasper leaned forward with steepled fingers. "So, thoughts? Is Ruby our killer?"

Having heard everything a second time, my instincts kicked in. "I know all we have is her word that she didn't leave the hotel, but I'm inclined to believe her. Otherwise, why ask for my help?"

Charlotte nodded her agreement. "Ruby knows Coco can get results. Why would she ask us to find the truth if she's the killer?"

"Hmm, fair enough." Jasper stroked his clean-shaven chin. "I'm assuming the police will be able to confirm whether Ruby left the premises. This place must be crawling with cameras and such."

I drummed my fingertips on the tablecloth. "They'll be able to access her room key activity, for sure. How quickly they'll be able to obtain a warrant, though, is the real question."

A devious grin spread across Jasper's face. "Well, *we* could find out right now."

"How?" Charlotte giggled nervously at his audacious comment. "It's not like we can just ask the front desk to hand over their security info."

"I didn't say anything about having to ask." Jasper's smile became even more diabolical.

I tilted my head, apprehensive at where this was going. "What are you thinking?"

He shrugged. "All we have to do is arrange for a hotel employee to vacate their computer. One of us can hop on and scope out Ruby's activity."

Charlotte choked on her iced tea. "Are you insane? What if we get caught?"

"We don't." Jasper's blue eyes narrowed.

I stared at him a moment. While I wasn't entirely against the idea of some underhanded snooping, I was amazed by Jasper's desire to meddle. "What's with you? You've never been this gung-ho before." Even when his freedom had previously been on the line, Jasper hadn't been this dedicated to a case. Had my rep coming under fire from the Internet sparked something protective in him?

A calculated gleam flashed in his icy gaze. "Come on, Cokes, you know the game. If we're able to clear Ruby's name, I'm sure she'd *love* to tell her story to my *Divulge Direct* audience."

And there it is. I felt somewhat foolish for thinking Jasper had noble intentions. Now it all made sense. My bestie wasn't in this for me or for justice. He was in it for the publicity boost. I shouldn't be surprised. This was Jasper, after all.

However, I wasn't about to reprimand him. I needed his help if I was going to dox a killer.

Before we could discuss a plan of attack, our food was delivered. Charlotte had ordered seared salmon, while Jasper and I selected marinated steak tips. Sleuthing Squad Rule Number One: It's always a good idea to treat yourself during a stressful investigation.

"So, what's the plan?" Charlotte asked after our server departed. She sounded resigned to her fate as a dutiful sidekick.

Jasper rubbed his hands together in anticipation. "All right. Char, you and I will cause a distraction in the lobby."

"Why am I always the distraction?" Charlotte frowned. "This feels very targeted. Are you Daphne-ing me or something? I'm more than a pretty face, you know. I can be a Velma."

Jasper chuckled at her *Scooby-Doo* reference. "Sorry, sweetie, but Coco is too recognizable for what I have in mind. That's the problem with having famous friends."

"Famously *delusional*, more like it." Charlotte glowered at him.

Jasper ignored her. "While we're creating chaos, Coco, *you* dart behind the desk and work your techie magic."

"Why me?" I complained. "I'd be happy to let Charlotte take the reins on this one."

Jasper rolled his eyes. "Because Charlotte is hopeless with computers, and *I* don't want to risk any fallout from getting caught."

"Gee, thanks." I snorted. Like I needed to cause myself any more trouble. "What makes you think a disturbance will work?"

"Um, did you see the front desk? It's huge. And like every other hotel, only one person is working it. They'll have to leave their computer station to check on a wounded guest."

"Wounded?" Charlotte grew alarmed. "Just what kind of distraction are you planning?"

"A big one." Jasper winked. "Although, I may be asked not to return…" He looked momentarily depressed but quickly brightened. "Let's eat and get this show on the road."

Charlotte and I did as instructed by scarfing down our food. Thank goodness we were in a secluded area of the restaurant with little chance of anyone capturing my less-than-graceful movements on camera and uploading them online.

Once we paid for lunch, Jasper looped his arm through Charlotte's. "I need to show you the ballroom they have here. Now that you and Deacon are taking the next step, we can take another and begin planning your wedding. Coco, why don't you get our ride from the valet?" He nudged Charlotte into action, and she handed me her ticket.

I gave my besties a hearty salute. Our plan was in motion. While I still wasn't sure what Jasper had up his sleeve for a distraction, I knew my marching orders. My instructions were to head to the lobby, pretending to be on my way to the valet. Once "The Thing" happened, I was to dash behind the registration counter and see if I could locate Ruby's room card activity. If I had time, I'd look up Miguel's and Katz's info, too.

I slowed my footsteps as I neared the revolving door, mindful not to look like I was stalling for time. *Okay, guys. You're up.*

A loud crash echoed behind me, followed by a shrill shriek. I whirled around, my heart in my throat. Holy Harry Styles, that sounded bad.

I spotted Charlotte lying at the base of the grand, carpeted staircase, her face contorted with pain. A handful of people swarmed toward her without a second thought. Even crumpled on the ground, Charlotte still looked flawless. The definition of a damsel in distress, and everyone around her took the bait, hook, line, and sinker.

Jasper, from the second-floor landing, had his phone in his hand. "Oh my

God. Honey, did you trip? What kind of deathtrap is this place?" From how he clutched his cell, it looked like he might be recording.

Although I was eager to see how the scene played out, my window of time was very limited. Hoping Jasper hadn't *actually* pushed Charlotte down the stairs, I hurried toward the reception desk. The dapper clerk on shift had abandoned his post the instant Charlotte's cry echoed through the lobby, and from the corner of my eye, I could see him profusely fussing over her.

I wiggled my fingers like a techie warm-up stretch and reached for the mouse. In the employee's rush to be Charlotte's knight in shining armor, he'd left the computer unlocked.

I scanned the screen, taking in the layout of the hotel's booking system. Despite the glitz and glam The Glades exuded, their archaic software looked like something out of *2001: A Space Odyssey*. With hurried clicks, I navigated through the different tabs: Check-in, Check Out, Room Assignment…the list went on, but I stopped on the "Guests" tab and selected it. A long list of names appeared before me, each a hyperlink to another application window.

Sweat prickled at the back of my neck as I searched for Ruby's name.

"Ahhhh!" Charlotte's plaintiff squeal nearly made me jump out of my skin. I risked a glance over the top of the registration desk. Charlotte and Jasper were the definition of "making a scene." Everyone in the lobby surrounded them. Jasper had his iPhone held in the air like the Statue of Liberty torch. The frantic clerk currently had his arm wrapped around Charlotte's waist.

Getting back to work, the name **Daniels, Ruby** leaped off the screen at me. I clicked, and Ruby's guest profile loaded. Her address and payment information were listed first. As I scrolled through the details, a red alert caught my eye. It was a room service order for twenty-eight dollars, and under "Payment" were the big nasty words, CARD DECLINED. I checked the timestamp. The transaction had occurred only two hours ago. Was this charge for Ruby's G&T order?

Focus, Coco. I could stew over Ruby's evident money troubles later. Right now, I had to see if I could find proof that she hadn't left the hotel the night LaTàge was murdered.

At the bottom of Ruby's guest profile, I found a hyperlink that triggered spasms of excitement. **Guest Activity.** I clicked, and another tab loaded, this one resembling a massive spreadsheet. Dates, times, and strange abbreviations ran down the columns. I checked the headers. **DATE**, **TIME**, **ACCESS**, and **AREA**.

"This has to be it," I whispered triumphantly to myself. This had to be a record of Ruby's keycard usage.

Sunday's data was at the top. It looked like Ruby had accessed her room for the first time at eight-o-seven. This confirmed what Ruby had told us out by the pool. The keycard was then used to access the fitness center at eight-thirty. *Ew, gross.* Working out after a long day of traveling was not my idea of a fun time, but Ruby's svelte physique was in much better shape than mine. At nine forty-two, Ruby entered her room again, and that was it for Sunday.

"Why don't I call the in-house physician, just to check?" a deep baritone startled me.

In a panic, I glanced up and saw Hunky Reception Guy slowly walking with his back to me, pointing over his shoulder in the direction of the front desk. *Yikes! I've got to get out of here.*

I was just about to navigate away from the keycard readout page when the timestamp following the nine forty-two Sunday entry made me do a double take. The change in date had me momentarily confused. The screen said Ruby had used her keycard to enter her room at two AM Monday morning. Ruby hadn't mentioned leaving her room at such an odd hour. Had she been coming back from a midnight ice bucket stroll…or from killing her former boss?

Whatever the answer, I had to put the questions to bed for now or risk getting caught by hotel management, and my reputation couldn't afford a hit like that. I didn't need The Glades putting me on blast. I backtracked from Ruby's profile, leaving the screen on the registration homepage where I'd found it.

I crept out from behind the desk, careful not to draw any attention to myself, but I needn't have worried. My friends still had the lobby enthralled by their Oscar-worthy performance. Once I was a safe distance from the desk, I leaned against one of the pillars near the front door. I needed to let Charlotte and Jasper know their distraction could conclude. We didn't need to suffer through an encore performance, either.

Jasper made eye contact with me first. "You know, on second thought, Ms. Bündchen's ankle looks fine. Doesn't it, Gerta?"

I raised an eyebrow in the direction of my friends. I had been too focused on my task to really listen in on their ruse. From the sounds of it, Jasper had really gone all out.

Charlotte bit her lower lip. "Well—"

Jasper cut off her horrible attempt at a Brazilian accent. "You're a klutz, sweetie. There's a reason why Sister Gisele made it big on the catwalk, and you didn't." With that, Jasper wrapped an arm around her, hoisting her away from Hunky Receptionist Guy's grasp.

"S-so sorry," Charlotte trilled as Jasper led her away from the curious crowd.

"*Limp.*" He hissed as they neared my hiding spot.

I stifled a honking laugh at Charlotte's terrible acting. Maybe their performance *hadn't* been so Oscar-worthy.

Rolling his eyes, Jasper motioned his head toward the entrance, and I took that as my cue to meet them outside.

I conquered the revolving doors, and a moment later, Jasper and Charlotte joined me on the curb.

"Gerta Bündchen?" I eyed Charlotte up and down.

Jasper shrugged. "Gisele has like five sisters. Gerta could be one of them."

Facepalm. "You know someone could very well Google that, right?" I then studied Charlotte hesitantly. "Jasper didn't actually push you down the stairs, did he?"

"How dare—" Jasper swelled with indignation as Charlotte and I dissolved into full-on giggles. The intensity of our mission had worn off, and it felt good to goof around once more.

I handed the valet ticket, still in my possession, to the uniformed woman working the booth. Once she disappeared to collect Charlotte's truck, Jasper turned his laser focus on me. "So? What'd you find out?"

I lowered my voice, mindful we were in public. "Well, everything Ruby told us adds up." I paused dramatically. "*Except* for the fact that she forgot to tell us she returned to her room from somewhere at two AM Monday morning."

"That seems like a gaping omission." Charlotte smoothed down her hair. "Do we know anything more concrete about when LaTàge was killed? Ruby's keycard activity certainly aligns with LaTàge's final Story uploads."

"Gavin didn't give me any breadcrumbs to follow on that front." Other than her social media activity, how else could we narrow down LaTàge's time of death? "Either way, we can't rule Ruby out. She lied to us." I also mentioned the recently declined charge on her credit card.

We didn't speak about the case again until we were in the privacy of the truck cab. "I think we should let Ruby remain under the assumption that we believe her and that we're out to prove her innocent," Jasper suggested. "You know, the whole 'keep your friends close, enemies closer' spiel."

I agreed. "Maybe we can get her to dish on Katz and Miguel. We need to know more about their movements, too. I didn't have time to check their hotel records."

"LaTàge's money problems could be motive for any of them, especially if all their cards are getting declined. Any one of the Squad could've been desperate for the cashflow." Charlotte turned her truck onto the main road back to Central Shores. "I can't believe LaTàge was broke. Didn't she just jet to Venice or something?"

Jasper stroked his chin. "I mean, celebs are the ultimate grifters. Free swag and trips from companies wanting to work with them? I believe it. It's not a hard ruse to keep up when everyone bends over backward to woo you."

I folded my arms as I settled against the backseat. "Yeah, but eventually, it catches up with you." I knew from experience. When I was twenty-five, I'd rapidly blown through a big payout I'd received from the acquisition of my college startup, LiveIt. My irresponsible spending was one of the catalysts behind the launch of Center of Attention Consulting. At the time, I couldn't afford to put my feet up and retire. Granted, nearly four years later, I knew better and was now thriftier with my funds, but I could see how the glam world Laila Jackson had immersed herself in had led her astray.

But she wasn't some wide-eyed, naive twenty-five-year-old, now, was she? She was in her thirties. Thoughts about LaTàge's hidden identity dusted off a possible theory. "We still have to consider where Laila fits into all this. She came back to Central Shores for a reason." I sighed. "I'm self-deprecating enough to admit that CoA's reputation isn't what drew her out here."

Charlotte met my gaze in the rearview mirror. "What are you thinking?"

"Well," I stretched the word out, "Ruby mentioned that LaTàge promised their paychecks would resume after this trip. What if *Laila* came back home looking for money?" My gaze drifted out the window, surveying the sweeping Atlantic to my left.

Jasper shifted in the front seat so I could see his arched brow. "A family reunion gone wrong?"

"It's possible." I stewed on the idea some more. "Laila needed cash and fast. Maybe she thought her dad would help her out of a tight spot."

"There's cash, and then there's *cash.* Does Omar really have that kind of money?" Charlotte asked. "I mean, I know he has several Central Sports gyms up and down the coast, so I guess he's probably living comfortably."

Jasper gave a flippant flick of his wrist. "There's living comfortably, and then there's having enough dough to bail out your super-in-debt daughter."

While Jasper and Charlotte discussed Mr. J's hypothetical finances, I typed his name into the search browser on my smartphone. Because I lived in a small town where everyone kept tabs on their neighbors, I already knew Mr. J resided in a nice residential area close to where my parents lived. While he wasn't a Mill Row inhabitant, it didn't mean he wasn't sitting on a secret fortune. Central Sports was a popular local franchise in the area, and after all these years, he still did good business. Mr. J had even been an honoree at the Chamber of Commerce Gala earlier this past spring.

I scanned the Google results for **Omar Jackson**, my eyes widening as I read a recent news article from the *Central Shores Gazette.* "Hey, guys, listen to this. *'Omar Jackson, 74, and Terrance Jackson, 33, of Central Sports gyms, announced a partnership this week with The Buchanan Group to bring exclusive,* *upscale fitness centers to the Delaware coast.'"*

Jasper whipped his head in my direction. "Upscale *and* exclusive? Go on, I'm listening."

I chuckled. Jasper, who spent almost as much time honing his John Cena-like muscles as he did expanding his media empire, had a personal gym in his condo to make up for the fact that the closest swanky fitness center to Central Shores was in Crestview. When Charlotte and I reminded Jasper he could get a membership to our local Central Sports, he not-so-politely declined.

"Where have I heard about The Buchanan Group before?" Charlotte glanced over her shoulder before quickly returning her gaze to the road.

I highlighted TBG and searched. "Ah ha! They're one of the development companies building out the woodlands. They're behind the Peach Blossom Grove and Strawberry Lane neighborhoods."

"Did they hire a Fruit-of-the-Loom marketing guy?" Jasper snorted.

I tapped back to the article about the partnership announcement. "So, Omar and his nephew are teaming up with a property developer to bring a bunch of posh fitness centers to the area."

"Sounds like it has the potential to be lucrative," Jasper mused.

I studied the date the article had been posted. Monday morning. *Hmm.* Odd to release such a big statement the day of Omar's scheduled heart surgery, but I supposed a business deal such as this must have been in the works for weeks, if not months. Amid her money troubles, had Omar's daughter gotten wind of this profitable opportunity? Had this been the siren's call to lure Laila Jackson home?

Chapter Sixteen

We spent the rest of the drive back to Central Shores mulling over our next steps. While I wanted to dig more into the Central Sports business deal with The Buchanan Group, I also couldn't ignore that Ruby had lied about being in her room all night. But my lingering questions would have to go on the back burner for now. I had some client work to take care of before heading over to Mom and Dad's for dinner, and I needed to rein in my sleuthing. My parents would not be thrilled to learn I had inserted myself into yet another mystery, so I intended to make sure they wouldn't find out.

Charlotte slid her truck into her private parking spot behind Brewed to Perfection. "Okay, so I'll poke around to see what I can find out about Omar's new venture from the other folks on the strip." She had the best street cred among us when it came to schmoozing with local business owners. "If the price was right, Laila might have come home to ask Dear Old Dad for a loan."

"And if that's the case," I added, "who knows what kind of tensions that stirred up among the Jackson clan?" Money was a powerful motive, after all.

Jasper nodded. "I've got a meeting later with a friend to discuss Katz's clothing line and how LaTàge was involved. My contacts in New York might also have some deets about its future now that she's out of the picture."

"Perfect. Thanks, guys." Charlotte and Jasper had offered their expertise without hesitation. I rubbed my hands together in anticipation. "I'll DM Ruby to give her the impression we've got her back. Maybe in return, she'll give us some intel about what Katz and Miguel were up to the night LaTàge was killed." I also planned to scour their socials to see if either of them had posted anything placing themselves near LaTàge's rental on Sunday night.

Outside Charlotte's café, we parted ways, and I had just buckled into Jolly when my phone rang. Reading the Caller ID, I answered via Bluetooth. "Hey, Manz. How's everything going?" Preoccupied with our shenanigans at The Glades, I'd forgotten about my text to Amanda, checking in to see how she was handling yesterday's terrible experience.

"Hey, Cokes." Even though her tone was friendly, Amanda's greeting failed to emulate her signature bubbly vibe. "Got a sec to brainstorm some brand motto ideas?"

I frowned. *Straight to business, huh?* Amanda must have been suffering more than I thought. I reoriented Jolly, heading for Millionaire's Row—or Canopy Cove, as its wealthy residents called it—rather than my home. I needed to check on my friend in person. "Sure thing. Which client are you working on?"

"The Twisted Candle Bookshop."

Drew Wilson was a new client who owned a collectible bookstore in Ocean Hollow, right on the Central Shores town line. Inspired by her namesake, Nancy Drew, the shop sold books and merchandise featuring everyone's favorite girl detective, as well as the Hardy Boys, Trixie Belden, Encyclopedia Brown, and more. Another big selling point was the store's escape room feature. Each month, Drew created an escape room boasting a popular teen detective as the theme. She'd been open for about five months now and was looking to expand her offerings into the eCommerce sphere, rather than just in-store. CoA was helping with her website and an online shop launch.

As I made the short drive over to Amanda's stately manor, I contemplated some ideas. "Hmm…how about 'The Twisted Candle Bookshop: Where Mystery Comes to Life.'" I loved that Drew had named the store after her favorite Nancy adventure, *The Sign of the Twisted Candles.*

"I like the mystery and life concept." Amanda went quiet for a minute. "But don't you think it's a bit wordy?"

"You have a point." Since the shop had a longer title, a shorter tagline would help balance it out, especially when it came to printing the motto on branded swag.

A figurative lightbulb dinged above my head as I parked in her circular driveway. "What do you think of 'The Twisted Candle Bookshop: Live the Mystery.'"

Amanda's sharp intake of breath rattled through the Bluetooth speaker. "*Live the Mystery*. Ugh, it's perfect! Thanks, Cokes."

"Care to celebrate with a drink?" I turned the engine off. "I'm outside."

"What—" She cut the call, and a moment later, one of her grand entryway doors swung open.

I climbed out of Jolly as Amanda skipped down the stairs. "What are you doing here?" she asked, shading her eyes from the afternoon sun. "Did we have a meeting I forgot about?"

I shook my head. "I wanted to check on you." I gave her a sympathetic smile. "You didn't respond to my text."

"Oh, yeah." Amanda twirled a strand of her silky blond hair. "Sorry. I meant to reply, but I guess I got a bit sidetracked." Her cheeks grew pink with embarrassment, and she hurriedly buried her face in her palms.

"Hey, no worries." I reached for her shoulder and squeezed. "Believe me, I get it. It's okay to not be okay."

Amanda reached for my hand. "Thanks. I'm fine, really. It was shocking, of course." She pressed her other palm against her forehead. "But I should be the one checking in on you. I mean, you're the one who f-found her," she stammered through her emotions. "Then there's all this stuff about LaTàge blowing up online."

I batted away her concerns. "Social media will get over it." *Especially once I find her killer.*

Amanda shuddered. "You're the expert." She ushered me inside the impressive foyer. "Let's sit out in the sunroom. I'll have Daphne bring us some drinks."

While Amanda went to speak with her live-in housekeeper (not the famous *Scooby-Doo* sleuth), I removed my shoes and made my way through the house as I had many times before. Despite its ostentatious size, Amanda's home had a cozy, welcoming glow to it, like she draped a cashmere blanket across your shoulders the minute you glided over the threshold.

I sat cross-legged on one of the white linen couches facing Amanda's manicured back lawn. She and Arthur had yet to close their swimming pool for the season, so the blue waters still sparkled invitingly in the sunlight.

"Here we are." Amanda entered the room carrying a silver tray. "Strawberry lemonade." She nodded to the pitcher. "And champagne to mix, if you're feeling it." A small bottle of some ridiculously expensive bubbly nestled next to two glasses.

Considering the champagne cost more than what I made from *Trending Topic* advertising in a week, I thought it would be rude to decline, especially since she'd already uncorked it.

Once our drinks were poured, we settled into a contemplative silence, admiring the natural beauty outside Amanda's window.

"So, have you talked with Gavin at all?" Amanda shifted in her seat, propping her elbow on the arm of her chair. "I know you kinda stepped back from being their spokesperson, but I'm sure the PD will need your services now more than ever."

"Actually," I began, tucking a loose strand of hair behind my ear, "given the scope, Chief McInnis has turned the case over to the Sussex County Crime Lab. SCCL is handling all media communications. But Gavin and the team are still working with Detective Forester."

Amanda bobbed her head. "Good. That must be a relief to have off your plate."

I took a sip of lemonade champagne instead of responding. I didn't want to lie to her about being involved, but I also remembered Gavin's warning about keeping Laila Jackson's identity under wraps. Jasper and Charlotte, I trusted with all my secrets. Amanda…

As if sensing my inner turmoil, Amanda narrowed her gaze at me. "You *aren't* getting involved, are you?"

A deadpan expression slid across my face before I could stop it. "What do you think?"

"Ugh, I hoped you'd prove me wrong." She reached for her temples and took a deep breath before confessing, "Once I saw #CocoClineisCursed trending, I figured it was only a matter of time before you tried to clear your name."

While I flinched at the unflattering hashtag, Amanda's less-than-enthusiastic reaction had me puzzled. "Why do you sound so disappointed?" She had been a great help to me during my last foray into murder. I'd been hoping to rely on Amanda again, even if I couldn't tell her the whole truth about LaTàge just yet.

"I'm not disappointed. I'm worried." Her gaze became pinched. "I know we had fun investigating together, but this time is different. I can't be there to help you." Her hands dropped to her stomach.

I was touched by her admission but confused at the same time. When I had been looking into the death of my neighbor, I couldn't pry Amanda from my side. Her declaration now left me feeling a little bummed. "Why not?"

A soft smile curled on her lips. "I'm pregnant."

I nearly dropped my cocktail on her flawless, white couch. "Preggers?" My focus darted to her drink glass, and it was then I noticed her lemonade was much pinker than mine. Her drink hadn't been diluted with champagne. She must have just pretended to pour. Some astute detective I was.

Amanda nodded, her face growing more radiant. "We found out last night. I felt pretty nauseous after our crime scene encounter, so Arthur took me to the doctor to help with my nerves. But instead of Xanax, they prescribed me prenatal vitamins." She cupped her flat belly. "I'm not even two months along, so we're keeping it quiet. But I thought you deserved to know why I can't play sidekick this time around."

"Omigosh." I jolted myself out of my speechless stupor and lunged forward to give Amanda a fierce hug. "Congratulations! I had no idea you were trying for a baby. What great news! You and Arthur are going to be wonderful parents."

Amanda chuckled awkwardly once I released her. "Thank you. I hope so. I mean, Arthur will be a terrific dad. Me, on the other hand…" She trailed off.

"What are you talking about?" I tilted my head, hearing her insecurities in her warbling tone. "You'll be a great mom."

Amanda wrapped her arms around her slender frame. "I just hope I can raise a little human who's much kinder than me."

I opened my mouth, but I couldn't find the right reassuring words.

She glanced my way and snorted. "I honestly don't know how you've done it, Coco." Amanda shook her head. "God, I was a complete monster to you in high school. And here you are, dropping everything to support me."

I swallowed, my anxiety spiking in anticipation. Were we really about to have this conversation? "Well, a lot's changed since high school. You, the most."

"I'd like to believe that, but…" Her chin quivered. "I've never told you how sorry I am. I've wanted to so many times, but saying sorry after all the crap I did just seemed so insincere. Once you moved back here, I tried to work up the courage, but I chickened out each time." Amanda wiped a tear from her bright blue eyes. "Instead, I just pretended like my bullying never happened, and you let me get away with it. Because you're a much better person than I could ever hope to be."

"That's not true." I held her gaze with loyal determination. "Your actions, since I've been back, have spoken loud and clear. Come on, Manz. Not many people would jump into the middle of a *murder* investigation, no questions asked. But you did. And I know the only reason you're not diving in with me now is that you've got a little person inside of you to protect."

More tears leaked from Amanda's eyes. "That means a lot to hear. And for the record, I really am sorry."

"I know, sweetie." I got up from my seat once more and settled beside her, draping an arm around her trembling shoulders. Hearing Amanda's apology made me realize that I had truly forgiven her a long time ago, but it was still nice, nevertheless. "Trust me, it worked out to my advantage in the end. I mean, I might still be going by Cordelia if 'Gourdy Cordy' hadn't become such a thing."

"Oh, God." Amanda buried her hands in her palms, mortified by the fat-shaming nickname she'd bestowed on me our freshman year.

Oops. I hadn't meant for my joke to make her cry harder. "I meant that in a loving way. Seriously, it's all water under the bridge."

"You sure?"

"One hundred percent." I smiled.

"Thank you." She leaned her head on my shoulder, still crying. "Gosh, these pregnancy hormones. I'm a mess."

We dissolved into happy laughter.

"Okay," Amanda began, collecting herself and wiping clean her cheeks, "so, I may be out of commission from fieldwork, but you can still bounce ideas off me." Her gaze turned inquiring. "Have you uncovered anything about LaTàge and her squad? One of them *had* to have killed her. It's not like LaTàge knew anyone in Central Shores besides…well, you."

I chewed on my lower lip, debating my next words for all of five seconds. I trusted Jasper, Charlotte, *and* Amanda with my secrets. "Oh, I uncovered something, all right, but you absolutely cannot tell a soul."

Her brow raised. "I'm a vault." She mimed locking her lips and tossing the key. "Spill."

I held up a finger, asking for patience. "First, what can you tell me about Omar Jackson and his family? You were besties with his niece back in school."

"The Jacksons?" Amanda did a double take. "What in the world do they have to do with anything?"

I emptied my flute and reached for more strawberry lemonade. "Just humor me, will you? What's Deja up to these days?"

Amanda scratched her head. "I don't see her much. Sometimes, I run into her at the club, but I tend to avoid her. Otherwise, I'm forced to listen to her talk on and on about her husband. Or her job." She rolled her eyes to show her disdain.

I stroked the stem of my cocktail glass in contemplation. "The Club" was the Crestview Country Club, one of the swankiest estates in the area. Its monthly membership fee was equal to a mortgage and more. "Who's her husband?"

"Judge Aaron Reinhardt."

I stared at her. "You say that like it means something."

"I forget politics isn't your thing." She giggled and then explained, "Judge Reinhardt was recently appointed a district court judge for Delaware. It's like one of three positions, *and* he was nominated by the *President*." She paused. "Of the United States."

A low whistle flew across my lips. "Wow." That did sound like a pretty big deal. "And I take it Deja is proud of her hubby?"

"That's putting it mildly." Amanda glanced at her French-manicured nails. "She loves to endlessly namedrop bigwigs in DC and all the people she 'lunches' with."

"What does Deja do?"

"She's a lobbyist for some tech company and commutes to DC regularly. Trying to push less restrictive data sharing laws." Amanda's expression turned into a scowl. "Arthur is not a fan."

I pursed my lips together. While I didn't concern myself with politics often, I definitely had skin in the data-sharing game. I believed in protecting an end user's privacy as much as possible, something Deja didn't seem to be concerned with. "Sounds like she's doing well for herself."

Amanda giggled at my dry remark. "Last she told me, she and Aaron were looking at buying a new home. In one of those fancy new developments north of Canopy Cove. A place to get away from the 'hubbub.'" She added air quotes.

So, Deja was interested in buying real estate in the same area where her cousin Laila had been staying. I felt my heart skip a beat. "What about Omar's daughter? Know anything about her?"

This time, Amanda held up a finger. "Nuh-uh. I've given you the deets on Deja. Now, what's she got to do with LaTàge?"

"Fineee." I lowered my voice in case one of Amanda's staff members wandered by. "You're not going to believe it, but LaTàge was really *Laila* Jackson. Deja's cousin totally reinvented herself."

My friend stared at me like I'd sprouted another head. "Um, Cokes? That's impossible. Laila Jackson is dead."

Chapter Seventeen

Had Amanda not heard me correctly? "I know she's dead. She's *LaTàge.*"

Amanda's hair swayed back and forth as she shook her head. "No. I mean, Laila Jackson died several years ago. Deja told me. It happened soon after her Aunt Trisha passed away."

I frowned. "I think you need to check your sources. Omar called Gavin at the police station earlier today to let him know LaTàge was his daughter." I folded my arms with confidence. "Detective Forester even confirmed it with a birthmark."

"What?" Amanda's face grew pale. "B-but…that's not possible. Deja told me—"

"What did she tell you, *exactly*?" I studied her shrewdly. "When was this?"

Amanda ran a hand through her hair. "I mean, gosh. It had to be during our college winter break, sophomore year. It was so awkward. We met for lunch, and when I asked how Laila was doing out in California, Deja just said her cousin was dead, and she didn't want to talk about it." She swirled her glass of lemonade, her forehead furrowed in concentration. "I was so taken aback by the news, I didn't know what to say. When I got home, I Googled to see what I could find, but nothing came up. Laila hadn't been active on social media for months, so I figured I should respect Deja's request and drop the matter."

I rose from the couch and began to pace around the sunroom. "This makes no sense. The police confirmed Laila *was* LaTàge. She wasn't dead. At least, not until yesterday. She was just living another life. Why would Deja tell people her cousin had passed away?"

Amanda tapped her chin. "I mean, you know how dramatic both Deja and I were back then."

"Are you saying she deliberately lied to you about Laila?" I paused my steps and placed a hand on my hip. "Why? To garner sympathy or something?" Had Deja reveled in the attention she and her family had received following her aunt's death? Despite being depicted in several fictional suspense thrillers in recent years, Munchausen Syndrome was very much a real personality disorder.

Amanda held up her hands in protest. "Whoa, slow down. I'm saying she *could* have meant it as 'Laila is dead *to me*,' and I read the situation completely wrong."

"Oh." That scenario was much less sinister and slightly more believable. How many times had Thea and I yelled something akin to "You're dead to me" during a sibling fight, only to take it back ten minutes later? "Even so, any idea what Laila might have done to warrant such a cold response from Deja?"

Amanda shrugged. "I have no clue. We never talked about Laila after that lunch, and within a few months, we drifted apart as our college careers took us in opposite directions."

I resumed my pacing, thoroughly vexed by the whole thing.

"So, if LaTàge was really Laila, are you thinking someone from Central Shores had a hand in her death?" Amanda held a hand to her mouth, agape in mild horror.

I shrugged. "We're pursuing a few different leads. It's totally possible LaTàge was killed by a member of her entourage. We haven't been able to confirm the squad's whereabouts, and we caught Ruby Daniels lying about her alibi."

Amanda's eyes widened. "Omigod. You *met* Ruby!" She clapped gleefully as a squeal wheezed out of her.

I grinned at her fangirling. "Yeah, Jasper, Charlotte, and I tracked her down at The Glades Hotel over in Crestview."

Amanda sank back against the cushions of her seat, looking more relaxed.

"Oh good. I'm relieved to hear you have the Dynamic Duo backing you up."

Her sincerity touched me. "With Hudson out of town, they're not letting me do anything on my own, I promise." I held a hand to my heart. "And I wouldn't want to, anyway. I need to make sure I'm around to play Auntie when the time comes." I pointed to her belly.

Amanda's eyes teared up again. "I know kids aren't really your scene, so that means a lot, Cokes."

"Being an aunt is the best. All the perks and no responsibilities," I teased. Both Amanda and Arthur were only children, so if their child needed a rogue aunt's influence, I'd happily fill the role. "But speaking of being an aunt, I've gotta get some actual work accomplished before heading to my parents' house. Mom summoned me to a family dinner."

Amanda chuckled at my theatrical moaning. "I'm surprised you're already taking a break from the case."

"Believe me, as much as I want to keep at it, I do need to eat." I reached for my glass to bring it into Amanda's kitchen, but she snatched it from me and placed it on the tray. "And the last thing I need is my mother breathing down my neck about ignoring my familial duties."

"Well, don't let me keep you." Amanda rose from her seat with enviable grace. "I appreciate you stopping by to check in on me. Honestly, with the news about the baby, I've been all over the place these past twenty-four hours."

I reached for her forearm and squeezed. "If you need anything, don't hesitate to text. Or call, even."

She laughed at my weak joke. "Same. If you need your calendar cleared, I can sub in for you at client meetings tomorrow."

"I might take you up on that." Having Amanda working with me was a true blessing. I didn't want to even think about losing her when the baby came, but the sad thought entered my mind unbidden.

Amanda escorted me to the front door. "And if you need me to do any couch recon—"

I cut her off. "You focus on you right now."

She hugged herself, her expression grumpy. "I'm kinda wishing I hadn't put myself on the sidelines. I forgot how fun this can be."

"Well, it's too late now because there's no way I'm letting a hot mama like you question potential killers." I winked. "*If* you feel like helping, I'd be curious what your dad thinks about Omar Jackson's new development deal with The Buchanan Group." Thurston Highgrove had long been one of Central Shores' most respected businesspeople. I bet he'd know more about the whole TBG deal than I'd found on the Internet.

Amanda gave her head a shake. "Wow, random much? Another lead?"

"I'm pursuing multiple avenues at this point." I felt a silly grin spread across my face. Look at me, sounding like a legit detective.

Amanda sighed as I stepped outside. "Whatever you do, be careful. Baby Bushman needs a fabulous auntie in their life."

I saluted at her orders and gave her one last wave before climbing into Jolly.

Three hours later, I cruised to a stop in front of my parents' craftsman home. Thea's SUV and her husband's sedan had already claimed the driveway, which meant Jolly was stuck with street parking. Luckily, my parents lived on a quiet residential road, so my car was safe.

My phone buzzed from one of Jolly's cup holders. A text from Jasper.

Just finished my chat with Brody. Apparently, since LaTàge invested no cash in Katz's line, only her face, investors aren't too concerned. In fact, Brody said her mag's already been approached about featuring Katz's line a full month ahead of schedule.

I gawked at the last line. **Bumping up release a month? Is that weird?**

Tryin to capitalize on publicity, I guess. Altho, word is Katz doesn't want to, outta respect for LaTàge. But investors hold the purse strings. Several side-eye emojis accompanied his words.

Seize the hype, so they say. Thanks for digging this up.

As I slipped my phone into my bag, I considered Jasper's fashion-insider intel. With no financial investments on the line, had Katz realized LaTàge was worth more to their brand dead than alive? It made for an interesting potential motive.

But my theories would have to wait. Family-time called.

I pushed our investigation aside and leaned into the backseat to grab the wine Mom asked for. Andre Nunez had recommended the brand when I'd swung by Vine on my way here. I'd nearly lost track of time, what with my afternoon consumed by emails and updates to my clients' social media profiles.

Thinking about CoA unleashed another musing. *I can't believe Amanda is having a baby.* She was the first of my close friends to procreate. As someone who'd vowed to live life kid-free, I couldn't imagine how she and Arthur must be feeling. I hoped they would announce their news soon because this made for a big secret to keep.

As I headed toward Mom and Dad's storybook front door, I tried to tamp down the nagging, selfish thoughts bouncing within my brain. Amanda and I were having so much fun building Center of Attention into a thriving business. Would our collaboration end soon, now that she had a baby on the way?

"Quit it, Coco. It's not all about you," I muttered. How Amanda wanted to proceed was her decision. I couldn't let my desires get in the way of her growing family, and I swore to keep my mouth shut about the matter.

Taking a deep breath, I rang the doorbell to announce my arrival. Although I could have knocked and let myself in, that wouldn't have been as fun of an entrance for the three little humans on the other side of the door.

The Ring cam's chime was drowned out by a chorus of shrieking yelps from inside. The door whipped open, and three sunny, screaming faces stared up at me like I was Justin Bieber.

"Auntie Coco!" Taran, Blake, and Parker shouted in triplet unison as they pounced for my legs, clutching me tightly with their surprisingly strong arms.

"Oh, wow, guys. You're going to crush me," I joked before bending down to speak with them on their level. "All those gymnastics classes must be paying off." I'd watched a few of their sessions over the summer, and the three were tumbling terrors.

Taran stuck his chin out. "I'm taking karate now, Auntie Coco."

Oops, I missed that memo. I winced at my clear misstep.

"*We're* in gymnastics still, Taran." Blake uttered her brother's name with enough sass to rival Jasper any day of the week.

Parker stuck her little pink tongue out. "Yeah, *we* didn't quit because we were scared of the balance beam."

Before World War III erupted, I patted them each on the head, ruffling their beautiful chocolate brown ringlets. "Well, you guys are so much more talented than I was as a kid. I could barely walk in a straight line when I was four-and-a-half," I pointedly emphasized their ages. The last time I'd just said "four," they'd given me a lecture about how they were *much* older than that.

My self-deprecating remark elicited a burst of squeaky giggles. "Auntie Coco!" The triplets continued to laugh as Parker took me by the hand and led me into the house. "Let's find the grownups."

I smiled at her comment. "Yeah, no adults here." Even though I was three years older than my sister, *I* still got put at the kid's table at family dinners. But mostly because my nieces and nephew loved hanging out with me so much and insisted that I sit with them.

We found Thea and her husband, Lucas, relaxing on my parents' sun porch. "Hey, guys. Long time, no see." I waved to the lounging couple.

Thea's lips turned downward in a disapproving frown. "And whose fault is that?"

Oh, jeez. We couldn't even get through greetings without some good, old-fashioned sibling bickering. I had to hide my rolling eyes from her, or we'd be in real trouble.

Lucas gently swatted his wife's shoulder. "Come on, Thea. Be nice. She just got here." He turned to face me with a wide smile. "How's it going, Coco?"

"Can't complain." I pulled the kiddos onto the couch with me so we could cuddle. "How's the new job?"

"It's great." He ran a hand through his brown curls. The kids were a spitting image of their tall, blue-eyed dad. "It's nice being fully remote to be around these little monsters more."

Thea shushed him. "If you keep reinforcing that label—"

"I know, I know." Lucas laughed off her annoyance. "It will imprint on their psyche or something."

Thea rubbed her temples with gritted teeth. Clearly, Lucas did not *know*.

"Mom and Dad out at the grill?" I asked, hoping to change the vibe of the room.

"Simon just put the ribs on." Lucas pointed over his shoulder. "Moira had to go next door for something."

"Johnny Green called." Thea leaned forward and lowered her voice like she had some juicy gossip to share. "He needed Mom's 'help' in the kitchen."

I snorted at the ridiculousness that Thea was alluding to. "When is that guy gonna throw in the towel?"

Thea shrugged. "Maybe since his marriage fell apart after thirty years, he's banking on the same happening to Mom and Dad." Johnny had been my parents' neighbor ever since I was young. He and his wife, Tess, had always been invited to backyard gatherings and parties, and the tradition had continued after Tess had left him for her yoga instructor. However, Johnny had clearly taken a liking to my mother in recent months and routinely asked for her help in the hopes of kindling a spark between them.

Of course, Mom was completely oblivious to his motives. She would reprimand Thea and me for our teasing and remind us he was just a lonely man, hence why she always rushed to his aid.

Lucas chuckled. "I can't believe Simon lets him get away with it."

"What's he gonna do? Fight the poor guy?" Thea scoffed at the notion. "If anything, Dad feels even more sorry for Johnny than Mom does."

"And he knows he's got nothing to worry about," I added. Even after almost forty years of marriage, Simon and Moira Cline were just as in love with each other as they had been the day they got married.

Our conversation was interrupted by the triplets telling me about Beeko, their kitten. He was a new addition to their family, and they had much to discuss. However, their attention spans being what they were, Taran, Blake, and Parker soon leaped from the couch and bolted toward the playroom to practice their "grilling" skills.

I stared after the figurative dust left in their wake. "Those little kooks make me feel old and young at the same time."

"They just make me feel old." Lucas stifled a yawn before taking a sip of the Sam Adams bottle he clutched.

Thea's blue eyes sparkled with intrigue. "Okay, now that they're gone, you've got to dish about this whole LaTàge thing."

I grimaced. I should have been expecting to be questioned like this. Mom and Dad might be totally social media inept, but Thea certainly wasn't. "What have you heard?"

"Nothing official, really. But TikTok is all over you." Thea pointedly stared at me. "People know she was here to see *you.* How could you not tell me one of your clients was *LaTàge*?"

I noted the slight tremble of hurt in her question. "Sorry. She wanted to keep her visit here on the DL." While LaTàge hadn't gotten around to making Amanda and I sign an NDA, Ruby stressed that they wanted the rebrand kept quiet so they could rock the online world with a surprise launch. Very Beyoncé.

"Yikes." Lucas gave an elaborate shudder. "If no one knew she was in town, how the heck did she end up dead?"

"That's the million-dollar question." I sighed. "Gavin had me give the police a rundown of LaTàge's influencer lifestyle, but that's the extent of my official involvement."

Thea's searching gaze lingered on my face, and I wondered if she could detect the lie.

Chapter Eighteen

"The trips said Delia was here." My dad's enthused comment preceded his appearance by a nanosecond. "Hey, sweetheart. How are ya?" Fifty-nine-year-old Simon Cline grinned at me as he ambled into the room, clacking a pair of grilling tongs with his right hand. Spry and goofy as ever.

"Hi, Dad." Thankful for the disruption, I hopped up to give him a kiss on the cheek, mindful not to get barbecue sauce on my outfit. "I'm good. How's the grill? Need any help?"

He waved away my offer. "Nonsense. We invited you for dinner. But your hand's empty, kiddo. What d'ya want? Beer? High Noon? Mike's?" Dad rattled off the drink offerings.

"I'll grab a High Noon." The flavored spiked seltzer would be a refreshing treat. "You guys want anything?" I asked Lucas and Thea.

My sister lifted a full wine glass, her expression still miffed that her LaTàge interrogation had been interrupted.

"We're good for the next ten minutes or so," Lucas joked as he took another sip of his beer.

I laughed and not out of politeness. Whether it was his new job or something else, Lucas had changed for the better since our last encounter. Normally, he acted a bit standoffish, but tonight, he seemed engaged in our conversation. I was happy to see it.

I followed Dad into the kitchen and grabbed a High Noon. "How's everything here?"

"Quiet." Dad shrugged. "Been doing a lot of projects before the season turns." As our family's resident handyman, Dad spent a lot of time working on the house when he wasn't down volunteering at the Central Shores Fire Department.

I bobbed my head in understanding before a sneaky idea popped up. "Hey, Dad. You're pals with Omar Jackson, aren't you?"

He accepted the beer I handed to him. "Yeah, he's one of my sailing buddies. Why?"

I searched for a believable reason to bring up Omar. "I heard down at Charlotte's that he was undergoing heart surgery. He doing okay?"

"Oh, that. Yeah, just a little routine maintenance work." Dad chuckled at his joke.

"That's good. After reading about his new deal with The Buchanan Group, I got worried something was wrong."

Dad tilted his head, his pale skin wrinkling with concern. "What deal?"

"I read about it online." I took a thoughtful sip of seltzer before continuing. "It looks like Central Sports is gearing up to launch a bunch of fancy fitness centers around the area."

"Huh? Are you sure?" Dad's blue eyes pinched with bewilderment. "Omar isn't one to cater to yuppies."

I stifled a laugh at my dad's obvious disdain over the "yuppification" of his hometown. His words, not mine. "The deal was just announced on Monday."

"The day of his surgery? Nah, that can't be right," Dad murmured. "As if we need *more* development around here."

"I take it you're not happy about the woodlands being bulldozed for more housing?" I raised an eyebrow.

"What's done is done, I s'pose." Dad scoffed. "But a lot of locals aren't thrilled. And unfortunately for your mother, they're taking it out on her and the rest of the town council."

"Are folks trying to stop it?" Mom served as Chairperson, having been appointed to the position earlier this year in a special election.

Dad shook his head. "It's only grumbles right now. But, hey, I gotta get back out to the grill." He pointed his tongs over his shoulder in the direction of the back deck. "You hang with your sister."

I obediently shuffled back into the sunroom.

"There you are." Thea clapped with anticipation. "Come on, Coco. You *must* be able to give us some more deets about LaTàge."

"I mean, other than she was staying at some house over in Crescent Hills, that's all I have." I plopped onto the same cushion I had vacated moments ago. "What do you guys know about the Crescent Hills area? Lots of new development going on, right?"

Lucas draped an arm around his wife's shoulders. "It's causing quite a stir with the school system. People are worried that the influx of families will overwhelm Central Shores Grammar and CSH."

"There's talk about a private or charter school coming to the area." Thea did not look enthused. "Makes figuring out the triplets' education all the more fun."

I gave her a sympathetic look. Thank goodness I didn't have to stress about such issues.

"But I *cannot* go down that rabbit hole right now. I came here to relax." Thea leaned against her husband's chest and shot a pleading glance my way. "You really have no dirt on LaTàge?"

I chortled. My sister's idea of relaxation was gossiping. "No, but I do have some Central Shores drama to share." I lowered my voice. "I was chatting with Amanda earlier today, and she said Deja Jackson told her that her cousin Laila died. Did you know that?"

"What?" Thea straightened in her seat. "Really? When?"

I shrugged, forcing my expression to remain neutral when, inwardly, I was celebrating. I had finally veered our conversation toward Laila without hinting at her connection to LaTàge. "According to Amanda, it happened during Deja's college sophomore year."

"Laila *died*? I had no idea." Thea gawked at her husband.

"Don't look at me." Lucas held up a hand in surrender. "I don't even know who Deja Jackson is." He hadn't grown up in Central Shores and wasn't as dialed into the community as Thea.

"She was in Coco's class in high school. Gorgeous, smart, and ruthless. I heard she's a lobbyist now." Thea stared at me pointedly. "She finally found her calling."

I smirked. Thea and I may not have been very much alike, but we both shared a traumatic history of being bullied. Our given names, Dorothy and Cordelia, had been fodder for our classmates—Thea more so than me—hence why we eventually decided to rebrand ourselves.

"How did we not know this?" Thea stroked her chin, clearly peeved at being out of the loop. "I mean, Trisha Jackson's death was all anyone could talk about for the longest time. Do you know what happened to Laila?"

"Nope. Amanda didn't, either. Deja wouldn't talk about it." I took a deep breath. "I'm honestly wondering if it's even true."

Thea gasped. "Why would Deja make up something that terrible?"

"Beats me." I shrugged. "The more we talked about it, Amanda began to wonder if Deja had just cut all ties with her cousin."

Thea frowned. "Sounds drastic. What could Laila have possibly done to have Deja figuratively kill her off?"

"No idea." It was time to play all my remaining cards. "Do you remember Laila at all? I know she was a lot older than you."

"Actually, I do." Thea lifted her chin. "She was a part of the Buddy-to-Buddy program. You know, high school students mentoring kids at the middle school?"

It was then I recalled that Laila's Buddy-to-Buddy work had been referenced in her yearbook feature.

"She was my friend Beth's mentor," Thea continued. "We always worked together because my buddy, Sage Hattape, was besties with Laila."

"Sage Hattape?" Her name brought forth an earlier memory from the day: my encounter with Rand Windham. He'd mentioned his wife, and I'd drawn a blank at the time. How could I have forgotten Rand married his high-school sweetheart, Sage, after graduating college?

These days, Sage owned Bright Auras, a healing crystal store on the west side of town. I'd stopped by once to offer Center of Attention's services when I was first building my client list but never heard back from her. "I don't remember Sage being friends with Laila." I tried summoning memories of the two together but failed. Any memories I had of Sage from high school were always accompanied by Rand, her linebacker boyfriend.

Thea twisted a strand of her ash blond hair. "They were tight until Laila's mom died."

"Why? What happened?" During such a time of emotional upheaval, wouldn't Laila have needed her bestie more than ever?

My sister lowered her voice dramatically, a fiendish grin enveloping her face. "Because Laila *slept* with Rand while she was home for the memorial."

"What?!" I nearly spit out my High Noon. "Rand cheated on Sage? No way!"

"Yes, way." Thea beamed, enjoying her role as an all-knowing gossipmonger. "Not sure how it all went down. I do know that Sage soon found out about it and dumped Rand."

"Yikes." Lucas shuddered as he drained his beer.

"Lies," I quickly snapped. "They're married! I just saw Rand this morning, and he was gushing about her."

"After a few years, Sage took him back, and *that's* when they got married." Thea blew a loose strand of hair away from her face. "He wore her down, always making a scene about how sorry he was."

I swirled the remaining contents of my seltzer can. "I had no idea their relationship went through a rough patch. Man, I missed a lot while I was living in Dover."

"It's like a soap opera," Lucas agreed.

Thea studied me with a shrewd expression. "You're not usually into town gossip. Why all the sudden interest in the Jacksons?"

I was saved from answering by my mother's harried arrival. "Goodness, that poor man needs a partner in his life. Or a cat. He's helpless," she grumbled, her voice floating down the hall from the entryway.

"Hey, Ma." I bounded off the couch, away from my sister's suspicious gaze. "Got roped into helping Johnny *again*?"

"You know, Delia," Mom said as she wiped her hands on her linen slacks, "I'm beginning to wonder if you're right about that guy. I mean, needing my help to boil pasta water? Could he be any more pitiful?"

"He just can't resist your charms." I laughed as I gave my mom a hug. "Who could? You're a total babe."

Mom tucked her shoulder-length brown hair behind her ear. "Oh, hush, you." She glanced over my shoulder. "Is your father still at the grill?"

"I think he's waiting for orders." My smile was teasing. "You know how helpless he is when you're not around."

"Just the way I like it." Mom grinned before shooing me away. "Now, go grab your sister, will you?" she instructed over her shoulder as she took off toward the kitchen. "We'll eat outside in ten."

Mom did love a good outdoor family picnic. "I'll wrangle the troops."

I returned to the sunroom to find Thea sitting on the couch solo. "Where's the hubs?"

"We heard one of the kids crying, so he went to investigate." Thea took a hearty sip of wine. "So, now that we're alone, you gonna tell me why you were fishing for information on the Jacksons?"

I cringed. Dang it, she wasn't going to let me off the hook.

"Come on, Big Sis." Thea scooted to the edge of her cushion, her round, blue eyes pleading. "I promise I won't say anything."

My hands went to my hips. "How many times have I heard *that*, only to have you rat me out to Mom or Dad?"

Her cheeks reddened. "Oh, give me a break. How many times do I have to apologize for telling them you kissed Tony Ramos behind Jewel's Ice Cream? I was eleven, for goodness' sake."

I giggled at her exasperation before a budding idea shut me up. Thea was a fountain of information when it came to Central Shores. Amanda might be well-connected, but the high-society social circles she ran in these days didn't necessarily cross-pollinate with a majority of the town's population. I needed more information on Laila and the Jacksons, and who better to get it from than my own sister?

"I need you to super swear you won't say a word. Not even to Lucas," I whispered, my lips drawn in a tight line.

Thea crossed her heart. "If I do, you can have my signed Justin Timberlake poster."

Ah, Thea's most prized childhood possession, still on prominent display in her home office. Good, she was taking this seriously. "Okay, here's the sitch. Laila Jackson reinvented herself after she moved to California. She became LaTàge."

Thea's mouth dropped open, but nothing came out.

I quickly shared with her about LaTàge being Omar's daughter and that the police were keeping her identity from the public until Omar had recovered a bit more from surgery.

"Oh. My. God." Thea enunciated each word with a theatrical flair. "So, it's totally possible LaTàge *was* killed by someone from Laila's world."

I nodded. "I mean, the Squad certainly isn't above suspicion, but the case is way more complicated than we initially believed."

"Yeesh." She hugged herself. "What do you make of it all?"

"I mean, it would be nice—if you could even call it that—if someone from Central Shores wasn't behind this." I reached for the back of my neck as a muscle twinged with tension. "But it would be shortsighted not to investigate why Laila was on such strained terms with her family. And now there's this thing with Sage. I had no idea she and Laila used to be close."

Thea clasped her hands together, wide-eyed. "Do you think Sage knew LaTàge was actually her childhood bestie?"

"If she did, she's certainly never blabbed about it."

Thea snorted. "Actually, I wouldn't be surprised if Sage didn't even know LaTàge existed. The last time I spoke with her, she was going on and on about how she doesn't have a cell phone because it would obstruct her chakra channels." She folded her arms. "There's no way Sage is on social media. That would totally clog her spiritual pores or whatever."

If that's the case, I guess it makes sense why Sage never reached out about a CoA engagement. "Do you run into her often?"

"Not really." Thea shook her head. "I only see Sage when I pop into the thrift shop next to her crystal store. Why?"

"I'd love to talk with her. See if she knew anything about Laila being back in the area." I mulled over a growing theory. If Laila and Rand really had an affair, maybe Sage was still holding a grudge that turned deadly.

Thea smiled brightly. "Well, I can arrange that. Come shopping with me on Friday. I have to get a gift for the trips' room mom. Trove has a great selection of scarves that are my go-to." Trove was the thrift store next to Bright Auras.

I studied my sister for a moment. Thea, a sleuthing partner?

"Sounds great." I dug my phone out of my pocket. "I've got some client meetings in the AM. Want to meet after lunch?"

"Sure thing." Thea rubbed her palms together. "Oh, boy, I can't wait."

Her excitement coaxed a tentative smile across my face. *I hope I don't regret this.*

Chapter Nineteen

"What a tangled web you've woven." Hudson's lip curled in a sexy grin.

I rolled my eyes at the FaceTime video. "I haven't been weaving anything. This is all Laila Jackson's doing." I hurriedly clarified, "Not that I'm victim-blaming her or anything. I'm just trying to figure out how her childhood and LaTàge are connected, if at all."

Hudson reclined against a sea of pillows. "Who would have thought Central Shores would produce such prominent influencers? Must be something in the water."

I giggled at his teasing before sobering. "I'm at a loss. Was Laila killed because she was LaTàge, or was she killed because she was Laila?"

"Why does it have to be one or the other?" Hudson raised an astute eyebrow.

I studied his handsome, slightly pixelated face. "I guess you could be right."

"Just be careful, babes. If you start asking questions, folks will get suspicious."

I bowed my head. "I know. Heck, I've even got Thea playing bodyguard."

My attention was momentarily sidetracked by a banner notification that popped up on my screen. Another Instagram DM.

You should be ashamed of yourself. Go hide in a hole and die!

"Why the face?" Hudson asked, his expression concerned.

I swiped away the nasty alert. "Oh, just another person calling me a harbinger of death." Every single one of my social media inboxes was filled with digital hate.

"Ugh. You shouldn't have to read crap like that." Hudson's scowl turned sympathetic. "This isn't your fault."

His worry for me tugged free a small smile. "I know, and I intend to prove it to the Internet."

"Keep me posted, will you?"

"Of course." My gaze flicked to the time. "Now, you've got to get going to your next interview." In a few hours, Hudson was appearing on a late-night talk show to promote *Crime Sweet Home*.

Hudson sat up in his hotel bed. "Oh, dang. You're right. Okay, call me if you need anything. Miss you."

"Miss you, too." I blew him a kiss and signed off the video chat. I dropped my phone onto the couch cushion, leaning my head back to stare at the ceiling. After returning home from a nice dinner at my parents' house, I'd hoped my chat with Hudson would spark an idea about what to do regarding my investigation: pursue Laila or pursue LaTàge? But it was beginning to look like I would have to do both.

A staccato buzz jolted me from my muddled thoughts. A text from Jasper. **Check your email, betch.**

My curiosity piqued, I swiped and tapped my way through to my personal Gmail account. Both CoA and *Trending Topic* had their own addresses, so I rarely visited my personal email. The astronomical number of unread messages proved it. I scanned the recent arrivals on the lookout for something from Jasper.

Seeing nothing that fit the bill, I followed a brewing hunch and switched over to my *Trending Topic* email. Any collaboration or sponsorship requests came in through this channel.

The words **YOU'RE INVITED** caught my eye in the subject line of an email from Kyūka, a chic, new sushi restaurant in Crestview.

I clicked, reading the personal message.

> **Ms. Cline,**
> **We'd be honored to have you dine with us as we celebrate**
> **our one-month anniversary. As someone the staff at Kyūka**

greatly admire, it would be a delight to host you. All food, drink, and valet will be complimentary on a date of your choosing.

I whistled at the clutch invitation from the restaurant's management. I immediately texted Jasper, **You get an invite too?**

Yup. Want to go tomorrow and make a thing of it?

I checked my Wednesday calendar. Like most workdays, I had client meetings scheduled throughout the morning, but my afternoons were clear to work on creative content for their social media, as well as my own. **I'm free but is Weds the right day to go? Won't it be dead?**

Duh. Then we'll really get the royalty treatment. Good for pics.

I smiled. Both Jasper and I knew the strings attached to this invitation for a free meal. Tags and posts featuring Kyūka. **Kk, what time?**

Let's make it 6.

With dinner plans in place, I prepared myself for bed. I couldn't help but wonder if Jasper had insisted on tomorrow so I wouldn't be on my own for the evening. I knew all my friends worried about me, given the sometimes-crippling anxiety I'd experienced after solving my first case. But instead of getting defensive about it, a warmth spread through my chest. I was so lucky to have them looking out for me.

Wednesday flew by in the haze of hashtags, boosted posts, and campaigns. Many CoA clients were transitioning to fall-themed sales, products, and promotions, so Amanda and I had our work cut out for us, updating websites and editing newsletter templates.

I also had to decide what to do about my weekly *Trending Topic* post, scheduled to go live on Saturday. I had originally planned to share an interview with a meditation specialist, complete with best practice tips, but it felt wrong to post the feature without acknowledging LaTàge. Anything I posted would be scrutinized within an inch of its life. The pressure made it incredibly difficult for me to figure out what to say.

I hadn't uploaded new content on any of my socials since the incident, either, and my silence was clearly beginning to raise the hackles of even my most dedicated followers. Their probing comments on my last post from Monday morning—before finding LaTàge—revealed the changing tide.

No tribute yet?

Why no LaTàge RIP?

Are you glad she's dead??

Where r u @Cococline?

I rubbed my temples as I scrolled through the angry mob. I *had* to say something. Ignoring her death would not make the matter go away. What's more, LaTàge deserved to be honored for all the joy and fun she'd brought to my newsfeed.

With an eye on the time, I sat at my iMac and composed a short message, lauding LaTàge for her work and how she was an inspiration to influencers everywhere. I made mention of how much her fans missed her, but I strove not to fawn over her because that would make me sound disingenuous. I wrote a message I believed came from my heart, a tribute to a relative stranger that I had always admired from afar.

Of course, it was tricky to be entirely genuine with all my buzzing questions surrounding Laila Jackson, but I tamped those down for now. I then pasted my words against a magenta canvas with a gold border, and my tribute graphic was complete.

I took a fortifying breath before blasting it across my accounts. My two-day silence on Facebook, Instagram, X, etcetera was about to end. I hoped I'd made the right call with my poignant words. Otherwise, it might be the end of influencer Coco Cline and *Trending Topic* as I knew it.

I shook my head at the incredible notion that one little action could have so much power. But that was the Internet for you. Just one remark, one comment, could make or break a public figure. I prayed my followers understood my stance and that this terrible situation would not break me.

Even if it did, Cokes, would it really be all that bad? The question wiggled through my mind, unbidden.

Four years ago, the thought of losing my online platform would have scared me senseless. My candid reaction now revealed just how much I'd grown to appreciate the life I had *beyond* the Internet. How much my family, my friends, and my CoA work all meant to me. It also indicated that my entire identity was no longer wrapped up in being "an influencer." Yet, at the end of the day, I still cared a great deal about my followers. I hoped my statement helped them process their grief for LaTàge.

To preserve my own mental health, I decided to mute all social notifications as soon as the tribute post was live. I wasn't in the right headspace to read any replies right now. I wanted to enjoy dinner with my bestie and not think about all the hate still trending my way. Although, Jasper would surely let me know if my online rep was crumbling all around me.

I dressed for dinner in a silky teal maxi dress and carefully painted on my makeup, very much aware Jasper and I would be subject to getting our picture taken. It was a small price to pay to enjoy a free meal at Kyūka. I might have been living comfortably, but even I couldn't justify thirty dollars for a *single* maki roll. Kyūka's expensive menu was one of the reasons I'd yet to visit. I also was not a fan of seafood, which made my sushi options very limited.

But if I wasn't footing the bill? Sold.

Jasper had spent the day working in Milton on his latest *Divulge Direct* segment, so we agreed to meet at Kyūka, rather than carpool.

"Ready to gorge?" Jasper rubbed his hands together as we waltzed along a pebbled pathway toward the restaurant's stained-glass entrance.

My stomach rumbled in answer. "I worked through lunch, so my body is ready."

Jasper chuckled. "Good." He held the door open for me, and the cool interior of the restaurant washed over us.

We stepped inside, admiring the maroon walls adorned with gold accents. The onyx-black floor tile caught the reflections of the twinkling Japanese lanterns hanging from the peaked ceiling.

"Wow." Jasper released a low, awestruck whistle. "Nice vibe."

We approached the podium, where a friendly man of Asian heritage smiled at us, recognition sparkling in his dark gaze. "Ms. Cline and Mr. Hastings, welcome. We're so delighted you've decided to dine with us. It is an honor to welcome such esteemed guests."

"Thank you." Jasper tipped his head graciously. "We're looking forward to experiencing Kyūka's charms." He then muttered out of the side of his mouth so that only I could hear, "Never gets old, does it?"

I discreetly nudged him in the side as I replied to our host, "Yes, thank you. We're thrilled to be here."

"Right this way." The man ushered us forward. "We have one of our private tables reserved for you."

We strolled through the main dining area and down a hallway lined with traditional Japanese sliding doors. Our host opened a door adorned with mossy green paper paneling and led us inside the cozy space. A U-shaped booth greeted us, its cushions the same maroon color as the lotus-patterned wallpaper.

"Your waiter will be with you shortly. Enjoy." With a bow of his head, the gentleman left us alone.

Jasper claimed the left side of the booth. "Swanky, right?" He relaxed and stretched his arms out.

I agreed as I slid into my seat opposite him. "Good date spot." I was already thinking about what I'd put in my caption when I posted a pic of the evening.

"Can you imagine us being on a date?" Jasper snorted.

I visibly convulsed. "Ugh, no! Why would you even say that? Especially before I've eaten." Jasper was the brother I'd never had.

"To get that reaction." He smirked as he placed a golden cloth napkin across his lap.

I rolled my eyes at his immaturity.

"And to put what I'm about to say into perspective." He steepled his fingers together, propping his elbows on the table. "Remember, Cokes, things can always be worse."

I stilled at his sudden seriousness. "What are you talking about?"

Jasper sighed. "Do you want the good news or the bad news first?"

"Oh, no." *My LaTàge tribute.* I'd done a good job blocking it out, but I should have known Jasper would bring it up. "I muted all my notifications. How bad is it?"

"It's not bad, per se." He grimaced. "For the most part, people appreciated your sincerity."

I tilted my head, worrying the relief I felt would be short-lived. "Then what's the bad news?"

"Some rando bot took a screenshot of your post and manipulated your message to make it look like you were celebrating LaTàge's demise." Jasper reluctantly held his phone out to me. "Because Elon Musk lets anyone be verified, lots of folks are taking this as gospel."

I grabbed his mobile and studied the counterfeit image of the graphic I'd made. Instead of my heartfelt wishes, it now read, *"Poor LaTàge. She should have known better than to mess with me. Come for me, and I will come for you."*

My hands shook with horrified rage. "What the actual—"

Jasper cut me off before expletives began flying. "Most news outlets are reporting that it's a fake, and both LaTàge's and your followers are demanding the post be taken down." He took his phone back and hid it away in his jacket pocket. "But still…"

"I should have stayed quiet." My face dropped into my palms. *I guess you get what you ask for.* The wishy-washy thoughts I'd been having about leaving the influencer space were about to come to fruition, and I was surprised by the sudden, deep ache in my chest.

"No, I think you did the right thing," Jasper hurriedly reassured me. "Your real message was expertly presented, and any prolonged silence would have been seen as cold and unfeeling. And besides, a ton of people are still supporting you. Unfortunately, grimy disinformation posts are just a pitfall."

We were interrupted by the arrival of our server. I ordered a Matcha Gin Fizz—extra gin—to help numb the anxiety building within me. While Jasper ordered a warm saké, I checked social media on my phone.

Unexpectedly, my spirits began to lift with each tap of my thumb. Jasper was right. I had thousands of encouraging comments attached to my statement. My followers shared how LaTàge had inspired them, and the post on X alone had over four hundred-eighty-thousand likes. However,

I saw the phrase **COME FOR ME** listed on the trending panel, and the budding warm fuzzies evaporated. I prayed the site's disinformation task force would remove the imposter post ASAP. Not only for my sake, but for LaTàge's. She deserved better.

I had numerous DMs from outlets across multiple platforms asking for me to comment. I left them unread. I'd said my piece, and that's what they could refer to. I wasn't going to give some lowly troll the satisfaction of getting under my skin.

Being the selfless hero that he was, Jasper kept my stormy thoughts preoccupied by regaling me about his latest *Divulge Direct* guest. Marnie Yates was an indie actress starring in her first Hulu original series, and part of her press tour involved appearing on Jasper's show.

"Ugh, girl needs a personality coach. She talked with absolutely no pizzazz." Jasper tossed back a little cup of saké. "Completely monotone the entire interview. She must be quite the actor, or otherwise, the show is going to be unwatchable."

I chuckled at his harsh critique. "It's great you booked her, though. There's a lot of buzz about her series."

"I suppose." He poured himself another drink. "I'd like to see our views for the live show increase. Right now, the podcast is doing the heavy lifting."

I noted the tremble of uncertainty in his voice. "What does Millie think?"

"She seems happy enough with the launch." Jasper shrugged. "But I can't help but be a little disillusioned. I think I had my expectations set too high."

I bobbed my head with understanding. "I get it, believe me. When *Trending Topic* first launched, I had, what, like ten followers?" I chuckled at the memory. "Building a following takes time. As long as Millie's willing to give it to you, you'll be fine."

Jasper's lips pursed. "I just don't want my on-air slot to get bumped for re-runs of Dad's show."

His nickname for Hudson tugged a wistful smile across my lips.

Our server returned with our appetizers, although, this time, he was joined by a beautiful woman dressed in a tailored hot pink suit. "Mr. Hastings, Ms. Cline, welcome. I'm Runa Akane, one of the owners here at Kyūka."

She extended her hand and gave us each a firm handshake. "I'm thrilled you were able to join us. Do you mind if we get a few shots for our website?" Her raven-black hair swept across her shoulders as she motioned to a young man behind her carrying a camera.

"Please, snap away." Jasper's suave demeanor oozed from him.

Runa chatted with us about our respective careers while the photographer grabbed some candid shots. After he showed Runa the fruits of his labor, she nodded with savvy triumph. You could almost see the dollar signs glowing in her eyes. "Wonderful. We'll leave you to enjoy your meal."

"Excuse me?" I spoke up, suddenly realizing the Matcha Gin Fizz had caught up to my bladder. "Could you point me in the direction of the washroom?"

Runa extended her arm. "We have private bathrooms at the end of the hall for our VIP guests."

I shot Jasper an impressed glance. *Ooo, fancy.*

I slid out of the booth and headed in the direction Runa had pointed. I'd just about reached the end of the corridor when a shockingly familiar voice reached my ears.

"Ugh, this is so unfair. It's like LaTàge is punishing us from beyond the grave."

Chapter Twenty

R*uby Daniels?* What the heck was she doing here? I whipped my head in the direction the complaint had come from, and my gaze narrowed on a closed, red paper-paneled door next to me.

"Don't be like that, boo," a silky tenor voice crooned. "We got this. We've kept this under wraps for this long. What's a few more days?"

I stifled a gasp as recognition flared within me. I'd heard that voice many times before, too. On Instagram Reels, not in person. Miguel Torres? As in, LaTàge's yummy arm candy?

Forgetting my pleading bladder for a moment, I leaned closer to the paper-thin door.

"A few more days?" Ruby snapped. "This isn't *CSI*, Miguel. We could be under scrutiny for weeks. *Months*, even. Ugh, we should have taken care of LaTàge before leaving LA."

My eyes widened, and I nearly choked on my shock. *Taken care of?* Did that mean—

"Hush, Rubes," Miguel cooed. "This will all blow over soon. And honestly, the optics will look totally better for us this way."

"How so?" she sounded doubtful.

"Well, instead of being seen as betraying LaTàge, we can now say our grief brought us together," Miguel murmured. "No one has to know we've been sleeping together behind her back for months now."

Omigod, omigod, omigod. I could not handle the piping hot tea being spilled on the other side of this door. Ruby and Miguel, lovers?

"From a PR standpoint, this whole thing is totally working in our favor."

Ruby scoffed. "Do you know how awful you sound? She was my best friend, Migs. It's like you're happy she's dead."

"So, what if I am? Tàge made our lives a living misery." Miguel's tone hardened. "She got what she deserved if you ask me."

A throat cleared behind me before I could catch Ruby's response.

I turned around, my cheeks already radiating molten fire with embarrassment, and found Runa staring at me with a raised brow.

"Do you need an escort, Ms. Cline?" she asked primly.

I shook my head. "Uh, n-no. I'm fine, thanks," I muttered before hightailing it into the ladies' room.

I stared at myself in the gilded mirror, my brain scrambling to process what I'd just overheard. Ruby and Miguel had been having an affair behind LaTàge's back? For how long? And what did Ruby mean by "taken care of LaTàge?" I swallowed the hard lump in my throat, thinking about the keycard activity for Ruby's hotel door. Had one or both killed LaTàge so they could be together?

I used the elegant washroom and hurried back to our table. As much as I wanted to spy on Ruby and Miguel some more, I couldn't risk Runa or someone else on staff catching me.

Jasper did a double take as I slid back into the booth. "What happened to you? Your face looks like you had a run-in with zinc oxide."

I did feel a little lightheaded, and no doubt, my face was pale. "You are not going to believe what I just learned."

Mindful that these "private tables" weren't actually soundproof, I quietly reiterated what I'd overheard.

Jasper grew pensive at my reveal. His icy blue eyes narrowed in shrewd concentration. "The plot thickens, my dear Coco. Ruby actually said, 'taken care of LaTàge?'"

I bobbed my head furiously. "I mean, that's practically a confession, right?"

"Perhaps." Jasper sipped his saké.

"So, what should we do?" I whipped out my phone. "Call Gavin and let him know about their affair?"

Jasper placed a hand over my screen. "Hold up. Let's not get ahead of ourselves. Why don't we just go chat with them and see what's what."

I studied my bestie for a moment, trying to decode his cool, calm demeanor. I had expected Jasper to unleash all the drama at this development, but instead, he almost seemed calculated. "Um, okay." I mean, I was all for questioning suspects myself, especially when I had formidable backup.

Jasper extricated himself from the booth. "Come on, before our waiter brings our entrees."

Needing no additional prodding, I led the way toward Ruby and Miguel's private room.

"How do we go about this?" I mouthed, trying to figure out a cover story.

Jasper, however, was a brazen step ahead of me. With a light rap of his knuckles, he then opened the door without giving the room's occupants any time to respond.

"Ah, we heard you were here—" Jasper gushed before dramatically cutting himself off as Ruby and Miguel's intertwined bodies greeted us.

Ruby squeaked and unwrapped herself from Miguel's heated embrace. "Knock much? What the he—Coco, is that you?" She squinted past Jasper's hulking frame, spying me hiding behind him.

I gave her a sheepish wave. "Hey, Ruby. We're dining a few tables down."

Miguel, with his deep copper skin and raven hair, glared at us. "Get out of here."

Ruby shushed him. "Don't be rude. This is Coco Cline, Migs. She's helping me clear my name with the police."

I tried to hide a wince of regret. I hoped Ruby's comment wouldn't make its way back to Chief McInnis or Detective Forester.

"Oh." Miguel's surly demeanor changed on a dime. "Sorry, I didn't recognize you." He leaned across the table, extending his hand. "This your bodyguard or something?" Miguel eyed Jasper's imposing frame.

"No, this is my friend, Jasper Hastings."

"I'm the host of *Divulge Direct,* the hot new crossover talk show," my bestie formally introduced himself.

Miguel snorted. "Crossover talk show?"

"Yes, we film live for TV and then stream across podcast platforms." Jasper gave him an icy stare. "And I'm sure my viewers would be very interested to learn that LaTàge's bestie and boyfriend were screwing behind her back."

Ruby choked on her drink. "What? No! What you saw—it's not what it looked like. Miguel and I were just…overwhelmed by our grief for LaTàge."

"Sure, Jan," Jasper mimicked the popular *Brady Bunch* meme.

Miguel, however, didn't appear as concerned as Ruby. "I was never LaTàge's *real* boyfriend. Our relationship was purely business. I played the role of her 'event companion,' and she got what she paid for."

"Except she hadn't been paying you," Jasper countered. "Is that why you killed her?"

Miguel slammed his fist on the table. "What?! No! Neither Ruby nor I had anything to do with LaTàge's death. I swear on my abuela." He reached for the gold cross hanging from his neck. A very familiar cross…

My gaze darted to Ruby, who wore the same necklace. She'd even used it to swear on her grandma's life earlier, much like her beau. "Then how do you explain Ruby's hotel door being unlocked in the middle of the night?" I folded my arms. "Right around the time LaTàge was murdered?" Okay, we didn't *know* that, but they didn't know what we didn't know.

"What? How—"

I cut Ruby off. "I can't help you if you keep lying to me, Ruby. You told me you didn't leave your room after ten."

"I didn't!" Her chin quivered.

"That was me," Miguel spoke sharply, draping a protective arm over Ruby's shoulders. "Rubes gave me an extra key to her room so I could visit her."

"At two o'clock in the morning?" Jasper raised an eyebrow.

Miguel shrugged. "I went out clubbing with Katz for a bit. We ended up at someplace called Cyprus."

I was familiar with the resort-like club. It was a popular nightlife hotspot over in Cherry Springs.

"It took me a while to shake off Katz. Had to wait until they found someone to entertain them for the remainder of the night." Miguel's lips curled in a suggestive manner.

"Does Katz know about you two?" I asked.

Miguel shook his head. "No way. Katz would have ratted us out in a second. They're more loyal to LaTàge than either of us have ever been."

"That's not true," Ruby whimpered. "I loved LaTàge like a sister."

Miguel scoffed. "You sure fought like siblings."

I interrupted the budding lovers' quarrel to ask, "What time did you leave Cyprus, Miguel?"

"Hmm." He dug his phone out and tapped the screen. "My Uber picked me up at one-forty AM. Dropped me off at the hotel at one fifty-six." He even let me check the details of his ride.

My heart sank. His car service itinerary didn't leave any room for a detour to kill his boss/fake girlfriend…unless he had only stopped by the hotel briefly to shore up an alibi before heading to Crescent Hills to commit the murderous deed.

I directed my next question to Ruby. "Did you see Miguel when he came into your room?"

"Um…" She gnawed on her glossy lower lip. "Well, not exactly. But he was in bed with me when I woke up that morning."

Jasper's brow wrinkled. "You didn't even hear him?" he asked, clearly unconvinced.

Ruby tucked a strand of hair behind her ear. "N-no. You see, I'd taken an Ambien. After telling LaTàge I quit, I needed help calming my brain. I was dead to the world until your coworker started messaging me about her."

Miguel's expression clouded over as he glared at his girlfriend. "I'm sure you can check security footage in the elevator or whatever." He paused, a sneer spreading. "Oh, wait. You're not the police, are you?"

A shiver went down my spine at his angered reaction. "I'm just trying to help Ruby."

"By accusing *me* of LaTàge's murder?" Miguel's nostrils flared.

Jasper held up a hand. "Look, we know you two were bumping uglies behind LaTàge's back. Now that she's out of the way, things become a whole lot easier for you two to go public, right? Instead of betraying her, you can now say your grief brought you together."

I shot a panicked glance at my BFF. What was his angle here, using the words I'd overheard Miguel say against him?

"I didn't kill her," Miguel reiterated. "I won't lie, it will be easier to go public with our relationship. But trust me, I wouldn't have had a problem stirring up a little drama."

I tilted my head. "What do you mean?"

"Come on, you know the influencer game." Miguel gave a condescending chuckle. "No publicity is bad publicity. I *had* planned to tell LaTàge about Rubes and me before she dragged us out here on this ridiculous rebrand trip, but Ruby insisted I wait until *after* we'd gotten paid."

Ruby's comment about "taking care of LaTàge" suddenly took on a new meaning.

A wistful expression softened Miguel's sharp features. "Me betraying LaTàge would have been all anyone could post about."

"Why?" I challenged. "Once it came to light that she was paying you, it would have just been seen as some dumb grift. A sham."

Miguel disagreed. "Well, obvi, I wouldn't have blabbed about our business arrangement, and LaTàge would never have admitted the ruse. She'd die of embarrassment." He didn't even flinch at his gauche words. Instead, he threaded his hands behind his neck, looking smug. "I could have ridden a wave like that for weeks." Miguel's dreamy expression returned.

"Are you serious right now?" Ruby smacked his arm. "Am I just part of some PR stunt to you?"

"No, boo. Don't be like that." Now looking somewhat chastened, Miguel tugged at his plunging collar. "I'm just saying it like it is. We could've handled any fallout with the press, whatever might've happened."

I shuddered at Miguel's sleazy attitude, but he had a point. In his world, you wanted, no, *needed* people talking about you. Breaking LaTàge's heart would have fast-tracked him to the top of the trending charts.

Ruby, however, was not appeased. "Can you be human for, like, a minute? I get things with LaTàge weren't great, but I know you cared about her as a friend. Stop burying your feelings and show some sympathy. This toxic machismo," she paused, motioning wildly toward him with a sassy hand, "is not going to go over well with anyone. Get a heart, Migs."

"I had one, sweetness." He reached out to stroke her cheek. "I gave it to you."

Jasper shot me a secretive glance and feigned a gag.

"All right." I decided to switch tactics. "If you had nothing to do with LaTàge's death, any idea who did?" Not that I believed in Miguel's innocence, but I wanted more deets on what was happening within LaTàge's inner circle.

He tapped his chin. "I mean, it's gotta be some rando, right? A robbery gone wrong? LaTàge knew no one here besides us." Miguel's lips curled into a smirk. "And you, Coco Cline. How do we know you didn't decide to off the competition?"

I rolled my eyes. "Puh-lease. I'm smart enough to know LaTàge was leagues above me. If anything, me working on her rebrand would have helped boost my profile even more."

Miguel frowned. "Hmm, that is true. I guess we are at an impasse."

His ever-changing demeanor was giving me whiplash. One minute, he was talking like a total bro, the next, a BBC talk show host. But whatever the case, I didn't think we would get anything else useful from Miguel. At least, not now.

"I wouldn't say that." A wicked grin flexed on Jasper's face. "In fact, I think a partnership is more in order. Coco will continue her investigation into who killed your friend while I provide you and Ruby a platform to share your side of the story with the world."

"A platform?" Miguel perked up. "I'm listening."

"You and Ruby have control of your narrative for the moment." Jasper pressed a palm to his chest. "Let *me* help you tell it."

Miguel chuckled. "And why should we go on your little fledgling show? Any newsroom in the country will give us airtime."

"But can you guarantee they won't attack you for dating behind LaTàge's back?" Jasper's gaze had a premeditated gleam to it. "That they won't vilify you? Even if your relationship was only for the cameras, many people believed it to be real. And the public doesn't like being lied to." Jasper folded his arms, striking a power pose. "The Internet is looking to put someone's head on a spike. If you're not careful, it might be yours. Why risk bad publicity when you can have it good?"

His persuasive proposal had clearly piqued Ruby's interest. "W-we could tell the story *we* wanted?"

"Of course," Jasper replied with a shrug. "I would merely be there for support. The Oprah to your Harry and Meghan."

And to rake in the viewing numbers to boot. As I heard Jasper's scheme unfold, the contrast between Hudson's journalism ethics and my bestie's couldn't be more apparent. Hudson's show pursued the truth. Jasper was all about entertainment.

Ruby sent a *What-do-you-think* look toward Miguel. His brow furrowed for a moment before a smile broke out on his lips. "I like your style, Hastings. You have yourself a deal, amigo." He paused, his gaze sliding to me. "*If* you guys can get us off the hook."

I gulped. I still wasn't one hundred percent sure we should be backing Miguel, but I knew how huge this would be for *Divulge Direct.* If Jasper snagged "The Ruby & Miguel Interview," it could launch his show into the celebrity stratosphere.

Jasper had the decency not to answer on my behalf, but I could practically hear his pleading thoughts, "*Please, Cokes. I need this.*"

"We'll continue looking into LaTàge's case," I confirmed, "but in return, you guys have to keep this all under wraps."

Miguel rested a hand above his heart. "Agreed." He then kissed his gold cross for emphasis.

"And if you need anything, don't hesitate to reach out," Ruby added. "We're open books."

I took her up on her offer immediately. "I do have a question. You mentioned earlier that Katz was extremely loyal to LaTàge. Why?"

Miguel shrugged. "LaTàge plucked Katz out of obscurity and made all their dreams come true." His tone signaled that this should have been obvious to me. "Ruby and I both had good stuff going on before LaTàge entered our lives. Katz didn't."

"What do you mean?"

Ruby cleared her throat. "When Katz came out to their parents, they were disowned. Tossed onto the street before they turned seventeen. Katz lived from paycheck to paycheck, barely able to keep a roof above their head. They made all their own clothes by repurposing old pieces found at thrift stores or Goodwill. One day, when LaTàge and I were walking down Sunset Boulevard, we encountered Katz, and LaTàge made a comment about how much she loved the romper Katz had on. We got to talking with them, and pretty soon, LaTàge invited Katz to join us for dinner. Come to find out, it was the first hot meal Katz had had in two weeks." Ruby broke off, her eyes growing wet with emotion. "Once LaTàge got Katz to open up, she immediately invited them back to our loft for a shower and a warm bed. After that, Katz never left."

I sucked in a breath. I'd had no idea Katz had experienced such hardship. Add to the fact that LaTàge opened her home to them…I could see why Katz felt indebted to LaTàge. It also spoke volumes about LaTàge—*Laila's* kindhearted personality. Beneath her wild antics and extra showmanship was someone who just wanted to help people however she could.

"But wasn't Katz angry that LaTàge was defaulting on payments?" Jasper asked.

Ruby nervously glanced at her lap. "I mean, Katz wasn't thrilled, but they believed LaTàge about the bank error. They didn't notice how much money LaTàge was constantly blowing through. Even on Sunday night, after our big fight, they told us to have faith in her."

"Have you seen Katz at all?" I pressed. Katz was the one squad member we had not spoken with yet.

"Briefly," Ruby responded. "I had to wake them up on Monday to break the news about LaTàge. But I haven't seen them around the hotel since, and they aren't answering either of our messages."

I frowned. Odd. One would think Katz would be leaning on their friends during a time of crisis. Although, given the harsh way Miguel spoke about Katz's loyalty to LaTàge, perhaps Katz wasn't as close with the other squad members as we were all led to believe. "I'd love to speak with them about all this. If you do see Katz, can you let them know?"

Ruby bobbed her head. "Sure."

"And if anything comes up that you think might be helpful, send me a DM." I cupped Jasper's elbow and pulled him backward. "I'm sure our food has arrived by now. We'll leave you be." Thank goodness we had ordered sushi rolls. A hot meal would likely be stone cold.

"My people will be in touch," Jasper said with a tittering wiggle of his fingers before sliding the couple's paneled door shut.

I jabbed him in the side as we returned to our private table. "You went in there solely to get them to come on your show, didn't you?" I hissed through gritted teeth and slid back into the booth.

Jasper stuck his tongue out at me as he rubbed the sore spot. "While I may have been working an angle," he admitted, matching my low tone, "I also knew it was the best way to get Miguel to talk to us. You know how hostile he can be."

Indeed, there were several videos online of Miguel spouting off in the faces of devoted fans. "Yeah. I don't even know if I believe him. He did have a lot to gain by getting rid of LaTàge."

"What about his alibi?" Jasper countered as he reached for his chopsticks. "Could Miguel really have returned to The Glades, went up to Ruby's room, then snuck back out to kill LaTàge?"

Hearing Jasper say it out loud made me realize how improbable it all sounded. "Well, if Ruby and Miguel didn't kill LaTàge, all that really leaves is Katz."

"Kinda sus behavior from them." Jasper picked up a dragon roll and popped it into his mouth. "Not acknowledging Ruby's and Miguel's messages or anything."

I munched on a mango sweet potato tempura maki roll. "Maybe Katz finally realized just how serious LaTàge's financial woes were and freaked. Their clothing company was on the line, after all. I know you texted that LaTàge didn't have any money invested, but if her 'brand' was in shambles," I said, using air quotes, "she might have been worth more to Katz dead than alive."

"Can't argue with that." Jasper bobbed his head. "We already know Katz's investors want to bump up the launch and ride the wave of public sympathy."

Even he recoiled at the stonehearted business move. "Let's hope Ruby can put Katz in touch with us."

As I ate a fresh asparagus roll, I replayed our conversation with Miguel. Conceited a-hole? Definitely. Cold-blooded killer? I wasn't so sure. His comment about capitalizing on whatever publicity came his way kept ringing in my ears. "I'm beginning to wonder if we're wasting our time on a red herring."

"You mean by focusing on LaTàge as our victim?" Jasper raised an eyebrow. "How literary of you."

I propped my cheek against my fist. "Until we can chat with Katz, I think we need to shift our attention to Laila. It's too big of a coincidence that she dies the night she returns to her hometown after years of being MIA."

"When you put it like that…" Jasper trailed off, his gaze staring into space.

I quietly shared the next phase of my sleuthing plan. "I'm meeting Thea on Friday for some shopping. We're going to stop by Sage Hattape's place to see if she has anything to say about Laila."

"Sage Hattape? That name rings a bell." Jasper's brow furrowed. "Why?"

I explained that Sage and Laila had supposedly been close friends while attending CSH. "Thea told me that Laila slept with Rand Windham, Sage's high school sweetheart-turned-boat-obsessed-husband, the summer she came back for her mother's memorial. If Sage somehow learned Laila had returned to Central Shores, she might have confronted her."

"Rand?" Jasper dipped his sushi into the soy sauce ramekin. "You think our resident yacht bro triggered this whole mess?"

I shrugged.

"I mean, he's a bit goofy, but he sure is studly." Jasper licked his lips. "I guess I could see Sage getting defensive over him if she heard an old flame was back in town."

"But would she have even known about Laila being here?" I rhythmically tapped my chin. "I mean, beyond Omar, no one seems to realize Laila and LaTàge were one and the same."

Jasper shrugged. "You'll have to find out on this sister-sleuthing outing."

"Don't pout that you're not involved." I rolled my eyes.

"I'm not pouting." He dabbed a napkin on his chin. "Besides, I'll be too busy prepping for my exclusive studio interview with the lovebirds."

I studied him, a pit of worry growing in my stomach. "You're really *not* going to reveal they'd been seeing each other behind LaTàge's back?"

"Me and the Truth have a testy relationship. I'm not as principled as dear old Dad," he said, clearly referring to Hudson. "I need something to put *Divulge Direct* on the map, and this is it."

"Remember Miguel's stipulation, though," I pointed out. "Only if we can clear his and Ruby's name."

Jasper grinned. "Better hop to it, Cokes. Once again, my future is in your hands."

Chapter Twenty-One

Ruby and Miguel must have snuck out of Kyūka before Jasper and I finished our meal because the panel to their private table stood ajar by the time we left. With promises to keep him apprised about my chat with Sage on Friday, I bid Jasper goodnight and drove home.

While I got ready for bed, I watched Hudson's latest interview. Again, he commanded the screen as he promoted *Crime Sweet Home.* Between Hudson's successful media tour and Jasper nabbing a blockbuster interview, WMTG producer Millie Stabler was sure to be over the moon.

Once the interview concluded, I texted Hudson my gushing praise.

He responded almost immediately. **Thanks, babe. Heading out for drinks with a few guys from college. One works as a defense attorney and might be able to help w/ the Roberta Jones case.**

Hudson had attended Columbia University, so it was great he could catch up with old pals still in the New York area. **Have fun! I'm heading to bed.**

Everything OK down there? Any news re: LaTàge?

Eh, kinda. Jasper and I ran into Ruby & Miguel at dinner.

Which squad members are they?

I typed, **Her BFF and boyfriend.**

Are they suspects?

Idk, tbh. Alibis seem to line up. Wish I knew exactly when she died…

Might be worth a trip to the station? Check in and see how the team is doing?

I grinned at Hudson's crafty idea. I'd been steering clear of the Central

Shores PD in an effort not to get underfoot and stay off the chief's radar, but when I'd done that during my previous case, it had still ended up raising eyebrows. **Good point. I'll swing by on Friday after my morning meetings.** I could head out a bit early on my way to meet Thea.

Knowing he had plans with friends, I sent Hudson a slew of kissy emojis and promised I would touch base with him tomorrow.

Another text notification popped up, this one from Hudson's sister. **Hey, gurl! We're psyched about the trip. Cannot BELIEVE all this stuff with LaTàge. Have you got deets to share with us???**

I shouldn't have been surprised Willow was asking questions. Anyone would be curious about the situation, but both Willow and Reade were serious true crime buffs. They'd even met at a CrimeCon convention, where love had quickly blossomed. **Can't believe it took you this long to ask.**

Was trying to be respectful!! I know you're probs overwhelmed.

A minute later, she followed up with, **Soooo, can you tell me anything?**

All I can say is that I'm looking forward to your visit.

No fair!

I laughed at the GIF she sent featuring steam coming out of a man's ears. But, to her credit, she didn't pester me further. Although, I had no doubt she and Reade wouldn't let me off the hook that easily in person once they arrived on Saturday.

Thursday flew by in a work-related blur. YouTube streaming services went down for one of my clients just as they were about to go live for an online event, so I had to help put out fires and get their webinar rescheduled. The only bit of sleuthing I achieved was digging into Miguel and Katz's Instagram accounts. I'd already missed the window to watch any Stories they posted from Sunday night, but Miguel had uploaded several pics from Cyprus that captured Katz's spiky hair in the crowd. Not exactly a solid alibi, given I didn't know LaTàge's official time of death, but it did support what Miguel had shared at the sushi restaurant.

By the time Friday morning rolled around, I was antsy about my lack of progress and ready to get some boots back on the ground. However,

I still had CoA meetings to wrap up before my next sleuthing operation commenced.

"Sounds great, Tom. I look forward to collaborating with you and Thomas on this exciting endeavor." I waved before signing off the Zoom call.

I'd spent the last hour chatting with a prospective client, and it felt like things were moving in the right direction. Tom Kingsley and his partner, Thomas Neumann, were in the process of procuring a storefront in the Central Shores area with plans to open a specialty chocolate shop. Tom had seen a Center of Attention sponsored ad and reached out to inquire whether CoA could help build the shop's website and social media pages. Since the store was still in its early concept stages, Tom didn't have much information for me, but I'd been able to charm my way into a follow-up meeting to help them determine their business name and branding. Tom had also requested a formal engagement, which meant I had to send the contract over before leaving to meet up with Thea.

Amanda had been managing most of CoA's new clientele while I continued to support our established clients, but I decided to keep Tom and Thomas— yes, their real names—for myself. With her baby situation, I didn't want to overwork her, and besides, a specialty chocolate shop? I'd been dreaming of one coming to town for the longest time. It would be a great experience to help these two build the tentatively named Sweet Resolutions from the ground up. So often, CoA was brought in to correct our clients' bad social media habits. With this engagement, I could train Tom and Thomas about best practices right from the start.

I sent a CoA contract over to Tom for signature, then swapped tabs on my browser. I'd decided to go ahead with my meditation post for *Trending Topic*, although I'd altered the opening paragraph to mention LaTàge's legacy and how meditation was a cathartic way to deal with grief. I doublechecked the post was scheduled to go live tomorrow, as my followers had come to expect a *Trending Topic* feature as part of their Saturday morning routine. In the rare instances I forgot to post, social media was quick to remind me.

With my work done and CoA's schedule cleared for the rest of the day, I had plenty of time to visit my friends at the police station before meeting up with Thea for some sleuthing and shopping. Unsure what scene awaited me, I made certain to look camera-ready in case reporters were still camped on the PD's lawn and caught a pic of me sneaking in.

Even though I thought I was prepared for anything, the raucous scene outside the station proved me terribly wrong. A huge mob containing many faces I recognized congregated at the PD's main entrance, some even holding picket signs. Having parked my car a few streets down to ensure anonymity, I had to squint to read the large, angrily scribbled words as I approached.

PROTECT OUR SHORES!

SAVE OUR CITIZENS!

ARE WE SAFE?

I hurried closer to the throng, my pulse racing. The first person I recognized was my friend and childhood babysitter, Lacie Burbank. I touched her elbow, drawing her attention toward me. "Lace, what's going on here?"

Her hands went to her hips. "What does it look like, girlfriend? We're trying to get some answers from Chief McInnis. This is the *third* murder in Central Shores in less than six months. Something needs to be done!"

I frowned at her near-hysterical delivery. Her demeanor was a complete one-eighty from earlier in the week when I'd run into her and her sister at Duneside. "Whoa. Deep breaths. You know the police are doing their best."

"Are they?" Lacie countered, more harshly than she'd ever spoken to me before. And I'd once tried flushing her homework. "We never had problems like this in the past. With the town's growing population, it's clear Chief McInnis and his officers are in over their heads."

I surveyed the crowd, shocked by the aggressive shouting. To my amazement, I spotted Bill Mendez, the owner of Zaddick's sandwich shop and official lunch provider of the PD, as well as Quincy Novak, who ran a high-end clothing boutique on the strip. Both entrepreneurs were reputable community figures with successful establishments. Yikes, this was not a good look for the chief.

"Who organized this?" I asked Lacie.

"It was a group effort." She stuck out her chin. "Bill and I were chatting with Ronny Durnst yesterday at Brewed to Perfection. Ronny's worried the rising crime rate is going to destroy sales in the new woodlands development, and he wants to know what the police's strategy is. We're all concerned." Lacie folded her arms across her chest. "More residents means better business, but we need our safety guaranteed."

I held my tongue. Nothing could be guaranteed in today's polarized world, but I understood where her fears were coming from. "Isn't this rally a bit counterproductive, though? I mean, the police can't devote all their energy to finding LaTàge's killer if they're dealing with an angry mob."

Lacie scowled. "We should have a competent police force equipped to deal with *both*."

I wanted to defend Gavin and the others, but it seemed futile. Instead, I slipped away from the chanting group and made my way toward the back entrance of the station.

I pressed the door buzzer since my consultant badge didn't have the proper security clearance to operate the lock. "Hey, Maude, it's Coco."

She didn't respond through the speaker, but the door zapped open.

I found Gavin, Deacon, and Adrian huddled in the conference room. Their defeated expressions nearly broke my heart. "Hey, guys. That's some crowd outside. How's everyone holding up?"

Gavin rubbed his temples. "Never been better."

Deacon and Adrian chuckled halfheartedly at his sarcasm. "Those poor folks don't realize they're barking up the wrong tree." Adrian shook his head. "The Community Safety Center is in the town council's hands, not the chief's. Of course, we need more people to support the town's growing population. It's not like McInnis didn't see this coming. That's why he submitted the CSC proposal the minute the woodlands development project broke ground. It's just been taking forever to get green-lit."

"Should you release a statement? I mean, we have Chief McInnis's vision listed on the website," I pointed out, going into PR mode. "Maybe the town just needs a reminder."

"That's what we were discussing." Gavin motioned between the three guys. "Unfortunately, the chief is in session with the mayor and council this very moment, arguing that we need to speed up the approval process."

Deacon snorted. "Honestly, if Mayor Sullivan took a look out his window, it might get us the results we need."

I tapped my chin in consideration. "Does anyone outside know the chief's in a meeting about the very thing they're protesting?"

The three officers shared looks. "Unless they're keeping close tabs on the town council's agenda, probably not," Gavin answered.

"Then why don't we enlighten them?" I said, snapping my fingers. "It might light a fire under Sullivan and the council." Mom had told me at our family barbecue that several council members were unwilling to adjust the budget to accommodate this matter. However, seeing a heated mob might change their minds, especially with elections looming in November. "We can tell them that Chief McInnis is fighting to improve their safety as we speak and that we need their support behind him."

Adrian's expression turned dubious. "It sounds well and good, but I'm not sure the chief would want us to take such a strong standpoint. What do you think, Gav?" He turned to his superior.

Gavin looked conflicted. "If I go out there and make a statement, it could cause more problems."

"What if I went out to speak with them?" I offered without hesitation. "Not as a police mouthpiece, but as a concerned citizen myself?"

Gavin cringed. "No way. Everyone in the tri-state area knows how much you've 'helped' our department in the past. Anything from you is going to look like it's coming from us."

I didn't appreciate the implied air quotes in Gavin's statement, but I understood his perspective. "Then what do we do?"

The conference room phone rang. Gavin pressed the speaker button to answer. "Hey, Maude. What's up?"

"One of the *protesters* has come inside. He'd like to speak with someone." Maude's disdain practically oozed from the phone.

Gavin sighed. "Send him back."

A few moments later, Ronny Durnst appeared in the doorway, dabbing at his brow with a handkerchief. "Hello, Officers. Thank you for seeing me."

"Hello again, Mr. Durnst." Gavin motioned for him to take a seat. "How can we help you?"

"Well, as you can see from the turnout, there are many troubled citizens that don't believe the Central Shores Police Department is doing everything they can to protect them." Ronny's gaze traveled around the room. "Case in point, there's a murderer on the loose and yet, not much detecting seems to be going on."

Gavin folded his arms. "As was announced by the Sussex County Crime Lab, they have taken over jurisdiction of the case. Our department is doing what we can to assist when our aid is requested. We have members of Mr. Lait's team at the crime scene with County as we speak." He motioned to Deacon, the department's lead forensic technician.

"Oh, I am aware," Ronny said with a condescending sneer. "That crime scene is *my* property, remember?"

"We have not forgotten, Mr. Durnst." Gavin's tone was equally curt.

In a surprise move, Ronny wiped the confident smirk off his face. "Look, guys, I'm on your side, really, I am." His gaze turned pleading. "I know how hard the PD is working, and I know the chief wants to expand the force. I just need some reassurances that it will happen soon. I've got nearly thirty houses getting ready to go on the market, and I'd like them to be listed before TBG gets their act together and breaks ground on their flagship project."

The mention of The Buchanan Group perked me up. "What do you mean, flagship?"

Ronny's attention landed on me, as if he'd just realized I was in the room. "Ah, Ms. Cline." He didn't elaborate more.

TBG getting their act together? Breaking ground? Did this have to do with the recent Central Sports announcement I'd read about online?

Gavin shot me a silencing look before addressing Ronny's audacious request. "We're not in the position to make those types of reassurances, Mr. Durnst. We're waiting for the town council to vote on the safety center initiative. So, unfortunately, it's out of our hands. Any concerns should be directed to your local representative."

My eyes widened at his charged remark. Gavin had decided to throw down the gauntlet, after all.

Ronny bobbed his head. "I see, I see. Well, gentlemen and *lady,* I appreciate your candor." He rose from his seat, brushing the wrinkles out of his suit pants. "I'll see to it that we take our concerns to the town hall, then."

What luck! Without having to make a public statement, Gavin had successfully been able to steer the protesters in the right direction.

"Oh, by the way." Ronny turned around just as he reached the door. "Do you have an idea when 713 Crescent Hills Drive will be released back to Derrick and me? We have numerous clients interested in the property."

His offhand remark raised several eyebrows. "Detective Forester with the SCCL will be in touch," Gavin answered stiffly.

With shoulders curled in defeat, Ronny nodded and left without another word.

Chapter Twenty-Two

"The nerve of that dude." Adrian scoffed. "Whining about how no one will want to move into his fancy houses, only to then reveal he's fielding multiple offers for the crime scene."

Deacon stroked his smooth chin. "LaTàge's death has clearly been a lucrative development for Durnst. Did his alibi check through?"

Gavin wearily bobbed his head. "Ronny's girlfriend says he was with her all night. Payne's alibi is that he was working late at Durnst Development. Harriet is waiting on cell phone location data to confirm both their whereabouts, but you know how long that takes." He rolled his eyes.

I sat there, soaking in all the juicy intel. The police had vetted Ronny and Derrick? I supposed it made sense. They were one of the few people who knew LaTàge was in town, beyond me, Amanda, and her friends.

I cleared my throat. "Have you guys made any progress with the LaTàge Squad?"

"Other than our initial interviews, no," Gavin grumbled. "Their lawyers were pretty quick to shut down our questions, saying that unless we had warrants, their clients were not to be disturbed during this time of mourning. We're still trying to piece together their alibis."

I debated a moment what my next move should be. I'd come here to see if I could get a more accurate idea about LaTàge's time of death, as it would help further my own search for the truth. But in order to get what I wanted, I needed to offer up something first. "Look, I have some top-secret info that might be of interest to you guys."

"Top secret?" Deacon arched an eyebrow.

Gavin's gaze narrowed. "How'd you come across it?"

"Totally by accident, I promise." I held my hands up defensively. "Last night, I was eating at that new Japanese restaurant in Crestview, and I saw Ruby and Miguel dining together. As in *together, together.*"

Adrian's jaw dropped. "LaTàge's boyfriend was hooking up with her best friend?"

"According to Miguel, he was never really LaTàge's boyfriend," I explained. "He was paid to make people believe they were an item."

"He failed to mention that." Deacon pointed at the whiteboard where the influencer's picture hung. "Miguel claimed LaTàge kept him on her payroll as her personal trainer."

I snorted. "Maybe that looks better on tax forms."

"He definitely played the role of grieving boyfriend when Harriet and I spoke with him. So, what's your theory?" Gavin challenged. "That Miguel killed LaTàge so he and Ruby could be together?"

"Actually, I don't think he was involved," I admitted, mentally preparing myself to take a huge gamble. "Miguel's alibi seems pretty solid. He partied with Katz at Cyprus for most of the night. He even showed me the receipts for his Uber ride back to his hotel. Right from the app, so they were legit. Miguel left the club at around one-forty and was dropped off at The Glades at two."

Adrian drummed his fingers against the conference tabletop. "I guess that does put him in the clear, considering LaTàge's TOD was one—"

Deacon coughed sharply.

I pressed my lips together, doing my best to look contrite, rather than triumphant. Adrian, bless him, viewed me more as a coworker than either Gavin or Deacon did, so I'd been banking on his slip of the tongue.

"Thanks for the tip, Coco." Gavin sounded more suspicious than grateful, probably because he'd seen right through my underhanded investigative tactics. "How interesting that Miguel shared all this info so freely with you when he barely spoke with us."

The tension in my shoulders melted into relief once I saw the corner of Gavin's lip twitch into a slight grin. He was holding up his end of our strange bargain by not calling me out for my sleuthing. "Will you pass this on to Harriet?"

Gavin glanced at his watch. "Yep. We're due for an interdepartmental briefing soon, so…"

I took that as my cue to jet. After all, I had to meet Thea at Trove. "Well, good luck!" With a chipper wave, I dashed out of the room before Gavin could pepper me with any more questions that I wasn't ready to answer.

As I headed down the hall toward the back entrance, I heard a heated yet unintelligible discussion erupt in the conference room. No doubt, Adrian was getting reamed out for his mistake. I felt bad for the guy. Gavin might not be opposed to receiving useful case info from me, but he clearly didn't view our arrangement as a two-way street.

So, LaTàge had been killed within the realm of one o'clock, soon after her last Instagram Story upload. Since Deacon had cut Adrian off, I wasn't sure if it was one, one-fifteen, one-thirty, etcetera, but whatever the case, Miguel Torres was off the hook. There was no way he could kill LaTàge in Central Shores, then be back at Cyprus to catch an Uber at one-forty.

And if Ruby's keycard timestamps were to be believed, she couldn't have done the deed, either. The only member of the LaTàge Squad left on my list was Katz. Yet, Miguel's Instagram pictures and his snide comment about trying to shake off Katz at the club so he could sneak away for a hook-up with Ruby, all but confirmed Katz wasn't LaTàge's killer.

The whole squad seemingly had alibis, so where did that leave me?

More and more, I felt deep down that Laila, not LaTàge, was the intended victim of this terrible crime.

By the time I rounded the front of the police station, the protesters had moved themselves to the steps of town hall. I hoped their unruly presence would tip the scales in Chief McInnis's favor and ensure the Community Safety Center got expeditiously approved.

Three murders in the past five months. I shook my head at the sad notion. Central Shores citizens had a right to be concerned.

Fifteen minutes later, I parked Jolly outside the small strip mall located on the northwest side of town. This section of Central Shores was off the beaten path for tourists, and its businesses catered more to locals. Besides Trove and Bright Auras, the building contained a liquor store, a dive bar, and a pizza place.

The smell of Saucy Sid's thick, doughy crust made my stomach rumble. While Thea and I planned to meet "after lunch," I'd been so busy this morning that food slipped my mind.

I scanned the parking lot, not spying my sister's Jeep among the parked cars. I checked my phone and noticed a text had come in while I'd been driving.

Running late. Be there in 10.

Thea had sent the message nine minutes ago, so I seized my opportunity to grab a pepperoni-filled stromboli from Saucy Sid's.

I leaned against the back of Jolly while I ate the yummy, cheesy handheld, enjoying the balmy September weather. It also gave me the perfect vantage point to survey Bright Auras while I waited for Thea's arrival.

Unlike the rundown storefronts of Saucy Sid's and Al's Liquors, Bright Auras had a fresh coat of paint and pretty artwork painted on its large windows. A flowery welcome sign adorned the front door, although it didn't look like the store currently had any patrons.

My phone vibrated, and I expected it to be another update from Thea. Instead, it was Amanda.

What do you think of this header? Accompanying the text was a link to our shared Google Drive.

We frequently exchanged messages like this, getting feedback from each other about our client projects. I tapped on the link and admired the beautiful vector image of a woven wicker tub full of peonies underneath the words THE FLOWER BASKET. **Love it. The font is on point.**

Thanks, she replied immediately. **Going to send for Viola's approval, but wanted your feedback first.**

Je'pproved. I sent her a smiley face emoji wearing a beret. **Everything ok?** We'd touched base about our client workload earlier in the morning during our daily Zoom huddle, but I hadn't heard from her since.

Just peachy. Once I'm done with this, I'm signing off for the weekend.

Btw, I talked with Daddy about Omar's business deal.

Oh? I'd honestly forgotten I'd asked her to look into The Buchanan Group's relationship with Central Sports.

Daddy was pretty surprised when the announcement came out. Omar hadn't mentioned it to him. He hasn't touched base with him post-op, either.

I licked some extra sauce from the corner of my mouth as I finished off my lunch. Interesting. Thurston Highgrove was usually so tapped into the business goings-on in Central Shores. It struck me odd that Omar hadn't discussed this huge venture with him. **Hmm, I see. Well, thanks for checking.**

Ofc. Will see you Monday!

I smiled as I typed out, **Happy Friday!** On Mondays, we met up and worked at either my place or Amanda's. It was so amazing being your own boss.

As soon as I sent the message, I heard the guzzling sound of an SUV approaching. Thea's Jeep made a sharp turn into the parking lot and skidded to a halt right in front of me.

"Sorry I'm late!" Thea called, having rolled down the passenger window. "Mom got held up at town hall with something, so I had to prep Dad to watch the trips." While our parents normally watched Thea's kids during the week, it was usually under Mom's supervision. I could only imagine the chaos our dad and the triplets would get into by themselves.

I waited for my sister to finish parking before responding to her initial comment. "I hope emergency services is on speed dial."

She chuckled dryly as she arrived at my side. "I told Dad no power tools, but I suspect it went in one ear and out the other." Thea hiked her massive purse on her shoulder. "You ready for Operation Rumor Mill?"

I eyed her bulging bag. "You got a tent in there or something?"

"Puh-lease. This is nothing." She sighed. "Just a badge of motherhood."

If I had wanted children of my own, I'm sure her comment would have stung. Instead, I just shuddered. "Better you than me. Shall we hit Trove first and get that out of the way?"

"For sure," Thea said as we headed toward the thrift shop with determined strides. "Jenny, the room mom we're shopping for, says she's a fan of your blog, so you pick out something according to your tastes."

I saluted my understanding. Trove's inventory often reflected the wide range of socio-economic statuses inhabiting Central Shores. From designer labels to department store brands, the second-hand clothing shop had a little bit of everything.

A perfumy musk washed over us as we entered. Miriam Hoyt, part owner of the store, greeted us from behind the counter. She appeared to be labeling a massive pile of floral-patterned skirts. "Coco! Thea! Well, how nice to see the Cline girls out and about together."

We smiled politely. Back when we were inseparable kids, we traversed the town as soon as Thea was able to ride a bike. But as we'd grown older, we'd also grown apart, so it wasn't often folks in Central Shores saw us as a duo. The sudden thought made me surprisingly sad.

"Hi, Miriam," I replied with a wave. Before opening Trove with her sister-in-law ten years ago, Miriam had worked as a part-time children's librarian at the Central Shores Public Library. She'd been the designated reader when Thea and I attended storytime. "We're on a mission to find some scarves."

"I just got some new ones in." Miriam dropped what she was doing and came around the counter. She smoothed back her flyaway gray hair before ushering us closer. "From a Mill Row resident." Her blue-eyed gaze twinkled knowingly.

Thea rubbed her hands in anticipation. Accessories from a Mill Row closet were bound to be divine.

Miriam escorted us to the back corner of the spacious room, where two display trees, draped with scarves, stood. "These branches contain the newest items."

"Jackpot!" Thea began sifting through the goods.

Miriam chuckled. "I'll leave you girls to the hunt. Just holler if you need anything."

I studied the huge collection. "Thanks, Miriam. We will."

She returned to her tagging at the front of the store, leaving Thea and I to make our selection in relative privacy.

"Can you imagine just giving this away?" Thea held a gorgeous cream Calvin Klein piece against her skin.

I was about to shake my head until I remembered my beloved Tom Ford shades, lost to Ruby. I glanced around the shop, spying a display of sunglasses on the far wall. "How about this for your room mom?" I held up a beautiful coral-and-periwinkle chiffon scarf. "Easy enough to handwash, too."

"Ooo, good point." Thea admired the watercolor-esque fabric. "Yes, this will go well with her complexion."

With my personal shopper duties completed in record time, I left Thea to check out the sunglasses. I could at least see if any of them resembled my favorite pair.

I was just sliding some white-framed Cole Haan shades up the bridge of my nose when Trove's front door opened. Out of the corner of my eye, I spotted a lean figure clad in black sporting bleach-blond, spiked hair cut short.

I nearly choked on my tongue as I did a double take. *Omigod.* Katz Keaton had just sauntered into Trove.

Miriam chirped a friendly greeting from behind the counter. "Hello, there. Anything I can help you with?"

"No, thank you. Just looking." Katz's low, gravelly voice was filled with melancholy.

Miriam dampened at their lack of enthusiasm. "All right. Holler if you need anything," she cheerfully added.

Katz bobbed their chin, listlessly surveying the store. I stood absolutely rigid, still a bit starstruck at seeing the much-hyped designer in the flesh.

Katz's blue gaze halted on me. They squinted before saying, "Coco Cline, is that you?"

I swallowed back my excitement at being recognized. "Yep! Hi, Katz. Fancy meeting you here." I motioned awkwardly around the sales floor, also hoping to flag down my sister in the back. I didn't want to make a big scene, but Thea would flip over meeting Katz. Unfortunately for my kid sis, it appeared that she'd chosen an inopportune time to visit the fitting rooms.

Katz reached for a rack that featured colorful bohemian-style blouses. "Thrift stores have always been a place where I can forget my problems." Sorrow pinched their pale, drawn expression.

My heart twinged for them, remembering the sad story Ruby had shared about Katz's upbringing. "I'm so sorry about LaTàge."

"Thank you." Katz hung their head. "I still can't believe she's gone."

I knew we all grieved differently, but Katz's emotive response felt like the first genuine reaction I had encountered amongst the squad. "How are you holding up?"

"Not well." Katz moved to another rack, this one filled with leather jackets. "I can't wait to get out of here." They paused and shot me an apologetic glance. "No offense."

"None taken." I smiled softly. "I can't imagine what you, Miguel, and Ruby are going through."

Katz scoffed. "Oh, you don't need to worry about Miguel and Ruby. They'll be just fine without LaTàge."

The lingering malice in their words made me think Katz knew all about Miguel and Ruby's relationship. Had LaTàge? "What about you? Will you be all right? I know you and LaTàge were close." I bit my lip from inconsiderately asking about Katz's clothing line.

"She was my family, and I was hers." Katz's eyes grew moist. "I have no idea what's going to happen to me now. LaTàge—" They broke off, clenching their fists. "No, I can't think like that," they said, almost to themselves, "I have to focus on making sure LaTàge is not forgotten."

Katz must have seen the myriad of questions floating through my mind, for they added, "So much is up in the air right now, but I have to bring the vision LaTàge and I had to life. I just have to."

"Vision?"

Katz held up an interesting pair of lacy white pants. "For my label. A label that will design fluid clothes for all identities and sizes. We wanted everyone to feel loved by my clothes, the way LaTàge said they made her feel. Wearing my designs, she told me she could forget all her problems and just feel happy, beautiful, and safe."

I got a little choked up hearing this moving mission. It also made me wonder what problems LaTàge—or Laila—was trying to forget. "I'm sure you'll find a way to make it happen, Katz."

They nodded. "Oh, you bet I will. If anything, I'm more determined than ever. LaTàge *will* launch, no matter what."

"LaTàge?" I repeated, raising an eyebrow.

Katz's cheeks reddened. "We were going to name the label 'Katzàge,' but I want her name to be remembered forever."

"A fitting tribute," I murmured appreciatively. As an awkward silence fell between us, I wondered what I should do. It felt grimy to question Katz about LaTàge's murder when Miguel had already provided them with a rather concrete alibi. Especially since they were clearly grieving.

"I'm sorry I didn't get a chance to meet her." I offered a sad smile. "LaTàge sounded like an amazing person. And friend."

"If only I had stayed with her." Katz's gaze grew haunted. "I'm going to regret leaving her at that house for the rest of my life."

"Where did you end up going?" I asked as innocently as I could manage.

Katz shrugged. "Some club in some town."

Very helpful. I bit back the response.

"I don't remember much about the night. I kinda drank too much." Katz's cheeks grew red with embarrassment. "I'd been planning to go back to LaTàge's rental after I was done at the club, but I was too out of it to remember her address for my Uber. All I could find in my emails were the deets for the hotel. God, maybe if I hadn't been so sloppy, I could have saved her."

I assessed Katz as they processed this startling realization. "Or you could have been attacked by the person who killed her," I reminded them.

Katz didn't seem to hear me. Instead, they grabbed a teal-and-pink zebra-striped kimono on a nearby hanger. "LaTàge would have loved this." They clutched the piece to their chest, tears leaking down their cheeks. "I should get going, but I'm glad we got to chat, Coco. I'm sorry it wasn't under better circumstances. I was looking forward to working with you."

"Me too." I wasn't about to ruin the moment by offering CoA's help with their label launch. Jasper would be so disappointed in me.

Katz bid me goodbye and went to pay for the wild kimono. Once Miriam bagged their item, Katz Keaton gave me a final wave and disappeared out the front door, leaving me to wonder if they were the one person in the world truly grieving the loss of LaTàge.

"Hey, what's with the sad face?" Thea's voice startled me from my pensive reverie.

I shook my head as I eyed the armload of clothes she carried. Shopping for the trips' room mom, indeed. "Have you been in the fitting room this whole time? You won't believe who you just missed."

I quickly filled her in on my conversation with Katz.

"Ack! Why didn't you come get me?" Thea stomped her foot.

"Katz was practically having a breakdown," I rebuked her thoughtlessness. "I didn't want to make things more uncomfortable for them."

Thea managed to summon a contrite look. "You said Katz touched these?" She held up the lace pants that were about two sizes too big for her.

I nodded and stifled a snort as Thea tossed the celeb-endorsed item onto her growing pile.

"Did you get any deets about LaTàge's murder?" she lowered her voice. Not that Miriam was paying us any attention.

I shook my head. "Katz was at Cyprus with Miguel when LaTàge was killed, so I didn't think it prudent to pepper them with questions."

Thea frowned. "They still could have provided intel."

Her reprimand made me question my decision, but whatever the case, it was too late now. "We're here to pursue the Laila angle, remember?" I muttered through gritted teeth.

"Fine, fine. But first, let me show you this amazing coat I found." Thea yanked my arm toward the back corner of the store.

Ten minutes later, we left Trove feeling the adrenaline rush a good shopping trip could incur. Thea had bought not one, not two, but *six* new scarves, five dresses, three pants, and four blouses, and I had found a replacement pair of Ray-Ban shades that fit the bill. Add to it that Miriam only charged twenty bucks for them, and I was riding high.

"Okay, ready to tackle Sage next?" I gave Thea a once over. My sister had never accompanied me on one of my sleuthing exploits before, and I was a little nervous about how she would handle the experience.

Thea straightened her shoulders and tossed her ash blond hair back. "Born ready. I spent all last night coming up with a plan to get her to talk without blowing the secret about LaTàge."

I raised my eyebrows. My little sis was leagues ahead of me. "Go on."

"Just follow my lead, okay?" Thea held my gaze. "Trust me."

To my own surprise, I didn't hesitate. I extended my arm toward Bright Auras. "After you."

If Trove's musty perfume had been strong, Bright Auras upped the ante. I stifled a cough as we strolled through the doorway, its main floor about a third of the size of the large thrift shop.

Contradictory to its name, Bright Auras was dimly lit and incredibly chilly. I had to stop myself from digging out one of Thea's new scarves and using it as a shawl.

We scanned the tight, slightly claustrophobic aisles, seeing no sign of human life. Only rocks of all shapes, colors, and sizes greeted us.

"Hello? Anyone here?" Thea called out, her voice trembling slightly.

I reached for my sister's hand, suddenly nervous. The last time I'd walked into an empty store, I'd found a dead body in the back. *Oh, God. Sage...*

"Helllllloooooo!" Thea raised her voice, drawing out the word. "Anyone? Sage?"

Sharing spooked looks, Thea and I inched our way through the shop, twitching at every moving shadow we encountered. No one stood behind the register, although there was a mug of tea, still steaming, left on the counter.

I pointed at the mug. "Someone's gotta be here." *Please, please, please...*

Thea gripped my hand harder. "Should we call the police?"

"Hold on, we haven't checked—" I broke off, nodding my head toward the painted midnight blue door at the back of the room. The carved wooden sign read OFFICE.

Thea inhaled so deeply, I'm sure they heard it two towns over. "Okay, let's check."

My mind whirling with a slew of terrible possibilities—*Sage had been attacked, Sage had suffered a fall, Sage had been killed by whoever killed Laila*—I took the lead and hurried toward the door.

Without even knocking, I grabbed the handle and yanked it open to find Sage Hattape sitting on top of her desk, completely naked.

Chapter Twenty-Three

"Omigod!" Thea, Sage, and I all shrieked in unison.

"Sorry. So sorry!" I slammed the door in Sage's face, trying to scrub the image seared into my eyeballs. Even though Sage was a beautiful woman with a body she should be proud of, I didn't need to have every inch of her ingrained into my brain.

"Uh, um, just a minute!" Sage's panicked voice squeaked from behind the door.

Thea tugged at my arm, and for a second, I thought she wanted to retreat. But her expression suggested otherwise. Her cheeks were bulging, trying to contain the laughter already flowing from her teary eyes.

Relief that we'd found Sage very much alive triggered the same reaction within me, and soon, the two of us were giggling as stealthily as we could. We couldn't risk Sage being completely embarrassed if we wanted to pump her for deets about her friendship with Laila Jackson.

A minute later, Sage opened her office door, still in the process of buttoning her floral maxi dress. Her dark bronze skin was flush, and she visibly winced when she saw us waiting. "S-sorry you had to see that. I must have forgotten to put the Be Back in 5 sign up."

I smiled warmly, trying to alleviate the awkwardness flooding the room. "We're just glad you're all right, Sage."

"Yeah, when you didn't respond, we thought something terrible happened to you." Thea bobbed her head, wringing her hands for emphasis. "You know, with a killer on the loose and all."

Sage smoothed back her luscious raven hair. "Oh my. I didn't even think…

I'm sorry to worry you. I had my AirPods in, and they block noise pretty well." A rosy blush returned with a vengeance. "I was just sending my husband a special treat."

Inadvertently, Sage had given us the perfect opening. "You and Rand celebrating something?"

"Yes. Today is the eighteenth anniversary of the day we met." Sage's gaze softened. "He transferred into my honors sophomore English class, and the rest is history."

"Such an adorable meet cute," Thea gushed. "I remember you telling me about it during our Buddy-to-Buddy sessions. Gosh, I couldn't wait to grow up and fall in love." She clasped her hands, batting her eyes in a dreamy manner.

Yeesh, tone it down, Thea. I chuckled inwardly at my sister's acting skills. "Well, it's great that you're still keeping things spicy," I added.

Sage giggled nervously. "I try."

"I hope Rand returns the favor." Thea folded her arms in a huff. "Goodness knows Lucas needs step-by-step instructions if I want him to do something romantic for me."

"Oh, Rand worships the ground I walk on," Sage said with a flippant flick of her wrist. "He's always been a doting hubby. He's taking me to Beaufort's tomorrow night for a special dinner."

"But isn't your anniversary today?" Thea's nose wrinkled.

Sage shrugged. "Well, Rand goes out to Harper's with the guys every Friday night."

I shared a covert glance with Thea. *Always the doting hubby, huh?* I debated how we should broach the subject of Laila without Sage clamming up or getting suspicious. We couldn't very well ask Sage outright if Laila and Rand had slept together, not without totally unmasking our true intentions for being here.

"Is there something I can help you with?" Sage, newly composed, tilted her head in question. "Or did my impromptu peep show ruin the chance of a sale?"

We all shared a polite laugh.

"Actually, I'm looking for something that might help calm the kiddos before bedtime." Thea's gaze did a quick sweep of the shop. "I'm a bit desperate, so I'm willing to try anything."

Sage's brow furrowed. "While I'm not thrilled with my life's work being labeled as an act of desperation, I do have some recommendations for children."

Thea grimaced at her faux pas. "Sorry, that came out wrong."

"Don't worry. I've learned to embrace the skeptics." Sage's lips curled upward. "However, part of a crystal's energy comes from its connection with the crystal holder. You might find you get a bigger benefit if you bring your children in to see which crystal speaks to them."

I visualized the destruction the triplets would leave behind being set loose in a store filled with sparkly baubles.

Based on Thea's pale face, she could picture the chaos, too. "You know, I was telling Coco about our time together during the Buddy-to-Buddy program. Such fond memories, right?"

Smooth, Thea.

Sage did a double take at the sudden change in subject. "I guess so. I remember being really happy I got you. Some of your classmates were total weirdos."

Thea snorted. "Yeah, remember when Gregg Morgan set fire to Arnold James's windbreaker with the lighter he brought from home?"

Sage shuddered. "Oh, God, yes. How could I forget? Your classroom smelled of burnt plastic for weeks."

"Luckily, Beth and I had desks by the window, so you and Laila Jackson didn't have to suffer as much when you visited." Thea paused and held up a finger. "Wow, now there's someone I haven't seen in forever."

I resisted the urge to high-five my sister right then and there. "Gosh, you're right. I haven't seen Laila since her mom's memorial." *And even then, I hadn't really seen her at all.* I hoped Sage bought the lie.

Thea turned her innocent gaze to her former mentor. "You guys were practically glued at the hip during high school. What's Laila up to these days?"

"I wouldn't know." Sage's reply was clipped, her lips drawn in a thin line. "I haven't spoken to her in over a decade."

"Huh?" Thea gawked. "Why? What happened? I thought you guys were going to take over the world. Always talking about wanting to write fashion articles for *Vogue* or something."

Sage clasped her hands in front of her, her expression neutral. Although, from the looks of her clenched knuckles, I could tell she was anything but disinterested. "We just grew apart during college, that's all."

"Oh, that's too bad." Thea stuck her bottom lip out in a slight pout. A move I'd seen the triplets do on many occasions. "Laila always seemed like such a sweetheart."

"Well, you'd be wrong." Sage's unaffected façade shattered, her features growing tight. "Laila showed her true colors a long time ago, and I certainly wouldn't wish that kind of negative energy in anyone's life."

Now we were getting somewhere. And based on her responses, it was also clear that Deja's strange remark to Amanda about Laila "being dead" had never made its way through the Central Shores gossip channels.

"Yeesh. Sounds like Laila did you dirty." I placed a hand on my hip, waiting for Sage to expound.

She bristled, then hugged herself. "I'm just glad she had the decency to leave town after her mom's funeral and never show her face again."

Thea reached for a nearby purple rock—amethyst, perhaps—and handed it to Sage. "You look like you need this."

Sage sniffed as she accepted the offering. "Ugh, sorry. I guess after all this time, I still haven't let go of what she did."

"Honey," Thea *tsked* like a wise old Southern woman, "unless she slept with your man, it's never worth it to hold onto such anger."

When Sage's gaze dropped to the floor, my heart skipped a beat. Man, Thea was killing it. "Omigod, Laila did not!" I gasped for effect.

Sage's expression grew panicked. "N-no! That's not what happened," she protested unconvincingly.

Thea draped a sympathetic arm around her. "Laila was like a sister to you. How could she do something so awful?"

Sage's fists balled at her sides. "Rand swore it was a drunken mistake. I mean, we all went to Rand's house and got pretty blasted after Trisha's funeral. I ended up falling asleep fairly early in the evening, and Rand said he was just trying to comfort Laila when things got out of hand."

I frowned at her hypocritical retelling of events. She'd somehow forgiven and gone on to marry Rand, yet still held anger toward Laila after all these years.

"Oh dear," Thea murmured. "When did he tell you?"

Sage placed the purple crystal back on the shelf. "Laila came crying to me at my place the next morning."

I resisted an eye roll. So, Rand hadn't even had the cojones to tell his girlfriend about his infidelity. What a stand-up guy.

"I thought Laila was crying over her mom, but then she told me what had happened. Or *her* version of the story." Sage scowled.

"What did she tell you?" I asked.

"That Rand came on to her, and that she was so drunk and upset about Trisha, she didn't try very hard to stop him."

Once quite high, my opinion of Rand Windham was now below sea level.

"I was so mad, I broke a tribal relic my dad had on display in our foyer." Sage stared down at her hands as if they had acted on their own. "I told Laila I never wanted to see her again, and that was that."

"You really haven't spoken with her since?" Thea raised an eyebrow. "What about when she visits home?"

Sage scoffed. "Like Laila would ever come back to Central Shores."

The certainty in her tone surprised me. "Why not?"

"Laila had major beef with her dad over how the Jacksons handled her mom's cancer diagnosis. Laila blamed him big time for Trisha's death." The contempt that had been in Sage's voice earlier had waned. "She almost didn't come home for the memorial in the first place. Her cousin, Deja, was the one who guilted her into it." Regret lingered in Sage's dark gaze.

"Deja?" Thea's brow wrinkled in confusion. "Why was she involved?"

Sage shrugged. "Deja and her brother, Terrance, didn't have the most stable home life growing up, and Deja was always super envious about how much Laila's folks doted on her. So, by the time Trisha passed away, Laila was barely speaking to her dad, and Deja tried playing peacekeeper to get into her uncle's good graces."

"How did Deja guilt her?"

Sage stuck her tongue out. "Money, of course. She told Laila that Omar wouldn't pay Laila's college bills if she skipped the memorial service."

"That's cold." I whistled in shock.

"It turned out to be a total lie, and when Laila discovered Deja had tricked her, she got super upset." Sage sighed. "That's why we went out drinking after the service. Laila needed to blow off steam. She'd lost her mom, she loathed her dad, and her cousins basically drew a line in the sand against her."

Interesting. A greater understanding of Laila began to take shape. With her best friend hating her guts and her family life in shambles, I could definitely see why Laila had sought to leave behind her old life and reinvent herself as somebody else. But had a decade-old family feud come back to haunt her?

Sage shook her head, as if just now realizing how much tea she'd spilled. "Sorry to unload all this drama on you. Normally, I try to stay above the rumor mill."

"Oh goodness, don't apologize." Thea batted the notion away. "The whole town's been turned upside down by this latest murder. Can you believe it involved such a popular influencer?"

"I don't really prescribe to 'influencers' or social media in general." Sage's nose wrinkled, looking like she smelled something foul. "All that online negativity is bad for our chakras." She gave a nervous chuckle. "Oops. Sorry, Coco. I didn't mean—"

"No worries. To each their own." I held my hands up in surrender. "I take it you weren't a follower of LaTàge?"

"La-who?"

"LaTàge," Thea repeated. "The woman who was *murdered.*"

"Oh, right." Sage tapped her chin thoughtfully. "Rand did mention her name when he told me the news. He was pretty shocked by it. Was she really *that* popular?"

"Um, is Michelle Obama an icon?" I countered.

Sage's clueless expression had me wondering if she hadn't turned on a TV or been outside her store in the last ten years.

"I mean, it is shocking. Another murder in Central Shores? What is this place coming to?" Thea wrapped her arms around her. "Makes me wanna get home and squeeze my babies. Which I actually have to do soon." She glanced at her watch. "We better get going. It was nice talking to you, Sage. I'll bring the kiddos by so they can pick out a crystal." Thea looped her arm through mine and dragged me toward the entrance.

"Bye, Sage. Good to see you—" I was momentarily assaulted with the memory of just how much of Sage I'd seen. "Hope you and Rand have a lovely anniversary." I gave her a teasing wink before the door slammed shut behind us.

"That was a quick getaway." I turned to Thea. "What gives?"

"I really do have to pick up the kids and take them to gardening club." Thea shrugged. "And it didn't seem like Sage had the slightest clue Laila was LaTàge."

"I think you're right." I mulled over our strange conversation. "Although, kinda sus she mentioned Rand being so torn up about it."

Thea tilted her head. "Yeah, our friendly neighborhood yacht broker doesn't seem like he'd go for LaTàge's makeup tutorials." She tittered at her own sarcastic remark.

A growing theory bloomed in the back of my mind. "What if Rand knew about Laila's transformation? What if he had been keeping in touch with her behind his wife's back all these years?"

Thea's lips pursed in the shape of an O. "Ooh, that would be a juicy secret to keep."

"Maybe that's why LaTàge kept Miguel on the payroll as her pretend boyfriend. She had to keep her real dating life under wraps."

A dubious expression spread across Thea's face. "Now, I think you're reaching, Big Sis. LaTàge's life was out in Cali. Rand has very much stayed in Central Shores. You can't tell me someone wouldn't have seen them cavorting around town in, what, the thirteen years since Laila left?"

"I didn't say they were carrying on *here.*" I rolled my eyes at her lack of imagination. "Laila could fly anywhere in the world as LaTàge. And how many times has Rand mentioned all those boat shows he attends."

Thea's jaw dropped. "Omigod, you're right. You think boat show is code for hook-up?"

I shrugged. "I mean, anything is possible."

"So, what?" Thea countered. "You think Rand got wind Laila was coming to town, met her in Crescent Hills, and killed her for some reason?"

That's exactly where my mind had gone. "I think it's worth talking to him to see what he has to say. If anything, he can tell us more about this beef Laila had with her family."

Thea deflated. "While I'd love to tag along, I really have to get going." Her disappointment was evident. "Sorry."

Her dejected response made me realize that this had been the longest my sister and I had gone without bickering in probably twenty years. "Hey, you were a rock star in there. I can't thank you enough for helping me with Sage. It's opened a whole new realm of possibilities." I wasn't embellishing, either. Not only did Rand and Laila's relationship require further exploration, Sage's comments about the Jackson family also warranted consideration. Omar might be off the hook, due to his surgery, but what if Deja or Terrance had gotten wind of their estranged cousin's return to town and it hadn't been a happy reunion?

Thea grabbed my arm. "You're not going to speak with Rand alone, are you?"

I smiled at her concern. "No way." A tentative plan hatched in my mind. "Sage told us Rand was forgoing an anniversary dinner tonight to hang with his buddies at Harper's. Should be easy enough to intercept them."

Thea clucked her tongue. "You going up against a bunch of drunk goons? Sounds like a *great* plan." Her tone suggested otherwise.

"It will be fine." I hurriedly calmed her apprehension. "I'll rally Jasper and Charlotte to help me. Now, get your butt over to *gardening club.*" I summoned my best highbrow accent. "And thanks for the help today."

"You're welcome." In a surprise move, my sister gave me a quick squeeze.

"Be careful. And keep me posted."

"Will do." With that, we climbed into our cars and went our separate ways. As I drove home, I dialed Jasper's number, hoping he wasn't in the middle of a work call.

"Is this what we do now? Are we old?" Jasper greeted me with a whine, making a joke about the fact I was calling him.

I giggled. "Sorry, I'm driving, and I wanted to catch you before any other evening plans popped up."

"They already have, but I need an excuse not to go." Jasper's tone was pleading. "I made them when I was feeling sociable."

I brought him up to speed on the chat with Sage and how I suspected Rand might still be in touch with Laila, given his reaction to LaTàge's death. "He's worth talking to, and I know where he'll be tonight." Unlike Deja, my former bully who was married to a federal judge, and Terrance, who I barely knew, Rand would be much easier to track down and approach.

"Harper's?" Jasper's distaste for the pub oozed through Bluetooth. "My pores are going to clog up just walking through the front door."

"We can eat someplace else ahead of time."

"Fine. Is Charlotte coming?"

I pumped my fist in victory. "I'm gonna call her right after we hang up."

"K, bye." Jasper dropped the call faster than Disney dropped a problematic actor.

Charlotte was even easier to convince. "Oh, good. I needed some dinner plans. Deacon is working overtime. Chief McInnis sent him to assist the county lab with their evidence processing."

"Ooo, has he shared anything helpful?"

"I haven't pestered him on it. I figured if I'm not asking him questions, he's not asking *me* questions. Trust me, I know from you and Hudson how annoying it is to have an overly concerned partner." She chuckled at her teasing comment. "But if we do uncover something useful to the case, we'll have to figure out a smart way to come clean, Cokes," she stressed. "Without getting you or Gavin in hot water with the chief."

Her remark hit home a somber point. I had uncovered absolutely nothing in my investigation so far to lead me to a killer. Rumors and gossip abound, but very little facts. "Come over for dinner at my place, then we'll head down to the strip together."

Chapter Twenty-Four

By the time I parked Jolly in the garage, I had a few texts waiting. Hudson checking in, a work question from Amanda, and a message from Willow.

Should be arriving around 10 AM tomorrow. Gotta love a red eye. Need us to pick up anything on our way from the airport?

I shuddered at the early-morning itinerary. **All set on my end. You guys gonna sleep off the trip tomorrow, or will you be up for an adventure?**

Always adventure. Show us where all your cases have been solved!!

I laughed, shaking my head at Willow's ghoulish enthusiasm. Both she and Reade had turned me on to just about every mystery-themed podcast out there. **Will be a short outing.** I sent several silly-faced emojis.

I'm sure you'll find a way to entertain us. See you soon xoxoxo

I messaged Hudson and Amanda as I made my way into the comforts of my home, checking in on Hudson's NYC trip and answering Amanda's question about LinkTree configurations. I had a few hours before Jasper and Charlotte arrived for dinner, so I made a beeline for my office to record a few collaboration videos. I had recently partnered with DrinkLee, an eco-friendly water bottle company. Each bottle contained its own filter, providing the user with clean, healthy water. Even better, DrinkLee's profits went to providing clean water in underdeveloped countries. Companies that strove to make a positive difference were my favorite kind to work with.

Beyond DrinkLee, I needed to record a comment for an anti-bullying campaign I'd been invited to participate in. The campaign, Kind4Good, was bringing together celebrities and public figures from all walks of life. We were supposed to record inspiring messages, and then Kind4Good would blast them across social media, reminding users—especially teens—the importance of being kind to one another.

My office was already complete with a "recording studio" (a.k.a. a well-lit corner with a blank wall), so the most time-consuming aspect was trying to film my remarks without flubbing my lines. Even with a teleprompter app I'd downloaded from the App Store, it took me five tries to get the water bottle sponsorship right and seven to get my ask for kindness across. By the time I finished, I'd given myself less than twenty minutes to prepare dinner for Jasper and Charlotte. Luckily, tapping an order into UberEats took me less than twenty seconds.

I opted for Thai food, ordering an array of dishes from Lemon Tree, a yummy place in Cherry Springs. With a pledge from Uber that our meal would arrive in half an hour, I raided the kitchen to make some cocktails for my friends. As I grabbed various ingredients, I begrudgingly checked X for activity. While the original doctored post about my LaTàge remarks had been deleted, it had not stopped the thousands of screenshot captures and uploads. The gross image popped up every few tweets on my timeline, most people calling out the cruel deep-fake. I had a ton of notifications, some supporting me, some believing the horrible, doctored words were real.

That's our girl. We luv u, CC!

Go get them, Coco.

You are a hack.

You're a disgusting, elitest fake.

Hope u die, too.

I shuddered at those last menacing words. This was how we treated people now? Tossing out death threats, willy-nilly?

I stared hopelessly as the barrage of comments went on. My account was a complete mess. Maybe I should do what so many people had done before and just delete it.

I quickly stopped myself from the rash action. I used X to promote amazing companies and people trying to do good in the world. I shared inspiring stories, fun fashion tips, and great books to read. I wasn't going to let some trolls put an end to that. I could stick out their nastiness until I cleared my name and found LaTàge's killer. *If* I ever decided to leave the platform, it would be on my terms, not theirs.

I muted the app and focused on my latest drink creation. I nestled a lime slice on the rim of each cocktail glass, assessing my work. While I may have been hopeless in the kitchen, I'd been known to concoct a yummy, boozy beverage or two. Tonight's feature was lime seltzer, vodka, Grenadine, and pineapple juice.

"A Sparkling Sunrise," I coined its name before taking a sweet sip. A play on a Vodka Sunrise, it was light, crisp, and refreshing. Perfect to give us liquid courage to talk to Rand and his pals.

Jasper and Charlotte arrived together, having walked from their homes up the street.

"If I have to play nice with Rand and his friends, I'm going to need a *lot* of liquor," Jasper announced as he strolled into my condo.

Charlotte tossed her messy braid over her shoulder. "You didn't exactly dress for Harper's." She eyed his pale pink slacks, white shirt, and paisley linen jacket with a smirk.

"If I ever *dress* for Harper's, have me committed." Jasper rolled his eyes as he grabbed a drink and took a swig. "Ooh, bubbly. I like it."

Charlotte perched atop a barstool before taking a glass. "Mmm, delish. Is this a new cocktail for *Trending Topic?*"

"You think it passes muster?" I countered.

"For sure." She grinned as she enjoyed another sip. "So, you really think Rand and Laila have been having an affair all this time? That's kinda hard to imagine, Cokes. Rand always speaks so sweetly about Sage when he comes in for coffee."

I drummed my fingers on the countertop. "I don't know what to think. It struck Thea and I both strange that Sage thought Rand seemed outta sorts about LaTàge's death."

"Mm-hmm," Charlotte murmured. "I'm not one to judge—"

"I am." Jasper snorted. "And there is no way Rand is watching LaTàge's videos for the *information* in them. If he's on her page, it's for the visual stimulation."

"But ogling women on the Internet isn't a crime," Charlotte pointed out. "Or we'd have more people *in* jail than out."

I waved a hand to get their attention. "We need to determine if Rand knew LaTàge was Laila. Or if Rand had kept in touch with Laila all these years."

Charlotte's brow furrowed in concentration. "If the LaTàge Squad abandoned her for The Glades, maybe Laila reached out to an old pal so she wouldn't have to be alone."

"Exactly." I gave her a thumbs up. "If we can get Rand's alibi for Sunday night, all the better."

"What about this drama with Deja and Terrance?" Jasper asked. "It's almost as if they wanted to push Laila out of her dad's life so they could swoop in and be his golden children. Omar's pretty loaded."

Charlotte shrugged. "Well, from that standpoint, their plan worked out. Terrance has been Omar's right-hand man for as long as I've been in town. He's set to take over Central Sports as far as I'm aware."

I mulled over the situation. "What if he found out from Omar that Laila had come back? Maybe Terrance panicked and thought his status would be in jeopardy if Laila and Omar reconnected."

"How very *Dynasty*." Jasper pressed his fingers together. "All right, now to address the elephant in the room." He glanced around. "I was promised dinner. Where is it?"

Charlotte and I laughed at his priorities. "En route. I got caught up making some content, so I ordered Thai."

Putting the case aside for the moment, we chatted about the busy workday and bombarded Charlotte with questions about her upcoming cohabitation adventure.

"Have you decided on a date?" Before she answered, my phone buzzed with an alert that UberEats was here. "Hold that thought."

I dashed to the front door, collected the bulging bag of food, and thanked the driver. Within two minutes, my friends and I had unpacked our feast.

"Okay, move-in date. Dish," I prompted Charlotte before stuffing my face with a sauce-drenched bite of pad cee eew.

Charlotte popped a spring roll in her mouth and chewed thoughtfully. "Deacon's lease is up October first, so we're aiming for the end of the month."

Jasper rubbed his hands gleefully. "This means a Halloween-themed housewarming party, right?"

"Housewarming? I've lived there for like, three years."

Jasper frowned at Charlotte's rebuffing. "All right. Then a Halloween-themed welcome to the neighborhood party."

"Why don't we just throw a Halloween party?" I tossed the idea onto the table. "Since you're so desperate for one."

Charlotte giggled. "Speaking of parties, are we really not having a big blow-out for your birthday?"

"Twenty-*nine*." Jasper pretended to choke.

I stuck my tongue out at him. "Please. *You're* going to be thirty before me."

Charlotte cleared her throat. "Thirty is the new twenty, I'll have you know." She was a year older than the both of us.

"Yeah," Jasper said with a snort, "when you *look* twenty." He eyed Charlotte's smooth skin with obvious envy.

She ignored him. "So, really no birthday party?" She stuck her lip out in a pout.

I sighed. "Nah, we're doing a celebratory dinner with Hudson's family, since they're in town for Irene's big award."

"Ugh, that sounds so adult." Jasper shivered with disgust.

Once our stomachs were filled to the brim with Thai cuisine, we cleaned up and had another round of drinks before summoning another Uber, this time to drive us to the strip. By seven, our friendly driver dropped us off in front of Harper's Pub, the smell of fried food hitting us at full blast, even from out on the sidewalk.

Jasper pulled a handkerchief from his pocket like he was some Southern gentleman. "Remind me why I'm here?" He dabbed at his brow.

"Bodyguard duty." Charlotte threaded her right arm through Jasper's and then grabbed my hand.

With our plan in motion, we breezed through the open doorway. Harper's was one of the oldest establishments on the strip, and its décor reflected as such. Faded, sea-green paint peeled away from drab walls adorned with fishing nets, lifeguard rings, and buoys. The sailor vibe was strong.

Jasper took a sharp intake of breath. "I don't even remember the last time I was in this place."

"Our first Christmas home after turning twenty-one." I recalled the memory vividly. Well, more like the painful morning after.

"Ahhh, yes." Jasper stroked his chin sagely. "Let's not have a repeat of *that* messy scene."

I didn't plan to. Our target sat at the bar in raucous conversation with five other guys sitting on the stools around him. Rand Windham didn't look like a person who'd murdered someone recently, but then, cold-blooded killers had an annoying habit of doing that. He wore Carhart pants and a long-sleeved t-shirt. His casual ensemble was night and day from the business attire we'd seen him in on Tuesday. His sleeves were rolled past his elbows, revealing a tattoo of a turtle on his left forearm. The symbol was very familiar to those in the Delaware area. It was the crest of the Lenape people, his wife's tribe. The tribute might have been cute if I didn't know he'd cheated on Sage by forcing himself on her best friend.

"Ready?" Charlotte glanced from Jasper to me. "Brent Porter's a regular customer. He's right next to Rand. Works for his dad's deep sea fishing company. I can break the ice, so Rand doesn't think we're here to interrogate him."

Jasper studied the guy sitting farthest away from Rand, his gaze suddenly sparkling. "That dude's delts could break anything."

I focused on the object of Jasper's attention. "Hey, that's Eli Holt." I recognized the ruggedly handsome face right away. He'd been in Thea's class.

"Eli, hmm?" Jasper's eyebrow inched upward.

Charlotte tugged us forward without warning. "Hey, Brent. How's it going?" She released my arm and flicked her hair back with a friendly smile. "Hi, guys." Charlotte nodded in acknowledgment to everyone sitting around him.

A grin broke out across Brent's sunburned face. "Well, hey, Miss Charlotte. Nice to see you out from behind the counter."

Charlotte's giggle held every man's attention. "Right? Happy Friday. What are we drinking?" She leaned forward to scope out everyone's drinks, strategically revealing her chest.

Brent and his friends all took the bait. All except Eli.

He waved at me. "Hey, Coco. Nice to see you. Thea doing well these days?" Eli had been in Thea's friend group and often hung out at our parents' house when we were younger.

"She is. In fact, I just went shopping with her earlier today." I beamed, pleased that I wasn't totally invisible while Charlotte worked her mesmerizing magic.

Eli's mahogany gaze slid to Jasper. "Hey, there, I'm Eli." He held out a muscular, tan arm in introduction.

"Jasper."

Eli's dark eyes widened. "No way, Jasper Hastings? Hey, man, long time no see. You might not remember, but we went to school together. Gosh, you look great."

"Thanks. I could say the same about you. What do you press?" Jasper placed a hand on Eli's biceps, his curiosity radiating from his porcelain skin.

Not interested at all in gym talk, I turned back to the crowd Charlotte had under her spell.

"And then the guy says, 'Sorry, I meant sugar, honey, not honey, sugar.'"

Her retelling of some coffee mishap got a better reception than Pedro Pascal hosting *SNL*. Rand and his friends howled with laughter at Charlotte's bland story. *Sigh.* Beautiful people really could get away with anything.

I listened to their conversation for a few minutes before gathering up the nerve to make my move. I tapped Rand's shoulder to try and tear his attention from Charlotte. "Hey, Rand. Congratulations are in order, I hear. I stopped by Sage's shop today, and she told me you guys are celebrating eighteen years."

Rand begrudgingly turned away from Charlotte and grunted. "Thanks."

"You two doing anything fun to celebrate?" I egged him on.

"We are." His response was clipped.

My forced smile felt like it was beginning to crack. What was going on here? The friendly camaraderie Rand had displayed earlier in the week was nowhere to be found. "Nice. It's so sweet you take the time to commemorate things like—"

"Sage told me about your visit, Coco." Rand's stormy gaze narrowed on me as he sipped his beer. "Sounds like she got a little chatty about the past."

I swallowed a sudden burst of apprehension. Had Rand guessed we were here to talk with him about Laila?

"I'd appreciate it if you didn't broadcast my mistakes on your little blog or something." His words were a low grumble. "I hurt Sage enough all those years ago. I've been doing everything in my power since not to hurt her again." His right hand went to the turtle tattoo on his other arm.

I examined his stern expression. "Your dirty laundry is not mine to share."

"Thanks." He dipped his head in gratitude.

As a strained silence settled between us, I scrambled to figure out how to bring Laila up naturally in the conversation without making Rand's hackles rise. Maybe I could peddle something about Omar's surgery—

"Yo, boss. Turn it up!" Brent motioned wildly for the bartender to jack up the volume on the TV hanging above the bar. "It's Gavin!"

My jaw dropped to see a clip running of Lloyd and Gavin McInnis standing behind Detective Harriet Forester on the national nightly news. While I couldn't really make out what they were saying due to the rowdy noise filling the pub, the big ticker running along the bottom of the frame told me what I needed to know.

The real life of LaTàge – Influencer was former Central Shores resident, known as Laila Jackson.

"*Laila?*" Jasper read the words off the flat screen for everyone around us to hear. He shook his head in pretend astonishment. "For real? How is that even possible?"

I felt a vibration against my thigh and realized my phone was going nuts with alerts. I pulled it from my romper pocket and skimmed the lock screen. Every major news app and outlet was blasting out the bulletin. Twenty-five-year-old LaTàge was actually a thirty-two-year-old Central Shores native.

The secret was out.

"Rand, you were tight with Laila back in the day, weren't you?" Brent knocked his pal's arm. "Did you know about this?"

Brent, doing God's work for me.

Rand didn't respond right away. He just stared, open-mouthed, at the TV.

"You in there, bud?" One of Rand's friends I didn't recognize waved a hand in front of his face.

"Huh? Yeah, wow. Sorry, guys." Rand rubbed his temples, looking a bit shaken. "No, I had no idea Laila—hang on." He stopped and whirled on me. "Is *this* why you went to see Sage?" Rand seethed through a harsh whisper. "Did you know the murdered influencer lady was really Laila?"

Gone was the appreciation for my discretion he'd shown earlier. Now, he was just angry.

"You trying to pin this on Sage?" Rand's enraged spittle misted my cheeks.

As I flinched, Jasper stepped in front of me. "Cool it, bro." Drawing himself up to his full height, he made for quite the imposing figure.

Rand's nostrils flared. "I'm not your *bro*, Hastings." He leaped from his barstool, and even though Jasper had a good five inches on him, he still flexed his fingers into fists.

"Now, now, gentlemen." A smooth, charismatic voice interjected. "Let's not ruin a Friday night, shall we?"

To my surprise, Ronny Durnst placed calming hands on Jasper's and Rand's shoulders. Dressed in a glossy navy suit, he looked almost as out of place at Harper's as my paisley-patterned bestie. Next to him stood another familiar and very concerned face: Noelle Paige, the library director.

Jasper folded his arms across his chest. "I couldn't agree more." But he still refused to relax his stance.

Rand blinked a few times as if finally seeing the disadvantage his smaller frame had. "Whatever. I'm outta here." He shrugged off Ronny's grip and headed for the exit.

"Hey, what about your tab?" Brent called after him.

The door slammed in response.

Chapter Twenty-Five

"What's got Rand's panties in a bunch?" Brent turned back to his pals, ignoring Jasper, me, and our unexpected savior.

Ronny arched an eyebrow. "Are you two okay?"

"I've never seen Rand so angry before." Noelle wrung her hands. "What happened?"

"We're fine." I thanked Ronny with a relieved smile before turning to Noelle. "And honestly, I'm not sure what just happened," I fibbed. "I made a comment about how Sage and Laila used to be friends, and Rand kinda blew up." I pointed at the TV, still broadcasting the news about LaTàge's identity.

Noelle's gaze skimmed the news ticker. "What? The girl who died was *from* Central Shores? Oh dear, that's not good." She glanced nervously at Ronny as she threaded her fingers through his.

"No, it's not." Ronny draped a protective arm around her.

It was then I put two and two together, remembering the gorgeous bouquet of flowers on Noelle's desk at the library. Ronny had to be the new man she was seeing. The two of them made a lovely couple.

But obvious alarm sprouted across both their faces. "What's wrong?" I asked.

Ronny sighed. "Call me crass, Coco, but I was hoping LaTàge had been killed by someone within her little circle. To learn she's actually got ties to the area…" He trailed off.

"Makes it harder for you to sell your Crescent Hills homes as beautiful, safe havens," I guessed, doing my best to keep disapproval out of my tone.

Ronny pinched his nose. "Actually, it makes me wonder if Derrick and I hadn't loaned her the 713 place whether she'd still be alive."

The remorse in his comment filled me with guilt for assuming the worst. "I'm sorry," I hurriedly interjected, "that was rude of me to say. Honestly, I know how you're feeling. LaTàge—Laila—was here to see me, after all."

Ronny was about to reply when his attention darted to the front of the pub. "Derrick?" He squinted. "What're you doing here?"

Derrick Payne, Ronny's business partner, hurried toward us, clutching a to-go bag. "Sorry to crash your date night, Ron, but I was grabbing food at Zaddick's when a call came in. We've got a problem. A big one." He nodded a wordless hello to Jasper, Noelle, and me before turning back to Ronny. "Jeffords is getting antsy about the project, what with the recent news." Derrick motioned over his shoulder to the TV, still reporting on LaTàge and Laila.

A tempest danced across Ronny's face. "If Jeffords pulls out, we'll be on the hook for the whole thing."

Jasper and I shared questioning looks, unsure who this "Jeffords" person was.

Derrick wiped invisible sweat off his brow. "I know. I'm sorry. This is all my fault. I never should have suggested this whole LaTàge setup. And I definitely shouldn't have turned off the security cameras for her." His skin had become sickly pale.

"Hey, I signed off on the rental deal." Ronny clapped his partner on the back. "Don't beat yourself up too much. It was a good promotional effort. As for the security cameras…well, you said it's what the client wanted. Who are we to say no?"

"Yeah, but if Jeffords pulls out—"

Ronny hushed him. "The business will be fine. We'll manage." Ronny then turned to kiss Noelle on the cheek. "Sorry, beautiful. Derrick and I should head back to the office and prep to deal with this."

"Of course." Noelle squeezed his arm in reassurance. "Feel free to come over when you're done."

Ronny and Derrick wished Jasper and me goodnight and left Harper's together in deep, troubled discussion.

"Poor guys," Noelle murmured as she watched them leave. "Ronny's been so stressed about selling those houses. Now, add a nervous investor into the mix."

"Is it really that bad?" I prodded. "Don't they already have several offers on the LaTàge house? Won't that quell any stakeholder qualms?"

"On *her* house, yes," Noelle countered. "But nothing on the other homes in the neighborhood." She twisted a loose strand of her dark hair. "I hope Ronny can survive this. He and Derrick really can't take any more bad press."

"More bad press?" I raised my brow.

Noelle sighed. "They've had complaints leaked about their construction sites. Not treating employees fairly and such. Ronny says it's just noise from disgruntled people they've fired. But add to that the heat they took from environmental groups for bulldozing the woodlands...he and Derrick certainly don't need anything else on their plate."

I bobbed my head in wordless agreement.

Jasper smoothed out the non-existent wrinkles in his jacket. "Well, I need a drink to soothe my nerves. Ladies?" He motioned toward the bar in invitation.

Noelle politely declined. "Ronny and I were just preparing to leave when Rand had his little outburst." She *tsked*. "I swear, that guy gets into it with someone every week."

"Really?"

"You bet." Noelle nodded. "We often come here for Happy Hour. We like the dive-bar charm," she admitted. "Rand's drunken tantrums, though, I could do without. Or being interrupted by Derrick with some work emergency. He tends to overreact at the slightest inconvenience, to say nothing of *his* temper if something doesn't go his way. It's become a real pain." She then chuckled, and I realized the irony of her words, given Derrick's last name.

"The guy does look like the poster child for Workaholics R Us," Jasper joked.

Noelle smiled, then released a weary sigh. "It would be nice if Derrick met someone who made him reexamine his work-life balance. Maybe then Ronny and I could actually enjoy some time alone together."

I was too engrossed by Noelle's remarks about Rand to comment. So, his anger issues weren't solely related to matters involving his infidelity. It seemed his personality became volatile with alcohol. Was that solely to blame for his earlier eruption, or had I hit a sore spot?

Rand's telling retort echoed in my ears. *You trying to pin this on Sage?*

Odd. His paranoid thoughts immediately had gone to his *wife*, not himself, as if he believed Sage was the one with motive to kill Laila.

Eli saddled up to Jasper and me once Noelle wished us goodbye. "Everything all copacetic here? Dang, what had Rand so riled up?"

"We were just asking ourselves the same thing," I answered with a weak smile. "I guess the news about Laila Jackson really hit him hard."

Eli placed a hand on his hip. "Well, I'm glad someone is mourning her loss. Heck knows the Jackson family won't be."

"What do you mean?" Jasper's eyes widened.

My heart skipped a beat. "You're close with the Jacksons?"

"You could say that." Eli rubbed the back of his neck, suddenly sheepish. "I'm gearing up to be one of the principal trainers for Terrance's new fitness clubs."

I tilted my head with confusion. "Terrance? Don't you mean Omar?"

Eli shook his head. "Nah. Terrance is the one leading the project, what with his uncle stepping back from the company. He's the one who hired me." He showed off his impressive biceps. "I make my living from these bad boys."

"Looks like you work them pretty hard." Jasper's lip curled upward.

I ignored their flirting, still processing what Eli had let slip about Omar stepping back from Central Sports. Neither my dad nor Thurston had suggested a change of leadership was in the works. "So, Eli, tell us about Laila. Did Omar or Terrance ever mention her?"

"Nope." He shook his head. "Only one who did was Deja."

Jasper and I shared interested looks. "I didn't know Deja was involved with Central Sports."

"She's not," Eli clarified. "But she comes around the office a lot to talk with her brother. That's when Laila usually came up. With Omar's recent health problems, Deja thought Laila should be summoned back to deal with her dad rather than leaving the burden on the two of them."

"Summoned back?" Jasper's brow furrowed. "From where?"

"No clue." Eli shrugged. "And that was always Terrance's reply. How could they bring her back when they had no idea where she was?"

I pointed at the TV screen. "Do you think they had any inkling Laila was *the* LaTàge?"

Eli burst out laughing. "Oh, God, no. Terrance would have been after her to be the face of the new fitness centers if that were the case."

Now, there was an interesting angle. Had Laila's death resulted from an endorsement deal gone wrong? Before I could ask Eli more about Terrance and Deja, Charlotte stumbled into our little huddle.

"Time for me to make a graceful exit," she whispered, her knowing expression sending me a telepathic message. She wanted to get out of there before the guys at the bar took her friendliness as a sign for them to get handsy.

"Oops," she gushed loudly as she straightened. "These drinks are starting to get the better of me."

I winced at her bad acting, but by now, most folks seated along the bar were a few too many drinks in to realize her tipsiness was all a charade.

"And that's our cue to get going." I looped an arm around Charlotte's waist, letting her lean on me.

She theatrically sagged against my side.

Eli chuckled. "Looks like someone went a bit too hard, too early. It was great seeing you, Coco. Jasper, nice catching up." He shook Jasper's hand.

I noted how their handshake lingered, neither seeming to want to let go. *What do we have here?*

Jasper, Charlotte, and I held off on any case-related chatter until our Uber driver deposited us in front of my condo.

CHAPTER TWENTY-FIVE

"Nightcap?" I offered. "We've got lots to dissect."

Charlotte shook her head. "I'm covering the café in the morning. But I will take something cheesy if you have it."

Swapping booze for brie, the three of us gathered around my kitchen counter, noshing on slathered crackers.

"What are our thoughts on Rand?" Jasper asked through a mouthful.

I drummed my fingers on the cool marble. "His riled-up response has me totally confused. He was worried I suspected *Sage* of Laila's murder, not him."

"Deflection tactic?" Charlotte posed.

"Or genuinely concerned husband?" Jasper added.

I chewed on the savory, smooth brie. "I'm inclined to think the latter. He'd clearly been drinking, so his uninhibited behavior would have been more reflexive than anything."

"Either way, Rand didn't do us any favors by announcing to the world that Coco's poking into the investigation." Jasper's brow furrowed.

Charlotte's eyes pinched with worry. "Don't go there. I was only a few seats away, talking to Brent and the others, and I didn't hear what Rand was getting so amped-up about. The pub noise drowned him out."

A tight thread within my chest loosened. "That's a relief." The last thing I needed was more gossip about me and LaTàge—*Laila*—finding its way to the Internet.

Jasper smeared another cracker with gooey cheese. "I guess you have a point. Eli was leaving for the restroom when Rand Hulked out, and he didn't seem to know what made Rand go berserk either."

"Speaking of Eli, his comments about the Jacksons were enlightening." Obviously, there was *much* more about Eli that I wanted to discuss with Jasper, but for now, I'd keep my focus on the case.

"That's just the tip of the iceberg." Jasper bobbed his head. "While you guys were chatting with Rand and his bros, Eli told me some pretty juicy details about the new Central Sports development project. Turns out, *Terrance* has been the one working with The Buchanan Group to rebrand the company with a super boujee name." He lowered his voice, as if revealing a scandalous secret. "The Atheluxe Club."

I choked on my cracker. "You're joking."

"Nope." Jasper grinned. "Eli says the rebrand campaign officially launches next week."

"That quickly?" I raised my eyebrows. "Will Omar even be fully recovered from his surgery?"

"Get this," Jasper continued, "according to Eli, Omar did some kind of temporary leadership transfer to Terrance before he went under the knife."

"What, like the 25th Amendment?" Charlotte scoffed.

Jasper nodded. "And while Omar was *in surgery*, mind you, Terrance set all these plans in motion with TBG. He'd been meeting with them for some time but downplaying the seriousness of their talks with Omar. Once Terrance had control of Central Sports, he went full throttle. And Eli told me that Omar was not happy with his nephew when he woke up from surgery and found out. Terrance had to shut down a staff meeting to go to the hospital and hash it out."

"This Eli guy seems to have been pretty chatty," Charlotte mused with a teasing grin.

Jasper shrugged off her remark. "You're not the only one who can loosen a man's tongue."

While they fondly bickered back and forth, I mulled over Jasper's stunning revelation. Terrance had made a major business decision while his uncle was having heart surgery? What the heck was going on with the Jackson family? Did Deja have any idea that her brother was going to basically usurp their uncle's legacy? And was Laila's return to Central Shores a catalyst or factor? My head spun with questions.

"With all this new info, our next move should be to chat with Deja and Terrance." I began to clean the crumbs off the countertop, our evening snack demolished. "See what they know about Laila's return to Central Shores."

Jasper nodded in agreement. "If she came back to get money from her dad, Terrance might have been worried how it would affect his plans to rebrand."

"How do we get them to talk?" Charlotte asked. "With the world finding out about LaTàge being Laila, I'm sure they're going to be flooded with interview requests and the like."

I skillfully arranged the dishwasher like a game of Tetris. "I'll think of something."

Jasper rose from his seat. "Be sure to loop us in, Cokes. No going off on your own, spur of the moment." He eyed me sternly.

"Hey, I've been a good girl, haven't I?" I held my hands up to defend my honor.

Charlotte chuckled. "Keep it up. And keep us posted."

I walked my friends to the front door. "Hudson's sister and her wife arrive tomorrow, so my hostessing duties will take priority for the weekend. We'll sync up on Monday to chat with the Jacksons."

I bid my besties goodnight and waited until they were out of sight before heading back inside. A twisting snake of paranoia wound its way up my spine as they vanished into the darkness. A killer was out there, and even though Charlotte and Eli hadn't heard Rand's abrupt accusation, someone else very well could have. I didn't need a target on my back. Again. Nor did my friends. I debated texting Jasper and Charlotte to let me know they made it home, when they both sent similar messages.

J: Good work tonight, #SleuthSquad.

C: We'll figure this out! Sleep well!

I smiled at their texts. They were only sticking their noses into this case because I was invested, and my rep was on the line. I was so grateful to have them in my corner, and I promised myself I would do everything I could to protect them.

Chapter Twenty-Six

I spritzed one last blast of floral Febreeze on the living room sectional just as the doorbell chimed a chipper greeting.

Smoothing my mint-green sundress and adjusting my high-top ponytail, I dashed to the front door and threw it open.

"Hey, ladies!" I beamed before opening my arms in warm welcome.

Willow Michaels squealed as she wrapped me in a crushing hug. "Eek, sis, look at you! Gorgeous as always."

"Me? Look at you!" With her pixie cut, high cheekbones, and smooth brown skin, Willow could be Zoe Saldana's twin. Irene and Winston Caruthers sure had some killer genes. "Both of you are just stunning." I turned to Reade and hugged her with equal fierceness. "I love the new color." I motioned to her lavender-dyed bob.

"Thanks. Thought it might be fun." Reade reached for her hair, her California-tanned cheeks blushing. She might have been a ruthless publicist out in LA, but outside of work, she was a total sweetheart.

"Come on in." I ushered them inside, reaching for their bags in the process. "You made great time."

Willow reluctantly released her duffle. "The drive here was perfect. No traffic for miles."

Reade nodded. "It felt great to be behind the wheel again."

"Oh, that's right. You've gone total public transit." I led them toward the stairs leading up to the barely used second floor.

Willow snorted. "Hardly. We end up Ubering everywhere. But still, it's better than paying an arm and a leg for the parking garage in our building."

Reade paused at the top of the landing, her eyes widening as she stared out the huge ocean-facing window that greeted her. "Oh, wow. I could get used to this."

I giggled at her admiration of the breathtaking beach view. "Please do. You guys have the whole upstairs to yourself." I dropped their bags in the guest bedroom I'd made up this morning.

"I'm so glad we could fly out for Mom's award." Willow draped an arm around her wife of two years. "Although I'm a bit miffed my little brother didn't drop everything to be here to greet me." Her tone was clearly teasing. Only a year-and-a-half apart, Hudson and Willow were extremely close.

Reade rolled her eyes. "I guess the allure of all those prime-time talk shows was just too strong."

"Hudson is really bummed that he's stuck in NYC until the end of the week," I admitted. "But I've got some tricks up my sleeve. You won't even miss him." I began to lay out an itinerary that included shopping, drinking, and spa treatments.

Willow flicked her wrist at all my hard prep work. "Um, this sounds lovely and all, but I don't hear anything about LaTàge."

Yikes, she had wasted no time getting to the point. "What about her?" I tilted my head, the picture of innocence.

Reade flopped onto the bed. "You're telling us you're not involved?" She arched a suspicious eyebrow.

I swallowed. "I'm not *involved*, per se."

"But you *are* looking into her death, aren't you?" Willow pressed.

I bit my lower lip. I didn't want to lie to either of them, but I didn't necessarily want to advertise what I'd been up to.

"Knew it. Pay up, sweet cheeks." Willow held a palm out toward Reade, who begrudgingly dug through her purse before slapping a twenty-dollar bill into Willow's hand.

Reade sighed. "I thought you'd want to stay out of the spotlight on this one, Cokes. The optics are pretty whack."

I winced at her assessment. As a publicist to several high-profile celebrities, Reade knew the ropes better than anyone. "Trust me, I don't like being labeled a harbinger of death any more than the next person, but if I can catch a killer and clear my name—"

"It's a win-win." Willow beamed as she plopped onto the bed next to her wife. "See? Told you. The girl's got a white-knight complex."

Reade folded her arms, struggling to keep a straight face. "The news about LaTàge's alter ego has really turned the tide against her. People in LA are ready to wash their hands of her."

I frowned at the harsh truth.

"It's ironic, really." Reade scoffed before continuing, "Celebs lie about themselves 24/7, but the moment *they* catch someone in a lie, the offender is dead to them." Her eyes widened as she comprehended her own words. "Oops, poor choice of metaphor."

"Do you think LaTàge's double life got her killed?" Willow turned her questioning gaze on me.

I could see that neither woman was going to let this go. Reluctantly, I replied, "The more I dig into things, the more I'm inclined to believe Laila Jackson's ties to Central Shores came back to bite her."

"Ooo, do tell." Willow eagerly rubbed her hands together.

I invited the girls downstairs for homemade iced coffees while I filled them in on my adventures over the past few days. As I laid out the LaTàge Squad's grievances, I also highlighted Laila's strained relationships between family and old friends.

By the time I'd finished, Willow and Reade wore matching expressions of confusion.

"I mean, this whole bankruptcy thing seems like the smoking gun." Willow pointed out. "You need *money* to keep up in LA, and if LaTàge—Laila—was defaulting on her payments..." Her words trailed off. "People have killed for less," she added after a moment. "We've seen it time and time again in our true crime book club, The Killer Reads."

Reade finished off her iced coffee with a smack of her lips. "Yeah, but according to Coco's findings, Ruby, Katz, and Miguel all have alibis."

"Ruby and Miguel have been pretty forthcoming about the case. I only chatted with Katz in passing." I recalled our run-in at the thrift shop. "I was too hesitant to ask them details about the murder. They seemed pretty upset."

Willow nudged her wife's toned arm. "Think you could get Katz on a call? Wasn't your firm trying to woo them for their new label launch?"

"Unfortunately, the account went to Irving." Reade stuck out her tongue after she mentioned her coworker. "I can't call Katz up without starting an internal blood feud."

"We wouldn't want that." I needed to switch topics. It wasn't fair of me to drag these girls into my investigation when they'd flown across the US to hang out and have fun. "So, it's a gorgeous day. Why don't we head down to the strip, and I can show you what's new since you last visited."

Willow's shoulders slumped. "We're getting benched as detectives, already?" She gave a defeated fist bump to Reade. "Guess we didn't bring our A-game."

"I appreciate your enthusiasm, but I honestly wouldn't mind taking a little break," I confessed with a shrug. "It's been a week, to say the least."

Reade came to my side. "Oh, gosh, girl. I bet it has." She shuddered. "That whole thing with the deep fake tweet must have been rough."

I nodded. "I'll be glad when another scandal pops up. You got anything you can leak?"

"Ha! I would if I could." Reade patted me on the forearm. "I'm sure something will break soon."

"Speaking of *Scandal*, I want to check in on Fitz and Olivia before we head out." Willow had her smartphone in her hand an instant later.

Fitz and Olivia were the Michaelses' two adorable Mini Shelties that they'd rescued from an Alabama kill shelter. "How are the fur babies?" I followed their account @fitzlivfurlife on Instagram.

"Precious, as always." Willow held out her phone. The screen showed a live feed of Fitz and Olivia snuggled in a posh pet hotel room.

Reade leaned over her wife's shoulder, making cooing sounds at the screen. "What a time to be alive, right? This cute pet boutique kennel on Wilshire Boulevard has an app that lets us see them whenever, wherever."

I studied the fuzzy canines with interest, although my mind wandered to

Hashtag, Laila's Miniature Pinscher. Was he staying at some fancy place like this? Would Laila's money troubles leave the poor little guy in the lurch?

The duo fawned over their fur babies for a few more minutes while I turned off the lights and grabbed my bag.

"Ah, best day of our lives, holding those pups in our arms for the first time." Willow sighed as she slipped her phone into her denim jacket pocket. "And that includes our wedding."

Reade laughed in agreement.

I felt a little pang of envy in my chest. *I'd love to have a dog* and *a wedding.* Someday…

As I herded Reade and Willow toward the garage, I caught sight of their rental car. A steel-blue convertible Mustang. How very Nancy Drew. "Um? Yes, please!"

Neither needed convincing to leave Jolly at home. My two-door MINI wasn't the roomiest passenger car, and the Mustang would let us drive around comfortably enjoying the mid-September sun.

I gave Willow directions to the strip from the backseat and settled in to check my blog comments. The meditation post had gone live earlier in the morning, and for the most part, the reception was positive. Of course, there were a few off-color comments about LaTàge's murder from usernames I didn't recognize, but a majority of my subscribers appreciated the information while also sharing their own meditation recommendations. Even though I'd been questioning my influencer life lately, those thoughts went out the window when it came to the incredibly supportive *Trending Topic* community. My dedicated followers always seemed to have my back.

Speaking of dedicated followers, I texted Amanda—a surprisingly huge fan of my blog—to see how she was doing. I hadn't heard from her since our Friday client check-in.

Willow had just turned onto the strip when Amanda responded with a video message. It was a selfie of her lying on a white-and-navy lounge chair beside a massive pool. Much bigger than the one in her backyard.

Lookin good. I replied. **Spa day?**

At CCC. Want to come join me?

I was about to politely decline her invite to the Crestview Country Club when something in the video message caught my eye. No, not something. *Someone.*

"Is that Deja?" I watched the short clip again, pausing when a tall, lithe figure appeared at the opposite end of the pool. I zoomed in on the frame and sucked in a breath. It *was* Deja Reinhardt née Jackson.

I debated my next move for all of a second. **Any chance I can bring my almost SILs with me?**

Of course! The more, the merrier. Would luv to meet them.

With Amanda onboard, I proposed a change of plans to my guests. "Remember what I was telling you guys about LaTàge's cousin IRL, Deja?"

"The one who married a federal judge?" Reade asked.

"And had some weird beef with Laila?" Willow added.

Dang, they had come to play. "Apparently, she's hanging poolside at the local country club today."

Willow and Reade shared knowing looks. "Where can we grab swimsuits?" Willow glanced at me from the rearview mirror.

I grinned at their willingness to play detective alongside me. "We can duck into Quincy's. She might have some on clearance." Quincy's Finds was a favorite haunt of mine, although, with designer-label inventory, the boutique tended to be on the pricey side.

Willow parked along the strip, and within five minutes, we were perusing clothing racks. As luck would have it, Quincy Novak, the owner, had two swimsuit displays still on the floor, even though the rest of her inventory clearly embodied the autumn season.

Willow selected a sexy red bikini that looked gorgeous against her bronze skin, while Reade bought a fierce neon orange cut-out one piece. I grabbed a rather conservative blue and white striped suit boasting a one-shoulder design. I wouldn't have minded something a bit more fun, but it was the only suit Quincy had in my size. I wasn't going to complain too much because it was a Ralph Lauren at a seventy percent discount.

"What a cute little shop." Reade gushed as we headed back to the car. "High-end, but with charm. A place like that would explode in LA."

I took her word for it. The wild world Reade inhabited as a publicist was much different than my small-town influencer lifestyle.

"So, what's our strat?" Willow asked as she zipped up the coastline toward Crestview.

I chuckled at her gusto. "You guys are going to enjoy the pool and relax a little bit. I'll strike up the conversation with Deja."

When Willow pouted, Reade *tsked*. "The three of us can't descend on this woman, Wills. Especially a lobbyist. She'll know we're working her for information." Reade adjusted herself in the passenger's seat so she could meet my gaze. "We'll be on guard duty. In case things go south."

From the rearview mirror, Willow's eyes widened. "You think she killed LaTàge—Laila?"

"I don't know what to think right now." My gaze drifted out to the glistening Atlantic. "With her brother making all these big moves at his uncle's business, I want to get a read on her. From what Sage—Laila's high school bestie—told me, Deja and Terrance did not get along well with her."

"Drama!" Willow announced with a singsong trill.

We chatted about the case during the remainder of the drive. I half-hoped talking things out with the girls would spark a better theory, but going through all the intel only made me realize how little I'd uncovered.

"If Ruby, Miguel, and Katz all have alibis," Willow began with a wave of her finger, "that kinda suggests that 'LaTàge' wasn't the target. Laila had to be the one the killer was after."

"You know, if the house she was staying at was really that fancy, you'd think there would be security cameras or something." Reade huffed.

I shivered, remembering what I'd learned from Ronny and Derrick. "Get this. Apparently, there was a camera system in place, but Laila asked one of the developers to turn it off to protect her privacy."

Willow nearly swerved the car off the road. "Are you serious? That's tragic."

I nodded sadly.

"It always drives us nuts when we listen to a podcast and hear that the security cams around crime scenes are useless." Reade tutted her disappointment. "Have any forensics been found?"

I giggled nervously at her question as Willow turned into the Crestview Country Club. "Well, I'm not *that* much in the know." But Reade's mention of the police had me wondering how Gavin and the others were doing, now that the news about Laila Jackson was out in the world.

While Willow followed signs for the valet drop-off, I sent a quick text to check in with my friend. **Hey, Gav. How's everyone doing? Do you need my help with the PD social accounts?** I recalled he'd mentioned me checking their online accounts once the news about Laila was made public.

Gavin sent me a GIF of an unimpressed child. **It's been a roller coaster. Your help sorting thru FB comments would be great. Monday?**

Ofc, I responded and checked my calendar. **I can come by around noon. Great.**

I watched as three little dots appeared on my Messages screen, indicating that Gavin was typing something else.

So, have you found anything?

I debated what I should share with him. I know Gavin had asked me to keep an ear to the ground, but other than gossip and hearsay, I had nothing concrete to back up any of my floundering theories. **Did you know Terrance made some big plays at Central Sports while Omar was in surgery? Launched a plan to rebrand?**

What does that have to do w/ Laila?

Idk, yet. Just thought you might be interested.

Willow pulled the car to a stop in front of an awaiting attendant when another text from Gavin filled my screen. **You suspect Terrance thought Laila's return might wreck the deal with TBG?**

No clue. As Willow, Reade, and I climbed out of the car and strolled toward the club's entrance, I shot off one more text to Gavin. **Have you spoken w/ him or Deja yet?**

Yes. We're capable of questioning next of kin, Coco.

I cursed under my breath. I hadn't meant to offend him. I just wanted to verify what or how much Deja Reinhardt knew about her cousin's death.

I sent a conciliatory thumbs-up emoji before pocketing my phone. I'd circle back with Gavin later.

Inside the luxe lobby, I greeted the club hostess with a friendly smile. "Hi, there. We're meeting Amanda Highgrove."

The young woman glanced up from her tablet, her bored expression breaking into a cheery grin. "Coco Cline, yes? We were told to expect you. Big fan of your content." Her head swiveled to survey Willow and Reade. "Could I get your names, please?"

"Willow and Reade Michaels," I introduced my might-as-well-be sisters-in-law.

"Lovely." The hostess flicked back her long blond hair, revealing a "Fiona" nametag. "Ms. Highgrove is currently at the VIP pool. I'll get someone to escort you." She then mumbled inaudibly into her unobtrusive earpiece.

Reade nudged my side. "Not gonna lie, this feels pretty baller."

I felt my cheeks warm at her sincere compliment. "Come on, you went to Heidi Klum's Halloween party."

Willow shuddered at the mention. "I ended up with cocktail sauce all over my costume. What a nightmare."

As we giggled, a tall, buff, dark-haired man in a khaki-colored linen suit appeared at Fiona's side. "Hello, ladies. Ms. Highgrove is waiting for you. This way, please."

Our guide led us through the main area of the club, allowing Willow and Reade to catch sight of the beautiful sand garden and koi pond that adorned the elegant space. "Who exactly are the Highgroves?" Willow whispered out of the side of her mouth.

I hurriedly explained Amanda's family ties to the area, omitting the fact that Amanda had been a total Regina George à la *Mean Girls* in high school.

For a September Saturday, the Crestview Country Club was bustling with people enjoying the last remnants of summer weather. Once October hit, the Delaware coast could go from eighty-degree days to low fifties in the blink of an eye. But as soon as we were ushered through a hallway marked VIP, the lively chatter and activity buzzing throughout the club died out. Regular club memberships were expensive enough. Not many, even in wealthy Crestview, opted for the VIP experience.

Our guide ushered us down the long hallway and out on a gorgeous white-stone patio deck. Ahead of us sprawled a massive pool, and I had a bit of déjà vu from my trip to The Glades.

The three of us had barely adjusted to the bright sunlight when we heard a melodic squeal. "Oh, yay! I'm so glad you girls could make it."

Amanda glided toward us, wearing a gorgeous navy halter bikini top and white high-waisted bottom. Her kimono cover-up billowed out behind her, making her appearance all the more dramatic.

Willow released a low whistle behind me. "Wow. She's stunning."

Amanda was, indeed, glowing, but I kept my thoughts about why to myself. I wasn't about to reveal her baby news.

"Hi, hi. You must be Willow and Reade." Amanda swooped in with air kisses as she greeted my guests. "So nice to meet you. I hope I didn't derail any fun plans by inviting you here." She turned to me for confirmation, her brow slightly wrinkled with worry.

"No way. The strip will be there tomorrow." I waved away her concern.

Reade shaded her eyes as she surveyed the pool. "I'll take this any chance I can get."

Amanda beckoned us to follow her to a cluster of four loungers she'd commandeered. "It's quiet here today, which is wonderful. I think a lot of folks are either out on the water—" She paused, motioning in the direction of the ocean, located a few minutes east of the club—"or on the links."

The links?" Willow wiggled her eyebrows at me.

I chuckled. "Yes, the very same." The Crestview Country Club golf course had played an integral role in my last investigation that had gone viral.

Amanda waved to a roving staff member. "Drinks, ladies?" She sipped on something pink, which I guessed was lemonade.

I ordered an iced tea, while Reade and Willow opted for Aperol Spritzes. "We're on vacay, and it's five o'clock somewhere, right?" Willow shrugged off my teasing look.

As we settled into our loungers and took a breather, I scanned the area for Deja. Had I already missed her?

"I know that look." Amanda's lips curled in a smirk. "Who are you trying to track down?"

I cringed with guilt. "I saw Deja walking around in the background of the video you sent. I wanted to talk with her about Laila."

"Deja?" Amanda propped herself up on her chair. "You saw her? She didn't say hello to me." Her lips grew downturned. "We might not be close anymore, but she usually keeps it cordial." Her head swiveled around, scoping the pool scene. "Maybe she was heading toward the outdoor restaurant? There's a VIP section that faces the pool." She extended a finger toward the corner of the club building. "The entrance is just over there."

"I'll scope it out." I hopped up from the lounger. "Want me to put an order in for lunch?"

Reade bobbed her head, and Willow licked her lips. "Yes, please. The only thing we've had to eat in the last ten hours is airline food."

I made note of everyone's meal preferences and headed in the direction Amanda had indicated. Although Willow and Reade volunteered to be my bodyguards, I assured them I would be fine talking to Deja in public and that they should go get changed into their swimsuits and relax.

It only took some minor prodding to send them on their way. I appreciated everyone's general concern about my safety, but I couldn't deny that it was a teeny bit annoying. I was perfectly capable of having a friendly conversation without needing an armada to protect me.

I followed the length of the pool before finding a pathway that led me to a covered outdoor seating area.

I spotted Deja's statuesque figure sitting at a nearby high-top table right away. It was hard not to. She was the only person dining outside. Clad in high-waisted linen trousers and a cropped corduroy vest, she looked like a total boss. With her dark hair buzzed close to her scalp and massive hoops dangling from her ears, Deja Reinhardt had to be the trendiest lobbyist I'd ever seen.

Summoning the courage to strike up a conversation with her, I straightened my shoulders and closed the distance between me and her table. "Deja? Is that you? Wow, it's been ages." I plastered on my most congenial smile, trying my best to make this seem like a happy reunion.

Chapter Twenty-Seven

Deja's large brown eyes narrowed as her gaze slid toward me. "Coco. How nice to see you."

I swallowed the horde of nerves that sprouted from hearing her cold tone. Yikes, Deja wasn't even pretending to be happy. "I'm here with Amanda. Highgrove," I clarified. "Just putting in a lunch order." I thumbed over my shoulder toward the outdoor bar.

Deja pressed her lips together and nodded. "I bet you are." She folded her toned arms across her chest.

I faltered under her intense scrutiny, my mind going blank. Deja was used to going up against politicians and activists. She'd eat me alive if she thought I was here to question her about Laila's death. Oh, jeez, I should have approached her with a more concrete plan.

Deja suddenly relaxed her fierce stance, dropping her arms to her sides. "I guess I should have expected this." Her voice rang heavy with defeat.

"Expected what?" I frowned.

She motioned at me. "You. With your questions."

"How do you know I have questions?" I lifted my chin defiantly, miserably failing to play coy.

Deja scoffed. "Come on, Coco. We haven't spoken in years. Then, my useless cousin gets murdered, and you suddenly show up?" She raised an eyebrow. "'The crime-solving influencer?'" Her air quotes felt like a personal attack.

I shuddered at the malice with which she'd uttered, "Useless cousin." She definitely wasn't hiding her disdain for Laila.

"I'm shocked it took you as long as it did to find a way to *conveniently* run into me." Deja sneered. "Some sleuth you are. Although, you're wasting your time. I have nothing more to offer the investigation, to you or the police."

My hands went to my hips in a power pose. "You've spoken with the police?" Of course, I knew she had, but I wanted to convince her to share more.

"Obvi." Deja rolled her eyes. "Or do you really think you're better equipped to handle their job than they are?"

"I just want justice for Laila," I replied softly. "I'd think, out of anyone, you'd understand that."

"Yeah, well, you'd be wrong." Deja reached for the near-empty cocktail glass in front of her. I wondered briefly what she was doing here, dining alone.

"I stopped caring about Laila the minute she blew up my uncle's life." Deja tossed back the rest of the drink. "I've pretended she's been dead for years, so I'm not about to actually start caring now that she really is."

I chewed on my lower lip, trying to make sense of the confusing scene. Deja's words were cruel and hurtful, but her expression and tone suggested that sorrow and remorse wormed within her. "Yeesh, Deja. Have some respect for the dead." I decided to fight fire with fire. "What happened between you guys? What did Laila do to ruin Omar's life?"

Deja flagged down the bartender, wordlessly requesting another drink. "That's none of your business."

My facial muscles went rigid. This was not going well. How was I going to get her to talk to me about Laila's relationship with the Jackson clan?

I took a shot in the dark. "Look, you might not care about getting justice for your cousin, but can you say the same about your uncle?" I used Gavin's earlier request to keep Laila's identity under wraps to my advantage. Omar Jackson had clearly been affected by the death of his daughter, so much so that the police feared it would impede his recovery from heart surgery.

At the mention of her beloved relative, Deja froze.

Bingo. I'd torpedoed her weak spot.

"And what does my private family drama have to do with Laila getting herself killed?" Deja swelled with indignation.

I held my hands up in defense. "I'm just trying to understand what happened in Laila's life that made her decide to cut ties with Central Shores and totally reinvent herself."

"You really think *you* can track down her killer?" Deja studied me, her agitation slowly beginning to fade.

I shrugged. "I've done it twice before."

She actually let out a laugh. "I guess you do have a history of getting results." Her gaze trailed across the deserted dining area, and she released a heavy sigh. "You remember my Aunt Trisha?" Deja motioned for me to take the seat opposite her.

I complied, both nervous and excited for what I was about to learn.

"Laila's mom got sick during her junior year at UCLA," Deja began, her tone quiet. "Aunt Trisha didn't want her illness derailing everything Laila had accomplished at college, so she told Laila she was fine and getting treatment and that all would be well. And at first, that was the truth. Aunt Trisha was responding well to her chemo. But unfortunately, by the summer, her health had taken a nasty downturn, and Laila discovered her parents had been keeping the seriousness of the cancer from her while she finished exams. From all of us, really. It was awful." Deja shook her head at the sad memory.

"That summer, Laila came home, thinking she'd get some quality time with her mom, only to find her struggling to breathe." Deja's gaze dropped as the bartender returned and placed a fresh cocktail on the tabletop. She didn't speak again until we were alone. "Laila was beyond furious, directing most of her anger toward her dad. She accused him of robbing her of time with her mom." Her words broke off as her expression clouded with emotion. "When Aunt Trisha passed away a few weeks later, Laila still wasn't speaking to Uncle Omar. She flew back to LA the next day, saying she didn't want to attend the memorial service with a…a traitor."

My eyes stung with unshed tears, both for Omar and for Laila.

"Trisha's death nearly destroyed my uncle. And then to have his own daughter blame him?" Deja's manicured hand balled into a fist. "I know Laila was in pain, but we all were. We all needed each other. Uncle Omar needed his daughter. But instead of being there, Laila clawed a gaping hole in our family. I knew Uncle Omar wanted Laila to attend the memorial more than anything, so I tried convincing her to come back."

I remembered what Sage had told me about Deja tricking Laila into returning. "How?" I wanted to hear the truth, straight from the source.

Deja took a sip of her drink and winced. "After getting ghosted by her, I got desperate and resorted to some pretty underhanded measures. I told Laila that Uncle Omar was going to pull her college funding if she didn't come home for the memorial." She had the decency to look ashamed. "Obviously, I came clean once she arrived and apologized for deceiving her, but I truly believed she'd left me no choice. Laila then accused me of taking Uncle Omar's side and said she wanted nothing more to do with a family who continually betrayed her. I never saw her again after she left Aunt Trisha's service."

Silence settled over us as Deja's story came to an end.

I scrambled to comprehend everything that had happened between Laila and the Jacksons. I could excuse Deja for her hurtful mistake; she'd been young and grieving the loss of a mother figure. And honestly, anger on Laila's behalf welled within me over how Trisha and Omar had handled the whole situation. I understood why Laila would've been upset with her dad. *Both* her parents had taken the choice away from her to put her college career on hold and spend more time with her ailing mom. But it also sounded like neither Trisha nor Omar had an inkling about how destructive Trisha's illness would turn out to be. Maybe if they had known how limited her time was, Laila's parents would have made different choices. It was a devastating situation, all around.

"Wow, Deja. That's really heavy. I'm sorry." The lies, the betrayal…had this somehow ultimately led to Laila's murder?

Deja shrugged. "Every family has their hang-ups, right?" She then met my gaze head-on. "I know mistakes were made, but Laila was the one who cut us out. Uncle Omar tried to fix things between them, but Laila wouldn't answer his calls or even tell him where she lived. He eventually was forced to give up. I saw how much pain Laila's silence caused him. It's tormented him ever since."

"Well, I appreciate your candor," I said, clasping my hands together. "It's given me a lot to think about."

The corner of her lip curled upward in a sad smile. "Uncle Omar deserves to know what happened to Laila. If you can shed some light on the situation, then by all means, please do. You're more equipped to understand the world Laila was a part of than I am."

I leaned back in my seat. "You really had no idea she was LaTàge?"

"Nope." Deja shook her head. "And I regret every single item I purchased using one of LaTàge's stupid collaboration promo codes. I can't believe I helped fund Laila's boujee lifestyle after all the pain she inflicted on Uncle Omar."

I mulled over her phrasing. It didn't sound like Deja had any notion about Laila's money troubles. "Have you spoken with your uncle recently?"

Deja's jaw tightened. "Of course. I came up from DC on Monday for his surgery. I've been to the hospital to see him every day. Like any good daught—niece would."

I didn't miss her stumbling to cover her awkward gaffe. But if Deja was telling the truth, this meant she wasn't even in the state when Laila was killed at the Crescent Hills house. Once we finished here, I would have to find some way to verify her arrival in town.

For now, I needed to see what more I could learn about Omar. "Did he know about Laila's return?"

Deja drained the rest of her drink. "Yes, although he didn't tell me until after the surgery, once he saw the news about LaTàge on his hospital TV." She set the empty glass down. "About a month ago, he called Laila's old cell phone number on a whim. Turns out, she still kept it active after all these years. When Laila actually answered, Uncle Omar told her that he didn't want to make the same mistakes again. He was having heart surgery to replace a faulty valve and wanted to let her know. To his surprise, she thanked him and told him how happy she was he had called her. Laila said she was so sorry for letting things get so bad between them. She missed him and asked if she could be there when Uncle Omar woke up from surgery."

This news made my chest tighten and each intake of breath felt like a knife. So, Laila's visit to Central Shores hadn't been about getting money from Omar, after all. She'd just been a concerned daughter, wishing to repair the wrongs of the past. Everything my friends and I had assumed about her being broke and needing money…God, I felt like utter garbage.

Tears suddenly trickled down Deja's dark brown cheeks. "But Laila wasn't there when he woke up, and when Uncle Omar saw LaTàge's face plastered all over the news…it was like Aunt Trisha all over again."

I reached out across the table and patted her arm.

"Look," Deja said, shaking me off, "Laila caused our family a lot of grief, but my uncle still loves his daughter after all this time. I want whoever's responsible for her death to be punished. For his sake." She hurriedly wiped her cheeks with a napkin.

Just for Omar's *sake?* I kept my thoughts to myself. "Do you have any idea who might've wanted to kill her?"

"Of course not," Deja snapped. "I have no idea what kind of person Laila became. I imagine one of her LA leeches had something to do with it."

Her comment was less than helpful, given the LaTàge Squad all had relatively concrete alibis. I took a tentative breath before asking, "How did your brother feel about all this stuff with Laila?"

"My brother?" Deja's demeanor turned on a dime. "I think we're done here." She stood to leave.

"Wait!" I reached out, but she batted my hand away.

Her nostrils flared. "Coco, I've been more than forthcoming about our petty family squabbles, in the hopes you'd help resolve this matter, not try to pin Laila's death on one of us."

"That's not what I'm doing," I pleaded as I rose from my seat. "I'm just trying to understand—"

"Understand this. Terrance and I love our uncle, and despite everything that happened between them, we know he still loves Laila. Neither of us would ever do anything to hurt him."

Never do anything to hurt Omar, huh? "What about The Atheluxe Club? Word is that Omar's pretty angry at Terrance about it."

"The *what* now?" Deja's nose wrinkled.

I paused. Her confusion seemed genuine. "While Omar was in surgery, your brother supposedly launched a big rebrand initiative with The Buchanan Group to give Central Sports a glam up."

"What on earth are you talking about?" Deja pressed. It seemed I was now the one in the hot seat. "Terrance wouldn't do something like that without Uncle Omar's consent."

Had Eli Holt lied to Jasper about the big changes happening at Central Sports? Or was Terrance keeping his sister out of the family-business loop? "Apparently, Terrance plans to launch a new marketing campaign next week with the announcement."

"You can't be serious." Deja dug her phone out of her trendy designer bag. "He wouldn't do something like—whatever. I-I need to get going. Bye." She brushed past me, knocking me back a step.

I stared after her, beyond intrigued by her sudden exit. Clearly, Deja was rattled by the news about her brother. But I couldn't yet see how Terrance's business decisions connected in any way to Laila, if they were connected at all.

"*Psst*, Cokes!" Willow's hiss jolted me from my thoughts.

I turned to see her waving from the gate separating the VIP dining area from the pool.

"Everything okay?" Her nervous gaze examined the empty tables that surrounded me.

I winced. I'd been MIA from my friends for too long. "I got carried away chatting with Deja. I'll put in our food orders and be right out."

Amanda and Reade sat with rapt attention by the time Willow and I strolled back to the pool. "So? Did Deja give anything up?" Reade patted the cushion beside her, eager for me to take a seat and dish.

I didn't feel entirely comfortable airing all of Deja's dirty laundry, so I opted for a quick debrief about Laila reconnecting with her dad after years of estrangement. "I've got more questions than answers at this point, ladies."

Amanda's pert nose wrinkled. "I hate to ask, but do you think Deja could've killed Laila, believing she was saving her uncle from more hurt?"

Her question prompted a Google search on my phone. Disappointment greeted me as I scrolled through the results. "At first, I considered the possibility, but Deja said she arrived in Central Shores on Monday to be with Omar during his surgery." I turned the screen so they could all see a *Washington Post* article. "I just checked the latest news for Deja Reinhardt, and she and her husband attended a big DC charity gala Sunday night as honored guests. I don't think she could have feasibly snuck away, driven to Delaware, killed Laila, and returned to DC in one night without raising any suspicion."

Reade nudged me in the side. "We've heard worse during an episode of *On the Case with Paula Zahn*. Just because it's improbable doesn't mean it's impossible."

I studied a glam photo taken of Deja and her hubby schmoozing at the gala. "I still think it's a big leap."

Willow stuck her lip out in a pout. "Well, what about her brother? She sure acted super sus about him."

"He's the only person left on my list to question." I aimlessly navigated to Instagram and searched for Terrance's handle. His personal profile revealed a collection of sailing pictures, but none posted recently.

Reade rubbed her palms together. "Should we try to track him down?"

I replayed my conversation with Deja in my mind. "This might shock you all, but no. I should sync up with Gavin first." I swallowed a defeated lump in my throat. "Deja guessed the moment I approached her that I wanted to talk about the case. While I don't think she'll rat me out to Chief McInnis, if I come knocking at her brother's door, I doubt she'll be as forgiving."

"I agree," Amanda chimed in. "You're playing it smart, Cokes. Deja isn't someone you want to cross." She reached for my hand. "Give Gavin the down low on everything you've uncovered, then regroup."

I stared at the pool tile, uncertainty beginning to eat at the back of my mind. What exactly did I have to share with Gavin? All my theories were drying up. There was still the Rand and Sage angle to explore a bit more; I'd yet to unearth an alibi for either of them. "Yep, you're right. I think I need to step back and give myself some breathing room. Come at everything with fresh eyes." I forced a smile to ease the concern on the three worried faces staring back at me. Willow and Reade had flown all this way for some fun adventures. It was high time I put my hostessing duties before my desire to snoop. "Since we're here, do you guys want to see where my friend Jasper and I took down a killer on live TV?"

Willow and Reade practically jumped out of their bathing suits. "Um, would we ever!" Willow did a shimmying dance.

Reade had the camera on her phone ready to go. "The Killer Reads are going to be so jealous."

I grinned at their morbid enthusiasm. Given my numerous exploits, true crime buffs were extremely easy guests to please.

Chapter Twenty-Eight

Willow, Reade, and I spent the remainder of the weekend enjoying each other's company while partaking in some good ol' retail therapy and revisiting poignant settings from my last two cases. For various reasons, Willow and Reade were fascinated most by Vine, the trendy wine bar that had once been a crime scene *and* the location of a very heated confrontation that had put Jasper on the hook for murder. The current owner, Andre Nunez, wasn't too thrilled by their numerous crime-related questions and picture-taking, but by the end of our visit, they'd bought a ton of wine to be shipped back to California as a monetary thank you.

Monday morning rolled around, and I groaned at my alarm for ending our weekend fun. Willow and Reade had plans to visit with Winston and Irene, leaving me to tackle my CoA client engagements before the three of us met for a late lunch.

Once the girls cleared out of the condo, Amanda came by for our Monday sync, bringing chai lattes and bagels.

"And with that, I think we're all caught up." Amanda snapped her laptop shut once we'd finished reviewing our client projects. Her eyes twinkled. "So, any updates since your chat with Deja."

I shook my head. "Nope. Although I did see this article over the weekend." I pulled up a link to *TMZ* on my tablet. It was a write-up about Katz and Miguel partying at Cyprus the night Laila Jackson had been murdered. The tone was super sleazy, as if trying to guilt the two friends for unknowingly having fun while Laila was attacked.

"Gross." Amanda grimaced for emphasis. "But what's so special about it?"

I pointed to the quotes from Cyprus goers, verifying they'd seen Katz partying into the wee hours of the morning. "It's even further confirmation regarding Katz's alibi. So now, the whole LaTàge Squad is officially off the hook."

"Which leaves?" Amanda prodded.

I sighed. "There's still Terrance to consider, but I can't risk speaking to him without incurring some serious wrath from Deja. I also haven't been able to dig up anything more on Sage and Rand. Sage isn't on social media, so it's hard to track her movements. Rand, on the other hand, is quite active, but was suspiciously quiet on Sunday night." I didn't dare mention how much his booze-fueled outburst at Harper's had spooked me. Otherwise, Amanda would be too concerned about my safety and try to talk me out of investigating him altogether.

"Have you talked with Gavin?" she asked as she tossed her empty chai latte cup in my small office recycling bin.

"Not yet." I reached for my phone in preparation to send him a text. "Since we've wrapped up early, I'll see what he's up to."

Hey, Gav. Wondering if you had time to chat about Laila while I work on the PD's socials? Might have some intel.

His response came quickly. **Sure. Can you come now? Chief just left for town hall so we're in the clear.**

I showed Amanda the message.

"Good. Maybe he can run with the Sage-Rand connection." She began gathering her things to leave. "I can handle the Threads webinar on my own, so take your time."

I put my palms together and bowed, eliciting a chuckle from my amazing and dedicated coworker. "Keep me posted if you need anything." My gaze warily flicked to her non-existent baby belly.

"You keep *me* posted." Amanda narrowed her eyes for emphasis.

We said goodbye, and I hurriedly got ready to head down to the police station. Not knowing how long Chief McInnis would be gone, I parked by the Commons twelve minutes later.

I texted both Jasper and Charlotte an update, as we hadn't connected about the case since Friday. **Going to talk with Gavin. Will fill you guys in after.**

Sounds good. Charlotte also sent a thumbs-up.

Jasper sent an emoji of a bee. Was he telling me I was being a busybody or suggesting I summon my inner Beyoncé? It was anyone's guess.

Without news crews swarming or angry mobs protesting on the lawn, it was nice to be able to breeze in through the PD's entrance like normal. I waved to Maude and wished her a Happy Monday as she buzzed me back into the inner workings of the building.

I found Gavin brooding at the note-and-picture-covered whiteboard in the conference room.

"Hey. Got here as soon as I could." I took a seat at the large table, eyeing the papers and files spread all around. "How goes things?"

With a weary smile, Gavin rubbed his temples. "Slow. I thought today we could get Aubrey and Jared's bios added to the website. I also want to scan the comments on our official Facebook post about Laila's death. See if anything pops up." He then lowered his voice. "But before we get to that…"

His unspoken question about my amateur investigation hung in the air.

I took a deep breath, hoping he wouldn't renege on his promise not to ream me out for snooping. "I've got some stuff to share. Maybe something will jump out at you that's been eluding me."

At this, I had Gavin's undivided attention. He listened patiently as I walked him through everything my friends and I had turned up over the past week, focusing my lingering suspicions on Sage, Rand, and Terrance. "I know Laila and Rand's affair happened over a decade ago, but maybe time didn't heal old wounds in this instance."

Gavin twirled a pen between his fingers. "What about your theory that Laila and Rand were still in touch with one another?"

"I haven't found anything to prove they were carrying on a relationship." My shoulders slumped with defeat. "Over the weekend, I scoured Rand's social media for signs of an affair but came up with nothing."

Gavin's brow wrinkled. "Signs of an affair? Wouldn't he do his best *not* to have any?"

"Sure, but people make mistakes." I flippantly swatted my hand. "Posting a travel pic with two drinks when there should be one. Two uneaten meals. A reflection showing more than one person. You know, small stuff like that." I sighed. "What's more, when I bumped into Rand at Harper's on Friday night, he seemed genuinely shocked LaTàge and Laila were one and the same person."

Gavin studied the whiteboard a moment before adding Rand and Sage's names in dry-erase marker. "This is good intel, Coco. Neither Rand nor Sage were on our radar, and while their motives are a stretch, it's something."

My spirits rebounded at his tentative praise, and I straightened in my seat.

"As for Terrance, we've actually been able to eliminate him as a suspect," Gavin offered, his voice low, clearly wary that Chief McInnis might return from the town hall at any moment. "Omar checked into the hospital Sunday night for his pre-op, so Terrance dog-sat for him. Omar's home security footage verifies Terrance didn't leave the property until Monday morning."

Security cameras actually *for the win.* I flexed my hand, frustration coursing through me. At least I had played it smart and not bothered Terrance. Otherwise, I could have found myself in hot water with law enforcement if either of the Jackson siblings had ratted me out.

Gavin used his pen to point at the other names and faces on the whiteboard. "Every person within Laila's immediate circle has an alibi of some type." With his other hand, he rubbed at the stubble marring his chin. "And without her passcode, we won't be able to gain access to her phone data until either the device manufacturer releases the information, or someone provides us with the digits to access it ourselves. With all the red tape we have to jump through, that could take weeks. Until then, we're just sitting ducks waiting for additional information to surface."

I felt for him. I knew how badly Gavin wanted to prove the Central Shores PD had what it took to solve a high-profile case. But what more could I offer?

I absently went to my phone, my mind on autopilot as I tapped open Instagram and scrolled through LaTàge's profile. Images of her friends and her fabulous life melted together, my chest gripped by sorrow. Laila, despite her troubles, had brought joy to so many people through her work as LaTàge. It was beyond tragic that it had all ended like this for her.

I paused as my thumb hovered over a seemingly out-of-place picture. It featured Laila without makeup, wearing jean shorts and a white tank. Nothing glamorous or fancy, but she still looked beautiful against the LA skyline. Nestled in the crook of her toned arm was Hashtag. The poor little guy was probably missing his dog mom terribly. What would happen to him now that Laila was gone?

As I moved on from the photo, the passing comment Willow had made about her own dogs the day she and Reade arrived popped into my head.

"Ah, best day of our lives, holding those pups in our arms for the first time."

Was the feeling universal among pet owners? I wondered...

"Hey, Gav?" My voice trembled with budding hope. "Have you tried guessing Laila's passcode at all?"

Gavin shook his head. "No. SCCL didn't want to risk the phone wiping itself if Laila had it set up to do so."

Before I could share more, the conference door swung open, revealing Deacon and Adrian in the doorway. "Hey, boss. Hiya, Cokes." Both men greeted me with tight smiles. "What's going on here?" Deacon leaned against the wall with folded arms. "Some type of venting sesh?"

"Coco and I were just catching up about the department's website," Gavin hurriedly explained.

I pressed my lips together. While Gavin wasn't technically lying, we'd sure covered a lot more ground than that.

"Relax, boss. I know she's had an ear to the ground for you." Deacon clapped Gavin on the shoulder and threw me a knowing look. "Charlotte just *happened* to mention it while helping me pack boxes yesterday." His tone was laden with suspicious snark.

I plastered an innocent expression across my face, inwardly relieved Charlotte had found the time to come clean to Deacon about our escapades this past week.

"Come up with anything for us, Coco?" Adrian joked as he took a seat at the opposite end of the big conference table.

Gavin cleared his throat. "Actually, she did. We should look into Rand Windham and Sage Hattape's ties to Laila."

"Sage Hattape? The crystal lady?" Adrian's brow furrowed. "Lana shops at her kooky store all the time. What's *she* got to do with this?" He sounded panicked at the thought of his beloved wife being linked to the eccentric entrepreneur.

Gavin held up a hand. "She's an old high school buddy of Laila's. Bad blood developed between them because of Rand's wandering…eye."

Grabbing a seat next to Gavin, Deacon whipped out his laptop and began clacking away on the shiny metallic keys. "That's some good intel." He shot me a tight smile. "Nice work."

"Now," Gavin said, turning back to me, "what's this about Laila's passcode? You got an idea?"

I bobbed my head, glad to still have his focus. "Ruby told you guys that Laila guarded her phone pretty fiercely, right?"

"She said Laila never let her use the phone unsupervised," Gavin confirmed.

I began snapping my fingers as the theory fully formed. "So, to make sure Ruby never accessed her phone without her approval, Laila would've needed a PIN that was something super personal, something Ruby wouldn't guess or know." I sat down at the conference table and resumed scanning LaTàge's Instagram profile. Hashtag had been her companion long before Laila ever made it big in the influencer space. I prayed the information I was looking for was somewhere.

"Yeah, and?" Adrian arched an eyebrow.

I didn't respond for several minutes, until—

"Ah ha!" I punched the air with a triumphant fist upon finding the obligatory "Gotcha Day Post" every social media-savvy dog owner uploaded. My thumb ached from scrolling through endless pictures, but the cramps were worth it. I memorized the date: six years ago, on June Fourth. "I think I might know a passcode we could try."

I rattled off the digits and presented my theory. "Laila adopted Hashtag years before Ruby ever came into her life. The date would be close to Laila's heart, but not necessarily something Ruby would know or ever need to reference."

Deacon stroked his chin as he glanced warily at Gavin. "One try wouldn't hurt."

Adrian nodded vigorously. "LaTàge had an iPhone. Those aren't configured to wipe until *ten* incorrect tries."

"It's worth a shot, right?" I stared at Gavin head-on. "Rather than just sitting here while a killer roams free?"

"Now, what have I walked into?" Detective Harriet Forester startled us as she strolled into the conference room, her expression both annoyed and curious.

"Detective." All three members of the Central Shores PD abruptly rose from their seats out of respect.

"What brings you down from SCCL?" Gavin asked curtly.

Harriet placed a hand on her hip. "Relax, Gav. I'm here to play nice. I was tasked with briefing Mayor Sullivan on our progress. I thought I'd stop by and see how you all were faring." Her pointed gaze settled on me. "I didn't realize you guys had opened this place up to the public."

Gavin held his chin high. "Coco was sharing some more information about LaTàge's social media profile, and we think we might have a hit on a valid passcode."

"*We* think?'" Harriet quoted back. "I don't remember bringing Ms. Cline permanently on board as a consultant for this case. Or have you forgotten this is *my* neck on the line?"

Gavin moved closer to her side, his tone low and compelling. "Come on, Harriet. Coco has proven herself when it comes to using social media to piece together a mystery. We'd be foolish to ignore what help she can offer."

Harriet held his gaze. "Foolish or foolhardy? Police work is no place for a civilian."

Before the tension between Harriet and Gavin escalated further, I cleared my throat. I didn't want Gavin and the others getting flack for discussing case details with me, but I wasn't going to drop my idea about Laila's PIN.

"Detective, I think I might be able to get you into Laila's phone." My theory tumbled from my mouth as I tried to persuade Harriet to give Hashtag's Gotcha Day a try.

Harriet's intense, inscrutable gaze moved from me to the whiteboard, where a glamorous picture of LaTàge was taped front and center.

Gavin placed a palm on her shoulder. "Come on, Harriet," he appealed. "It could take weeks before the manufacturer releases the iCloud backup data. Do you really want the media lens on you and the team *that* long when we might have a code worth testing right now?"

Harriet folded her arms as we all stared her down. She didn't flinch at the attention. "A pet's Gotcha Day? Really? You expect me to take this to the crime lab director?"

"Just one crack at her phone. That's all you'd be asking." I quickly added, "Just tell Director Morrison that you came across some new information buried in LaTàge's socials."

Harriet's lips pursed for a moment, but she then reached for her cell. "What's the date again?"

Resisting the urge to share a victorious grin with the guys, I relayed Hashtag's adoption date.

Harriet tapped her phone before sliding it back into her jacket pocket. "Glad to see your team is hard at work, Gav." The corner of her lip twitched as she gave us all a stiff nod and left.

We didn't speak until we heard the station's back door slam shut. "Think she'll act on it, Boss?" Adrian cocked an eyebrow as he assessed Gavin.

"I honestly don't know." The lieutenant ran his fingers through his hair. "That woman is so frustrating sometimes."

I opted to change the subject. "Well, my work here is done. Although, I do have those website updates to make." For my regular CoA clients, I could usually edit their webpage from anywhere I had Internet access, but for the Central Shores's dot-gov site, I had to be connected to the PD's network to access the government domain. "I'll get to work adding Aubrey and Jared's bios." As part of the department's community outreach, I'd encouraged Chief McInnis to let me introduce new hires on social media and the PD's homepage. "Or do you want me to search Facebook for comments first?"

Gavin checked his watch. "If you could make the updates now, I'll help you scan Facebook after lunch."

Deacon pushed his laptop across the table. "Feel free to use mine."

I accepted his helpful offering, glad I wouldn't have to kick Maude off her computer out front.

Adrian thumbed over his shoulder toward the door. "I've got patrol in thirty. Wanna grab food down at Zaddick's?" he asked the others.

Gavin halfheartedly agreed while Deacon checked with me. "Can we pick you up anything?"

I shook my head. "Hudson's sister is taking me out later to some new Italian place over in Ocean Hollow, so I'm saving myself."

The guys wished me good luck with my work and said they'd be back by twelve. I logged onto Deacon's computer as a guest user and pulled up the police department's webpage to begin my edits. Having two new hires meant reconfiguring the layout, which was a bit more laborious than I expected. I couldn't get the text to line up the way I wanted, so it surprised me that Gavin and Deacon returned from their lunch run—minus Adrian, who was now on patrol—before I'd finished.

"Still at it?" Gavin peered over my shoulder at my handiwork.

"Looks great," Deacon commented from my other side.

I stared at the page, a frown growing. "Aubrey's bio is a few sentences longer than Jared's. I don't like them being uneven."

Deacon bit into an apple he'd pulled from his Zaddick's bag lunch. "Jared's got a bunch of certifications to his name. Why don't you add them to his bio and call it good?"

"Genius." I held my hand up for a no-look high five. "What are they?"

Deacon rattled off the forensic certs while Gavin sat down and unwrapped a massive sandwich.

I'd just saved the final website changes when Gavin's phone rang. "Lieutenant McInnis," he answered without looking at the caller ID.

He bolted upright in his chair a second later. "What? Really?" His hazel eyes were as big as baseballs as he laid the device on the table and hit the

CHAPTER TWENTY-EIGHT

Speaker icon.

"Yep, we've got access." Harriet's voice rang out, her tone both excited and bemused. "So, please let Coco know her contribution was greatly appreciated."

"What?" I choked back my astonishment. Not so much that I'd been right—although that did feel incredibly cool—but that Harriet had actually listened to my advice and followed through. "Hashtag's Gotcha Day was the answer?"

"Ah, hello, Coco. Yes, we're in Laila's phone." She paused, and we all heard muttering in the background. "Why don't we get on a Zoom? Our technician can share Laila's screen. I'd be interested in any insights from the Central Shores team. You might recognize something I don't."

Gavin looked absolutely giddy. "That'd be great. Send us a link. We're already in the conference room."

A few minutes later, a Zoom window projected onto the blank wall opposite the door. The conference room was already equipped with a webcam and speakers, so we could see Harriet standing in an SCCL workroom, and she could see us. Beside her, there was also a small, slender man hunched over a computer in the corner of the Zoom frame.

"This is Mateo." She introduced her associate. "He's mirroring Laila's phone."

Soon, Harriet became a small box in the corner of the Zoom window, and a huge, blown-up image of an app-filled home screen was plastered on the PD's wall.

"What have you reviewed so far?" Gavin asked.

"We started with her text messages," Mateo answered in a trembling tenor voice. "She didn't have a lot coming in the night she died, but she certainly sent a lot."

The cluttered home screen transformed into the Messages app.

"Ruby Daniels." I read the name associated with the active conversation.

"The contents support Ms. Daniels' claims that she had quit her role as LaTàge's personal assistant," Harriet summarized, but Mateo displayed the blue messages for us to read ourselves. Some of Laila's final words to Ruby.

How can you do this? I thought we were ride or die!

I promise I'll get the money.

Just give me a week, that's all. This rebrand will put us back in the black. Coco is so good!

Plz babe, don't leave me. We can work thru this.

Rubes, you're my fam. I luv you.

Plz don't do this to us.

You can't do this to me.

Gurl??? Plz! I need you.

Emotion blurred my vision as I sensed the visceral pain and panic Laila expressed in each message. The mention of Ruby being her family hit particularly hard. Given Laila's tumultuous relationship with Omar, Deja, and Terrance, to have Ruby abandon her must have felt like another heart-wrenching betrayal.

The messages further proved that Laila hadn't come back here for Omar's money. She'd returned to Central Shores to support her dad and to work with me. It took all my willpower not to bawl my eyes out in front of my colleagues.

"Ms. Daniels did not respond to these messages," Mateo explained. "The victim also tried reaching out to Mr. Torres and Mx. Keaton, but received no replies."

"Everyone ghosted her," I croaked, my throat tight.

Deacon moved closer to the projection on the wall. "Did Laila reach out to Omar? Or any of the Jacksons?"

"The last communication she had with her father was right after her plane landed on Sunday," Harriet informed us as Mateo pulled up the conversation.

L: Hi, Daddy. Flight was delayed so I won't make visiting hours. LAX is the worst. Sorry I won't be there tonight to get you settled in. I'll see you tomorrow evening when you wake up. Lots to catch up on.

O: I understand. Travel safe. I'm just so happy you're coming, sweet girl. I can't wait to see you.

L: Do you want me to bring anything to the hospital? Sneak in some HoneyBuns or something.

O: LOL, haven't had one of those in years. Would love one but my doc might not be happy. Probably why I'm here in the first place.

L: Will D & T be there? Do they know about me?

O: Haven't told them about anything about you or your alter ego. I didn't know if you still wanted things to be kept "on the DL" with the fam.

L: LOL! Oh, how trendy of you. Gosh, I can't believe you knew all this time.

O: I'd know my own daughter anywhere, no matter what.

L: I love you, Daddy. I'm sorry I didn't realize how much you loved me.

O: Always, honey.

Gavin glanced my way. "This aligns with everything the Jacksons have told us."

I nodded, no longer able to keep the tears from streaming down my cheeks. I hurriedly wiped them away, grateful Gavin didn't make a comment. While there was clearly a lot of love emanating from this text chain, the fact Laila and her dad never got the chance to reunite in person left me gutted.

Mateo sighed. "Certainly not the gold mine we were hoping for. But maybe her emails will provide a lead."

"Have you checked her DMs?" I spoke up hesitantly. "Influencers communicate heavily through direct messages, almost as much as texts." My cheeks warmed as I felt Harriet's electronic gaze on me. "Her social apps might reveal more intimate intel than her Gmail." Whether she was Gen Z LaTàge or Millennial Laila, neither generation was known to send juicy personal deets through email.

The Zoom webcam revealed Harriet drumming on the worktable, but the mic didn't pick up on the sound. "Let's start with Instagram," she instructed Mateo.

Gavin sent me a covert thumbs up as the screen transformed for us again, revealing LaTàge's profile.

Chapter Twenty-Nine

"Holy Eras Tour." I gasped at the astronomical number of notifications. If I'd ever thought I had it bad, it was nothing to the thousands upon thousands of alerts, DMs, and comments LaTàge received.

Deacon's jaw dropped. "What a mess. How's anyone supposed to navigate this nightmare?"

Once again, I felt all eyes on me. "Go to her messages and click the Primary tab." Instagram helped content creators by intelligently filtering their inboxes. Laila would have marked ongoing or important conversations as Primary while relegating others to the General or the Requests tabs.

Mateo did as I instructed. While Laila certainly had an overwhelming number of active convos on her LaTàge profile, it slightly narrowed down our scope. A little.

"This is going to take a lot of resources to comb through," Mateo muttered.

Harriet pursed her lips. "Ms. Cline has a point about email. If Laila wasn't communicating with anyone via text, she would be doing so here."

I straightened my shoulders at the detective defending my suggestion. "Why don't you start with the last read messages? The ones Laila would have seen before she died. Scroll past all the unreads for the moment."

"What if Laila's killer messaged her account after she died to throw off suspicion?" Deacon arched an eyebrow in challenge.

"What if they didn't?" Gavin countered.

Harriet sighed. "Let's not get tunnel vision, guys. We don't even know if Laila was messaging her killer at all."

"Here we go," Mateo announced, interrupting their back-and-forth. "Looks like the last read message is an exchange between a user with the handle @katzouttathebag."

"That's Katz." What would we find here? According to *TMZ*, there were several witnesses placing Katz at Cyprus around the time of Laila's death. Since Katz wasn't responding to Laila's texts, maybe Laila messaged Katz about their plans through Instagram.

Harriet leaned over Mateo's shoulder. "Pull up the conversation."

Mateo clicked, and our screen changed to show the direct messages between @LaTàge and @katzouttathebag.

My heart sank with disappointment as I scanned the images spewing from the projector. "These are just memes and Reels."

Gavin muffled a snort as he read one featuring Michael Scott from *The Office.* "Hardly incriminating."

Mateo scrolled through the conversation, but there was nothing to suggest anything remotely nefarious. "Not a lot of recent activity on this chain. Laila was the last one to send a DM. Two days *before* she arrived in Central Shores."

I deflated at the digital dead end.

Harriet folded her arms, her dismay evident. "Mateo, pull a team together to go through each and every one of Laila's unread LaTàge conversations. Even general DMs and requests." Her sharp gaze landed on the camera. "Thanks, guys. We'll take it from here."

"Are you sure we can't help?" Gavin hurriedly asked before Harriet ended the conference call. "Deacon and I can drive up to the crime lab and be an extra set of eyes."

While Harriet debated his offer, Mateo backed out of the DM between Katz and Laila. He was still sharing the iPhone screen, whether knowingly or unknowingly. As I stared at the list of messages LaTàge's account had received, one of the unread messages a few rows above Katz's exchange caught my attention.

I'm outside.

"Hey, guys!" I burst out, interrupting Harriet mid-sentence. I ran to the wall and pointed at the timestamp next to the message. "LaTàge received this message at one twenty-six AM." I then realized Harriet and Mateo couldn't see what I was pointing at. I couldn't see the username because it was cut off by the screen, so I said, "Check out the conversation at the top of the frame marked 'I'm outside.'"

Harriet wordlessly urged Mateo to comply. A new DM filled our screen, and I finally caught sight of the username. It made my tongue go dry.

@durnstdevelopment.

What was Ronny Durnst's business account doing DMing LaTàge close to the time she died?

Silence settled over our conference call as we all read the most recent string of messages.

@durnstdevelopment: Hope you're enjoying the house.

@LaTàge: Omg luv it so much. Thank you for letting me stay here. And you were too kind to give us such a thorough tour.

@durnstdevelopment: No worries. Glad for the chance to collab. Will def help when the place goes on the market.

@LaTàge: And here I thought you did this outta the kindness of your own heart LOL

@LaTàge: There must be something I can do to thank you. Interested in a nightcap?

@durnstdevelopment: Won't say no to that. Need to finish up something, tho. Be there in an hour?

@LaTàge: I'll be waiting.

I gulped at the numerous winky and kissy face emojis LaTàge had sent. Just what had she meant by "nightcap?"

Ronny's **I'm outside** message had come in exactly an hour later. Laila must have seen the notification on her lock screen, but not read the text within the Instagram app.

"So," Harriet began once she'd concluded reading, "this suggests Ronald Durnst was at the crime scene near Laila's time of death."

Deacon grunted. "Something he very much failed to mention."

Out of the corner of my eye, I saw Gavin's jaw clench. "But what about his alibi?" he asked. "Noelle verified he was with her, right?"

"Ms. Paige said they had a nice evening together and went to bed around eleven." Harriet placed a hand on her hip. "We can't discount that Durnst's girlfriend could have been lying to us."

"Noelle wouldn't do that." I bristled in defense of the library director. "Maybe she didn't realize Ronny snuck out for a late-night rendezvous."

Harriet frowned at me through the Zoom. "Coco, you've provided invaluable insight into Laila's personal communications, and for that, we are grateful." Her gaze flicked to Deacon and Gavin. "I'm going to brief Director Morrison about this new information. Gav, why don't you have your team pick Durnst up and bring him here? We'll question him together."

"I'll radio Officer Riley and head over to Durnst Development now." Gavin shifted on his feet. "But what if he refuses? We really don't have enough to get a warrant yet."

Harriet shrugged. "If he won't talk, we'll just have to expedite a request for Durnst's phone location data. We have probable cause, what with the Instagram DM. From there, his phone should show us he was at the Crescent Hills home."

Harriet and Gavin exchanged a few more words before ending the Zoom call.

"Wow. What a break, right?" Deacon rubbed his chin, his jaw a bit slack.

Gavin shut down all the conference room tech and rubbed his hands with anticipation. "No kidding. Great job, Coco." He met my gaze, his expression full of sincerity. "We're gonna nab this slimebag because of you."

I only managed a half-hearted smile. I was still reeling from the revelation about Ronny Durnst. Sure, he gave off an overly enthusiastic salesman vibe, but he and Noelle seemed genuinely happy together. Had he really gone over to the Crescent Hills house to cheat on her with Laila? And if so, how had Laila ended up dead?

Moreover, I was troubled by Noelle's potential involvement. I really liked her and thought her presence had been good for Central Shores. Had Ronny asked her to lie to the police about his alibi? Did she suspect something? My head spun with questions.

Deacon came to my side. "Hey, you okay?"

His concern shook me from my stupor. "Yeah…" I felt my cheeks grow hot. "I guess I'm not used to uncovering a murderer with so little fanfare."

He chuckled. "Well, the chief will be happy not to have another nationally televised takedown, that's for sure."

"Don't worry. As soon as the press gets wind of Durnst being on our radar, they'll be all over us again." Gavin strode toward the door, dialing a number on his cell. "So, what we've talked about does not leave this room. Is that clear?" He lanced me with a severe stare.

"Got it."

Gavin eyed me a moment longer before turning his focus to Deacon. "Track down the chief and bring him up to speed? He's probably still at town hall."

"Will do, Boss." Deacon saluted as Gavin brought his phone to his ear.

"Hey, Adrian, there's been a development. Can you swing by the station, pronto?" Gavin's voice echoed as he left the room.

Deacon placed a hand on my shoulder. "To reiterate what Gavin said, you did good, Coco. You saved us some valuable time."

I could tell he was kindly asking me to leave. Now that they had Ronny in their sights, I needed to get out of the way and let them do their job. "Happy to have helped." And I was. I was also deeply touched by how much Gavin and Deacon valued my insights. They'd put a lot on the professional line, vouching for me with Detective Forester, so I was glad I hadn't messed things up for them. But why wasn't I feeling more ecstatic about finding Ronny's ties to Laila?

As I left the precinct, I had an honest moment with myself. I missed the theatrics of solving a mystery, Coco-style. I hadn't confronted a killer on broadcast TV or put together the puzzle pieces in the nick of time. Heck, I wasn't even going to be there when Ronny was arrested. Rather, the whole thing felt like a big letdown.

"Ugh, what is wrong with me?" I mock-punched Jolly's window as I sidled up to the car. Here I was, complaining about *not* having put my life in danger. No wonder my friends and family were worried about me. It was unhealthy to thrive on drama the way I seemed to thrive on mystery.

I tried to shake myself out of my funk as I drove back home. If Willow or Reade sensed something was amiss, they'd pepper me endlessly with questions. Actually, they'd already do that anyway. They knew I'd made a trip to the police station because I texted them to let them know about the spare key under a chair on the back patio. Not wanting to break Gavin's confidence, I fumbled for a blanket statement to avoid spilling the deets about Ronny.

In an effort to prolong the inevitable, I made a pit stop to get gas and pick up some groceries at the local market. My houseguests had healthier eating habits than Hudson and I did, so I made sure to grab some snackable veggies and fruits, forgoing my usual staple of Cheez-Its and popcorn.

Thirty minutes later, I parked Jolly in the garage. The Michaelses' rental car was nestled in Hudson's usual spot, meaning the girls had returned from visiting Willow's parents. I marched sluggishly toward the front door, hoping I could divert attention from the status of Laila's case. With a deep breath, I entered the condo and called out, "I'm home—"

"Omigod, Coco, did you see the news?" Willow shrieked as she darted into the kitchen to greet me. She danced on the balls of her feet. "The police have arrested LaTàge's killer! We're watching it on TV right now."

She dragged me into the living room, where Reade sat mesmerized by the scene on the big screen.

I stared in amazement as TV crews captured live footage of Ronny Durnst being escorted inside the Sussex County Crime Lab. I skimmed the ticker along the bottom, which confirmed Ronny had *not* been arrested, but that the police were speaking with a new person of interest.

"Deets, now!" Willow begged.

Her pleading expression made my stomach flip with guilt. If the story about Ronny had already broke, was I *really* betraying Gavin's confidence by sharing what I knew?

Eh, don't answer that.

I opted for a glossed-over version of the truth. "Turns out this guy," I began, pointing to a freeze-frame of Ronny now displayed on the TV, "had been messaging LaTàge's Instagram account the night Laila died. Since he failed to mention said actions, the police are bringing him in for questioning. He's not actually under arrest."

"Oooh, so her killer was sliding into LaTàge's DMs? I bet *you* helped the cops figure that one out, right? Why aren't you there for the arrest?" Willow didn't appear to have heard the last part of my statement.

I chuckled. "I appreciate your faith in me, but my role in this case is done. I've taken my final bow."

A frown grew on Reade's glossy lips. "That's all you can give us?"

"Sorry, ladies." I winced apologetically.

Willow would not be deterred. "Come on, Cokes. Our friends are gonna hound us when we get back to LA. We need more tea than this."

"I wish I had it." Other than his late-night visit to Crescent Hills, I understood nothing about the resolution to this case. I didn't even know why Ronny had killed Laila.

Reade stared at the screen, continuing to soak up the information from one of Hudson's WMTG counterparts. "The dude worked in Central Shores, right?"

I nodded. "Yeah, his company has a small office on the other side of town. Near his development project." Yikes, I wondered what would happen to all those homes in Crescent Hills. Would Derrick Payne and the team at Durnst Development be able to survive with Ronny on the hook for murder, or would The Buchanan Group swoop in and take over?

Willow perked up. "I see what you're doing, babe." She squeezed Reade's shoulder with obvious affection. "Can we swing by this creep's office? I want to see where a killer works."

"You guys have a problem." The words were out of my mouth before I realized how hypocritical I sounded. I couldn't fault Willow and Reade for being fascinated by a high-profile murder investigation unfolding right before them, especially when we were in such close proximity to the action. "But if it will appease you, we can do a drive-by."

Chapter Thirty

Willow gleefully clapped, and Reade pumped a fist in the air. "Gotta get some pics for the 'gram."

I shook my head, bemused by their enthusiasm, but then again, these were the young women who'd proclaimed a Jack the Ripper tour was the highlight of their UK honeymoon.

Fifteen minutes later, I slowed their Mustang rental to a stop in front of the small building Durnst Development occupied. What had once been a lighting store with big windows was now a sleek, ultra-modern structure that looked like a mini-version of many of the Crescent Hills homes.

"Kinda an odd spot for a business, don't you think?" From the passenger side, Willow surveyed the quiet residential area surrounding us. "Why not try to be closer to the strip?"

I pointed up the road. "The big housing project Ronny's company is overseeing is located just up that way. I imagine he wanted to be near the construction."

Reade gripped my shoulder from the backseat. "Can I take a few pics out front? Please?" She added several syllables to stress her point.

Sigh. What was the harm? "You guys are weird." I pulled into the gravel parking lot beside the office, noting a green sedan parked in the shade. "Try to be respectful, will you? Looks like someone might be around." I pointed to the car.

Willow's eyes sparkled. "Think they'll dish about their crooked boss?"

"I'd love to get a comment," Reade added, her publicist mind clearly at work.

Maybe this hadn't been such a good idea. "Let's not cause a scene," I pleaded. "I imagine the news about Ronny has really shaken the company." I remembered how overworked and stressed Derrick had been when I'd run into him Friday at Harper's Pub. I hoped Ronny's business partner was doing okay.

The three of us climbed out of the car and ambled around the front. I snorted at Willow and Reade's attempts to be covert with their actions, but their true-crime fangirling had totally taken over. Reade snapped several selfies, and Willow recorded a video on her phone *with narration.*

"We're standing outside the workplace of Ronald Durnst, the man responsible for LaTàge's murder..."

I tried ignoring their antics, instead choosing to admire the stately Victorian across the road.

"Hey!" Reade gasped. "I see someone moving around inside."

Without giving me time to rein her in, she whipped open the door. "Hi!" Reade's cheery California drawl called out.

I cursed under my breath and hurriedly trailed after her and Willow.

"Uh, hello." Derrick jumped up from his desk, cementing a customer service smile on his tired, pale face. He looked like he'd been put through the wringer. "How can I help you?"

I closed the door, a jingling noise from behind startling me. I glanced over my shoulder and found a keyring still in the door. Derrick must have forgotten them after unlocking the place.

The jangling keys drew Derrick's attention my way. "Oh, hi, Coco." His confused gaze slid to Reade and Willow. "Friends of yours?"

Before I could introduce them as my guests, Willow chirped, "Yep. And I'm in the market for an investment property, so Coco suggested we come by."

"She did?" Derrick's eyebrows pinched. "Well, unfortunately, it's a bit of a bad time."

And that's a bit of an understatement.

Reade tilted her head. "Oh dear, that's too bad. Is there an issue with one of your properties?"

I realized what my crime-obsessed cohorts were up to. Playing dumb in the hopes Derrick would reveal some juicy details about his business partner.

"Uh, no, it's not that…" Derrick trailed off, his gaze surveying the room.

I, too, glanced around the open-concept office space. The client waiting area faced four metal desks. One of those, I imagined, belonged to Ronny.

"Our CEO, Ronny Durnst, has run into a bit of a legal issue," Derrick finally admitted, underplaying the severity of the situation once more. His marketing expertise was really working overtime.

Willow and Reade murmured their sympathies, linking their arms through Derrick's in a comforting, if flirty manner.

When I eyed them suspiciously, Willow winked. The phrase *'catch more flies with honey'* trilled through my mind.

As Reade batted her eyelashes and Willow amped up her charms, I suppressed a laugh at the couple's antics, noting that they each hid their wedding-ring-adorned hand behind their back. Derrick seemed to be buying their charade, though, so I left them to their devices.

Made completely invisible by the two gorgeous women in front of him, I was free to meander around the office and explore. I spied a box next to the desk Derrick had leapt from. Inside was a potted plant, some folders, and an Everyday is Earth Day coffee mug. Had he been laid off? Or had he seen the writing on the wall and was planning to jump ship? I glanced back at Derrick. He did seem somewhat anxious, but who wouldn't be if their business partner was a suspect in a huge murder case?

Derrick had also left his expensive laptop open, an Internet browser window on display. I narrowed my gaze at the screen, taking in the familiar site. It was the logout page for Instagram. Derrick must have been in the process of logging out of personal accounts and decommissioning his laptop when we interrupted him.

I was gearing up to pry Willow and Reade off the poor man when my brain registered the user handle listed on the logout notice. The button said, "Continue as @durnstdevelopment," giving the user the chance to log back into the website.

@durnstdevelopment? The same account that had messaged LaTàge about coming over for a nightcap? A *business* account.

Oh my God.

I'd asked myself earlier why Ronny would be flirtatiously messaging Laila from his business's Instagram account, yet hadn't given it much thought. But what if Ronny hadn't been the one communicating with Laila? What if Noelle had been telling the truth about Ronny's alibi?

My heart skipping a beat, I skimmed the other open tabs on Derrick's laptop. The header "EXPEDIA – SEPT. ITINERARY" caught my eye. Itinerary? Was Derrick planning a vacation?

Glancing quickly at Willow and Reade, I saw they were still in animated conversation with Derrick, even though their backs were all to me. *Perfect.* I leaned over the desk and clicked on the travel service tab.

I swallowed a gasp as my eyes widened. Derrick had a flight to the Maldives scheduled to take off in less than two hours from Baltimore/Washington International Airport. Holy Ice Spice. Derrick wasn't jumping ship from Durnst Development. He was skipping town.

Panic rising inside me, I pulled out my phone and texted the group chain I shared with Gavin, Deacon, and Adrian. I couldn't risk calling them in front of Derrick.

Think you've got wrong pup. Darren Pain is the one who massaged Laila. At the place now.

I cringed at my autocorrected spelling mistakes, but my fingers were shaking too fiercely to be able to fix them. Hopefully, the guys would understand. Gavin could track me through Find My Friends if they needed further clarification. I sent the message, my mind whirling. I had to get Reade and Willow out of here. If Derrick was capable of killing Laila, who knows what he would do if he realized I'd figured things out.

Swapping the active browser tab to where Derrick had left it, I backed away from the desk, my ears clueing in on the trio's bubbly conversation.

"Poor thing," Willow gushed. "You deserve a vacation. I can't imagine the shock."

Derrick certainly looked like he'd warmed to their company. He practically radiated with confidence. "Yeah, I never would've thought Ronny capable, but now, looking back, I suppose I did see some signs about his violent streak."

Reade held a hand to her chest, aghast. "Was he ever violent against you?"

"Oh, no," Derrick hurriedly assured her. "Ronny would never mess with me. He knows how much I work out."

I rolled my eyes at his not-so-humble brag.

"But he'd sometimes go off on the contractor or the construction teams," Derrick added. "We've been getting a lot of flack for it. It's been a nightmare dealing with the negative press."

I recalled Noelle telling Jasper and me about the company's recent string of bad publicity. How could Derrick possibly think *murder* wouldn't cast a pall over Durnst Development? Just how delusional was this guy?

"Sounds like you deserve a break. Where are you vacationing?" I asked sweetly, startling Derrick with my question. Clearly, he'd forgotten about me.

"The Maldives. I hear it's beautiful this time of year." He clumsily tried to shrug off Willow and Reade, who'd threaded their arms through his. "I'm actually heading out right now."

Crap. I glanced at my phone, checking to see if Gavin or the others had received my message.

Nothing.

Ugh, they must all still be busy with Ronny. If Derrick left and made the drive to BWI, there was a chance he could be on a plane before the police had even received my text message.

My only option was to let him go and call 9-1-1, praying the operator would take my accusation seriously.

But neither Reade nor Willow seemed ready to release Derrick from their crime-loving clutches. "Can't you tell us a little more about your boss and LaTàge?" Willow begged. "How did he even get on her radar?"

Derrick swallowed. "Well, LaTàge reached out to us about renting a place while she was in town. Ronny saw the value in having a celeb client and offered one of the Crescent Hills homes, free of charge."

Liar, liar, pants on fire. Derrick had told a much different story to me that first day at the police station. He'd said *he'd* been the one to propose comping LaTàge's stay to Ronny, a claim he'd later reiterated during our run-in at Harper's Pub.

I decided to play along with his lies. "How did LaTàge reach out?" I twirled a strand of my hair, trying to keep my expression neutral.

Derrick snorted. "How else? She DMed the company account." A smug look enveloped his face as Willow and Reade made appreciative murmurs. "*I* was the one who actually facilitated the arrangement. Ronny just took the credit with her."

Now, we were getting somewhere. Derrick was already changing his story to impress the girls by linking himself to the famous LaTàge.

"Did you get to meet her?" Willow bounced on her toes like a kid outside a candy shop.

"Briefly. Ronny and I gave her a tour of the house when she arrived. Showed her all the bells and whistles."

Were my eyes playing tricks on me, or had Derrick's grin become a sneer?

"She must have been really grateful." I met his gaze head-on.

Derrick shrugged. "You know how those celeb types can be. They expect the red carpet to be rolled out for them." While light and breezy, his tone held a hint of malice. Much different than Ronny's down-to-earth impression of LaTàge during the same encounter.

A disturbing possibility clicked into place. What if Laila had assumed—much like me—that handsome, suave Ronny had been the one DMing her about sharing a nightcap, only to have Derrick show up in his stead? Had Laila reacted badly? When we'd chatted with Noelle at Harper's, she'd offhandedly mentioned that Derrick was known to lose his temper if things didn't go his way…Had Derrick's ego been so hurt that he killed her in a fit of rage?

My phone vibrated in my hand.

On our way from SCCL. 20 mins out. Be careful and get out of there.

I sagged with relief at the notification from Gavin. The cavalry would arrive.

"I sure do," I finally responded to Derrick's lingering comment. "And no doubt, you need that vacation. So, we should let you get going." Taking an assertive step forward, I grabbed both Reade and Willow to wrench them from Derrick's side. "Happy travels."

Willow opened her mouth to protest when I sent her a withering glare. I prayed she'd forgive my rudeness, but I needed to get my friends out of here.

Reade handed Derrick her business card. "If you need any image rehab services to erase your ties to Ronny, just let me know. My firm excels in scrubbing away scandal."

"Thanks." Derrick waved as I dragged the girls outside.

Willow huffed when I finally let go. "What was that about? He didn't seem too bothered by the attention. Gosh, he painted Ronny out to be a real creep."

"That's because *he's* the killer," I hissed, even though we were alone in the parking lot.

Reade and Willow halted in their tracks. "What?"

I kept my voice low as I hastily explained what I'd seen on Derrick's laptop.

By the time we were buckled in the Mustang, Willow's jaw was hanging slack. "Omigod. *Derrick* was the one messaging LaTàge right before she died?"

"And now he's packing up to head halfway around the world." I gripped the steering wheel, my anger rearing.

Reade wedged herself between the two front seats. "Guys, the Maldives doesn't have an extradition treaty with the US. If he's able to make that plane..." She glanced worriedly between Willow and me.

I knew the police were already en route, but I couldn't stop myself. "We can't let him get away." I dug through my bag, spying the tie-dye pocketknife Hudson had given me for safety purposes. I grabbed it and bolted out of the car, heading toward the green sedan parked only a few spots down.

By the time Willow and Reade caught up to me, I was squatting by the back passenger's wheel. Summoning all my strength, I jabbed the pocketknife into the tire, puncturing the rubber. When Hudson had told me to use the knife to keep me safe, I doubted this was what he had in mind.

"Go, go, go!" I shooed my companions back into the convertible, gunning the car into drive before they were buckled.

Several minutes later, we shared a triumphant high-five as I drove toward home, passing a screaming squad car heading the opposite direction. With our help, Derrick Payne wouldn't be making his plane, after all.

Chapter Thirty-One

"What a total wastrel." Irene Caruthers held a hand to her chest, completely aghast as we completed our harrowing tale.

Hudson frowned at his mother's remark. "Not the word I would've chosen, Ma," he said as he draped an arm around my shoulders. "More like a disgusting f—well, you get it."

From his spot in the driver's seat, Winston Caruthers's concerned gaze found mine in the rearview mirror. "It's a good thing you kids got out of there when you did."

"We tried to make Coco turn around and let us see the arrest," Willow said with a dramatic sigh from the backseat of the three-row SUV. "But she refused, Pop. Can you believe it?"

"Because *you* would have streamed it for all the world to see," I countered, shifting in my seat to stare her down.

Willow shrugged defensively. "Didn't you *want* the Internet to see how kick-butt you are? A livestream from me would have totally cleared your name."

I lovingly rolled my eyes. "My name was cleared in the court of public opinion once the truth about Derrick hit the news." Not only had the social media cesspool finally stopped telling the world I was a psychopath, but also, Jasper had teased a clip from his upcoming sit-down interview with Ruby and Miguel that featured the couple sharing how helpful I'd been as they navigated the fallout from LaTà—*Laila's* murder.

"At least we got all those great selfies with the guy," Reade pointed out.

Willow bobbed her head gleefully. "The Killer Reads are gonna flip!"

Hudson chuckled at his sister's behavior. "You certainly picked the right time to come to town, Wills."

I nestled my head on Hudson's shoulder, so glad to have him back home. The past few days had been completely exhausting, what with the aftermath of Derrick's arrest.

According to Gavin, the police had found Derrick cussing out his car in the Durnst Development parking lot. Slashing his back tire had given Harriet, Gavin, and the team the time they needed to descend on him, avoiding a potentially dangerous car chase toward the airport. Once Derrick was in custody, all Gavin had to do was put the incriminating DMs in front of him before Derrick confessed to circumvent premeditated charges. He swore up and down that he hadn't gone to Laila's rental to kill her. He thought she had invited him over for a hook-up. However, things quickly turned south when she opened the door to find him standing there, rather than Ronny. Derrick admitted she tried to play it off as kindly as she could, but her disappointment was evident. Nursing a major blow to his ego, he said something vile came over him, and he tried forcing himself on her. When Laila pushed back, he feared she would report him and bring more bad press to Durnst Development, a company he had a lot of money tied up in.

Derrick "claimed" he didn't realize he'd strangled Laila until she'd stopped struggling. Petrified by what he'd done, instead of calling 9-1-1 and possibly resuscitating her, he took her wallet to make it look like a burglary gone wrong and left. He already knew that if anyone questioned his alibi, Derrick could claim his phone location data showed him working late at the office, since Durnst Development used the same cell tower as the Crescent Hills homes. What's more, it turned out that Laila never asked Derrick to turn off the security cameras in the first place. He'd just deleted all the footage of her stay to cover his tracks. He'd lied to Ronny about her asking for privacy to explain why the incriminating footage didn't exist in their system. Derrick also believed he could delete his DMs with Laila, and no one would know he'd been in communication with her that night. Yet, he didn't understand the tech enough to realize that the messages wouldn't show as deleted on Laila's end.

When Gavin had filled me in on the details, I'd been left feeling empty. Not because I was bummed about missing the official takedown, but because Laila Jackson died over a man's wounded ego. What an utter waste of a vivacious, talented life. It made me sick now thinking about it. Murder was never the answer, but Derrick's motive was the lowest of the low.

Ruby, Katz, and Miguel had all been truly devastated when the grisly truth behind their friend's demise came out. Despite the squad's ups and downs, it was clear they all cared about Laila in their own way and missed "LaTàge" deeply. Ruby had already welcomed Hashtag into her home, her online posts brimming with love for the little animal and how she was grateful to have a piece of LaTàge still with her. Katz announced a partnership between their clothing company and a domestic violence organization dedicated to helping LGBTQIA+ individuals. And most surprisingly, Miguel had kicked off an awareness campaign about male toxicity with the hopes of helping prevent terrible dating situations like the one Laila found herself in.

The squad's swift responses lifted my spirits, even if some critics claimed their actions were only PR stunts. Whatever their intentions, it was heartening to see some good come from Derrick's lecherous act of evil.

"Well, I'm just glad everyone is here, safe and sound." Irene smoothed out the non-existent wrinkles in her maroon gown. She looked lovely, ready to accept her professional award.

In fact, everyone in our group looked stunning in their various takes on cocktail attire. I squeezed Hudson's hand, looking forward to a fun evening with the Caruthers clan.

Winston pulled into the parking lot of the event venue. Irene had informed me that the university had sprung for a banquet hall located off-campus in an effort to glam up the celebration.

"Lots of people here already," I observed, glancing out the window. I left my concerns about arriving late unsaid.

Willow snorted. "We'll be fine. We've got a few minutes to spare. We've got the guest of honor with us, after all." She winked.

While everyone else chuckled, I pressed my lips together. Her last-minute wardrobe change was the reason we'd left ten minutes behind schedule.

Winston parked on the outskirts of the lot, and we all tumbled gracelessly out of the SUV. We were a few paces out when a sharp intake of breath came from Hudson. "Shoot. My tie pin fell off."

"Where?" Reade asked. "In the car?"

Willow raised an eyebrow. "Are you sure you even put one on?"

"Kids," Winston grunted, "your mother needs to get inside." He impatiently rocked on his heels, elaborately tapping his watch face.

"Hush, Win. It's all right." Irene patted her husband affectionately on the chest. "Hudson, sweetheart, why don't you and Coco look for the pin while the rest of us grab our seats?"

Hudson nodded absently, already looking on the ground around the SUV.

I smiled apologetically. "We'll be quick."

With a wave, the Caruthers crew ambled toward the entrance while Hudson and I got to work, searching in and around the SUV.

"Didn't think I'd be on another case this quickly." I stuck my tongue out as I stuffed my hand in between the seat cushions.

Hudson patted himself down, digging into his pockets. "Oh jeez, if only all of them could be this easy." He held up the gold tie pin that had belonged to his grandfather. "It was in my suit jacket."

I playfully swatted his arm. "You goon. You just wanted some time alone together, didn't you?"

He wrapped me in his strong arms. "You're a regular Sherlock, milady." He pressed his lips against mine.

I savored the spine-tingling kiss. With our houseguests, Hudson and I really hadn't had a private moment to connect after his whirlwind return from New York. "I missed my Watson."

"Well, lucky for you," Hudson murmured in my hair, "Millie wants a full slate of eighteen episodes for *Crime Sweet Home,* so I won't be going anywhere for a while."

I threaded my arm through his and began to lead him toward the banquet hall. "All thanks to your *killer* press tour."

He gagged at my bad joke. "Now, I just have to track down the leads Roberta's former sister-in-law provided. There's a real shot I can prove the brother did it." Hudson gave me a sidelong glance. "Are your crime-fighting days over, or would you be willing to help your fiancé out?"

"Of course, I'll help you—" My brain short-circuited as I processed his words. "Wait, what did you say?"

Before I knew what was happening, Hudson was down on one knee in the middle of the parking lot, holding a Tiffany blue ring box. "I planned to do this later, after the award ceremony, but I just can't wait a moment longer." A giddy smile stretched across his face, threatening to break it in two. "Coco Cline, I want to spend the rest of my life with you, and it would be the greatest honor in the world to be your husband. Will you marry me?"

"Yes! Omigod. Yes! Of course, I will!" Tears streamed down my face as I laughed and squealed at the same time. My whole body shook as Hudson slipped the ring onto my finger.

A perfect fit.

"Is this real life?" I clumsily kissed him while staring at the gorgeous princess-cut diamond.

Hudson squeezed me hard. "Surprised? I stopped by their landmark store while I was in New York. Totally boujee. You would have loved it."

"I seriously can't believe this is happening." Every inch of me thrummed with blissful joy. "How am I supposed to focus on the rest of the evening? We can't drop this news before your mom's big moment."

Hudson stroked my cheek. "You're too sweet, you know that? Just hide your hand in your pocket for now." He brought my fingers to his lips. "We can tell everyone later." His sexy smile sent shivers down my spine.

"Oh, God. I'm a mess." I wiped at my cheeks. "We've got to get inside." I felt like a teenager trying desperately to make curfew.

Hudson checked his phone. "Oh, shoot. Willow just texted. The ceremony's already started."

My neurosis kicked into overdrive. "Ack! Let's book it." As fast as I could wobble in heels, we made our way to the banquet hall entrance. Beautiful strands of yellow lights greeted us, and it looked very romantic and elegant. Kinda an odd vibe for a professional university event.

The entrance hall was dimly lit, a clear sign the program was underway.

Hudson held a finger to his lips to be quiet and ushered me toward a set of large double doors.

Carefully, we inched it open. I prayed to the hinge gods that the door didn't make a loud creak.

Dark silence greeted us. "I think we're in the wrong—"

"SURPRISE!"

The crowd's cheers washed over me as the lights flashed on, revealing a decked-out room full of familiar faces. Jasper, Charlotte, and Amanda waved pink flags. Arthur, Deacon, my parents, Thea, Lucas, and the trips all blew on noisemaker horns. Winston and Irene tossed confetti while Willow and Reade shimmied in place with ribbon wands. And that was just the first row of folks who greeted us. I spied Gavin and Adrian in the big crowd, along with Andre Nunez, Lacie Burbank, Noelle Paige, and Ronny Durnst. Several longtime CoA clients waved in greeting, as well as Millie Stabler from WMTG.

"Happy Birthday, Coco." Hudson kissed my cheek, his hand pressed against the small of my back as he moved my stunned frame toward the awaiting partygoers.

Jasper and Charlotte dashed forward. "Cheers, betch." Jasper handed me a flute of champagne, which I gladly accepted.

"Wh-what is all this?" I glanced wildly around the room, still trying to process everything. "What about your mom's award?" I turned to Hudson.

Irene laughed as she approached. "Oh, darling Coco. You think too highly of me. I received the award in the mail earlier this week. The cost of postage was the amount of fanfare the university was willing to spend."

"The whole ceremony was a ruse?" I gawked at Hudson, amazed he had pulled this off.

"Indeed. I knew I had to make the night about someone else, or otherwise, you'd sniff out the truth." Hudson chuckled. "But of course, I had help." He motioned toward Jasper, Charlotte, Willow, and Reade.

"You guys knew about this?" I stared accusingly at my two besties. Willow, I could excuse for doing her brother's bidding, but Charlotte and Jasper?

Jasper scoffed. "Obvi. And you're lucky we did. Hudson would have bought keychain party favors if we hadn't intervened." He quivered with faux disgust.

"We thought you'd figured it out, given how you walked in on us party-planning last week at the café." Charlotte nervously giggled. "Thank goodness we had a mystery to keep you preoccupied."

I swallowed back a lump of emotion, staring at the happy scene shimmering all around me. At the veiled mention of our recent murder investigation, my heart went out to Laila Jackson, knowing she would never again get the chance to see the people in her life who cared for her. It didn't seem fair.

Charlotte seemed to note her words had brought on a melancholy change in attitude. "Come on, let's get you something stronger than champagne."

She led me toward the throng of people, my mom and dad stopping us along the way.

"Happy Birthday, Delia." Mom threw her arms around me.

Dad patted me on the back. "Cheers to twenty-nine years around the sun, kiddo. Golly, it's still hard for me not to think of you as a moody seventeen-year-old."

I teasingly stuck my tongue out at him. "You're only as old as you feel, right?" Seeing Thea approach, I absently swapped my drink into my left hand, preparing to give my sister a one-armed hug.

Her eyes doubled in size. "Oh my God. What is that?!?" she shrieked, pointing at my glass.

Thinking a bug had fallen into the bubbly or something, I wildly checked the champagne flute, only to find nothing. "What's what?"

Jasper grabbed my wrist and whistled. "Dang, you did good, Hudson. I thought you were going to do this during the party?"

It was then I realized everyone around me was staring at my engagement ring.

Hudson reached for the back of his neck, smiling sheepishly. "My bad. I just couldn't wait."

As Jasper tutted his disappointment, news about Hudson's proposal spread through the crowd. Charlotte and Amanda descended on me, begging to see the ring, while Willow and Reade already started rattling off wild bachelorette party ideas. A whirlwind weekend in Las Vegas sounded the *most* tame.

Mom hugged Hudson so fiercely I thought she might squeeze the life out of him, while Dad shook his hand and said, "Well, it's about gosh darn time, son."

"Ack. Simon stole my thunder," Jasper muttered out of the side of his mouth. "I have so many jokes about how long this took all queued up for my birthday toast. But now, I think I have to go in a different direction…" He tapped his chin as he meandered off into the crowd.

I floated through most of the evening, receiving well wishes about my birthday and our engagement. I really couldn't have been happier.

Thirty minutes into hors d'oeuvres, Omar Jackson cupped my elbow, pulling me aside from a group of college friends who lived in the area. Laila's dad brandished a very dashing cane to help him walk. "I'm touched Hudson invited me to this joyous event. I wanted to thank you in person, Coco." Omar's face grew tight with sorrow. "Deja told me about your involvement in Laila's case. I'm very grateful for everything you did to help find my daughter's killer."

I couldn't imagine the pain he must be in, so I simply gave him a hug.

"I know things were difficult between Laila and me for a long time," he continued sadly, "but with the videos she made as LaTàge, it always felt like she was right there, talking to me, making me laugh with her silly antics." A small smile curled on his lips. "I doubt she knew her dear old dad was one of her biggest fans. She'd probably be horrified." A garbled laugh escaped him before his eyes clouded with tears. "I-I won't ever be able to forgive myself for what happened—"

"Her death was not your fault, Mr. J." I placed a comforting hand on his forearm. I could almost feel the guilt writhing within him. If Laila hadn't come to Central Shores to be at his hospital bedside…

I'd asked myself similar "what if" questions when the Internet had blamed me for her death, and it did no one any good. "Laila came to Central Shores to be with you. Cherish her love. Remember that, above all else."

He bobbed his head wordlessly as he dabbed his eyes with a handkerchief.

Moments later, Deja and Terrance materialized on either side to support their uncle. They each gave me a curt nod before helping Omar shuffle to his seat. Omar hugged them both before he sat down to regain his strength. I was happy to see them all together. Whatever business drama brewed behind closed doors, it seemed it had not destroyed their family bond.

"The chief sends his regards." Gavin tipped an imaginary hat as he and Adrian approached me. "He offered to take an extra shift so the night crew could come." Gavin pointed to my friend Rita Yoon, who stood with her partner, Heather, as well as Elise and Peter, the other nighttime officers.

"Tell him he's missed." I raised my glass in greeting.

Adrian took a sip of his cocktail. "You say that now, but wait until you hear about the rebranding campaign he wants you to implement for the new Central Shores Community Safety Center. It's got, like, eighteen phases."

Instead of balking at the number, I gasped with excitement. "The initiative got approved?"

"Just this morning." Gavin nodded, his expression proud. "Both Harriet and Director Morrison put some extra pressure on Mayor Sullivan to make it happen. They're continually impressed by the results our team *and* our consultants deliver." He held my gaze a moment to let his words sink in. "Just think what we'll accomplish with more resources."

I beamed at the small role I'd been able to play to help make our beloved hometown a little safer. "That's awesome, Gav." I clinked his glass.

"Just think what *I* will be able to accomplish with my own desk," Adrian teased.

Gavin clapped a hand on his shoulder. "I'm expecting big things from you, partner."

"Partner?" I tilted my head.

Gavin and Adrian both grinned. "What with the department's structural overhaul, Adrian and I both decided to take the detective's exam," Gavin explained.

"If we pass," Adrian added, "you're looking at the new Central Shores Dream Team."

"Oh, wow! That's incredible news, guys." Before I could pepper them with more questions about the big changes coming the PD's way, I was pulled into a lively conversation with Daniel Wu, Lacie, Noelle, and Ronny.

"I hear we have you to thank for foiling Derrick's plans to escape." Ronny held out his hand. "Thank you, Coco. For everything."

As I shook his outstretched palm, I knew Ronny wasn't out of the woods yet when it came to his troubles, but I appreciated his encouraging sentiments. His company had taken a major hit from its association with Derrick. Luckily, Reade had offered her firm's savvy services to help Durnst Development navigate the murky PR waters.

Overwhelmed by all the people here to celebrate my birthday, I finally made my way to my assigned table at the front of the banquet hall and collapsed into my chair. Jasper, Hudson—eek, my fiancé—, Charlotte, Deacon, Amanda, and Arthur all eyed me worriedly.

"Since when has Coco Cline not been able to handle the spotlight?" Jasper asked in mock horror.

I laughed. "Since she's been running on an empty stomach. I didn't have lunch today. I'm starved." I grabbed a cloth napkin and fanned myself for dramatic emphasis.

The night continued in a happy blur. Hudson, my parents, Jasper, and Charlotte all gave speeches, filling the room with laughter and joy.

As I bit into a slice of chocolate cake with peanut butter frosting—my fav—I took a moment to appreciate the extraordinary sight. I'd built an incredible life since I'd moved back to Central Shores. Total girl boss goals. But even with all my professional wins, I wouldn't be anywhere without the love and support of the amazing community around me. No matter what challenges I faced, I could always count on my friends and family to be in my corner.

And with their happy faces smiling back at me—not to mention my glittering engagement ring—well, the future looked even brighter.

Acknowledgements

There was a time when I wasn't sure Coco and her friends would ever get into the hands of readers. Now, as I celebrate the release of book three in the series, I am overwhelmed by gratitude. Thank you to Shawn Reilly Simmons and the team at Level Best Books for championing this series and being such invaluable partners. Many thanks to my agent, Dawn Dowdle, for her unwavering support of my career and my creativity. And thank you to Laura Darrell for bringing Coco and her friends to life in the Trending Topic Mystery audiobooks.

I must express my gratitude to *The Bookish Hour* community, and all the support our viewers have given us as our little podcast empire has grown. And of course, many thanks to my Sisters in Crime siblings, my BRLA family, and the *Writers Who Kill* blogging team.

Thank you to J.C. Kenney, Lori Robbins, Sarah Wu, Melissa Green, and Leah Dobrinska for your support and encouragement.

Just as Coco has her followers to thank for her success in life, I am truly grateful to the readers who enjoyed their time in Central Shores. You're the reason why I am here; thank you for spending your time with me.

About the Author

Sarah E. Burr lives near New York City. Hailing from the small town of Appleton, Maine, she has been dreaming of being Nancy Drew since she was a little girl. After not finding any mysteries in corporate America, Sarah began writing some of her own. She is the author of the Trending Topic Mysteries, the Book Blogger Mysteries, and the Court of Mystery series. Sarah is also the author of the award-winning Glenmyre Whim Mysteries. *You Can't Candle the Truth* was a 2022 NGIBA Best Mystery Finalist and a 2022 Silver Falchion Best Supernatural Mystery Finalist. *Too Much to Candle* was a 2023 NGIBA Best Paranormal Finalist.

Sarah is a member of Sisters in Crime, currently serving as the social media manager for the NY-TriState Chapter. She is also the creative mind behind BookstaBundles, a content creation service for authors. Sarah is the co-host and producer of *The Bookish Hour*, a live-streamed YouTube series featuring author interviews and book discussions. She writes as a member of the *Writers Who Kill* blogging team. When she's not spinning up stories, Sarah is singing Broadway show tunes, video gaming, and enjoying walks with her dog, Eevee.

SOCIAL MEDIA HANDLES:
Instagram: @authorsaraheburr

Facebook: https://www.facebook.com/authorsaraheburr

AUTHOR WEBSITE:
https://www.saraheburr.com

Also by Sarah E. Burr

Trending Topic Mysteries:
'#FollowMe for Murder
#TagMe for Murder

Glenmyre Whim Mysteries:
You Can't Candle the Truth
Too Much to Candle

Book Blogger Mysteries:
Over My Dead Blog

Court of Mystery:
The Ducal Detective Mysteries
Paradise Plagued
Burdened Bloodline
Sovereign Sieged
Crown of Chaos
Harrowed Heir
Ravaged Reign
Innocence Imprisoned
Ardent Ascension